A
CURE
FOR
SORROW

ALSO BY JEN WHEELER

The Light on Farallon Island

A CURE FOR SORROW

... A Novel ...

JEN WHEELER

LAKE UNION
PUBLISHING

Published by Lake Union Publishing, Seattle

www.apub.com

Amazon, the Amazon logo, and Lake Union Publishing are trademarks of Amazon.com, Inc., or its affiliates.

ISBN-13: 9781662517143 (paperback)
ISBN-13: 9781662517136 (digital)

Cover design by Shasti O'Leary Soudant
Cover images: © Nicole Matthews / Arcangel; © Amundsen Productions, © balounm, © KBel, © sociologas / Shutterstock

Printed in the United States of America

To Neil Tierney, for your long-standing patience, kindness, care, support, love, and humor (among so much else)—and for double-checking your PO box way back when . . .

"Life, although it may only be an accumulation of anguish, is dear to me, and I will defend it."

—*Mary Wollstonecraft Shelley*, Frankenstein; or, the Modern Prometheus

CONTENT WARNING

This novel contains depictions of medical procedures, violence, natural and accidental death, murder, self-harm, and suicide. It also portrays neurodivergent characters in a nineteenth-century setting, when they would have been less well understood and often treated in ways we might find uncompassionate today.

You can find a more detailed list of potential trigger warnings on my website, www.jenwheeler.com.

CHAPTER ONE

New York City
October 1875–January 1886

The first time that Leonora Harris saw a freshly shelled human brain, she was ten years old. It was in the basement of the three-story brick row house across from Washington Square Park, where she had always lived.

She'd seen brains before—in illustrations and as artistic models and even the real thing, preserved in spirits, looking rather like an oversized rubber walnut bleached of color. She'd seen tiny animal brains, too, extracted from bodies not yet in rigor mortis, but never the organ so newly liberated from a person.

Though she had known for some time about the nature of the things that happened in the basement, until that day, the door had remained locked against all her attempted intrusions, stealthy and otherwise.

Nora had seen her father permit entry to small groups of young men with slicked-down hair and nervous energy animating their limbs; or usher in his own older friends and colleagues, perfectly relaxed; and admit private patients of all ages and dispositions, seeking minor surgical procedures outside of a hospital, which many did not trust. On more than one occasion, Nora had been physically held back from following by their housekeeper, Calista.

But at last, having convinced her father that she was ready, or perhaps having simply worn him down, Nora too was granted entry. She had little time to marvel over the specimen jars along one wall of the dissection room, but even at a glance, she saw that their contents were more recognizably human than the abstract masses displayed in the study upstairs.

An entire ghost-white baby floated in one jar. Vying for her attention, a full-grown human skeleton hung like a suit of armor from a stand in the corner. There were tall shelves of books and surgical instruments that Nora desperately wanted to inventory.

But most intriguingly, in the middle of the room, there was a porcelain table, and upon that, a remarkably fresh corpse.

Nora, who had been instructed not to make a sound, nor to move a muscle—except to run immediately upstairs if she felt faint or ill or frightened—perched silently on a stool near the cadaver's feet.

From there, she watched her father open the head, a process both brutal and refined. With a few quick movements in hidden cavities, he severed the brain's tenuous connections to the rest of the body and finally, carefully, took the organ out.

He cradled it so that all might see. Its glistening folds and ridges seemed to faintly quiver in the light from the gas jets. It was a thing that should have been scooped from a tide pool, Nora thought, not out of a person's skull.

Its overall hue was a pale pink just a touch too drab for nursery drapes or ladies' gowns—yet vastly more interesting than either.

"This," her father said to his assembly in his faint Scottish burr, "is—in essence—everything that we are. In each one of us, this fragile lump of tissue, this . . . gelatin mold of nature's own making—not even half as tough as a cow's tongue, and connected by such a thin thread of nerves all our lives—*this* is the wondrous thing that not only makes us live but makes us *us*."

In the hushed laboratory, Nora imagined that every young medical student's throat felt as tight as her own, and every pulse beat as heavy.

She sensed a syncopated thrum, a flutter, among the warm, close press of male bodies, even though she sat apart from them.

"Our brain," her father continued, "contains every single thought and emotion and dream and impulse we ever have—every memory, every hope, every fear—which we can no more excise after death than we could in life, though we may prod and poke and slice the thing to pieces. And in that way, each brain's physical characteristics can tell us a useful and fascinating story. *But*—it can never betray one-billionth of what it once contained: the entirety of a unique human being. Now, that purported seat of the soul—the heart, which we will get to in due course—well, that is a muscle, an engine. And yes, clearly, it is equally critical to life—some might say more so—but unlike the brain, it's no great mystery."

The congregation drew slightly closer as Nora's father's voice dropped just a little lower. She leaned forward on her stool.

"The dead heart," her father said, "is nothing but a clenched fist of flesh that has stopped working, that has lost its fight. But the brain— well, what of all those thoughts and fears and dreams, all those things generated by and held safe within it—*now*, when it is no more animated by the spark of life? Where do you suppose all those secret things have gone? Have they escaped the body with the last vapor of its breath and floated up to heaven? Or dispersed into the ether? Or are they still imbued in the very cells that make up this mystifying organ—only of no substance that we may ever measure, too minute to discover under even the most powerful microscope?"

In that moment, he seemed more like a mystic or a priest than a surgeon, and Nora felt the transcendent devotion of a disciple, the fervent desire to become an acolyte, even if she didn't know what those things were yet.

"No matter what you believe, my good men," he said, "I hold that *this* is the sacred seat not only of wisdom but of humanity itself. Treat it accordingly. With reverence. With humility. Never forget that every man is as vibrantly real and complex as yourself, and yet—no matter how deeply you delve into his body, he will keep his deepest secrets. As will the world. No matter how much you learn, or how much you discover, a frustratingly great deal of knowledge will stay locked away from you. And one day, every bit of it that you have gleaned—and not written down or passed on—will be stripped away.

"For there," he said, as he shifted the brain into one cupped palm and pointed his free, bloody forefinger at the cadaver, "there, independent of any grace of any God, shall you all go. Some day. In the interim, gentlemen, may I suggest, live good lives and do good work?"

A murmur of appreciative assent, which Nora's father allowed to settle before concluding, "With that said, let us begin."

∿

The brain's hidden realms would remain inaccessible until it had been soaked in a preservative solution for a couple of weeks—cutting it apart now would destroy it—but Nora watched her father's hands as he indicated the visible parts of that venerable object. Silently, she chanted the same words he intoned: *dura mater, arachnoid mater, pia mater, cerebellum, cortex, medulla.*

It was science, yes, but no one could have told her that it was not also an incantation.

And Nora was fully under its power from that day on.

∿

Eleven years later, she had handled more than her own fair share of delicate brains and precious dead bodies. But the one that lay before her now, in the second-floor bedroom just down the hall from her childhood room, was different.

This one, she had loved. This one, Nora had known intimately, long before it became a corpse.

If asked, she would have said, even as she sat there, that she still believed her father's gospel—that the brain was the mechanism that made human beings what they were in some essential way. That it was, or it contained, what many called the soul.

Yet it was Nora's heart that felt like the locus of her own being, and had for some time now. It was no fist but an open hand, reaching for another that could no longer reach back.

All the same, it strained with the effort. It ached so intensely that she thought she might die—desperately hoped she might.

But Nora's life did not flash before her eyes as some said it did just before the end; only one perfect part of it struck her like lightning.

In September of 1883, she was eighteen, and Euan Colquhoun arrived at the Harris household, the latest in a lucky line of medical students whom Nora's father took under his wing and into his home.

There was a new one every other year or so; sometimes more frequently, depending on how long they lasted in the program—or how badly they wanted to move out from under their teacher's roof. They came recommended to him by various peers and acquaintances and colleagues. Most couldn't afford to pay their own tuition, in which cases her father covered that as well. Euan was vouched for by Dr. Burns, an old friend who currently practiced in the upstate town of Hoosick Falls.

Nora's father read his introductory letter aloud at the dining table. According to Dr. Burns, Euan was smart and sensible, hardworking but not hardheaded—at that, Dr. Harris gave his daughter a pointed look—and reasonably well versed in Greek and Latin. He'd studied various practical matters of medicine in an unofficial capacity with Dr. Burns himself, but Angus thought the boy would benefit tremendously from a proper education. He trusted that Duncan would find Euan both able and amiable.

"And what else?" Nora asked as she buttered a roll. "Is *his* father also a good friend of the good Dr. Burns? Or some equally prominent member of the Hoosick Falls elite?"

"His father is dead," Nora's father answered, with another significant look leveled at her.

"Oh."

"Poor boy's an orphan, in fact. Angus says he was raised by his older brother, on their family farm outside town."

"Farm?"

"Yes. But Euan went to school—excepting harvest days, of course."

"Oh, of course. How old?"

"Twenty. Twenty-one soon. He finished high school."

"But no college?"

"No."

"He hasn't written you his own letter," Nora observed.

"Well, I'm not entirely certain he knows Angus wrote to me on his behalf."

"Hmm. And yet he's already in, of course—your latest chosen one, appointed whether he knew he was in the running or not."

"Is that so?"

Nora turned a perfect copy of her father's freighted stare back upon him. "Dr. Burns is never wrong, in your opinion. He could recommend an illiterate fifteen-year-old who faints at the sight of blood and you'd still give him a chance."

Her father snorted and set the letter aside to pick up his wineglass. "And he could recommend an honors graduate from Edinburgh with awards from Harvard and Yale and you'd still cast aspersions."

"Aspersions?" Nora echoed, with a note of offense only partially put on. "I demonstrate a little healthy skepticism, perhaps, but that is not the same thing."

"Well, what makes you skeptical of this one, specifically? That he's done manual labor?"

"No."

"Because if he hadn't, then *that* would be it—he's had it too easy all his life and—"

"Why has this discussion become about *me?*"

Nora's father leaned back in his chair with a smile and one hand raised in a gesture of retreat. But as he took another sip of wine, he added, "Whoever gets picked, he will be your classmate, after all. Perhaps you should have some say."

She gave a twitchy shrug of one shoulder and speared another mushy green bean. "It hardly matters to me."

At the time, she'd believed that to be true.

CHAPTER TWO

New York City
September 1883–June 1884

Dr. Burns had said nothing about Euan Colquhoun being handsome, but he was. Strong and compact, about Nora's height—five foot eight. He had thick auburn hair with a slight wave in the front, and dark-blue eyes that gave a pensive impression, until he smiled and his whole face looked disarmingly boyish.

He'd come to medicine because he'd seen too many people die. He didn't hesitate to say so, and sounded neither solemn nor self-pitying, just matter-of-fact as they sipped their first coffees after he arrived from the train station.

Dr. Burns had accompanied him, more for the excuse of visiting Nora's father and the city itself. The four of them sat in the parlor, where Calista served biscuits with cinnamon and raisins, her approximation of—and, in her opinion, improvement upon—the scones Dr. Harris favored.

Nora perched on the piano stool, her saucer on the closed lid of the keyboard, her biscuit untouched. Her father and Dr. Burns relaxed into the pair of armchairs by the unlit fireplace, while Euan sat ramrod straight in the middle of the sofa and was gently interrogated.

When Nora's father had finally run out of questions, he mentioned that his daughter would be a fellow student. Euan looked at her with an expression that Nora couldn't decipher—partly because she couldn't look at his face for more than a fleeting second at a time.

"Yes," he said, "Dr. Burns told me—that you're the first female student they've admitted. That's wonderful."

"They crumbled in the face of Leonora's insistence," said her father, proudly, yet also a touch amused.

Nora blushed and smoothed her skirt. "Of course, it's only because of who *you* are that they actually admitted me. I'm the exception that proves the rule. I'm an indulgence on their part, really."

"You met the same entrance requirements as everyone else," her father countered. "And exceeded the bulk of them, I know that."

"Still." She sipped her coffee.

Dr. Burns addressed her with a twinkle in his eye. "You don't put much faith in the women's colleges, then?"

"Of course I do," Nora answered. "But Dr. Jacobi herself still advocates for integrated instruction. In the end, that's the only way to ensure that everyone receives an equally sound education—and hence an equal quality of medical care."

"Oh, to be sure," said Dr. Burns, with what Nora took to be a patronizing smirk.

"Why should there be separate schools in the first place?" she asked, neither wanting nor waiting for an answer. "It *seems* so admirable, to found and fund a women's institution, but on the other side of that coin—as prettily progressive as it is, doctor—it is shameful. To create divisions where there need be none."

"Hasn't God Himself created the divisions?" Dr. Burns answered.

"No," Nora said. "Not in any way that matters. Are women so delicate that they require special instruction? That's obvious nonsense, so then it must be the men who tremble at the idea of intrusion into their so very tightly closed ranks. Yet if women are the weaker sex, then what is there to fear? Competition? Most doctors—male doctors, even—see the value in nurses. They know what they're capable of, and yet they would deny them the chance to be their true equals. In status, and in salary. And thirty years after Elizabeth Blackwell, at that. Clearly, it cannot be a matter of aptitude. As we've already discussed, there are entrance requirements—which I believe could stand to be far more rigorous—but administer them blind and I'm certain you would end up with a far less homogeneous student body. In fact, I believe that bodies are precisely it."

"See what you've started," her father muttered into his coffee, through a grin.

Nora continued with barely a pause, "Cut open a feminine rival, after all, and you will find an identically formed brain in her head, will you not? Disguise her living body—as Dr. Miranda Stuart disguised her own self for so many years, and she was hardly the only one—or have the college adopt a new uniform of Muslim robes from head to toe for all, and in most cases, I warrant, most men would never even know the difference."

Dr. Burns, looking pleased with himself, said, "Well, I suppose it would depend on the pitch of the lady's voice."

Nora's had risen to a rather strident tone, far more emotional than she'd allowed herself to become in her appeal to the college's admissions board. "Any *man* too distracted by the female form in his class, let alone her voice, is surely not cut out for his chosen profession. And any man who is simply too intimidated by a woman seeking the same knowledge as himself—well, he's not only a plain fool, but spiritually feeble."

"Hear! Hear!" her father said, and raised his coffee.

Euan, whom Nora had momentarily forgotten, lifted his own cup and murmured, "Well said."

She took a deep, steadying breath and bit down on a smile.

With a sigh, Dr. Burns nodded and made his own toasting gesture, which seemed more like a conciliation. "I'm hardly surprised that you convinced the board, Miss Leonora. In fact, I believe they might have admitted you even if you were not your father's daughter."

If only to shut you up, Nora imagined he dared not add.

She gave him a rough approximation of a smile and excused herself on the pretense of getting more coffee. But rather than proceed to the narrow kitchen at the back of the house, she slipped into the dining room and crept softly to the pocket doors that were closed between it and the parlor.

". . . been that way since she was little, of course," she heard her father say. "Tell her *no* or that she cannae do something and she'll only be more determined to prove you wrong."

Dr. Burns laughed. "Best *not* warn her away from our young protégé, then."

Nora's father might have chuckled to be polite.

Nora herself flushed with embarrassment, even before Euan sputtered, "Oh, but I—of course, I would never . . ."

"No, no," her father said. "Dr. Burns is only trying to be provocative. And I wouldn't worry about Nora, anyway. My lass is not what you'd call a romantic. Never has had her head in the clouds."

~

Yet that was exactly where Nora's head—and heart, and entire body—began to float before long. Because, despite what even she had begun to suspect in recent years, it turned out that she was not immune to love, or attraction.

They set in and became a fever, with measurable physical symptoms. She often grew lightheaded and breathless and hot. Her pulse pounded in her veins and her heart fluttered. Her mouth went dry even as her underarms produced too much sweat. She found it fascinating, and terrifying, and exhilarating all at once.

Even when Nora could administer a dose of self-restraint and focus for a whole afternoon on histology lectures and chemistry labs, she felt the threat—the promise—of her ardor working silently away in her deepest tissues, her blood and bone marrow.

And Euan, no matter how neutrally civil he tried to be in most of their interactions, was clearly suffering similar symptoms—or so Nora thought, though she allowed it might only be her hope. And she knew she shouldn't wish for that. She should pray for him to shun her, scorn her. Like a not insignificant number of their other male classmates did.

It was a terrible idea to even entertain the notion of becoming involved with Euan in any way beyond a friendship. Even that was probably fraught.

But there was no stopping nature on certain courses, and Nora comforted herself with that fact. Or perhaps she sought to excuse herself with it.

Sometimes, she wondered if she'd have felt the same about anyone who would have come to stay with them that year—if it was just the timing. She didn't think so. It was true that she didn't resent Euan the way she'd automatically resented the others, because she was able to join him instead of watching him live out her own dream. But that alone wasn't enough to move her so monumentally, even combined with a pretty face, which he certainly had.

He was genuine, and kind, and not conceited. Yet he didn't underestimate himself, either. Nor did he underestimate Nora; if anything, he was *too* impressed with her. But because he expressed it entirely without mockery—or jealousy—that was endearing too.

Still, she didn't throw caution to the wind at once, though there were countless occasions on which she wanted to, and easily could have. They talked all the time, not just to study and trade theories and opinions on ethical dilemmas and scientific questions but to get to know one another better. They sat up late in the parlor exchanging histories and confiding hopes and dreams. They ate almost all their meals together while they chatted away at the dining table with books and papers spread between them, or out in the back garden—or standing in the tiny kitchen when they only had time to snack.

Outside of the house, they were still constantly in each other's company. Nora occasionally joined her cousin Bette for tea and had social reform meetings and tennis matches with Alice Edelstein, but nearly every day, she and Euan walked to and from classes together and strolled for pleasure in Washington Square Park in the evenings. On Sundays, they often took excursions throughout the city, Nora excited to show him all the places she liked best.

They even sat beside each other at the opera, which neither of them really enjoyed—but Nora's father had paid fifty dollars for the box, and he wanted it filled. So much so that he even bought Euan a tuxedo, in which he looked rather breathtaking.

Nora would have been embarrassed by her inability to stop staring, except that Euan had a similar reaction to seeing her in a sumptuous silk evening gown instead of her usual dark skirt and pale blouse. Cousin Bette would have wanted Nora to dress her chestnut hair more stylishly, and their grandmama would have ordered her to powder her face in an attempt to diminish the freckles sprinkled across it, but Nora didn't mind them. Apparently, neither did Euan.

Even when they began blatantly flirting, they both strove for a casual affect, as if their words, and the act itself, were of no consequence. No different, really, than the jocular affection that many of their male classmates showed each other—in fact, markedly less intimate and forthcoming. And so what if they were of the opposite sex?

When they took turns looking through a microscope, bent close enough to catch each other's scent and the radiance of body heat, their proximity was incidental. Their breath was bated in simple concentration, nothing more.

When they practiced bandaging each other's arms and heads in the parlor, it was purely educational—Nora's father was right there, after all, offering pointers and laughing along with them as he sipped his nightly Scotch.

But there was no such way to ignore or deflect the frisson of accidentally brushing fingertips with Euan when they passed each other books and plates, and soon, they were clearly doing it on purpose. Creating more sparks to smolder until they eventually went out—or flashed over.

$\sim$

They slept on separate floors, of course. Nora and her father were on the second level, where she had the main bedroom at the back, connected to the bathroom, a generous amount of space. Her father had turned the former dressing room at the front of the house into his study and claimed the smaller adjoining bedchamber as his own.

A modest guest room occupied the middle of that floor, but Euan, like every resident student before him, was relegated to a meager cell in the attic, originally intended as servants' quarters. Two other such rooms had been given over to storage, since the Harrises no longer kept a proper staff.

Besides Calista, there was only John Garrett, the groom and driver, who lived in the carriage house behind the garden, with Asclepius and Paracelsus, the horses, and Dr. Harris's private landau.

Occasionally, Nora had spied Calista going to and from the carriage house at odd hours, but officially, she slept in the attic's largest room, formerly the nursery. The erstwhile nanny, in constant disagreement with Dr. Harris about what little girls should be allowed to do, had been dismissed when Nora was six. Her small attic bedroom was renovated into a water closet, which Calista would have enjoyed more if she hadn't had to share it with a string of strange young men.

When Euan and Nora went to bed at the same time, after they said good night at the landing and he continued to the top floor, she could often hear the water running above her head as she stood splashing her face and brushing her teeth, pulling the pins from her hair.

She couldn't help but picture Euan's reflection as she looked at her own. She imagined his equally unguarded expression as he prepared for bed, his shirt unbuttoned, or at least with the cuffs and collar loosened.

Nora wished, sometimes, that their bedrooms were stacked as well, but his was directly over her father's chamber on the other end of the house. Probably for the best, lest she lie awake all night listening for the smallest sounds, trying to interpret them.

She did still think of Euan as she went into her own room, leaving a trail of clothing. Her skirt and blouse—or, more rarely, gown—usually spent the night draped over the side of the tub, in a halfhearted effort to save Calista from ironing. Nora's bustle and petticoat and bloomers lay crumpled on the floor. Her stockings were generally flung in opposite directions, her corset cracked open and tossed onto her chair. Normally, she exchanged her chemise for a nightgown. Sometimes, with increasing frequency after Euan's arrival, she simply stripped it off and climbed naked beneath her covers, shivering at the cold linens against her skin.

That chill jolt always made Nora think, for an instant, of the morgue. But when she thought of Euan's skin, how warm it would be, how vibrantly alive, it was not only her heart that fluttered.

It was curious, she thought. How, although he was the object of her adoration, she felt like both a magnifying lens and the thing on which it was focused—while Euan was the source of light that she was capturing and concentrating.

The smoldering heat continued to build inside her, and Nora wanted, like a phoenix, to burn.

CHAPTER THREE

New York City & Newport, RI
June–September 1884

For nine months, though, nothing happened between them that anyone could have taken exception to.

In June, everything changed.

It was fitting, since it was the month that marked another milestone: the end of their first year at school. To celebrate the close of final exams and the temporary reprieve from forty hours of practical anatomy and physiology and materia medica every week, a faction went off to McSorley's, where women were unequivocally not allowed.

Nora had no wish to be humiliated by being physically blocked from entering or bodily carried out if she managed to push her way in, so she decamped with another group, including Euan, to a more welcoming alehouse, where they toasted to their hard work and mutual good luck.

Everyone got slightly tipsy. Some of them got downright drunk. Paul Billings passed out cocaine tablets like candy—"For all the good children who've made their marks!"—and James Whitmore distributed cigars to all and sundry. Nora took a good-natured puff of hers but despised the taste and gave it to Pruitt Townsend, who made a show of smoking two at once. She noticed that Euan only gestured with his, occasionally tapping the ash into one of the heavy crystal dishes ranged down their communal table, among the plates of cheese and crackers and pickled oysters.

Nora and Euan left before they disgraced themselves, but were laughing and loose-jointed as they swayed down the street in the dusky light.

"We'd better walk a while," Nora said. "In the park or someplace, I mean. Until we sober up a little. My father would *not* approve of the state we're in."

Euan chuckled. "Neither would my brother."

"Good thing he can't see you, then." But Nora knew he would soon. Euan was due to go home for the summer break, to help out on the farm. They wouldn't see each other for months. She sighed. "I can't believe it's already over."

"Not technically," he said. "Not until the ceremony."

"Hmm. But then you're off, aren't you?"

"Duty calls."

They'd ambled into the center of the park to the fountain. Euan looked at Nora and added, "You'll be calling to me, though. While I'm gone."

She blinked at him and felt a smile slowly spread across her face. "Will I?"

He laughed—his grin obliterating the deeply earnest and slightly apprehensive expression that had been on his face. "Nora, I miss you the moment you walk out of a room. I'll be beside myself the whole summer."

"Be beside me, then," she said. "Come to Newport. There's plenty of room."

"I can't," he said, and stepped closer, leaving almost no space between them. "But I'll think about you every second. I already do."

Still, he didn't touch her, and Nora couldn't stand it any longer. She leaned up and in and kissed him. She felt the tension in Euan's body as she gripped his arms, the momentary stiffness of surprise in his mouth—but then he relaxed and his own hands went to Nora's back and waist.

And that was that.

~

They made the most of the few days before his departure, discussing the myriad ways in which they were making a colossally stupid decision—usually while they were still kissing, pausing only long enough to get a few more words out and take a heaving breath or two, or to check that no one was around to catch them.

Their parting at the station was necessarily more chaste. Since Nora's father hadn't come, she did embrace Euan on the platform. She'd long prided herself on not being sentimental and tried hard not to cry—but it was hopeless. Euan smiled and kissed the tears from Nora's cheeks, then kissed her lips so she tasted the salt. She would touch her mouth with sea-dipped fingertips in Newport all summer, so as to relive the moment. He promised to write, and she did the same. And then, in no time at all, he was gone.

Nora abandoned all pride and sobbed on her way home. She found something romantically thrilling about her anguish at being parted from her lover. And something pleasing in the way her face, post-crying, looked a little as it did after they'd kissed for half an hour, attractively flushed, lips slightly swollen.

True, her hazel-green eyes were also horribly red, but at least they sparkled. Anyway, there was no one to see her now whose opinion Nora cared for.

~

A few days later, as she had since she was little, she joined Grandmama, Aunt Birdie, and Cousin Bette for the journey to Rhode Island, where her maternal clan had a massive summer home.

Grandmama had come from money, not very old and not very much, but enough—when combined with her distinguished beauty—to attract the attention of a wealthier husband. Unfortunately, he was a scoundrel who abandoned her with two young daughters, in dire straits. His family had provided a monthly stipend to help smooth over hurt feelings, if not the scandal itself, but stopped the allowance when Grandmama married a far kinder man with much smaller coffers. He loved the girls—Nora's mother and aunt—as his own.

When they were nearly grown women, their biological father finally died. To Grandmama's great shock, he left her a contritely vast sum in his will, which she accepted only for the sake of her daughters, though she still wanted them to marry well.

A few years later, when her dear second husband was dying, Nora's father had come to the house to attempt a miracle cure. Though it had failed, he'd won the broken heart of Grandmama's eldest daughter, Emma.

Dr. Harris had barely been established then, and though he had a solidly middle-class family background, he was no great prize where his pockets were concerned. Luckily, Grandmama could see his potential, as well as his genial, steadfast nature, and she blessed the union. She did so with far more gusto when Birdie soon married a man with a Fifth Avenue mansion and the acquaintance of the Astors. The Newport house had come courtesy of him too.

Uncle George had died when his daughter was only a baby—so Cousin Bette, like Nora, had grown up with only one parent.

Unlike Nora, Bette had always been a romantic, rhapsodizing about her mother's pure love, so great that she'd never entertained the idea of a second marriage. Bette never mentioned the money that ensured her mother didn't have to seek another husband, just sighed and skipped ahead to her own hazy future, in which she hoped that she would find her own heart's true half, but that he would be luckier and live.

Historically, Nora's response was to roll her eyes and, when she couldn't bite her tongue, remark, "Maybe you should marry someone you're not that fond of to start—it seems like the first one always dies. So find your best prospect and then pick your *true* love for number two."

She didn't believe in the matrilineal curse, of course; her own father was proof that marrying into the family wasn't fatal to men. In more fanciful moments, however, Nora wondered if her mother's death from childbed fever had saved him—and perhaps even changed the fate of all future husbands. Once she became besotted by Euan, she stopped teasing Bette about such things. And Bette, who'd had too many romantic entanglements to keep track of in her twenty-two years, guessed Nora's secret before anyone else.

She'd been annoyingly pleased. "Our little late bloomer Leonora Jane, finally blossomed! Or blossom*ing*."

"*Little?*" Nora jeered. "And *late-blooming?* I'm *nineteen*."

"And in love, at last," said Bette. "With something other than science, I mean. Something that can love you back."

To her credit, Bette hadn't said anything to anyone else, but she'd teased Nora relentlessly ever since.

On the train that summer, rather than trying to read as she usually did, Nora gazed vacantly through the window, stifling sighs and missing every other thing Bette said.

She poked Nora in the ribs and rightfully accused her of pining. "Parting *is* such sweet sorrow . . ."

"There's nothing sweet about it," Nora groused.

"But when you're reunited . . ." Bette smiled knowingly and settled back in her seat as she fanned her face. "You know what they say about absence and fondness . . . I bet you won't stay so timid, once he's finally just a floor away again."

"No one has ever accused me of being timid," Nora said, and turned toward the window to hide her blush.

"Only in love," said Bette, and tried to peer at Nora to see how annoyed she was. But when Nora continued to hide her face, Bette said far too loudly, "He kissed you!"

"Shh!" Nora hissed—but couldn't keep from laughing, pressing her face to her cousin's shoulder to try and muffle her own foolish giggles. "I kissed him, in fact," she murmured near Bette's ear. "Then he kissed me."

"Of course," Bette said. "And then?"

"Well," said Nora, "it all gets a little blurry after that."

In fact, she felt she had never seen the world so clearly—let alone noticed how exquisite so much of it was. That whole summer, Nora herself was distant and dreamy. She wrote an excess of letters to her beloved and sketched everything with new eyes: the seashore and its strange, enchanting creatures, from armored horseshoe crabs to soft-bellied starfish; its less intriguing figures, too, from common seagulls to the monied men and women who descended in similarly great and raucous flocks.

Nora was aware that she was counted among their number, yet ever since she was a young girl, she'd felt set apart. By ten, she'd begun actively cultivating that division—gleefully asking her grandmother's party guests if they'd ever noticed how closely cauliflowers resembled human brains, and walnuts even more, with right and left hemispheres, relishing the most offended reactions—but she'd also learned well enough how to blend in when she wanted to, when it seemed important. The others in her set knew how to play along as well. However prickly Nora's attitude could be, and however off-putting her interests, she came from a Good Family with significant wealth, and thus was due a certain amount of respect.

Rather than mere tolerance, however, she sensed that people were more genuinely welcoming that summer.

"Because they can tell you're happy," Bette said.

To which Nora replied, "Because I seem to have lost half my wits."

Yet, instead of being insulted by the friendliness of people who had never genuinely warmed to her before, Nora only smiled and floated along on a cloud of contentment.

She still preferred to spend time alone. Nora was happiest reading in the open window seat, dozing on the porch swing, or wading through tide pools, daydreaming about Euan all the while. But she did attend several of the dinner dances, and some of the tennis matches, and nearly all the picnics.

When she thought of Euan dripping with sweat, breaking his back in the fields—a thing Nora still couldn't quite picture, his hands blistered and dirty, wrapped around the haft of an axe—she felt, after a thrilling pulse of excitement, shamefully guilty. She should have been attending rounds at a hospital during the break in classes, or serving in a dispensary. Her father, when most of his well-off clientele fled the city in the summer, devoted more time to visiting those who couldn't afford to pay him much, if anything—those who couldn't really afford to be ill, much less loaf about for mere pleasure.

Dr. Harris could have, of course; he made an impressive income now, on top of the money that his late wife had brought to their marriage. But he had no interest in vacations. He only deigned to visit Newport for a handful of days every season, mostly because he got lonely without Nora at home. Even then, he wasn't very good at relaxing. After two days in Rhode Island, he began looking for minor ailments to diagnose in his dinner mates, which seemed to give him some measure of comfort, at least.

She couldn't imagine Euan ever joining her for whole months of idleness, nor abandoning his family's farm, not even once he was officially licensed to practice medicine.

It was the one thing that gave Nora pause when she thought of their future together.

You must think me terribly selfish, she wrote.

And I know that I am. But I wither at the thought of returning to Manhattan at its most sweltering and smelly, even (especially) to do something as noble as check up on children in the tenements or distribute public-health pamphlets—much less assisting the city's most devoted doctors. I love this stultifying summer indolence. Especially now that I have the memory of your lips upon my skin, which feels sun-warmed even late at night when the moon peeps through my bedroom window.

I only wish that you were here too. If for no other reason than I might make you forget everything you know about my lesser qualities. But then, I wouldn't want to imperil your own best impulses. Truly, I fear (I know) that you are far too good for me. I should hope that you realize the same, while you're toiling away to feed your family and I'm feeling unduly sorry for myself with my toes dug into the sand. I should hope that you return to Manhattan with a resolution to push me away—however gently—to end what has only barely begun between us, before it's far too late. But what I want—and, alas, I am a creature of rather earthshaking desires—is for you to take me straight into your strong arms again and press your open mouth against my throat, where the pulse is strongest . . . and then, to do the same in every place where my heart drum-beats through my body.

∿

Nora considered tearing up the tortured confession and writing something less passionately pitiful, but decided that Euan should know the full truth. When she received his response, she was gratified by both his sweet reassurances and his emboldened forays into reciprocal fantasy.

Having to improve upon each previous letter, they worked themselves into paroxysms of passion on the page that astonished Nora. She posted her envelopes with thudding pulse, and tore open Euan's replies prematurely flushed.

Upon their reunion in New York that September, as per Bette's prediction, neither one of them remained timid.

～

They comported themselves as appropriately as ever in classes and clinics. Behaved almost as impeccably in mixed company both at home and out with friends. In certain social situations, they might have sat a bit closer together than before, or allowed themselves to casually brush each other's sleeves, and probably exchanged openly adoring looks, but even Whitmore and Townsend, their closest allies at school, weren't certain they were romantically involved.

Meanwhile, they stole every moment alone that they could, whenever Nora's father was called away in the night, and the sacred Sunday morning hours while he and Calista were at church.

Nora acquired a womb veil. One of the benefits of being an especially liberal-minded doctor's daughter—and, crucially, acquainted with several likewise liberal female physicians—was that Nora knew all about such things and was able to access them fairly easily without having to worry about Comstock laws.

Still, they were cautious. "I don't intend to start on the third generation of Harris doctors until I have my own degree in hand."

"*Harris* doctors?" Euan echoed, with an exaggeratedly furrowed brow and his hands on her hips.

"Harris-Colquhoun?" Nora offered.

He smiled and sat up to pull her closer. "That's better, yes."

～

They talked of the future like that—half seriously, or perhaps couching their utter seriousness in repartee for fear that their visions would at some point deviate.

Ever since she'd first considered pursuing medicine, Nora had assumed that she would set up a private practice in the city after graduation, and perhaps teach—at the women's college, most likely. That still made sense.

Euan, she knew, had vague notions of taking over for Dr. Burns in Hoosick Falls, but not until some distant day when the man finally retired. In the interim, he could surely find a place in New York City.

But that would always be temporary, and no matter how far off the prospect of his moving back home might be, Nora couldn't imagine herself joining him, at least not on a permanent basis. Still, the two places weren't so far distant. And however provincial she might have expected Euan Colquhoun to be before they met, he had already proven amenable to unconventional arrangements. She hoped that he would remain so, that they could both have everything they wanted. If not, she was certain they could come to some other agreement.

CHAPTER FOUR

New York City & Newport, RI
September 1884–January 1886

In the shorter term, Euan regularly fretted about their precarious living situation. Even if they weren't caught, it felt dastardly to do what they were doing while Nora's father was funding his education and everything else. "Buying my food, for God's sake, having my collars starched!"

But Euan couldn't afford to live elsewhere, at least not without getting a job—which he had no time for, unless he stopped sleeping completely. Anyway, Nora refused to entertain the idea.

"I want you here, at all times. A floor away from me, at most. Even when it's torture."

And so he stayed, and they passed another academic year entwined, in semi-secret—except for the winter break, when Euan went home for his customary week at Christmas.

~

In Manhattan, with her entire family gathered around Aunt Birdie's twinkling tree, Grandmama asked why on earth Leonora looked so gloomy. Cousin Bette made a teasing remark about missing her friend.

Piqued, Nora impulsively announced that they were far more than *friends*, and when everyone else gave her startled looks, she declared that, in fact, they were getting married.

Bette squealed at the same time that Nora's father said, "You *what?*" Birdie fiddled with her brooch and murmured that it was a lovely surprise. Grandmama, Nora thought, was not quite sure what had happened, judging from the confused look on her face.

With her cheeks burning, Nora focused on the half-unwrapped present in her lap. "It isn't official—*yet*—but we planned to announce the engagement after graduation. *Next* year's, I mean."

Grandmama blinked at her. "You intend to marry. The *farmer?*"

"The *doctor*," Nora corrected. "He will be, by the time it happens—and that'll make the pair of us."

Her grandmother's neck tendons stood out as she took a deep breath through her nose and gave a slight shake of the head that looked more like a shudder.

∾

Euan wasn't upset, exactly—a bit taken aback to find out that their clandestine romance wasn't a secret anymore, and rather nervous about how the news had been received, particularly by her father—but once reassured, he confessed that he might have told his family a similar thing.

And Dr. Harris was honestly delighted. Like Nora herself, he'd warmed to Euan far more than he had to any of his previous protégés. Euan's Scottish extraction, perhaps, having something to do with it. If her father suspected them of getting ahead of their eventual wedding night in any way, he hid it well. And Nora supposed that he trusted her—her determination to construct a very specific future and career as much as her basic intelligence.

She assured him that she would have her medical degree before her marriage license, and to him, her word was her bond.

∽

In June, since Nora had shaken the cat from the bag, Euan received a formal invitation from Aunt Birdie to summer in Newport. To Nora's great joy, he said that he supposed he could cut his farmwork a bit short and join them for the last few days.

She went about, as she had during their first summer spent apart, in the grip of a lovely sort of delirium that made everything else a bit less real. She didn't feel her feet touching the ground, so whether it was sand or Turkish carpet beneath her soles she couldn't say.

They each filled reams of stationery, their letters by turns torrid and teasing but always tender. They faithfully described their days and their daydreams. Nora sent more sketches, mostly of her own body, parts of which looked oceanic, like the ridged tip of a cone shell or the frilled edges of an oyster.

You're driving me to distraction, Euan wrote. *I've taken to opening your letters far off in the woods. I'm tempted to bury them in a secret cache, but I can't stand to have them too far away from me. I cannot see you in the flesh soon enough.*

∽

And then, for a blessed few days at the end of August, Euan joined her in that wonderful place. He had never seen the ocean and splashed about the shallows like an overgrown boy, hesitant to wade out any farther until Nora promised she'd keep him safe.

When everyone else was asleep, they familiarized themselves with several of the secret niches in Aunt Birdie's house, seemingly designed by an amorous architect expressly for rendezvous. And on their last night, with the moon spilling quicksilver across the black ocean, they sneaked off to a sheltered cove where they waded without the encumbrance of clothes.

Standing with shimmering wavelets gently lapping about their shoulders, Euan tucked a lock of Nora's dripping hair behind her ear and studied her face with one of his beautifully serious expressions.

"Leonora Harris," he said, with all the reverence that he would have given a proper taxonomic name. "You are far more than I ever dreamed of, you know that? *All* of this . . ." He waved a hand toward the houses on the cliff, the general direction of New York, the rest of the world. "But *you*," he said, "you're the very best of it."

Nora wrapped her arms around him. "So are you."

The two of them glowed with warmth in the cold, salty sea.

~

As summer waned, their third and final year of school commenced. Along with the regular roster of anatomical dissections and practical clinics, they began the study of more specialized subjects: obstetrics; mental disorders; diseases of the eyes and ears; childhood afflictions; fracture setting.

Only a few weeks into the first semester, rumors echoed back to them that they'd gotten engaged, but they refused to confirm or deny it, even when Whitmore and Townsend asked them outright. Nora wondered if her father had shared the news with one of his colleagues and someone had overheard, or if it was just a natural extension of the hearsay that had always swirled, even before it became true.

In any case, it didn't matter. Soon enough, they'd be earning their degrees and striding across the stage. And after that, walking down the aisle, into their shared future. Meanwhile, they began to work out the details.

In their second year of school, they undertook the writing of their wills, discussing the drafts as they worked on them at the dining table. Euan declared—with no bravado or provocation but as a simple, logical statement of fact—that he would donate his body to the medical college. Nora barely blinked before saying that she would too.

"Although, perhaps I'll leave mine to the women's college."

Euan murmured approval and touched the end of his pen to his chin. "Of course, you should get whatever's left of me—if that's not too morbid?"

"Not at all," she answered. "'For into your hands I commend myself, body and soul.'" Seeing Euan's surprise, she added, "If that's not too sacrilegious?"

"No." He scribbled down another note for his will, smiling as he did so.

The planning of their marriage went far less smoothly.

Nora suggested they wed in Hoosick Falls so his family could easily attend—and her own would have something to gossip about later.

But Euan said it would be far finer in Manhattan, and he was sure his brother Mal, at least, would brave the city for the wedding, especially if they had it in the winter when farmwork was lighter.

Then they could visit the farm itself, Nora suggested, on their way to Niagara Falls, where they might honeymoon.

Euan was noncommittal—he always was, in fact, whenever she spoke of visiting the farm. At first, she found it charming, but eventually, it distressed her. When she expressed concern that Euan wasn't sure about marrying her at all, he swore that wasn't true—"It's just, that *place*—as much as I love it, it . . . it's not where you belong."

"But you do?" Nora asked.

"I did," he said. "I could, still. But we'll make a new home now."

∾

And she believed him. That winter, he left for his usual Christmas week away, but returned in time to celebrate New Year's Eve at Aunt Birdie's annual extravaganza.

Euan wore his opera tuxedo, Nora her mother's diamonds. At midnight, they kissed, unconcerned with who might be looking on.

❧

On January 4, they returned to classes. Some of their schoolmates had clearly extended their festivities over the long weekend. Michael Babcock was the worst off. He smelled like a freshly opened jar of ethanol and looked wan and queasy even before Dr. Ratliffe appointed him the honor of draining their patient's abdominal abscess in one of their first practical sessions of the day.

Nora pursed her lips; it was all very well to teach Babcock a lesson, but not at the risk of the innocent man on the operating table. Still, she held her tongue, and couldn't suppress some petty satisfaction in watching the reeking, supercilious young man—one of the handful who had never even pretended to respect her presence or her person—thickly swallow against his rising gorge as he positioned his scalpel.

His incision released a foul gush of pustulant matter. Babcock jerked back with a guttural sound that clearly communicated not only disgust but the impending threat of vomit.

Several students standing close enough to observe collided in their haste to step clear as Babcock whirled around, the scalpel still in one raised hand, the other clamped over his mouth with its oily black mustache.

One second's hesitation, one millimeter's, and it might have happened very differently. As it was, that shining, disease-slicked blade flashed through the air and caught Euan's face, opening a bright red line along his jaw and angling down beneath it.

Nora felt a full-throated scream ready to erupt, but all she emitted was a gasp, drowned out in the commotion.

The abundance of blood was even more striking for the white shirt beneath Euan's jacket, quickly turning crimson. When he met Nora's eyes, the fear in his expression was palpable. She sprang into action much sooner than it felt like—the eternity that she remained paralyzed lasting only a second or two, in fact.

Facial lacerations did bleed freely, with so many fine vessels so close beneath the surface of the thin skin; they all knew that. Upon closer inspection, Euan's cut was shallow. Mercifully angled, too.

"It doesn't even need stitching," he said, a clear note of relief in his voice.

"But it needs disinfecting," Nora said. *"Now."*

Dr. Ratliffe told her and Whitmore to see to it, then took over at the surgical table, stepping wide around the mess that Babcock had spewed all over the tiled floor.

An orderly tended to that. Meanwhile, several other students had fled to the lavatories to clean themselves up. Those who remained were divided between watching Dr. Ratliffe and seeing that Euan was really all right.

"It's fine," he said, and let out a shaky sort of breath that wasn't quite a laugh. "Near miss."

$\sim$

No artery had been nicked. It couldn't have been more than a minute, maybe two, before they applied the first antiseptics.

But that was more than enough time for the germs introduced by that fine-edged, flashing blade to delve deeper and begin destroying Euan's very cells.

CHAPTER FIVE

New York City
January 1886

At first, all they could see was that the superficial wound had become infected, despite careful cleaning and dressing with carbolic acid. The skin beneath the lighter copper stubble that Euan couldn't shave just then became red and warm and swollen.

But he was young and healthy. They cleaned and disinfected the cut again and trusted that he would easily fight off the threat, thus assisted.

There was nothing else that they could do—or should do, at that. Any more drastic curative actions would be as likely to harm as to help.

~

Euan attended school as usual for the next few days. Then he grew feverish and clammy, and slightly disoriented. Alarmingly quickly, he became so weak that Nora and her father had to help him up the stairs.

They didn't take him to the attic but arranged him in the spare bedroom on the second floor.

It had no windows, but Euan didn't seem to mind; when he opened his eyes at all, he tried to focus on Nora's face.

"What a pointless way to die," he murmured once.

She squeezed his hand too hard and shushed him sharply. "You're not going to die. Don't be stupid."

~

In the hallway, Nora whispered of blood transfusions and saline injections and even leeches to her father, anticipating the precise objections he would raise to each idea. It was a time for desperate measures, and she took them.

She only hesitated before giving Euan her own blood. Nearly half of all transfusion recipients died—but if he was doomed anyway, there was no reason not to try.

For hours, Nora sat beside him, refusing to weep even as silent streams of tears rolled down her cheeks. She only left the room to use the toilet. Calista brought her food that she didn't eat. Her father came to check on Euan, and on Nora too.

"I sent a telegram to Dr. Burns," he said at one point, but she pretended not to hear.

Sometime later, seeing that she intended to sit there through the night, her father dragged in the plush armchair from his study. When Nora stood to let him take the hard, straight-backed chair she'd been using, they locked eyes and she saw tears welling in her father's too.

Yet when he tried to hug her, she pulled away and shook her head. Accepting comfort would mean accepting what was happening, and she wouldn't. Not that she thought rejecting it could keep it from occurring, but perhaps she *hoped*—against all hope, and against all knowledge.

She pulled the armchair closer to Euan and sat down, resolved not to move again until he got up. Sat up, at least. Opened his eyes. When Nora took his hand, her stomach dropped at the limpness of his fingers.

She wanted to say his name, but was too afraid he wouldn't respond. His pulse was terribly fast, she noted, his breathing likewise rapid.

Nora's sped up to match. But they could not keep pace forever.

~

An hour or so later, when Euan's breath and heartbeat finally slowed, then stopped, Nora's only paused for an awfully protracted moment.

Far worse was the instant when they started up again, her heart lurching and her breath scraping back into her lungs. The irrepressible sobs that followed were like a siren that brought her father and Calista upstairs.

Nora would not look at them, would not lift her head from beside Euan's body as she knelt on the floor with her arm clamped around him and wept into his shirt.

~

She couldn't say how long she kept vigil even after death, but Euan's body had become cool and begun to grow rigid, so several hours at least. She'd moved back into the soft chair and taken his hand again, kissed its rough knuckles and whispered that she loved him so many times she'd lost count of that too.

He was so very still, and still so very lovely, if already somewhat strange.

Nora saw more clearly than ever how death stole some vital essence of familiarity along with life. A human being, even one immensely beloved, so quickly became a human body, and there was a marked difference.

But she gazed fondly at that body, Euan's smooth brow, his dark auburn hair, so soft. She pictured his deep-blue eyes forever veiled behind his pale eyelids and thick fringe of lashes. She caressed his calloused fingers that weren't particularly graceful but had been surprisingly capable of deft and gentle movements: neatly suturing a laceration in their Saturday surgery clinic, tenderly cupping her breast in their Sunday bed.

She had adored his brain, too, of course, and everything that it made him, but it was *not* all he was. Nora placed her palm upon his perfect chest and pictured his kind heart, sitting as shallow and inert as an ungerminated seed beneath the surface.

Her own heart felt frightfully imperiled, wrenched out of place, crushed in some cruel grip.

But it was resilient, that useful muscle in her chest.

It kept beating, and her heart-sprung sorrow kept sending tears streaming down her face.

~

Sometime later, a soft voice from outside spoke her name—only, the way it carried through the cracked-open door and bounced off the wall made it seem as though it came from just beside her: "Nora?"

She started, and blinked at Euan's bloodless visage. It took her a second to realize that it was her father, out in the hall.

"He's here," he said, and Nora frowned.

Uncomprehending, she stood and sniffled, swiped at her cheeks, then opened the door wider—and started again.

Over her father's shoulder, she glimpsed a familiar face, a man standing a few paces behind him in the evening gloom of the hall, just on the edge of the pool of light from a sconce. His hair was a shade or two lighter than Euan's, more fiery threads in evidence—though there were also ivory streaks at his temples. He was slightly taller and broader, his suit not as nice as the ones that Euan had taken to wearing in Manhattan. His eyes were almost the same dark blue as his brother's, but the skin around them was webbed with fine lines, for he was nearly twenty years older.

Nora couldn't speak, staggered by her gullible brain, her thoughtless heart, which had really believed for a moment that she beheld a ghost.

Malcolm Colquhoun opened his mouth, but it, too, was filled with silence. And Nora couldn't bear it, or his face, for another second, so she turned and rushed into the study, the closest room that didn't require brushing past Malcolm to reach.

From there, she went through the connecting passage to her own room, where she stopped short in the middle of the rug. Her instinct was to curl up on her bed, but she couldn't bring herself to even perch on the edge atop the covers. It was a sacred site that Nora could not possibly disturb.

Instead, she sank to the floor. She could hear her father and Malcolm murmuring in the hall. Then one pair of footsteps moved into the middle room, while the other approached her door, but moved away again, went down the stairs.

~

Somehow, Nora dozed off. When she came to it was fully dark, and preternaturally quiet.

She rubbed her sticky, crusted eyes, stretched her sore back and hips, flexed her tingling-numb legs. There was a half-hopeful, half-dreadful sense that she might have been dreaming for a long time now, that she might only have imagined all the terrible things that so quickly came slithering back to her consciousness.

She stood with one ear against her door and listened for any intimations of movement in the hall: the faint creak of a board, the whisper of a breath.

But she heard nothing, and when she eased the door open, not even a chill waft of air disturbed the empty corridor.

Nora looked into the spare bedroom, where Euan's body still lay. Another horrid pulse of hope thudded through her, but she could plainly see, without even turning on the light or stepping into the room, that he was gone.

~

Downstairs, she discovered that Malcolm had gone too. He'd already headed back to Hoosick Falls, her father informed her, though he'd been invited to stay the night.

It made sense, Nora supposed, since there would be no funeral.

Euan had always spoken of Malcolm as a fair-minded and deeply kind man, who had been more like a father than an older sibling, but Nora was surprised that he hadn't overridden Euan's unconventional wish to donate his body; people defied the dead every day. She certainly would have understood if he'd insisted on taking Euan home to be buried.

Nora herself wanted nothing more than to veto Euan's will. Though she had been impressed by his decision, now she couldn't stand the thought of his body being dissected. Whatever was left being shipped off to be cremated in Buffalo, the ashes mailed back to Manhattan via parcel post, delivered like something from a catalog. A ghastly prospect, not romantic in the least—what callous little fools they'd been. What arrogant tempters of fate.

Sitting at the same table where they'd drafted their wills, her father on the other side now, neither of them touching their plates, Nora asked with a faint quaver in her voice, "Do you know what class he'll go to?"

Her father looked up at her and sighed, scratched beneath the bridge of his spectacles. "You needn't worry about that, love."

"I'm not worried, I'm just asking."

Delicately, her father answered, "Well, I think we'll send him to another school."

"What? No. That wasn't what he wanted."

"I know, but . . . it seems kinder—"

"To whom? To me? To go against his last wishes?"

"Yes. To everyone. Do you really think that's what Euan would want? For his own friends to . . ."

Cut him open, he didn't say, didn't have to. *To peel back his skin and crack his ribs? Reach in and pull out his insides? To weigh his heart, his lungs, his brain? To look through the last remnants of sustenance in his stomach?*

Nora stood, rattling everything on the table as she pushed her chair back. She hurried upstairs to kneel by Euan again, while she still could, while she could still entertain a wild fantasy of circumventing decay and destruction altogether. She imagined filling the tub with spirits and submerging his body so he might be held in stasis forever. A box of bone fragments and powdery ash would never be enough of him.

Nor would a lock of hair suffice. Nora might clip one and then keep going, take a paring of his fingernail, a taste bud from his tongue, a length of tendon, a knob of spine, a sliver of his heart.

What she really wanted, of course, was Euan *alive*. Failing that, she yearned for his bright, gentle spirit to stay with her. But even right there beside his body, Nora felt no trace of what had once inhabited it. And, despite what she'd thought she'd seen only a few hours before when she first encountered Malcolm, she did not believe in ghosts.

All that was left of her love, besides memories, was the meat of him, and all that could feed was the writhing worm of her despair.

CHAPTER SIX

New York City
January–March 1886

When men came to shroud Euan's body and carry it off, the secondary theft, even anticipated, felt somehow more terrible. Nora watched closely and followed them downstairs. In the parlor, as they carried him from the house, she finally came apart in an explosion of racking sobs and blinding tears.

Her father tried to comfort her, but Nora rounded on him and demanded that he *do* something—have Babcock held responsible for murder, or manslaughter at the very least, have Dr. Ratliffe fired for his poor judgment, have someone punished.

Though he looked wretchedly sympathetic, her father didn't even placate her with false promises. Once, Nora would have appreciated that. But when he only said, so softly, "It was an accident, love," she was unable to bear it—the idea that no one would suffer for Euan's loss, except herself and everyone else who'd loved him.

"I'll kill them, then," she cried. "I'll kill them both myself, and then—oh, God, I want to die."

Having no memory of her mother, Nora had only ever mourned her in an abstract way. No one else so close to her had perished since, so although she could speak quite logically and even eloquently of death itself, Nora was not fluent in the guttural language of grief. If she had been, perhaps she could have communicated the wrenching pain that overwhelmed her in that moment in some other way.

But all she could express was her wish to die, because it was the only remedy that she could imagine for what ailed her. Her father looked utterly helpless, but embraced Nora as she let herself go limp. He followed her down to the floor, where he supported her and shushed her and rocked her slightly, as he must have done when she was a wee, wailing babe.

He cried, too, but she was only dimly aware of that: a wet warmth on the crown of her head, his body shaking as he held her.

Had her father's sympathy extended only that far, everything might have been different, after.

But Nora came to sometime later, dressed only in her chemise, tucked in bed with a bittersweet taste in her mouth. The sky outside the window was violet. Her vision wavered when she sat up, her stomach bobbed. On her bedside table sat a long-spouted porcelain feeder cup designed for babies and invalids, full of an amber liquid—and though her mind was somewhat hazy, Nora felt a spike of alarm at the sight. She swung her legs out of bed and searched the insides of her arms for telltale pinpricks or bull's-eye bruises, but her father could have administered an injection in the same site from which Nora had drawn her blood to give to Euan.

When she sipped the cold, unbearably oversweetened tea in the spouted cup, she knew for certain.

Her father had given her laudanum, that alcohol-and-opium concoction so useful for blunting pain and bringing calm. Addictive to many, deadly in the wrong dosage. He'd known what he was doing, of course, with regard to not only the proper amount but the sagaciousness of administering the drug at all. He'd acted as both doctor and father and been well within his rights in both capacities. Some lingeringly serene part of Nora's mind told her that, but it was drowned out by her fury.

She stormed downstairs to find him and was only more incensed that he seemed to think her reaction irrational, overblown. "You were in a terrible state, love. Distraught. You hadn't slept for two days. You needed rest. Frankly, you were hysterical."

Nora balled her fists to keep from seizing his collar or shoving him against the wall. "How long has it been, then? What day is it now?"

He tried to evade, elide. When she demanded to know, he finally sighed and said it was Tuesday.

She nearly collapsed again in shock. "Six *days*?" Nearly an entire week removed from the world without her knowledge or her consent. "What about school?"

"What about it? They understand that you needed leave—"

"I didn't want that!"

"No, you wanted to murder Babcock and Ratliffe—"

"I didn't mean that. Not anything I said, of course—I was only overtired, and—"

"And you needed relief. You'd have done the same if you were in my position, if you'd seen yourself like that."

"Maybe for a day or two," Nora allowed, "but *six*? That is not relief; that's control."

He scoffed, a bit desperately. "Every time you came to, you were still distressed. You said . . . such troubling things, love, about curses, and—"

"Did you not think that might have been the laudanum itself?"

"I was frightened for you, Nora."

She pushed past him and strode back up to her room to dress, to throw more clothes into a valise. But first, she locked all three doors that granted access to her bedroom—from the hall, from the bathroom, and from the passage that connected her chamber to her father's study.

He did come after her, though not at a run. He knocked as gently as he normally would and said her name with a calmness that Nora found

45

insulting. She didn't reply. When she finally yanked the hall door open, he flinched, then frowned at her valise.

"Where do you think you're going?"

"Aunt Birdie's." She shook her father off when he tried to stay her passage past him toward the stairs.

He followed her down, but she outpaced him; to compensate, he raised his voice. "Nora, you cannae leave the house like this—"

"You can't stop me." She whirled around halfway down the front entrance hall and stood at full height, a grown woman in every sense, though she felt like a shrinking child throwing a tantrum—and resented her father all the more for that. She made herself sound firmer than she felt when she said, "If you try, I'll call the police. I'll tell them you drugged me and held me against my will."

He scoffed again. "I'll tell them that myself—I'll have to do it again, too, if you work yourself into another state."

Nora's stomach plummeted; her skin went cold. "*No*. Try to touch me and I'll break your fingers."

"Nora!" Her father's frown deepened, but there was fear in his eyes again. "Do you know what could happen if you say things like that? Let alone try to do them."

Tears wobbled in Nora's eyes. "Are you threatening me? With what, Blackwell's Island?" The women's mental institution in the East River, but that was for poor people. "Or no, I suppose you'd send me to Bloomingdale Asylum instead—unless you didn't want word to get out."

Her father stared at her for a petrifyingly fragile moment before Nora said, "I'd rather Aunt Birdie's, if it's all the same to you. But I have to get out of here. *Now*."

His shoulders slumped as he sighed and rubbed a hand over his face. "Let me get the carriage, at least."

"No, I'll find a cab."

"Nora—"

"You've done enough already. Leave me alone."

～

She considered going to Bette's grand new marital home uptown, but detested the thought of seeing her cousin with Ernest, smiling at him, even in passing, casually touching his arm or accepting a kiss on her cheek.

Nora hated them. She hated everyone and everything. She hoped—only slightly appalling herself, only half believing it wasn't really true—that the family curse was real and Ernest would soon die too.

The anger was a balm, in its way, a distraction from the pain that Nora knew would seep back as soon as the fury faded. But surely the solution was not to make herself insensible, unaware. Not unless it was to fully commit to death. Her father should have fed her a whole bottle of laudanum. Then she realized she could easily get one herself. That, too, was a strange comfort.

If life became unbearable, it could always be ended.

～

Nora had expected Aunt Birdie's warren of massive, echoing rooms to be preferable to the cozier confines of her own home, where Euan had occupied nearly every inch of space at some point and Nora could only be conscious of his absence.

But even within the engulfing emptiness of the Fifth Avenue abode, she had no choice but to bring her body along. Holding herself around the middle, she couldn't conjure the sensation of Euan's touch. Closing her eyes, no matter how hard she tried, she couldn't convince herself that any breath of air against her neck was the brush of his fingers.

Though she was still furious at her father for rendering her unconscious, Nora yearned for the temporary reprieve. She wept often, in the same frighteningly uncontrollable way as before, which rid her of nothing in the long term, yet at least hollowed her out and exhausted her enough to sleep for a while.

Awake, she refused to see or speak to her father, no matter how many times he came to Fifth Avenue to try to appeal to her. Aunt Birdie and Grandmama said he was only worried, only trying to help, but they didn't force Nora from her borrowed bedroom, nor did they allow her father access to it.

They must have reassured him that she was fine, all things considered. And they did deliver notes and letters that he brought by. Nora didn't open the ones in her father's hand, or even the ones from her most cherished friends and acquaintances. She couldn't bear to be subjected to them, so she set the growing stack of papers aside.

The sight of *Hoosick Falls* on one envelope, however, made her breath catch. She broke the seal with trembling fingers and read:

> *Dear Ms. Harris—Leonora, if I may call you that,*
> *Please forgive me for leaving so abruptly the other day,*
> *without even speaking to you, but I did not wish to*
> *intrude upon your sorrow. Nor did I know (or, indeed,*
> *know now) what to say in light of such devastation, other*
> *than that I am inexpressibly sorry for your loss.*
>
> *Our loss, it is—and yet our experiences of it must*
> *necessarily be separate and distinct. My brother loved you*
> *very much. He was never happier than after he met you;*
> *therefore, those of us who loved him cannot fail to love*
> *you too. It is all the more regretful that we cannot remove*
> *your pain, or even fully understand it.*
>
> *Your father told me that you tried valiantly to save*
> *Euan, and I thank you (most inadequately) for that.*
> *Though I know it must have been difficult, I am glad*
> *that you were with him at the end. It was undoubtedly*
> *a great comfort to Euan. Someday, I hope that it will be*
> *one to you as well.*
>
> *Despite it having the ring of a terribly cheap plati-*
> *tude, I suspect that time will be the only thing that truly*

helps. I do not think that God Himself can leech every drop of poison from the blood, nor expertly set straight everything that has been knocked askew and torn asunder. We shall suffer certain twinges and telltale signs that betray the ways in which we have been harmed and broken ever after, for as long as we live. But we will live, and we will be mended—I trust the truth of that, even when it feels otherwise.

I pray for your peace, and for your comfort. For whatever it is worth, I keep you in my thoughts.

With deepest sympathy & sincerity,

Malcolm Colquhoun

∼

His letter made Nora cry again, but also soothed her, as nothing else had. Somehow, his assertion that she needed time was far less galling than when others said the same—because he acknowledged that it would never be quite enough, perhaps.

Everyone else seemed to want to pretend, or at least to make Nora believe, that she would return to normal someday.

She knew better, and suspected they did too. People loved to think that lies were kinder than hard facts. But she had always wanted to know what was real, however grim and gruesome, had always believed no truth should be withheld from her, or from anyone who sought it.

∼

For over a month—the last snowy stretch of January and all the freezing February that followed—Nora barely left her aunt's lavish guest room, reading and rereading Malcolm's letter, never finding any of her own words substantial enough to reply.

And she became fixated on the idea that there *was* one perfect healer: Death. She had attended church as a child, but the literal concepts of God and heaven had seemed too farfetched to be real. She had come to believe, as her father did, that such biblical fables were ways to cope with uncertainty; it must be a lovely comfort to imagine the promise of reunion in another, unending life beyond this one, instead of simply being snapped off like a light switch at the moment of death. But to him—and then to Nora too—the prospect of oblivion itself was beautiful. The great blessing of ceasing to be conscious, the total erasure of all suffering and pain. The only pity being that one could not be conscious of that very state of *not* being.

So while there was probably no great sentient being, benevolent or otherwise—no heavenly Father who took notice of or interest in the ant colonies of humanity, much less waited to welcome each unyoked soul up to a realm of golden clouds and harpsichords—what immense awe to think of being returned to the universe, being elementally reincorporated into all existence.

Nora could still see the beauty in that, and yet, now more than ever, she wanted greater things to be possible on earth.

Since she did not believe they were, the most comforting prospect was death.

Not only for its promise of senselessness, but for what might happen in the moments before that final nightfall. Nora had questioned her father, once, about the abundance of people who seemed to see long-lost loved ones while on their deathbeds. Could that not be proof of something beyond? He'd smiled a little sadly. "It could. I cannae prove otherwise. But I suspect it's hallucination—that if we're lucky, the brain plays all sorts of kindly tricks on us as we slip away."

There was one way, then, that she might see Euan again, and it was all she thought of in between painful memories of him.

～

One afternoon, when she knew her father would be out, she ventured back to Washington Square. She startled Calista, who hugged her for a long while in gracious silence.

Before Nora went about her primary business, she roved around the house. She pressed a few keys on the piano as she passed by, brushed her fingers against the china cats on the dining room sideboard, idly tried to turn the engraved brass knob of the basement door.

It was stuck fast. She tried again, a bit more forcefully. The knob jiggled slightly, rattled faintly, but it was locked.

Nora was immediately furious, and ashamed, to think that her father had barred her, had envisioned her floating downstairs in a daze—or perhaps marching, grimly determined—and taking up his bright scalpels in the cellar's gloom, setting them to the insides of her elbows or just under her jaw. It seemed he could no longer trust her.

And of course, he shouldn't.

On her way to her room, she gazed into the windowless chamber where Euan had died. The bed had been remade, of course, and the air was perfectly still and scentless.

Upon continuing up to the attic, she feared finding Euan's old bedroom empty too—or worse, full of some new student's things— but it was just as he'd left it, which broke Nora's heart anew. The flint arrowhead that he'd brought from home sat on his nightstand. His shaving kit and slippers were still in place, his notebooks neatly squared with the edge of the dresser. Beside them was his leather roll of surgical instruments. Nora took one scalpel, wrapped it in her handkerchief to conceal in the bottom of her valise.

She lingered to survey the walls, covered with most of the sketches that she'd ever given Euan—except the ones of a more intimate nature, which Nora knew he'd cached in a Runkel Brothers chocolate box inside his own valise.

She knelt and pulled it from beneath the iron bed, surprised— relieved—that Malcolm hadn't taken it. He hadn't taken anything, as far as she could tell.

In a waft of old vanilla, she opened the hinged lid of the wooden box and found all the letters that she and Malcolm had ever written Euan. She plucked one out at random—dated November 1883—and read a portion:

> *It is cold here too, a dusting of snow already sticking to the ground and the fenceposts. We can see the cows' breath in the mornings, and in the evenings too. The troughs are forming their icy skins as fast as we can break them; soon, I suppose, the pond will freeze over. The woods have lost all their lovely colors and the foundry smoke in town hangs heavy. But we are content, of course.*
>
> *Jasper threw a shoe the other day and Kirsten cracked a double-yolked egg just this morning—good luck, she says, or a sign that someone will be having twins, or maybe getting married. I suspect it simply means we were blessed with a heartier breakfast. And that is about the sum of our recent excitements.*

~

Nora took the entire box back to Aunt Birdie's, where she read each of Malcolm's gloriously ordinary letters to his brother in order, two and a half years' worth of endearments and encouragements and gentle admonishments, news of the farm, vivid pictures of the seasons. She found references to herself, as well—to what was now her past, which, at such a distance, seemed as much like something from a storybook as everything else in those missives.

Finally, she wrote to him, apologizing for the delay in replying to his wonderfully kind letter, and thanking him for his much-appreciated regard.

Though she didn't mention reading his other letters, she admitted: *I find myself envious that you have so many more years' worth of memories of him—I wish I could know everything that you know, but then I wonder if it would only feel worse, having lost that much more. I hope that the memories comfort you, as does the knowledge that he admired you greatly. It is abundantly clear why.*

~

Having written that, Nora felt better than she had in many weeks.

And when Malcolm Colquhoun wrote back in a matter of days, though she wept to read his letter, that made her feel better too.

She began to live for his words, for the way they seemed not to bring Euan back to life but to make her almost believe that he had never died.

CHAPTER SEVEN

New York City & Newport, RI
March–August 1886

Although the initial intensity of Nora's despair slackened as trees budded and temperatures rose, it was still deeply entrenched, and she was insulted when her relatives looked at her with pleasant expressions of approval or encouragement or, worst, hope.

She wanted to tell them that if she seemed calm, it was only because her grief had thoroughly drained her vitality and continued to do so, as any parasite leeched nutrients from its host. There was no method of completely purging it. It had to work its own way through a body, and probably always left parts of itself behind—splinters of sorrow snagged in one's guts, or broken off in chambers of one's heart.

But those pains did dull and could be borne.

Nearly three months after Euan's death, Nora began to feel something she had almost forgotten: boredom.

~

She refused to be pressed into social engagements, only went for short strolls in Central Park or on the occasional trip with Grandmama to her milliner. There always seemed too many people and noises outside, and when Nora did find a quiet pocket within the park or in the halls of the natural-history museum, her melancholy was only amplified—for she had been in those places with Euan, and he was still not there.

But she did begin to venture more often from her room, if only to sit in Aunt Birdie's library or parlor while she read or wrote—letters to Malcolm Colquhoun, of course, and she started in on *Frankenstein* again, an old favorite. As a younger girl, Nora had marked certain passages: *It was my temper to avoid a crowd and to attach myself fervently to a few.* And: *None but those who have experienced them can conceive of the enticements of science.* Now, she underlined other parts: *I was new to sorrow, but it did not the less alarm me.* And: *I was doomed to live.*

Cousin Bette often visited, mercifully without Ernest. She sometimes played piano but never convinced Nora to join. Likewise, no one could entice her into card games or conversations. She was willing to engage enough to allay her family's fears for her languishing condition, but she wouldn't pretend to be happy.

At family dinners, which her father began to attend, though his careful delicacy made Nora bristle more than any blunt-force questions could have, she barely tasted the morsels of food she managed to eat.

She braced herself for pointed inquiries—chiefly, when she planned to come home, and when she would go back to school. But apparently there was still concern enough that it quelled such questions. Somehow, that was irritating too.

~

Nora did mean, every morning, to take Aunt Birdie's carriage back downtown. But she rarely even made it down to breakfast.

She was paralyzed by the thought of stepping into the stream of other students—laughing and calling to each other, or chatting seriously, or lost in their own thoughts, but all moving with great purpose, as if nothing at all had changed, as if the whole world wasn't tilted off its axis.

The moment that Nora inserted herself back into their midst, they would look at her—every one of them—with varying degrees of surprise and pity. Some with hunger. Ghouls, greedy for tragedy and pain. A few eager to see her crack and confirm their belief that she had never belonged among them.

But she could endure it, she thought. And Babcock wasn't there, she knew; he'd dropped out or transferred to another school—a detail gleaned from a note from Townsend, which Nora had finally opened but to which she had still not responded.

She worried, too, about whether she could stomach morbid anatomy class, where she might be distracted, inclined to gaze at the strange, vacant face of the cadaver. She wouldn't be able to stop wondering who that body had once been, how it had lived. If it had been loved, and by whom.

The thought of practical surgery sessions was worse. Nora wasn't sure she could touch a syringe again, much less slide the needle into someone's flesh. The prospect of watching bright-red blood spring up in the path sliced by a blade, even wielded by someone else, made her pulse jump wildly in her throat, just there beneath the fragile surface of her skin.

She tried to make herself believe that that was why, locked inside her Fifth Avenue room, she finally unwrapped her secret scalpel and touched it to the inside of her arm. She knew how little pressure was needed to part the flesh, and was careful to only open a line in the top few layers of her skin. She'd arranged cloths to catch the blood and bandages to stanch it from bleeding through her sleeve.

The urge to cut her jaw was almost overwhelming, but that couldn't be hidden, so she refrained. Instead, she touched the blade to the clean, straight cut in her arm and made it deeper—the sting of pain made her suck in a breath, along with the surprise of how much farther this second incursion went. Nora wiped the blade and pressed the cloths tightly to her arm, thinking she should have gotten catgut and needles. She hadn't meant to need them.

Eventually, the bleeding did stop, and Nora carefully disinfected and bandaged the surgically precise wound, dim thoughts of therapeutic bloodletting in her head. That was all she'd done, really—not tried to tiptoe up to the sheer, steep verge of death.

And she'd passed another test, she thought. She'd shown herself that she could handle flesh and blood and fine blades. Yet she was in no hurry to return to school.

≈

The next time that her father came for dinner, if only to soothe some of his unspoken worries, Nora announced she'd decided to enroll at Dr. Jacobi's college in September—still almost six months away. If there was any flicker of disappointment in her father's face, she didn't catch it. He only smiled and said that was a sensible decision and he was glad to hear it. No one asked what she might do in the meanwhile.

No one knew that she had a long, thin cut healing on the length of her left forearm.

≈

Nora pondered what to do for the next half year. It wasn't quite enough time to travel, not to anyplace she truly wished to see. Anyway, such halfhearted daydreams all dissolved before gaining one-tenth as much texture and vibrancy as her mental images of the Colquhoun farm. And Malcolm had already extended an open invitation.

You are always welcome to come visit the farm—whenever you wish, and for as long as you like. We consider you family.

Once the idea of visiting the place was planted, it grew. Tendrils sprouted and spread and soon choked out thoughts of so much else.

But Nora made constant excuses to herself.

Late winter was hardly the ideal time to visit such an isolated northern landscape, and as March melted toward spring, the thaw would bring travel-delaying, boot-sucking mud that could keep her stuck in town for several days.

Once it dried up, it would be their busiest season; she couldn't possibly intrude then. She would either get in the way or, worse, remain apart and idle while everyone else worked themselves weary—and would likely still feel as if they had to entertain her too. She wouldn't be a parasite.

But mostly it was the fear that even in the place where Euan had been born, and where he'd *lived*, she would find no significant traces of him—at which point there would be nowhere else in the world left to look.

There were, of course, traces of Euan in Malcolm himself. Not just his kind and stalwart nature. Nora still recalled the shock of seeing Malcolm's face in the dim hallway when they'd met.

Part of her wanted to see him again, if only to discern how great the physical resemblance truly was, and how much her mind had exaggerated it in retrospect. But that prospect was unnerving too.

In June, with Cousin Bette enormously pregnant and the graduation that Nora would not be part of looming, she convinced Aunt Birdie and Grandmama to leave early for Newport.

Nora took full advantage of the empty beaches and unpeopled lanes, knowing that once the jolly crush of vacationers arrived, she would hide herself away again, come out only very late and very early. She'd be whispered about, occasionally glimpsed beneath the moonlight in a pale robe, haunting the clifftops and skimming over the beaches below. It would suit her, she thought, being a ghost.

June and July passed in a haze of heat and sun. She spent long, curtain-dimmed afternoons indoors and lingered on the starlit sand at night, cold surf around her ankles.

She plodded through *Frankenstein* again, and was arrested by different passages now: *Heavy misfortunes have befallen us, but let us only cling closer to what remains and transfer our love for those whom we have lost to those who yet live.*

The moment that Nora underlined the sentence, she wanted to cross it out. But even when she shut the book, the words drifted through her head.

All the while, the steady exchange of letters between Newport and Hoosick Falls continued, despite the fact that Malcolm must have been exhausted from fourteen-hour days of labor; Nora pictured Euan in the fields beside his brother, or in the barn milking cows, or at the table eating meals. He wasn't so far away after all.

One morning, as the mail was distributed in the breakfast room, Aunt Birdie smiled and said, "I feel a bit of déjà vu, don't you?"

Nora blinked at her.

Grandmama remarked, "Yes, you certainly have a great deal to say to one another."

Heat rushed through Nora, rose up to tint her skin as she stood from the table. "And you all have an awful lot to say in general. Most of which you could stand to keep to yourselves."

Even the maid looked shocked, but it was hardly the worst thing Nora had ever said, so they all let it go without further comment.

Nora's father wrote regularly too. She opened his envelopes, though still didn't write back, because she had nothing to say—until early August, when he mentioned that he'd received Euan's ashes and asked if there was anything Nora wanted him to do with them.

Bring them to Newport, she replied, *or ship them to me—first class, express; send a courier posthaste.*

Instead, her father came to present them in person, in a beautiful lacquered box of shimmering abalone shell that he must have found in some wonderfully fanciful shop. Nora was touched that he'd gone to the trouble.

Inside she found a disproportionately unlovely rough cotton bag in which the Buffalo crematory had placed the ashes. It looked like a miniature flour sack; Nora had a fleeting thought of baking its contents into a batch of bread and eating every last crumb.

In fact, though she'd wanted the remains in her possession as soon as possible, she had no idea what to do with them.

In private, she stroked the smooth, iridescent box, its oily rainbows seeming to promise an equally enchanting treasure concealed within, but the gritty, whitish powder in the rough-spun bag was oddly humdrum. It was human gravel—yet bore no relation to Euan, or to any living thing. Nora licked her fingertip and dabbed the substance, then touched it to her tongue. No transubstantiation occurred. It might have been a bit of especially coarse sand, except there wasn't even a trace of salt.

$\sim$

The next morning, she wrote to Malcolm to let him know that she had his brother's ashes and to propose that she bring them to the farm that fall, *to keep or to disperse however you see fit,* she added.

He might think it was selfless generosity, but in truth, Nora simply wanted to rid herself of the curiously unmoving material, and satisfy her desire to see the farm—and Malcolm himself.

Then, she thought, she could move on; she would have to, even if she didn't know where the rest of her life might take her, or if she would consent to endure it for much longer.

CHAPTER EIGHT

New York City & Hoosick Falls, NY
August–September 1886

Bette's impending delivery meant they all left Newport early that summer, which annoyed Nora, who didn't see why she couldn't stay there alone. Her father mentioned that he wouldn't be hosting another student that year—at least, not in their house.

Nora bit her tongue to keep from snapping that she'd never said she was coming back there. She did have to return to Washington Square at least long enough to exchange her coastal wardrobe for warmer clothes more suited to the country.

~

But Nora felt strangely out of place. Sleepless in her own bed, intimately aware of the quiet in the next room.

Some nights, she heard Calista overhead in the attic bathroom and held her breath. She tried to picture Euan's face, but it seemed indistinct in her mind's eye, as if glimpsed through a steam-occluded mirror. Yet if she tried to swipe away the haze, Nora feared she would obliterate his image entirely.

With every day that passed, she felt more and more afraid in that woefully unhaunted house.

Yet even as she was eager to escape it, she felt increasingly anxious about her trip. No matter how vivid and familiar the farm was in her mind, it would be different in person. And her presence would change it, would create an imbalance—a string of imbalances—even if she only stayed for a few days, or a week, which was the plan.

If she could visit while everyone else was gone—save, perhaps, Malcolm himself—then Nora would have no trepidation. She could walk about at leisure and not feel an intruder, nor worry about what impression she might make. But the other people on the farm never left, because they never stopped working, even when the fields grew fallow and the snow set in.

And no matter how many details she'd gleaned about their characters and histories from Malcolm and Euan, they were all still strangers. While Malcolm said they considered her family, Nora understood that he could only speak for himself.

The old Nora wouldn't have cared, would have waltzed confidently into their midst—hoping to be liked—but not truly concerned how they perceived her. Now, it felt essential that they find her pleasant and yet impossible that they could.

Even Malcolm, she worried, would be disappointed, would find her completely unlike the person he'd pieced together from letters. She confessed some of her fears to him in writing; naturally, he did his best to allay them, but Nora remained nervous.

~

When her father saw her packing, he looked alarmed, then disappointed. "You're going back to Birdie's, then?"

"Maybe," Nora said. "Eventually. But first, I'm going up to Hoosick Falls."

"You are? Since when?"

"Since I arranged it with—Mr. Colquhoun. I'm taking Euan's ashes to the farm. And all his things."

"Ah. Well, that's . . . that's a lovely thing to do. And you'll be back in plenty of time for the start of term."

Nora was unable to suppress a flash of fury. "Maybe. Maybe not."

He cleared his throat. "Well, surely, they'll allow a bit of a delay, but—"

"I don't know if I'll reenroll."

"You what?"

"I might not go back."

"But you said—"

"I know what I said. But honestly, I don't . . . I don't think I care about it anymore. Being a doctor."

Her father scoffed. "Oh, aye, it's only been your ambition since you were a wee thing. Only what you've worked your whole life toward."

"But *why?*" Nora's gaze was as serious and troubled as her father's. "Because I wasn't supposed to, isn't that right? And because of you. I mean, if you'd been a lawyer, then I would have petitioned to sit the bar exam. A banker, and I'd have barged my way onto Wall Street. A farmer, and I would have tried to till a thousand acres on my own. But I never would have thought of medicine. Because it's never been for the right reasons."

"The reasons hardly matter—"

"Don't they? Doesn't it matter if I have no passion for it? That I've never been a noble person?"

"That isn't true."

"It *is*. Not like Euan, and not like you. I was only ever . . . resolute. Now I'm not even that."

"Of course you are." Her father frowned, tried to put his hand on her shoulder, though she jerked away. "But you're still in mourning, Nora—I know. You cannae be expected to feel like your old self yet."

"And I never will."

"No," he said. "Not entirely. I know that too. But you'll live a good life yet. You'll still do what you've dreamed of."

"What if I don't? Then it's just a waste?"

"Of course not, love—"

"I know you'd be disappointed—"

"I will always be proud of you, Nora. Always. I only want you to be happy. And I promise, no matter how it feels just now, you will be."

~

She resented his certainty in a way that she hadn't resented Malcolm's. Yet she hoped they both were right.

Nora only knew that if it was possible to be glad again, it would never be in that house or city, never in that life, forever bereft of Euan.

It might only be possible in the place where she was headed.

~

And then she was on her way.

It wasn't a particularly long or taxing journey. She only had to change trains once, in Troy. Barring delays, she would arrive in Hoosick Falls by the late afternoon. She had three pieces of luggage to contend with and would have taken less, but every skirt was voluminous enough to fill half of a normal valise, and then there were all of Euan's things to deliver to his brother.

Nora kept her capacious, tooled leather bag—fit for a doctor— upon her lap. Among other things, it contained the abalone box of Euan's ashes.

During the ride, she pictured how her first visit to the farm should have gone: Euan looking at her across the space between their seats with a reassuring smile, taking her hand in his and gently squeezing, telling her what to expect.

But those insubstantial visions easily dissolved with the faint jouncing of the train as it rolled and clacked along the tracks. Nora couldn't concentrate enough to read and couldn't fully relax even as she gazed out at the small towns and fields and forests rotating by. And though the trip became interminable after a mere few hours, it was over far too soon.

~

The last portion of the journey took the train along the south bank of the Hoosick River, with fine family homes on the other side of the tracks, until they curved into town among more densely packed commercial buildings. There was no grand station in Hoosick Falls, no open-air platform, no great bustle of crowds to wade through. Nora simply stepped out beneath a shingled awning—and saw Malcolm right away.

This time, there was a much gentler jolt of recognition. He looked familiar even from a distance, but in broad daylight, not quite so much like Euan, or anything like a ghost.

He approached with a hulking, white-blond man whom Nora recognized as Axel, a farmhand and the younger sibling of Kirsten, widow of Stephen, the middle Colquhoun brother. Euan had told her that Axel was extremely quiet. Indeed, he only nodded at her as he hefted her trunk in his huge hands and turned immediately for the farm wagon waiting nearby, before she could even say hello or thanks.

Malcolm began to speak at the same time as Nora. They stopped short to let the other go on, then talked in unison again a second later, laughed a little.

It was so ordinary, so unmonumental. Nora took a deep breath and felt herself relax as they commenced with the usual pleasantries. Then Malcolm picked up her valise and they crossed the road to the wagon. Axel gave another nod and walked away.

"He'll stay in town for a night or two," Malcolm said. "Did you want to see any of it before we head onward? Or freshen up? Get a bite to eat?"

Nora scanned the buildings; Hoosick Falls was technically a village, but that word seemed too quaint for what looked to her like a proper small city. It was picturesque enough, except when she turned toward the massive Walter A. Wood Mowing & Reaping Company just a few hundred feet down the bank of the river, spouting black smoke from its chimneys. "I'm all right," she said to Malcolm. "There's always Friday for the full tour, anyway." Their market day, she knew.

He nodded and offered his hand, broad and blunt-fingered, breath-takingly like Euan's, but markedly rougher. Nora took it to help her to the wagon seat, glad of her gloves, and settled herself with her bag upon her lap. The ears of the great chestnut draft horse twitched as Malcolm unhitched the animal and then stepped up onto the seat, the wagon rocking slightly beneath his weight. He left plenty of room between his tweed trouser leg and Nora's plaid skirts.

"There's a blanket if it gets too chilly. Just washed."

She smiled and thanked him, then looked out at the town as they began slowly moving forward and through. It was a Wednesday after-noon, but plenty of people were walking about. Other horse-drawn conveyances rolled steadily along the streets. A group of gleefully shriek-ing children ran home from the small school. Nora glimpsed multiple steeples and the top of a fairly large hotel.

Several people acknowledged them with waves or smiles or hat tips. Some called out greetings. Malcolm returned them all. Nora wondered if they knew who she was, if they'd expected her. It was a small town, after all. News must spread fast. But who would have started the talk? Dr. Burns was a likely suspect. She hoped they wouldn't run into him and be obliged to stop. Her father had probably asked him to look out for her, send a telegram to let him know she'd arrived as scheduled.

But she didn't see him as they turned north onto River Street. The wagon trundled over one of the bridges that spanned the Hoosick, its water burbling as briskly as hot fat in a cast-iron skillet below. On the other side, Nora turned in her seat to look back at the town.

It seemed much smaller now, a modest clutch of human industry and habitation carved out from a great deal of wilderness.

When they turned onto a dirt track that led into the countryside, she glanced back again. Hoosick Falls was already partially obscured by distance and trees. Nora felt a flutter of something like panic, which was absurd, because she had absolutely nothing to be afraid of. She was grateful when Malcolm distracted her. "Let me know if you'd like to stop at any point. I'm sure this isn't as comfortable as the carriages you're used to."

She smiled and shrugged. "It's all four wheels and a horse or two."

"Unless it's a chariot, I suppose," said Malcolm.

She chuckled, felt that pleasant buoyancy in her chest again.

They rode in an easy silence.

The afternoon was cloudy but mild. It was colder in the deepest pockets of forest, where a gentle breeze rustled the abundant leaves, most of which were still green, though they'd begun to change in places—speckles of yellow and rust, a few spots of crimson.

"Does it all look how you pictured it?" Malcolm asked.

"Even lovelier," Nora said. "It's so peaceful—and so nice to hear all the songbirds. And it smells so fresh, so *green*."

"Well, the cows aren't far off now . . ."

But Nora found the sweetish stench of their manure rather pleasant. Not that she would wear it for perfume, but there was something comforting and pure about its grassy nature.

There would be more cows on the Colquhoun farm, she knew, and chickens, a few pigs, even some sheep. Kirsten and Marie carded and spun wool to sell and to knit and crochet with; they all sold and traded whatever bits and bobs they could, including excess eggs, milk, cheese, and butter. But these days, theirs was chiefly a subsistence enterprise in which they grew and raised their own food and fodder and made as much of what they needed as they could, from soap to maple syrup.

Any money they generated went straight back into the land, or toward the immediate needs of the family.

But they weren't struggling, per se. Weren't wanting, at least. Malcolm was well dressed, Nora noted—in his Sunday best, she thought—but when she looked closely, she could see places where the clothes were shiny and threadbare and others where they'd been carefully mended. She felt self-conscious in her pristine dress, worn only twice before.

~

They'd traveled for the better part of an hour at a fairly leisurely pace when Malcolm said, "Almost there now."

Nora's stomach lurched, not only from the sensation of rattling over a rutted section of road.

She had just glimpsed the house through the trees when the clamor of a dinner bell rang out.

"That'll be Marie," Malcolm said. "And Solomon," he added, as barking began to blend with and overtake the bell's fading echoes.

Nora tried to match his smile, but her pulse was thundering in her neck, sweat prickling her underarms. She had a brief vision of jumping off the wagon and pelting into the woods.

But she gripped her leather bag tighter to steady herself and took a deep breath. And then they took the final turn out of the trees and pulled toward the farmhouse.

CHAPTER NINE

Hoosick Falls, NY
September 1886

The two-story home was large but far less ostentatious than Nora had expected from Euan's descriptions. A long porch wrapped around the front and sides. Gingerbread trim edged the eaves. The simple black shutters looked somewhat severe against the snowy-white facade, otherwise punctuated only by a cheerful red door.

The original Colquhoun home, by contrast, a single-floor log cabin that nearly blended into its surroundings, was just visible a little way behind the newer house.

Before she could take much of it in, however, and before Malcolm could even rein in Jasper, a woman ran down off the porch toward them. Nora recognized her the same way she'd recognized Axel, from secondhand descriptions, which felt slightly surreal, like seeing a fictitious character in the flesh.

Marie was Nora's age, and quite beautiful, of short stature and ample flesh, with thick waves of chestnut hair and merry, dark eyes above plump pink cheeks. Her teeth were rather small, set in a broad expanse of gums, but her unrestrained smile was contagious. She practically pulled Nora down from the side step, babbling all the while in a high, girlish voice with a northern English accent—Lancashire, Nora recalled.

"Oh, *hello*, how do you do? It's so good to meet you!" Nora lost some of the next words, but thought Marie was complimenting her hat and dress and brooch in rapid succession. "And I love your sprinkles!" Nora wasn't certain she'd heard that correctly until Marie quite freely reached out to touch her cheek.

"Marie," Malcolm said, his tone gentle but enough to make her take a step back with her hands tucked behind her.

"Sorry."

"That's all right." Nora laughed. "My goodness. Thank you for such a warm welcome."

The dog had finally stopping running half circles, so she stooped to pet him, then straightened as a tall, leanly muscled man approached from the barn.

Erik was Marie's husband and the half brother of Malcolm and Euan—a Magnusson, not a Colquhoun. His clothes were work-worn, his dark-blond hair overlong; a lighter beard bristled over the bottom of his face but couldn't obscure his surprisingly plush pink lips. His eyes were a pale, piercing blue, and squinted at Nora in a sunbreak.

"Howdy, doc. I'd shake your hand but those look like expensive gloves."

Before she could respond, he tipped the brim of an invisible hat and sauntered around to the wagon bed. He hopped up to take one end of the trunk. "Jesus Christ, you movin' in or what?"

Nora saw Malcolm shoot a look at his brother, and her own cheeks flushed. "Most of it isn't mine," she mumbled.

"We'll take it up to the spare room," Malcolm said as he lifted the other end of the trunk, and Erik jumped down to back toward the porch steps, his eyes on Nora all the while.

She turned to survey the landscape: fenced pasture and open fields, scattered outbuildings and animals, and dense stands of forest bordering it all. The sun was quite low in the sky already, would soon dip below the tops of the rustling trees.

"Did you want to see the animals?" Marie asked. "Or the house first?"

Nora peered at the scattered cows grazing in the pasture, one massive bull, sharp-horned and heavy with muscle, among them. *Old Nick*—she even knew his name. And that he had the habit of breaking the fence, though he looked placid just then. His sheer size made her uneasy, though, so Nora chose the house, and Marie threaded an arm through her elbow and led her up onto the porch and inside.

∾

Wide wooden planks creaked in the wainscoted vestibule and broad entry hall.

The men were already coming downstairs, having deposited the trunk. "I'll be right back with your valise," Malcolm said.

Nora thanked him as Marie took her into a long parlor papered in flocked burgundy damask with a paler purple background. It ran the full length of the house and was arranged into two sections, lavish rugs in each. Nearer the front windows, a sort of library nook held tall bookcases and a small table and chairs. "Do you like games?" Marie asked. "We have lots, but hardly anyone ever wants to play."

Without waiting for an answer, she drew Nora to the other end of the parlor, where the bulk of the furniture was arranged before the hearth, brightly embroidered pillows on the settee and armchairs. French doors opened onto the porch where it wrapped around the right flank of the farmhouse, and paintings hung in abundance from the picture rail. Nora's eye was drawn immediately to one in particular, but before she could look too closely, they moved onward across the hall.

A study sat snugly at the front of the house, its walls covered in a print of dark-red and bronze floral medallions. A rifle was mounted above the mantel, and two brown velvet armchairs huddled before the hearth. A stuffed fox stalked a glass-eyed pheasant atop one bookcase.

More tomes were haphazardly stacked on the table and desk. "Mal does his figures in here. Best knock if the door's closed—but it hardly ever is."

Next, Marie showed Nora the adjoining dining room, which contained a long, polished table and a hutch full of vividly painted china with a riotous pattern of birds and plants. The gold-accented chinoiserie wallpaper was a striking turquoise, the bold hue tamed somewhat by dark wood trim. Even Grandmama would be impressed by the decor, Nora thought. Another set of french doors opened onto the left-side porch.

"The pantry's through here," Marie said, and led Nora through it into the kitchen, amply sized, outfitted with a dry sink and a black cast-iron cookstove beneath a window.

"She's here!" Marie announced.

The tall, rail-thin woman at the stove turned to sweep her gray eyes over Nora. "Miss Harris."

"Kirsten," Nora said. "Hello."

Kirsten had been married to the second-eldest Colquhoun son, Stephen, dead for over five years now. She'd stayed on to help run the farm and keep house. She'd been something like a mother to Erik and Euan when they were younger, though not necessarily the most demonstrative. Euan had once recounted how she'd scrub his scraped knees *like she meant business—that always hurt worse than the fall itself. And then she'd kiss my forehead—but that was like getting pecked by a slightly friendlier than average chicken.*

Nora had laughed and hoped to meet her someday. Now, she couldn't hold Kirsten's gaze.

Marie gently tugged her toward the far corner, where two dark-haired little girls, about three years old, sat on the floor, sorting a pile of buttons into like-colored groups.

"That's Bea and that's Addie. Girls, this is Miss Nora. She's come to stay with us for a while. They don't talk yet, but they ain't deaf. Ain't changelings neither."

"Of course not," Nora said, then offered a greeting to the twins.

They didn't even glance up. They seemed entirely unaware of anyone else's presence, which Nora had known to expect, but still found strange—and intriguing. She knew that Euan had cursorily examined them and found nothing obviously wrong to prevent them from speaking. Not tongue-tied. No cleft palates. He'd thought the issue was some developmental disorder, likely congenital.

Marie is extremely kindhearted, he'd written, *and the most naive woman I have ever met.*

> *Rustic, certainly, and barely educated, but I believe there is something more to her lack of sophistication than that. Some natural deficit, which seems too harsh a term; a difference, then, readily apparent within a few moments of meeting her. She also happens to be the daughter of the mill owner who employed Erik in England. As she has no siblings, Erik now stands to inherit that mill.*
>
> *It wouldn't be the first marriage for financial gain, of course, but it strikes me as somewhat distasteful—though then I wonder if it should. Marie is a grown woman, after all, and clearly capable. She seems perfectly happy with their arrangement too, even though Erik resides in the cabin while she and the girls stay in the house.*
>
> *When I asked Erik if he loves them, he wouldn't give me a straight answer. Mal thinks the fact that he brought them home is proof enough. Perhaps that is true. At least he isn't unkind to them, as far as I can tell. Only distant, which may be for the best.*

However unlikely and unconventional their union, Marie did indeed seem happy. When Kirsten said, "Why don't you show Miss Harris upstairs now?" she enthusiastically obliged.

As they left the room, Nora noticed another interior door with a hefty padlock on it. "What's that?" she asked Marie.

"Oh—just the basement. It's dark, and the stairs are steep."

"Can't have the girls falling down them," Kirsten added.

Nora nodded, but the lock was a serious-looking thing that might have secured the gates of a cemetery. It sent a strange twinge of unease through her.

She had little time to think about it, though, before Marie led her upstairs.

~

At the closed door nearest the second-floor landing, she said, "That's Kirsten's room. We don't go in there. But you can come into ours whenever you like."

She towed Nora a few steps down the hall to look into the next room, which had three narrow beds and two homely rag dolls, which Marie proudly announced she'd made. They continued a few more paces toward the front of the house and paused outside another open door.

"This one's yours! It used to be—oh, well. Never mind."

But Nora already knew, and stepped cautiously to peer inside before crossing the threshold. The space was small and somewhat cramped with a bed, armoire, and desk, and though several surfaces seemed to have been recently cleared for Nora's use, it hadn't been stripped completely.

The walls were a pale yellow, with several of her own drawings hanging up, much as Euan had decorated his attic room in Washington Square.

The blankets were the same ones that had covered him, she guessed. The mantel held more arrowheads and other treasures found in the fields and forests, from birds' feathers to wasps' nests.

She placed her leather bag upon the foot of the bed and nodded toward a vase of purple asters and canary-colored black-eyed Susans. "Those are lovely."

"I knew you'd like them," Marie said.

When Malcolm appeared in the hall, behind Marie's shoulder, Nora startled slightly.

"There you are," he said. "You got the grand tour, I expect?"

"Yes; it's such a lovely home."

"His room's just across the hall," Marie said. "It's the nicest, but that's only fair."

Before either of them could stammer a response, she continued, "You can see the cabin now, and the barn and the animals, and—"

"There's plenty of time for all that," Malcolm gently interrupted. "Miss Harris might like to rest—she's had a long journey."

The *Miss Harris* sounded jarring coming from him; he only ever called her Nora now, though she realized that he'd only ever called her anything in letters.

"I'm fine," she said. "I'd like to see everything else—though I suppose it's almost time for milking. Can I help? With anything?"

"No, no; please, just settle in until supper. That is, you're welcome to go where you like, of course. Make yourself at home."

Nora smiled and said to Marie, "The barn, then?"

The interior of that massive structure was dim already, but the air was warm and sweetly fragrant, a little fermented and earthy too. "Axel sleeps up in the loft," Marie informed her, which Nora knew was by choice, though she thought it strange. "But he has Solly so he isn't lonely," Marie said, of the dog.

She introduced the two draft horses, "Matilda—and Jasper, of course, you've already met. Then Aggie's Malcolm's mare, and Erik's gelding here is Odin. I'd like my own pony but there's no need. Nor money. I did have a donkey at home, at least. Old Bob. I miss him. I bet Gran and Dad don't ever scratch his neck."

Even speaking of homesickness, however, Marie looked content. Nora watched her rub Matilda's glossy neck, the size of a tree trunk, and felt a sudden spike of sorrow that threatened to undo all the morning's happiness. Euan had lavished similar affection on Asclepius and Paracelsus, had asked countless cab drivers in the city if he could say hello to their horses, and what were their names, and weren't they gorgeous. It was one of the millions of things about him that had so charmed Nora, and though it ached to remember, she reminded herself how glad she was to finally be here, in the place where he had lived.

Marie showed her the grazing heifers next, but Nora had no hope of retaining their names, much less recognizing them. Nora backed away from the fence when a number of the cows came toward it at Marie's summons, as did Old Nick—though the bull seemed entirely without aggression.

The sheep and pigs were likewise friendly. Marie reeled off all their names too.

The only creatures that hadn't been christened, in fact, seemed to be the feral cats that slunk about the barn and streaked occasionally across the landscape, seeking the mice and birds that kept them fed.

Nora dissuaded Marie from showing her Erik's cabin; it felt too prying, and besides, he might be inside. She wasn't eager to interact with him again. She'd expected a certain prickliness, but not the alarming jolt she'd felt when he turned his piercing, pale-blue gaze upon her.

It was just the unusually arresting color, Nora told herself. And the directness of his attention.

Euan had rarely spoken of his half brother, had deemed him temperamental, with a wild streak. They'd been closer as boys, separated in age by only one year, but as young men, their relationship had grown strained. At seventeen, Erik had left the farm, over two years before Euan departed for Manhattan and medical school. From occasional postcards, they'd known that Erik was alive and overseas, but little else.

Then, almost a year and a half ago, he'd returned without warning, with a wife and twins in tow, stunning everyone. Euan had received the news in a letter. He'd seemed excited—encouraged—but once he'd visited home and met Marie and the girls, he'd confessed the complicated truth of the matter to Nora.

Now, she followed Marie to the springhouse, a squat, whitewashed stone structure built over a stream. They used it in lieu of an icebox to store perishables, and drew their water from a pump just inside.

The long, low hut's thick walls radiated a damp chill and made Nora think briefly of some crude medieval morgue. She only peeked inside; with no windows, the space was already dark, even with the door propped open, for dusk had fallen.

On moonless nights, Euan once said, *you can't even see your hand in front of your face.*

"I'd better get back to the barn now," Marie said, and Nora was glad, for she suddenly wished to be safe inside.

CHAPTER TEN

Hoosick Falls, NY
September 1886

Don't be daft, she told herself—in her father's voice. There was nothing dangerous out here.

There are bears, Nora's own inner voice answered. But they were rarely seen, much less encountered. It was just so much darker than she'd imagined.

She heard Euan say, from deep within the past, *You might be scared.*

Well, she'd said, in the same half-teasing tone, *I'll have you to protect me.*

But now, she was alone.

Not really, she thought; the others were within shouting distance, and later, Malcolm would be just across the hall. Nora blushed at the idea, and felt absurd for that as well.

She thought it prudent to duck into the outhouse while there was still a bit of natural light. The whitewashed walls helped brighten the close confines of the odiferous wooden hut, and Nora was relieved to see an actual roll of toilet paper—no Montgomery Ward catalog pressed into service.

There was, however, a spider dangling in one corner. She only noticed it mid-business, and hurried to finish, her attention torn between the arachnid and the half-moon slit carved into the door, non-sensically expecting an eye to appear in the space at any second.

Outside, there was a place to wash her hands. The water looked fresh, and the homemade cake of soap smelled pleasantly astringent from rosemary. That soothed her nerves considerably—but saddened her, too.

The same soap had faintly perfumed Euan when they first met, then faded with successive launderings of his clothes in the city. Each time he'd returned from visits to the farm, he'd carried a fresh waft of the pungent herb. Nora had smelled a whiff of rosemary on Malcolm when they rode in from town.

As she walked toward the porch steps, she held her own knuckles to her nose, and her heart felt so heavy she feared it might fall from her chest.

~

Inside the farmhouse, oil lamps and fireplaces lit the rooms; there were no gas pipes, let alone electricity.

She waded through pools of shadow toward the back of the house, where faint clatters drifted from the kitchen.

Before Nora could speak from the doorway, Kirsten swiveled her steel-streaked blond head. "Did you need something?"

Nora jumped at the sharpness of her voice. "No, thank you. Can I help with anything?"

Kirsten pressed her thin lips together and turned back around. "I'm sure you're not normally called on to do such things, and I wouldn't dare. You're our guest."

"Well, I don't mind," Nora said. "And I can cook, a little. Our housekeeper tricked me into learning. She pointed out how it was just as much science as anything in my father's books. How liquids turn into solids, and sugar—"

"I wouldn't know anything about that," Kirsten interrupted. "*Science.* I'm used to managing by myself."

"Of course."

Humbled, Nora left the kitchen. She considered going to the barn to help with milking but feared she would be a hindrance there too.

On her way through the dining room, however, she decided that she would set the table—as quietly as she could, lest Kirsten bustle out to stop her.

Nora didn't usually perform such chores, it was true, but she was perfectly capable, and would rather not feel so utterly useless. She was pleased with her work, though partway through, Kirsten poked her head in and said, "We don't normally use the fine china."

"Oh." Nora felt her stomach sink, then straightened her shoulders and gave Kirsten another perfunctory smile. "But I'm sure you do for guests."

Kirsten's gray eyes narrowed slightly, and the fissures around her mouth deepened, but she went back to the kitchen without further comment.

Nora imagined making furtive eye contact with Euan, stifling laughter until it burst from them anyway. Her heart made its weight known again, but even lonely, and alone, she felt her lips tremble in a smile.

~

The meal itself was pleasant enough, though Marie directed Nora to the chair immediately beside her own, which put Erik directly across from her. Malcolm sat at the head of the table, to Nora's right; Kirsten took the foot, with the twins situated on either side.

Axel's chair, beside Erik, remained empty. Nora wondered if he'd made himself scarce because she was there.

She bowed her head while Kirsten said grace, but felt Erik's eyes on her. To distract herself, she watched the girls from her peripheral vision. They had climbed into their seats on their own, at a prompt from Kirsten, but seemed otherwise disengaged—or rather, interested only in looking at minute areas of the table, or something past it that no one else could see.

Nora had expected an interview of sorts, if not an interrogation. Her own family would have probed—politely, for the most part—into the life of any new guest on their first night among them. But Marie was the only one who reeled off questions, with a charming artlessness and wildly free associations. She already knew a great deal about Nora, which meant that Euan—or Malcolm, or perhaps both men—had spoken of her, and she was touched. Still, she felt somewhat awkward being the center of the mostly one-sided conversation.

At one point, Marie said, "I wish we had a piano so we could hear you play!"

"Oh, I'm terribly rusty," Nora said, and despite the fact that it meant she had to address Erik, she seized the chance to bring someone else into the discussion. "You play the violin, don't you?"

"Fiddle."

"Are they different instruments?"

He smirked. "Technically, no. But *violin* makes it sound like I can saw out Vivaldi. Whereas *fiddle*, well, that sets the proper expectations."

Nora emitted a genuine chuckle.

Erik grinned. His eyeteeth were pointed. "I keep waitin' for Kirsten to pull out that old zither of hers," he said as he shoveled in a mouthful of food.

Nora had never heard of Kirsten playing music. She was intrigued, but sensed it was a subject best left unexplored, even before Erik added, "This used to be a pretty lively house."

Malcolm asked, "Was there anything in particular that you wanted to do tomorrow, Nora?"

She wondered if he meant the memorial ceremony, but only said, "Not really, no. I thought I might just get the lay of the land, wander the woods a bit."

Erik snorted. "Wander too far, you might not find your way back out again."

"The woods aren't that thick," Malcolm countered. "But I could go with you. Or Marie's a fine guide, too. Just to be safe."

"We can look for chestnuts!" Marie's broad smile quickly slid into a frown. "Oh, but—tomorrow's a butter day."

"It's fine," Kirsten said. "You show Miss Harris about if you'd rather."

"Nah," Erik said. "You'd better let Mal do it. I think he's a mite anxious to have some more time alone with the doc."

It was not one wave of prickling irritation that washed over Nora then but an entire sea, turbulent with embarrassment, too, and perhaps a glimmer of hope. She caught Malcolm giving Erik a censorious look, and caught Kirsten pressing her lips flat again, while Marie seemed to bite down on a giggle.

At least Erik finished before the rest of them. He mopped his mouth and beard, then threw his napkin on the table as he stood. "Well, it's been a pleasure, but I'll leave you all to it."

He cast a pointed look at his wife before he turned and left by the french doors. Nora's cheeks flamed again, and she kept her eyes on her plate.

When the rest of them were finished, Malcolm complimented the meal and asked if they should adjourn—it was a script of sorts, Nora sensed, and she dutifully rose along with the others.

When she moved to help clear the table, Kirsten raised a hand—a gesture that one would use to command a dog, which Nora obeyed, though she felt rankled again when Kirsten announced, "I'm worn out from today. I'll turn in early and take the girls up. Marie, you can do the dishes."

Marie opened her mouth as if to protest but then seemed to think better of it and silently followed Kirsten to the pantry with an armful of dirty crockery.

Nora hesitated to leave the girls alone, though she doubted they would attempt to toddle away or climb on the furniture unsupervised. They'd barely moved even to eat, and hadn't fed themselves but had been ministered to by Kirsten. Now, they remained seated, paying no mind to anything else in the room, including each other.

From the way their eyes moved, in tiny flicks across the tablecloth, Nora knew that their brains were working and wondered if they were in some sort of waking dream. She could see why more superstitious and less-educated people might think them enchanted. She wanted to speak to them, to know the magic phrase that would get them to respond, but suspected there was none, and held her tongue.

"They'll be fine," Malcolm assured her, so, tearing her attention away, she followed him across the hall into the parlor.

There, he hesitated. "I shouldn't assume you want to sit up—if you're tired . . ."

"I'm all right," she said. While he kindled a fire, Nora drifted over to the painting she'd meant to look at earlier. An oil portrait of a red-haired, blue-eyed child of ten or so—it could easily have been Malcolm, or even Stephen, yet Nora knew it wasn't. Euan's essence beamed from those beautifully painted eyes, a giddy intelligence and warm curiosity that pierced her heart.

"Stephen painted that," Malcolm said, from where he bent before the hearth. "Most of the other ones too. He used to take lessons with an artist in town after church on Sundays, but he always had a natural talent."

"I didn't know that," Nora said, truly surprised that neither Euan nor Malcolm had ever mentioned their middle brother's artistic bent, much like they had never mentioned Kirsten's music.

"You're quite a gifted artist, too," Malcolm said as he stood up before the now-blazing fire.

Nora tried not to look startled as she turned from the portrait, but some of the sketches that she'd so recklessly sent to Euan flashed through her mind. Malcolm hadn't taken them from the attic room in Washington Square, but that didn't mean he hadn't come across them the night Euan died.

But then he never would have alluded to them—and her shell studies and seascapes were on the walls. She finally stammered, "Thank you. I always liked to sketch. I started out copying the illustrations from fairy tales, but found I liked my father's anatomy textbooks better."

She stopped short, realizing that wasn't conventionally appropriate, either, but Malcolm was familiar with her history, and only smiled.

Too late, Nora realized that she should have said she was tired and shut herself away in Euan's room, but it wasn't unpleasant to pass the time in Malcolm's company. Only somewhat awkward, thanks to Erik's earlier comment, and the fact that they both knew Marie was no longer in the house but had slipped out to meet her husband.

Nora couldn't choose a book, knowing she wouldn't be able to stay focused on a story, but finally took a slim, soft volume off the shelves near the round table at the far end of the room and carried it back to the settee before the fireplace.

Malcolm had already brought a novel to one of the armchairs. He smiled to see her selection of the town directory.

Once she sat, she became acutely conscious of the darkness outside the windows and french doors at her back, and of the oil portrait's gaze from the wall. But Malcolm's proximity was reassuring, even as it was its own source of slight discomfort. The warmth that wavered upon Nora's skin from the fire seemed slightly too intense, and though the silence that enveloped them, underscored only by crackling logs and the ticking grandfather clock, was companionable, she felt it thicken.

She read intently and found that Hoosick Falls seemed to offer everything one could want: farm implements; oysters; ammunition; ale, wine, and imported liquors; silk stockings; fur capes; feather mattresses; musical instruments; hot and cold baths; hairdressing services;

steamship tickets; ice cream; upholstery and undertaking. The village had one newspaper, two photographers, three dentists, six livery stables, eight meat markets, ten notary publics, and twelve physicians, not including the veterinary surgeon also listed in the directory.

When she began to yawn, Malcolm seemed rather relieved. "I'm sorry for keeping you up," she said, but he assured her it was only just getting to be his bedtime.

She wanted to wait for him to douse the lamps and break apart the logs, but it seemed inappropriate, and childish besides. So they said good night and Nora climbed the stairs alone.

She let herself into Euan's empty room, much darker now.

As she undressed, she peered out at the stretch of cleared land before the forest, where a paltry gap marked the road.

Hoosick Falls still lay somewhere beyond, and Nora was not so far outside the bounds of that robust society. Yet she thought the opening in the woods looked smaller now. As if the trees shuffled closer together at night, might seal the way out entirely.

She hurried to close the curtains and burrowed beneath the bedcovers in her flannel nightgown. Malcolm had offered to lay a fire for her, but she'd declined—and though it was chilly, she was glad, for she felt that the flames would have made her too visible, exposed her to something, as the house itself looked so exposed from outside.

Nothing was there, of course, and when Nora's eyes flew open at a heavy tread in the corridor, she reminded herself that it was only Malcolm, going to his own bed.

~

But she had to open her eyes again, because with them closed, she began to picture other things she didn't mean to. First, flashes of Euan's milk-pale skin—his strong back beneath her palms; the way she'd once tried to touch her mouth to every single gingery freckle smattering his chest and arms; his parted lips, seen from below the angle of his chin, his thick fingers twining deep in Nora's hair, raising gooseflesh on her limbs.

It happened then, even as warmth pulsed through her body.

But then, instead of Euan's eyes, she saw Erik's piercing, ice-blue stare and pointed canine teeth.

When Nora pushed that figment away and cautiously shut her eyelids again, it was Malcolm's faintly furrowed brow and paler lips that flashed through her mind. Through the rest of her flashed the phantom feeling of his short russet beard rasping against the inside of her thigh.

She bolted up from the bed and went back to the window, opened it to the dark thicket of forest that blotted out the world beyond the farmstead. A night chorus of crickets and other hidden insects sang; the sheer magnitude of them made the sound less soothing and more unsettling. But at least the chill air was helpful as it seeped into Nora's skin and flesh and cooled her blood.

Anesthetized, she thought, as she finally closed the window most of the way and went back to bed.

CHAPTER ELEVEN

Hoosick Falls, NY
September 1886

The first hint of daylight and a faint smell of bacon trickled into Nora's sleep and woke her. She could tell it was still early, but also that she'd probably slept later than anyone else. She hurried to dress in yesterday's clothes, then raked her fingers through her hair and twisted it into a hasty chignon.

As soon as her bootlaces were tied, Nora raced downstairs and straight for the outhouse. If she'd woken in the middle of the night, she would have used the chamber pot beneath the bed, but she hated the thought of being seen emptying it.

She said good morning to the spider.

❧

While she washed her hands, she gazed at the barn, but decided to head toward the small orchard instead, planted on a slight rise past the closest field.

Just beyond the apple and pear trees, which screened the view, lay the family cemetery. Nora's breath grew shallow at the first glimpse of headstones, and caught when she got close enough to read the largest marker.

Euan had been named for his father; he'd told her several times how strange it was to visit this place as a boy and see his gravestone—*like Ebenezer Scrooge.*

Now, she read it for herself:

EUAN COLQUHOUN

LOVING FATHER AND HUSBAND

DEARLY MISSED AND FOREVER IN OUR HEARTS

APRIL 7, 1813–AUGUST 19, 1862

She took a deep breath and made herself move on to the other stones, the earliest one for the first child Euan Sr. and his wife had lost:

HAMISH COLQUHOUN

GONE TO GOD

JUNE 24–JUNE 28, 1849

Then one for their only daughter, who'd been born the year after Malcolm:

MAISIE COLQUHOUN

OCTOBER 21, 1845–DECEMBER 10, 1856

OUR SWEET LITTLE ANGEL

WITH HER BROTHER AT THE HAND OF GOD

Such pitifully short lives, Nora thought. Even Euan's parents had died fairly young—his father first, and his mother on the same day as her second husband. A fever had taken them within hours of each other. Nora regarded their markers now:

HANNAH COLQUHOUN

DEAREST MOTHER, DEVOTED WIFE, AND SERVANT OF GOD

ONCE OUR ANGEL, NOW HIS OWN

JUNE 13, 1823–AUGUST 26, 1870

GONE TO HER REWARD

By contrast, Erik's father's memorial inscription was shockingly brief:

O MAGNUSSON

2/2/26–8/26/70

The stone itself was far smaller and plainer, too. *Strange*, Nora thought, and certainly jarring, to not even inscribe the man's full name. She knew that he hadn't been the kindest person, but it was such a stark contrast to the others. She noted, too, how they had given Hannah back her former surname. She had died a Magnusson but been memorialized as a Colquhoun. Nora wondered if it stung Erik, to be denied that connection to his mother. If it had felt lonely to be the only one of his kind left in the family, before he married and made new Magnussons of his own.

The final pair of headstones, for the last people who had perished in this place, bore dates that also almost matched:

Johan Colquhoun

Pure of spirit

September 10, 1870–December 31, 1880

And only one day later, his poor father had followed:

Stephen Colquhoun

July 15, 1847–January 1, 1881

Husband, father

Beloved brother and loyal son

May God rest his soul

Nora knew that Johan had drowned, trapped under pond ice. Euan said Stephen had died of a broken heart. She'd never pressed, but always suspected he didn't mean an actual coronary event.

Partially sunken into the grass between their markers was a much smaller rock, irregular but reasonably flat, and crudely inscribed—by Kirsten's own hand, Nora guessed:

My heart lies here

She felt a sharp pang of sympathy for the woman, and a hot welling of tears in her eyes.

But then something almost like hope coursed through her. For Euan was not in the ground like the rest of them—he'd been burned, and breathed out into the world, and what scant physical traces of his body were left were currently in his childhood room, where Nora was welcome to stay as long as she liked.

~

Malcolm raised the subject after breakfast, when they went for a walk, Marie rather glumly left behind to help Kirsten make butter. Nora would have liked to observe, but didn't want to be a bother.

She'd brought some art supplies from home and retrieved her sketchbook before they set out, though she didn't actually stop to open it as they ambled among the trees.

"There's a hill near here," Malcolm said after a little while, and gestured vaguely. "I thought it might be a good place to . . . well, Euan used to like to take in the view from there."

It was the first time, Nora realized, that either of them had spoken his name aloud in the other's presence. She nodded, not trusting herself to speak.

After another moment, Malcolm said, "I've been thinking, though. I know it's all symbolic, but . . . I'm not sure we should scatter all the ashes here. Because, as much as he loved it, Euan always wanted to leave."

Nora tried to swallow the painful lump in her throat. "Yes, but—he always wanted to come back too."

"What if we divide them, then?" Malcolm asked. "Scatter half here, and . . . you can take the rest wherever you like."

"If you think that's best. But I'm not in any hurry."

"No. And I don't intend to rush you. I just . . . wanted to say."

~

And then they didn't speak of it again for some time.

~

After breakfast the following day, everyone except Axel went into town. Erik saddled Odin while Malcolm hitched up the wagon and the others loaded it with the modest cargo they hoped to sell or trade in town.

Addie and Bea struggled somewhat, mewled weakly when Kirsten lifted them up. Malcolm noticed Nora's frown and said in a low voice, "They've gotten much better—they used to squirm and scream. Kirsten's good with them."

Nora nodded and hesitated to take his hand when he offered it to help her up. "Does anyone else usually ride up front?"

He glanced at Kirsten, who, although Nora hadn't known she was listening, said, "I'm fine in back." She cut Nora off when she tried to insist that she didn't mind and boosted herself into the wagon bed with a bitter air of triumphant suffering.

Nora suppressed a wave of annoyance and let Malcolm hand her up onto the side step. She scooted over on the spring-supported bench seat, though not as far as she had on the ride in from the village only two days before.

It seemed an age ago. Nora tilted her head back as the sun streamed down, rather hot already in the open portions of the path. The birds sang complicated choruses and counterpoints around them, and the turning leaves rustled on the trees. The horse's tack jangled, and the animal itself huffed periodically. Soon, Nora had relaxed into a state of drowsy contentment, though she had to grip the edges of her seat when they jostled over the rougher sections of the dirt roads. A few times, she bumped into Malcolm, and he stiffened, but chuckled along with her too. She forgot all about Kirsten's bony frame jouncing against the hard wood of the wagon bed.

❧

They lost sight of Erik as he galloped ahead, but met far more traffic than they had on the ride in from Hoosick Falls. Sundry other farmers drove their wagons and smaller carts or rode on lone horses laden with saddlebags. Nora smiled and nodded at them all.

She felt an unexpected surge of excitement when town came into sight, the sort she imagined made a sailor cry *Land ho!* Soon, they crossed the bridge over the burbling river and plodded toward a busy street, where Malcolm helped her down, then hitched the horse outside a mercantile.

"If you'll excuse me, I have a little business to attend to, but Marie can show you where to find anything you need—and then we can all meet back here in an hour, if that suits you?"

"Certainly," Nora said, and glanced back at the girls, who now stood on the street beside Kirsten. Upon closer inspection—and she had to look twice—they were attached to Kirsten's waist by means of ropes threaded through loops on the backs of their plain dresses. They were leashed.

Kirsten raised her chin. "Can't have them wandering off, can I, darting under the wheels of some carriage? But they won't let you hold their hands for more than a second."

Nora flashed a smile. "Clever solution." And it was, she supposed, if jarring at first glance. Just like the oversize lock on the cellar door. Particularly when she had only seen the twins move at a glacial pace.

The regular residents of Hoosick Falls must have been used to it, for no passerby looked twice, and only a few looked askance—at *her*, Nora realized, not at the twins. But then, she was a new face in town.

She returned the greetings of everyone who gave them, and reminded herself that those who scrutinized her did it out of sheer curiosity. They knew nothing about her, especially all the ways in which she had changed.

∾

Her first order of business was to buy a postcard. She felt she owed her father that much. She jotted down the first thing that came to mind:

This city mouse is feeling quite content in the country! Give my love to everyone. Hope all is well.

Filial duty discharged, Nora set out to buy a gift for the family to show her appreciation for welcoming her to the farm. Her father had sent her off with a generous purse, despite her protests. *What on earth am I going to buy out there?* she'd asked.

Your return ticket, at the very least, he'd said.

Now, Nora felt an urge to spend every cent on frivolities.

A cake from the bakery, which sent delicious fumes wafting down the street, would offend Kirsten, and any household trinket seemed presumptuous. Something practical might be appreciated, but abysmally boring. Even fancy French-style confectionary, which some of the stores stocked, seemed too ostentatious. But surely no one could object to simple penny candy. Sweet and special without being precious, it was something to share among everyone for a short time without overstaying its welcome.

While they waited for a clerk to fill a two-pound bag, a little brown-haired girl, about six, wandered over and cast an envious eye upon the bounty.

"Hello, Annie," said Marie.

Annie smiled and mumbled hello back.

"A handful for her, too, please," Nora said.

The clerk raised his eyebrows but deposited a small scoop directly into Annie's palms.

She giggled and scampered toward the back of the store, where a clamor immediately arose. Two children bickering, and a woman's voice rising over them. "There's more than enough for you to share—and where did you get that, anyway? Did you sneak behind the counter again?"

"No! The lady gave it to me—*me*, not *you*."

The other child squealed.

"Be *nice*," the woman ordered.

"It's my fault," Nora called, and stepped around the shelves separating them. "I didn't realize . . ." She trailed off, struck by the sight of the family: a tall brunette woman maybe ten years older than herself, with a wispy-haired baby on her hip. At her skirts, Annie, and a boy of about four, with white-blond hair and bright-blue eyes.

Nora had to force herself to look away from him. "Well, I'm sorry. I didn't mean to cause a squabble."

"It doesn't take much. And it was kind of you. Miss Harris, isn't it? You're staying at the Colquhoun place?"

"Yes. Nora."

"Grace Murphy. Pleased to meet you. Say thank you," she told her children. They did.

"You're welcome," Nora said, and lower, to their mother, "I am sorry."

Grace chuckled. "Throw me a piece and I'll forgive you."

Nora smiled and offered her the bag, from which Grace plucked a lemon drop. "Thanks." She shifted her gaze over Nora's shoulder. "Hello, Marie."

"Hello, Grace! And hello, Ezra! And little Alvie."

The older blond boy waved, his mouth too full of sweets to speak politely. Nora couldn't help glancing between him and Marie and Grace, but she sensed no awkwardness, and scolded herself for jumping to silly conclusions when there was hardly only one blond, blue-eyed man in town. In fact, there were two on the farm alone.

Grace made baby Alvie wave, and said she'd see Marie on Sunday, and hoped to see Nora too.

~

Back at the wagon, Nora discovered that the twins weren't interested in sweets, and Kirsten declined to partake. Erik was still nowhere to be seen. But Marie and Malcolm gladly accepted some candy, and Nora held a piece of horehound in her own mouth as they began their journey back to the farm.

Its faintly medicinal flavor nagged her with familiarity. Only as town slipped away behind them did she realize what it evoked: the aftertaste of laudanum.

She felt a twist of dark emotions, the equivalent of clouds passing before the sun, but then sat straighter in the wagon seat, glad to be going back to the farm, to not be going home yet.

CHAPTER TWELVE

Hoosick Falls, NY
September 1886

When they arrived, a ghost of mentholated bittersweetness still lingered on Nora's tongue. She had placed the abalone box of Euan's ashes in the center of his mantel, surrounded by his boyhood things, and when she went up to get her sketchbook, she paused to lay her bare palm upon the cool, polished shell surface.

She despaired to think of how thoroughly she'd stripped his attic room in Washington Square. *A clean slate,* she'd thought, but it seemed misguided to have erased so much evidence of his habitation. She was immeasurably grateful for what Malcolm had preserved.

Still, it would never be enough, and she cast a thought out to Euan: *I miss you.*

A faint creak outside the room made Nora turn her head, but no one looked in, and when she stepped closer to the door, there was no one in the hall.

As she stepped into the corridor herself, another faint creak sounded—again, from behind her, inside the room now.

Nora held her breath as she looked back at the empty space, hand on the silvered-glass doorknob, covering its distorted reflections. Old timbers shifted in strange ways, she reminded herself. Still, she peered in for a moment longer, something like hope flickering in her chest, and alongside it, something like fear.

Finally, gingerly, she closed the door, as if to allow the room some privacy, some time to gather itself.

~

Outside again, Nora sketched the buildings and the animals. While she was finishing a quick study of Old Nick behind the pasture fence, Erik reappeared on Odin. When he dismounted outside the barn, he listed to the left.

But he reported promptly for evening milking, and Nora, emboldened by the convivial nature of the day, asked to help. Marie offered her own low wooden stool. "Sit here and I'll show you!"

Nora hesitated. The cow seemed enormous and would only loom larger once she crouched beside it. "She won't kick me, will she?"

Marie laughed. "Not Bitty, no! Goosey might. Or Ethel."

"Any one of 'em might," Erik said. "Unpredictable creatures. Changeable as everythin' else out here."

Nora glanced at him when he spoke, a simple reflex, but looked away again and tried to ignore the zing of fear she felt at his words.

Marie dropped to her knees, heedless of the hard ground and dirty straw, much less the massive cow, to get a better angle as she positioned Nora's fingers upon the teats. Marie covered them with her own fingers to demonstrate the proper pressure and angle so that the milk jetted straight down into the pail.

It was harder than it looked, and Nora was humbled; for all the finely skilled movements that her hands had learned to make—with sutures and scalpels and simple palpations of human tissue—they were clumsy at this strangely intimate task.

Soon, she and Marie were both laughing. But after a while, Nora began to get the hang of it, and to be lulled by the asynchronous hissing of milk streaming into metal pails, and the other animal noises: soft moos and huffs and hoof scuffs, tails twitching, cats lapping up their share of milk. Even Erik's presence didn't mar the peacefulness, though when they carried the milk canisters to the springhouse, Nora smelled a thin reek of alcohol trailing off him.

Not as if you never drank, she reminded herself. Though it had been a long time.

It had been a long time, too, since she'd had real exercise. Her arms and neck and lower back ached by the end of the hour-plus it took to milk all the cows. But the pain felt strangely satisfying for the fact that it had been well earned.

All hands washed, they went inside for supper. As a rule, it was a much smaller meal than their midday dinner—they'd only made an exception when Nora first arrived, to welcome her with an evening feast. She hadn't properly appreciated the accommodation then. When she made sure to sincerely compliment Kirsten's cooking, though, the woman only murmured noncommittal noises that made Erik half laugh into his bread.

That evening, he shoveled in his food as gracelessly as always, but didn't seem as drunk as Nora had initially thought. He asked how she'd liked their little hamlet.

"Quite well. It doesn't seem to lack anything I could want in Manhattan, and it's far friendlier."

Erik smirked.

"She met Grace!" Marie said. "Had Mr. McArthur give Annie a handful of candy. She was so pleased. But Ezra put up a fuss."

Nora glanced at Erik again. His expression betrayed no concern at the mention of Ezra, but with a jab of his fork toward Malcolm, he changed the subject. "You hear Pat O'Shea's havin' a huskin' bee next month? Second Saturday in October—that's only the ninth. No way in hell the corn'll be dry by then."

"Well," Malcolm said, and hesitated, perhaps simply because he was averse to gossip, perhaps because the subject itself was delicate. "I heard Fiona's sick. I don't think she has much time left. And Patrick wants to spend as much as he can with her. But he wants to get the harvest in before he leaves, so—it's a compromise."

Erik snorted. "So, what, he can come home from a dead sister to a whole load of spoiled corn? May as well jump in the grave with·Fee and not come back."

Malcolm and Kirsten both clamped their lips tighter.

But Marie said brightly, "We're going, then, aren't we? To the bee?"

"Of course," Malcolm said.

Erik scoffed. "Hell, I'll fiddle while Rome burns. Or while O'Shea wastes his whole damn crop, long as he's got somethin' to drink."

Nora didn't bother to hide her expression of distaste, not that Erik noticed.

Nor did Marie, who turned in her chair. "You'll come, too, won't you? It's such fun!"

When Nora wavered, Malcolm said, "It's a month away yet."

He might have been speaking to Nora as much as to Marie. There might have been some hint of a question in his tone. Unless that was only what Nora wanted to hear.

She looked at him. "I have always wanted to go to one."

"Oh, have you?" Erik asked, the cutting edge in his voice surprisingly hurtful.

"Yes," Nora said, just as sharply, then looked down at her plate and added in a softer tone, "Since I learned they existed."

"Oh, do come, then!" said Marie.

A brief moment of delicate, careful quiet seemed to stretch between Nora and Malcolm, even as the rest of the table clattered with supper sounds. When he finally spoke again, it was hard to tell if there was some strain in his low and gently husky voice. "You could always come back for it."

Nora was surprised at the immediate twinge of disappointment she felt, but before she could speak, he added:

"Or you're welcome to stay, of course. As long as you like."

Erik snorted again, and Kirsten's fork chimed so loudly against her plate that Nora started. But she held Malcolm's gaze and said, "Maybe I will, then. Until the bee, at least."

"Oh, *yay.*" Marie clapped a few times, until Kirsten gave her a sharp look.

Erik said, "I thought you had to get back to school," surprising Nora—that he knew at all about her plans, much less cared.

"I can stand to miss a week or two," she said, and glanced at Malcolm again, grateful that he'd kept her confidence about the uncertainty of her future.

He gave her one of his measured smiles—a bare lifting of the corners of his lips, a softening of his eyes. "We'll be glad to have you."

And Nora was glad to have a reprieve, more time before going home.

In the parlor that evening, she sketched Marie as she sat on the rug near her girls and reeled off recollections of past dances and parties. Nora drew Kirsten, too, silently mending, stiff-backed in the armchair opposite Malcolm's. She refrained from drawing him, not wanting to cause him the discomfort of being studied—she could see his body tense in anticipation—but also fearing it might turn out not to look much like him at all, that something in his eyes would make it seem like Euan was peering out.

Later, when everyone had said good night and gone to their rooms, Nora changed into her gown with her gaze on the abalone box atop the mantel.

She recalled the first time Euan had attended the opera, in the fine tuxedo her father had given him. They'd gone to see *Faust*. During intermission, as they'd trailed behind Nora's family on their way to the glittering, gilded lobby, she'd asked how he was liking it.

Not half as much as you, he'd said, and she'd laughed. When he'd added, *I think I'm more at home at a husking bee,* she'd wrinkled her nose and asked, *What's that?*

A corn-husking party, he'd answered, and when Nora still looked befuddled, he elaborated: *It's when a big group gets together to help shuck all a farmer's field corn before he stores it, and they're repaid in pies and music and merriment after. Moonshine, maybe. Dancing, always. Whoever finds a red ear gets to kiss the girl they think is prettiest.*

Nora had nearly tripped on her hem, stopped a moment to gather herself and glance at Euan. *And if a girl finds it?*

Then she's afforded the same privilege, of course.

How egalitarian, Nora had answered, and arched her eyebrows at Euan. *And how much more exciting than the opera.*

They'd both laughed then, and avoided looking at each other until some of the color had faded from their cheeks.

Nora should have grabbed his hand that very night, kissed him right there in that crowded theater. She would never forgive herself for squandering so much irretrievable time.

And yet she hadn't felt like she was making such a mistake in the long months since Euan had died. Shutting herself away, giving up school and socializing, letting all her passions wither away to nothing had been shockingly easy, all told.

It hadn't mattered what Nora was missing out on because nothing left in the world was of any great importance—except for Malcolm's letters. At first, that was only because they conjured Euan, and allowed her to do the same. But in the process, she had come to know Malcolm, too, and to cherish his kindness.

She'd come to the farm, in part, for him—to see a friend. But he was something more than that—like family. And, of course, like Euan in many ways, as Euan had been like him.

Nora couldn't deny that that was one reason why she felt so drawn to Malcolm, though it was also the largest part of why she felt she shouldn't be. Surely it wasn't wrong to love him, yet she was afraid to study the precise nature of her affection.

Distracted, she climbed into bed without closing the curtains. With no firelight to bounce the room's reflections off the window glass, the frames were gaping holes through which anything might crawl. But Nora forced the notion from her head. And when a floorboard creaked off in the corner near the desk, she forced herself to look into the shadows, to prove to herself that nothing was there.

Though the corner was empty, the darkness felt substantial, aware. Not malevolent—nor quite benign; just *present*—and yet still frightening for its uncanny nature.

Nora turned her back on it and tried to calm her racing heart. *Nothing's there,* she told herself. *Nothing's there.*

But hadn't she wanted there to be?

And did she not want that any longer?

CHAPTER THIRTEEN

Hoosick Falls, NY
September–October 1886

Nora attended church on Sunday partly for the sake of appearances. And she preferred not to be alone with Erik. Even if he made himself as scarce as the barn cats until milking time, she suspected that she would sense him, and be unsettled.

She also wanted to mail a letter to her father, inform him that she was extending her stay, request that he send some items from home, including her bicycle. It would be useful for visiting the village whenever she wished, without troubling anyone for a ride. And it might please her father to know that she was interested in cycling again.

He would worry, of course, at the length of her visit, even though she had warned him, in a way. A month did sound surprising, but Nora didn't think it excessive. Except for the fact that it meant she would miss the start of school, which would perturb him. But that didn't matter. She couldn't make decisions based on how they would affect anyone else. Selfish, perhaps, but necessarily so. It was her life, and it must be lived as she saw fit.

In town, she sat beside Malcolm in his Presbyterian pew on Church Street. Kirsten and Marie attended the Episcopalian St. Mark's with the girls, who presumably sat as obediently and disinterestedly as they did at the dinner table. Nora would have preferred to be outside, but only her body was stuck in the pew; her mind was free to wander.

After the service, she and Malcolm strolled to Main Street, where a host of congregants from multiple denominations mingled, including the Methodist Dr. and Mrs. Burns. While Nora stopped to chat with them, Grace Murphy and her family streamed out of the Church of the Immaculate Conception.

Nora only noticed when Annie pelted over and nearly crashed into her legs to ask if she had any more candy.

"I'm sorry to disappoint, but I promise I'll fill my pockets up before we come in next week."

Annie smiled, as did the Burnses, though the distinguished doctor's brow furrowed in apparent surprise. He'd hear from her father soon enough, Nora suspected.

She was glad when Grace and the rest of her clan ambled over. Her husband, Benjamin, had brown hair and brown eyes, but he palmed the cornsilk-colored crown of Ezra's head with the fond familiarity of any father. It occurred to Nora that she'd never seen Erik so much as give a prolonged glance at either of his daughters.

The following Sunday, as promised, Nora did bring sweets, but word had spread among the junior members of the flocks of Hoosick Falls, so she was mobbed by far more children than she had enough candy to placate.

Dr. Burns scattered them with a declaration that she wasn't a sweet-shop, for pity's sake. Benjamin Murphy slyly smiled and said, "Anyone would think you were a dentist drumming up business, Miss Harris, and not a doctor."

"Oh," Nora said, glancing toward Dr. Burns with a fiercely embarrassed blush, "I'm—I'm not—"

"Soon enough," said Dr. Burns. "That is, if you get back to the city in time . . . Dr. Jacobi's school starts up again next week, doesn't it?"

Nora gave a brittle smile and said yes, but she could obtain permission for a late enrollment, which was likely true, though she felt increasingly certain she would never request it.

Despite the possibility of encountering Dr. Burns, and the gnawing awareness that she would soon miss the beginning of what should have been her final year of college, Nora enjoyed visiting the village, which was far easier once her father sent her bicycle. He paid for a courier to deliver it to the farm, where Marie was fascinated by the thing.

"It's not a pony," Nora said, "but at least you don't have to feed and water it."

Marie laughed as she wobbled upon the bicycle, her feet on the ground for the first little while. She managed to pedal it in wide arcs across the barnyard amid a great deal of shouting and laughter that made Kirsten scowl and shake her head before going straight back inside, away from such indecorous foolishness.

"It is fun," Marie said, "but my poor fanny! And it makes my legs burn something awful—and feels like my teeth are about to rattle out of my head."

Nora didn't mind, though, and on afternoons while Marie and Kirsten made butter or polished windows or washed laundry, she pedaled along the now familiar roads that led to and from the village. Closer to town, she drew a mix of reactions from scathing stares to shouted alarm and cheering approval, but most people seemed at least amused. Not that she cared, she told herself. Not that she should, any more than she should mind whatever rumors circulated about her. But in the interest of avoiding collision in the streets or having too many people see her knees as she pedaled down Main, she usually dismounted before walking the bicycle across the bridge.

In town, she sketched the war monument and the storefronts, the factory towers and the modest cascade that gave the village half its name.

Everyone seemed pleased to see her memorializing their hometown. *But next, they'll be saying I studied in Paris,* she thought, and smiled to herself.

On her second Sunday in town, Grace Murphy had extended an open invitation to drop by her house, so Nora did that, too, a few times. She tried not to look too long at Ezra, but having her sketchbook at least gave her an excuse, and she made a portrait of him with his baby brother, Alvie. Annie was off at school.

"She'll be cross if she sees she was left out," Grace said, when Nora tried to give her the portrait. So she kept it for herself, and promised to return some Saturday or Sunday when she could draw the whole family.

"I'll bring my pastels, so you'll all be in color."

Back on the farm, Nora sketched feverishly, feeling an urgent need to fix the days themselves in place, in some more tangible form than mutable memory. She drew the animals, and the gravestones, and Axel pitching hay, and Kirsten scrubbing clothes on a washboard. Nora didn't offer to help with laundry, though she did wash her own under-things in her room, and hung them over the furniture to dry.

She sketched Marie, her most willing subject, at various pursuits: picking mushrooms, collecting eggs, churning butter, and once, nap-ping in the cow pasture, propped up against the side of a dozing heifer on a rare idle afternoon, both of them gilded with late-summer sun.

But the season was waning, and Nora tried to capture the slug-gish, smokeless fire of the autumn forest, too, the brilliant blaze of orange and red and gold spreading from treetop to treetop, leaf by leaf, each day.

One gloriously crisp afternoon, Malcolm took her and Marie fish-ing, and Nora sketched him frowning at a tangled line; having the knot to focus on seemed to make him more comfortable under her sustained gaze, or perhaps it was being out in the open, away from anyone else's observation. And since he didn't look at her, she wasn't afraid of making his expression more like Euan's.

Erik, naturally, didn't care when Nora sketched him cleaning his fingernails with a pocketknife on the side porch or twisting the knob on his bow to tighten its strings.

She couldn't help but be drawn to his hands, just as large and long as the rest of him, powerful and raw—but not inelegant. Not without the potential for elegance, anyway. If they hadn't been roughened and dirtied by work, they would have looked at home on a crystal decanter or a carriage door. As it was, they looked just as right upon the neck of his fiddle as upon a shovel.

They would look right, too, Nora thought, upon a woman's body.

She couldn't help but wonder if he'd had a dalliance with Grace Murphy, as incredibly unlikely as that seemed. Not impossible, because Nora had asked Grace for Ezra's age, then done the math to figure that the boy had been conceived not long before Erik left home. But she couldn't imagine them together.

She couldn't quite stop herself, however, from imagining Erik and Marie—acutely conscious of the fact that he often summoned his wife to his cabin, which Nora pictured as close and dank as the den of a wild animal. But Marie went gladly, and came back humming. It would have been easy to assume that Erik pressed her into service, was perfunctory at best in taking his pleasure from her, but perhaps he repaid it. Perhaps he was even tender with her in private. Not that tenderness was always necessary, Nora knew.

In the post-supper parlor, while Nora sketched or read, if Marie was there, she might sew or sit on the floor to gaze at her girls, who traced the intricate patterns of the carpet with their eyes or sorted buttons until Kirsten took them up to bed. She seemed to have usurped the role of mother, yet Marie never complained; in many ways, she behaved almost like another ward of Kirsten's. But some nights, Nora heard her murmuring to her daughters in their room, the only place they ever got to be alone.

She supposed every family was composed of smaller, shifting sub-groups, and followed its own peculiar patterns. No doubt they would have found her Manhattan clan strange in many ways.

Axel rarely joined them in the parlor—he even took his supper back to the barn some evenings—but Erik occasionally plopped himself onto the settee beside Nora, the only free spot before the fire. If she scooted farther against the arm to avoid his sprawling leg, he only oozed closer. Often, then, she rose and suggested a game to Marie, who was always eager to play hens-and-chickens or war or slapjack.

But one evening, Erik stood by the mantel and played his fiddle. A slow, melancholy song that Nora felt wend through her body like a deep-seated memory, and then a faster, toe-tapping tune that Marie got up and danced to, pulling Nora along, her joy as infectious as the music.

Malcolm placed a finger in his book to mark his page and smiled at them from his chair, while Kirsten jabbed her needle through the cloth clamped in her embroidery hoop and pulled the thread taut, until it snapped. The twins, of course, seemed oblivious to the commotion, though during another mellifluous song while the women rested, Nora thought the tilt of their heads was telling—that they listened to the music as if it drifted from some distant place.

Nighttime came a little earlier each evening, but in communion with the others in the barn or the parlor, Nora didn't mind so much. She still tried to make her last visit to the outhouse before supper, and felt unease creep over her once everyone had retired to their beds, when even Malcolm seemed far away across the hall.

Alone, even with the curtains drawn, she could feel the resonant darkness outside, the miles of thick black forest encircling them. Occasionally, strange sounds pierced the night—the shrieks of foxes and cries of owls, made even more unnerving for how they were disembodied in that deep, dense dark.

Worse was the persistent sense of a nameless presence within the room, no matter how absurd Nora continued to tell herself that was. Part of her still hoped she might be wrong—that some immaterial yet indelible part of Euan did dwell there—but she kept her eyes closed now, didn't look into the shadows even when she thought she heard the desk chair creak like someone had just sat down in it.

Sometimes it was a relief when other insidious emotions overcame her; sometimes she deliberately conjured them. And though she tried to imagine her own wandering hands were only Euan's, they often became his brothers'—Malcolm's, then Erik's, then both at once.

And then all three.

The deep burn of shame was only one facet of the fire that consumed Nora. She told herself it was like the inflamed matter filling a boil. She didn't willingly summon such filth, but when it arose, it only took a practiced mechanical action to drain the noxiousness and return her flesh to its normal quiescent state, with the added benefit of calming her brain enough to sleep. It seemed to stop strange dreams from coming, too, to wring them all out of her before she drifted into unconsciousness.

In the mornings, she felt no trace of unease; dawn scrubbed the room clean and lent a faint glow to its pale, buttery walls. While she dressed, the space felt perfectly calm and airy again, if quite chilly still. The sense of an unseen presence only slowly gathered throughout the day. It thickened with the shadows—because it was all in her mind, Nora reasoned.

What was real was the smoke in her clothes from the cozy wood fires, so much nicer than the coal hearths and radiators of Washington Square and Fifth Avenue, and the tinge of rosemary from Kirsten's soap. They made Nora feel marked, as one who belonged.

And yet the day of her departure came ever closer. With its approach, her equilibrium wavered even in the daylight, when a sudden shortness of breath—her throat clotted with the threat of tears—would strike her as she watched the sheep graze or listened to the leaves of the apple trees rustle around her.

She and Malcolm had agreed to scatter half of Euan's ashes on the Saturday afternoon before the husking bee, because they both wanted to wait as long as possible, she supposed, though it freighted the day with an even greater finality.

On her last Friday visit to the village, Nora left her art supplies behind and bought a postcard from one of the shops. She wrote on the back: *Shall return home on Sunday.* But then she couldn't bring herself to relinquish it to the post-office clerk. Instead, she slipped it into her pocket, where she obsessively fingered the edges of the card until she ended up crumpling it in her fist.

Nora drew no pictures at all that evening, and excused herself quite early from the parlor, only to lie staring at the abalone box of ashes, which now held only some jumbled half of Euan, Nora having transferred the other portion to a rosewood box that Malcolm provided.

I miss you, she thought, but this time no promising creak of boards replied. She felt a nonsensical flutter of panic, that she had disrupted something by separating the ashes. Maybe the bone dust of Euan's feet had gone into the rosewood box, and he could no longer stand upon the floor.

It was preposterous, and Nora's alarm soon subsided, but her grief only grew. It would continue to metastasize once she left this place, she thought. Until it killed her.

CHAPTER FOURTEEN

Hoosick Falls, NY
October 1886

The following morning, after breakfast, they tromped to the top of the rise that Malcolm had selected. Kirsten insisted the girls wouldn't go willingly and stayed behind to watch them, though she'd gotten up even earlier than usual to pack a picnic complete with an apple cake.

"He always liked that," she murmured as she smoothed the napkin atop the wicker basket, as gently as she might once have petted a child's hair.

Nora began silently crying before they even reached the forest, and continued until they crested the chosen hill with its view of the valley, now fully engulfed in the flames of autumn leaves.

~

Everyone said a few words, beginning—to her surprise—with Axel, who read almost inaudibly from a folded scrap of paper, a short intonation in German that Nora wouldn't have understood anyway. Even so, she sniffled, and Marie shuffled closer to pat her arm.

Erik seemed agitated, impatient—and smelled as if he'd already had something to drink. When Malcolm asked if he wanted to say something, Erik looked at the rosewood box. "Yeah—we sure that thing's not just full of whatever some barkeep dumped out of his ashtrays?"

Though Nora was shocked, she felt no anger—just a surprising pang of empathy for Erik, even some sense of comfort, to think that he still loved his brother. Malcolm, however, looked as stormy as she had ever seen him, and Nora cast her gaze toward the ground.

Checked by Malcolm's stare, Erik expelled a harsh breath. "Fine. All right. I don't know. Even when he was little . . . Euan always wanted to know *why*. He always . . . he wanted to make sense out of a senseless world. And he would have done a hell of a lot of good in it, if it had given him what he deserved. But of course it fuckin' didn't."

"Language," Marie murmured.

Malcolm looked slightly disappointed, but Erik only stalked off a few paces toward the edge of the hill and fished a flask from his trouser pocket.

With a muffled sigh, Malcolm looked to Nora, who tensed even before he asked, "Did you want to say a few words?"

"Yes," Marie said, saving her for at least a few seconds. "I'm so sorry Euan's gone, and that everyone's still so sad, but he's with the angels now. It's a much softer place. That's what Mum used to say. And she's there too. And one day, we'll all see them again. We should be glad of that."

"Yes," Malcolm said, his eyes glazed now with tears. "Thank you."

He waited a moment, but Nora continued staring at the ground, an ill-prepared student hoping to avoid being called on.

With a gentle clearing of his throat, Malcolm recited a stanza from a much longer poem: "One morn I miss'd him on the custom'd hill, / Along the heath and near his fav'rite tree; / Another came; nor yet beside the rill, / Nor up the lawn, nor at the wood was he."

After a pause in which he steadied himself with a deep breath, he went on, his voice more strained, "But he is here—in this place, and in all of us. May that be a comfort. And may God rest his soul."

And then there was no one else left except Nora, but her mind was empty of any words beyond *I'm sorry* and *I love you* and *I'm such an idiot; I could have written something, at least.*

But if Euan was in her, then she supposed that he could hear those thoughts, and sense her feelings, which was good enough. If he wasn't, then there was no point in speaking anyway, so she shook her head as she began to cry in earnest, unable to hide her tears now.

Marie put an arm around her as they followed Malcolm toward the edge of the hill, where he opened the rosewood box and awaited another strong breeze before he shook out the ashes, which were visible for a brief moment. They dispersed too far and too suddenly to tell where they settled as they drifted down toward the valley.

Still sniffling, Nora sat beside Marie on the blanket that Malcolm had unrolled for Kirsten's picnic lunch. Though her stomach had felt leaden since they started walking, as she began to nibble the apple cake, she grew hungry enough to eat two slices.

None of her appetites stayed suppressed for long in this place, it seemed. And soon enough, her tears dried.

Back at the house, they had a little time before evening chores, but Nora skipped milking for the first time in weeks, too afraid of falling to pieces again if she tried. She apologized, said she still hadn't packed. She would help in the morning, at least, she promised herself.

Upstairs, the pale-yellow walls of Euan's room were already going grayish in the waning daylight. Nora dressed in the nicest thing she'd brought—the same plaid ensemble that she'd worn on the train from Manhattan—and went downstairs before Marie could be sent up to fetch her.

She had never been in the woods at night. She'd never left the farm-house after true dark at all, except to scurry to and from the outhouse with a lantern. But when they set out for the O'Shea farm for the husk-ing bee, they traveled through a land of writhing darkness.

They had no carriage, just the broad wooden farm wagon with its open bed, which Nora thought they might have taken solely for her benefit—for Kirsten, Axel, and the girls all stayed behind. The rest of them could have paired up on the two riding horses, but besides the fact that Nora had almost no experience in the saddle, it remained beyond the bounds of propriety to share one with Malcolm.

She might not have minded, though. In fact, the thought of being nestled close against his back, arms fast around him, thighs aligned— or vice versa, held steady by his limbs, knowing she could lean back and feel the solidity of his body behind her—sent a glowing pulse of pleasure through Nora. She never would have said so, of course. And Malcolm, even if he might not have minded, surely never considered suggesting it either.

Sitting beside him, she shifted closer and felt if not less spooked by the mysterious night sounds and wavering shadows all around them then at least more confident that she was safe from any truly dangerous thing that might leap or lurch out of the black recesses between the murmuring trees.

She wondered if Marie felt similarly protected, sharing a blanket in the back with Erik, the closest that Nora had ever seen them together.

There was only a sliver of moon, but the stars were sprinkled as freely as the freckles on Nora's own cheeks, and when they went through a clearing, she tilted her head back to take them in, bathed in their cool, silver radiance. Out of the clutches of the forest, the night was breathtakingly beautiful.

Still, the beacon of the O'Shea farm was a welcome sight—light spilled forth from the barn and the modest house, and merry voices swelled above the rustling of trees and unseen animals.

~

The faces in the barn were friendly, though only some were familiar. In the center of the space was the largest pile of corn that she had ever seen, its sweet, musty fragrance mingled with the scent of hay and all the animal smells to which she'd become accustomed.

Off in a corner, a couple of musicians were already playing. Erik went to join them with his fiddle. Malcolm was waylaid by a neighbor while Marie led Nora to one of the open hay bales that served as auxiliary seats, the chairs, barrels, and overturned buckets ranged about the periphery of the barn all taken.

Marie showed her how to shuck a desiccated ear without detaching the innermost layers of the husk, which were simply peeled back so their papery, trailing ends could be braided together and great garlands of cobs could be hung.

It was a far easier task to pick up than milking, and Nora was able to divide her attention between the work and the ebb and flow of chatter in the barn; she caught snatches of jokes, general gossip and laughter, political discussion, reminiscences—nothing terribly different from an average party at Aunt Birdie's, really.

Several people came to talk and work by them for a while before moving on to other spots or breaking for a drink, but Nora was glad when Malcolm eventually came to join them. And she was struck by how much easier he seemed. She'd seen him relaxed enough on the farm—where he was in his element, after all—and yet outside the confines of the Colquhoun homestead, he seemed as if he could potentially be a new person.

~

Once the corn was shucked, half a dozen pumpkin pies were laid out along with other food. The musicians moved outside, near a bonfire that cast a light almost equal to that of afternoon, though it was an unstable illumination, and the darkness at its edges flickered too.

Nora tried not to look. After she ate, she danced with Marie in the light. They joined a larger group, men and women on opposite sides, passing partners off in quick succession, leaving Nora dizzy and laughing.

When she broke to catch her breath, she went to Malcolm, sitting alone. "Don't you dance?"

His smile seemed to want to stretch wider, but he kept it contained. "As a rule," he said, "no."

"Hmm. And you're not a rule-breaker, are you?"

He chuckled. "I'd break your toes, I'm afraid, if I made an exception."

Nora grinned. "I'm nimble enough to escape danger. Anyway, I know how to set a bone. But it's all right, of course. I won't bully you into it."

"No. But—on second thought—you've convinced me. When else will I get the chance?"

So he joined Nora for the next song—not that it was always easy to tell where one ended and another began—and as they twirled about, she barely felt her feet touch the ground.

She was suffused with the sort of happiness that left no room for any other feeling, but the very enormity of it was overwhelming. When they finally came to a breathless stop, she made a half-mocking curtsy and excused herself to get a drink—weak cider, which she sipped at the edge of the bonfire's glow, her back to it only to hide her tears, though it meant she had to confront the flittering silhouettes of corn stubble and distant trees, the dark fields ripe with shadows.

～

They left soon after. The pies were all but gone and people had begun to disperse. Erik had clearly had a good deal to drink, though his fiddling hadn't suffered, and he kept it up all through the ride home, unfurling a banner of music through the dark woods.

The instant the wagon came to a stop in the Colquhoun farmyard, Erik stopped playing and sprang from the bed, helped Marie down—and kept hold of her hand, nearly jogging toward the cabin, both of them laughing.

Nora felt a lump in her throat and heat in her cheeks as Malcolm offered his own hand to help her down. Not wanting to let go once on the ground, she raised her arm, and he obliged to give her a twirl as he had earlier.

She stumbled slightly in the dark and laughed, caught herself against his chest, their faces so close they could have felt each other's breath, if either of them had been able to breathe just then.

Before he could pull away, Nora raised her chin and kissed him, softly. He tensed for a fraction of a second, then put his arms around her and returned the gentle pressure of her lips.

When she moved her head back to look into his solemn eyes, she whispered, "I don't want to leave."

"You don't have to. I meant it when I said you were welcome to stay."

"But not as a guest," Nora answered.

Malcolm only looked at her, faintly shook his head as if he didn't understand, or maybe didn't quite believe.

"There's no one else in the world who cares for me like you do," she said. "And I've come to care for you too. Very much."

"Nora."

The softness of her name in his mouth made it feel like he caressed her heart—but in the next second, he might crush it, however gently.

She drew away, gingerly. "I suppose there's a reason you never married." Euan had thought it was due to the tragedies that befell their siblings and parents, that Mal hadn't been willing to risk his heart that way. But he had just kissed her and had never denied her any kindness. "Maybe you'd make an exception? For me?"

He looked sorry even before he said, "I couldn't."

Nora held herself very still. "Oh."

"I couldn't let you make that decision."

She scoffed, the sound like someone had knocked the wind from her. "Couldn't let me?"

"No," Malcolm answered, not without regret. "I'm . . . I'm so old, Nora. And so serious, and staid. I'm far better on paper than in person—"

"That isn't true."

"I'd bore you."

"You don't."

"I would, eventually. And this place—you don't know what it is to live here yet. One month, in the fall—it's just a glimpse. And compared to where you came from . . . I have nothing to offer you."

"Except kindness," she countered, rather wildly. "And compassion, and companionship, and those are no small things. They're everything. They're what I want, what I need. But if . . . if you find me unsuitable, then of course you can say so. I would understand. I'd rather have the truth—"

"That isn't it," he said. "Nora, you . . . you have become immeasurably dear to me, but I would never dream . . . You deserve so much better."

"There is no better," she insisted. "Not for me." *Not anymore, at least,* she thought. "I *love* you—I think I have for some time now. I tried to tell myself it was only as a friend, but that isn't true. And you say you care so much for me, but—you wouldn't want me for a wife?"

"I would. If I were someone else."

"But you aren't." Nora held Malcolm's troubled gaze. "And I want to stay here with *you.* Because you're wonderful."

He swallowed, spoke cautiously. "I'm afraid you don't know enough of me, that you see someone else when you look at me. And when you realize that—how disappointing I am—I want you to be free to go."

She ejected a mirthless laugh. "Well, there's always divorce." When he didn't react, she looked away, embarrassed. "Oh, God. I'm sorry. I didn't mean to spoil the evening; it was so lovely. But if that's how things are, then that's fine; I'll leave tomorrow, as planned, and—"

"You can come back, whenever you like."

Nora turned to look at him again. "I won't, though. I might not write you anymore either."

"Nora—"

"I'm not saying it to be cruel, or vindictive. I just don't think I could, after this. If I have to go, then . . . it has to be far. And for good."

Malcolm looked pained, and Nora thought he might step closer, touch her cheek or even take her in his arms again, brush his lips against her forehead, if not her mouth—but if he wanted to, he restrained himself.

"I don't want you to go," he finally said. "I don't want to lose you. But I'm afraid that . . . you don't really know what you're asking. That you won't be happy here."

"I *am*. Back there—*home*? I'm miserable. But here . . . with you . . . there is no other happiness."

Malcolm studied her for another excruciatingly long moment before he nodded and said, not without resignation, "All right, then." And because he still made no move to touch her—and she couldn't withstand the weight of his expression—Nora stepped forward and wrapped her arms around him.

When he readily returned her embrace and kissed her temple, she shuddered. But a cold breeze had gusted just then and set the surrounding woods to whispering.

～

They said good night in the starlit yard. He still had to put away the wagon and stable the horse. Nora tiptoed upstairs through the dark house and stepped tentatively into Euan's room, eyes drawn not to the windows but the dim shape of the abalone box. She tried to ascertain if there was any new charge in the air—disappointment, perhaps, or disbelief, if not outright anger. But though she felt that familiar sense of perception in the room, it conveyed no judgment. And when she stared into the shadowed corners, they betrayed no spectral forms.

Strangely, Nora felt no great inward censure, either, though she thought she should be racked with guilt, at least somewhat conflicted to imagine what Euan might think. But the terrible truth was, it didn't matter, because he was gone.

He would want you to be happy was the thought that ghosted through her head, like a ribbon of smoke on the breath of a blown-out candle.

And what she'd told Malcolm was true: she had been happy on the farm, with him. She believed that she could remain so.

She hoped she could. Desperately enough that she had staked her future on it, finally forfeited any thought of another life.

CHAPTER FIFTEEN

Hoosick Falls & Manhattan, NY
October 1886

The next morning, she was up in time to catch Malcolm in the hall. He looked somewhat wary, which made Nora's stomach drop.

"Last night . . ." he said. "That wasn't all a dream, was it?"

"Not only that," she answered, and was gratified to see him smile.

She bit her tongue to keep from asking—even jokingly—if he'd changed his mind, but half feared he might say something similar, offer her another way out.

Instead, he only asked if they should make the announcement at breakfast, and Nora said yes. They walked downstairs together, then outside and down the packed-dirt path worn through the grass toward the barn. As they set to milking, Malcolm asked Axel to join them for breakfast. Nora cut her eyes toward Erik for any hint of suspicion, but he seemed uninterested; perhaps he assumed his brother simply wanted them all assembled to say goodbye to their guest.

Marie was clearly dispirited by the prospect, but Kirsten seemed brighter than Nora had ever seen her. She almost felt guilty when, at the end of saying grace, Kirsten tacked on a wish for her safe travels.

After *amen,* Malcolm cleared his throat. "We have some news . . ."

Before he could continue, Erik looked between him and Nora, who had averted her eyes, and half laughed. "Holy Christ, hell's frozen over."

Nora glanced up long enough to see Marie's confusion and Kirsten's dawning dismay.

"What news?" Marie asked.

"Miss Harris and I—Nora and I—we're getting married."

After a second of gaping shock, Marie squealed so enthusiastically that Nora thought even the twins flinched. Kirsten still seemed frozen in place. Erik chuckled again, not altogether kindly. Axel murmured, "Congratulations."

"Thank you," Nora said, and sipped her coffee for something to occupy her hands and mouth, then stared down into the dark well of the cup and wondered if she hadn't been pulled back from the edge of a void but in fact had finally jumped.

～

She told Malcolm that she thought she should still go home that morning—she wanted to break the news in person, as soon as possible. When he asked if he should join her, Nora balked. "You can't be away from the farm. Not on such short notice."

"For this, I think it's fine. For a day or two, at least."

"But it's not really necessary. I'll be back in—well, I'm not exactly sure, but soon. This is mostly just to tell him our decision and get my things. No need to trouble yourself."

"It's no trouble," Malcolm said, but began to frown as he peered at her. "You don't expect him to be pleased, then." It wasn't quite a question.

"No, I do. Once he gets over the initial surprise." Nora meant it; or at least it was another thing that she hoped was true.

～

There was no sense in taking anything back with her, so she carried only her leather bag, into which she tucked two nearly full sketchbooks. The abalone box of Euan's remaining ashes stayed on the mantel in his room.

On the ride into Hoosick Falls, where the others would attend church as usual, she and Malcolm discussed the business ahead. There would be forms to sign and licenses to obtain, which could all be done in the village—"and I don't think we need a ceremony," Nora said. "If you'd like one, I'm perfectly willing, but . . . well, neither of us much enjoys being a public spectacle, do we?"

"No," he agreed. "If you're sure . . ."

"I am. And rings don't make sense, do they? We'd only be taking them off every other hour to do another chore."

They fell silent for the next stretch of leaf-speckled road before Malcolm said, "I can't help feeling, though . . . shouldn't I speak with your father?"

Nora raised her eyebrows. "What, to ask his permission? I think you know I'm very much my own person. So does he."

"Yes, certainly. Still. It's—respectful."

"Not to me."

He seemed to stop himself from saying something else, only looked at Nora and belatedly nodded. But a moment later, he asked, "Are you against my writing him a letter, at least? He might like to know that . . . well, that I love you."

Nora held Malcolm's dark-blue gaze for a moment before smiling and scooting closer on the bench seat. "That sounds nice. I love you too."

In town, she promised to be back by Friday, at the latest. And then she bought a ticket and was soon on a train speeding her away, back toward a city that seemed strangely foreign.

It was late when Nora reached Manhattan, weary from the tedium of traveling for most of the day. She had just enough money left for a cab from the station to Washington Square, where she let herself in the front door and found the parlor empty, as was the dining room and kitchen.

As she passed the basement door, she tried the knob. This time, it was unlocked, but Nora only cracked it wide enough to see that no lights were on. She spared a thought for the farmhouse's padlocked cellar door and decided that she would look there too once she was the legally appointed lady of that house. No one would doubt that she belonged there.

Upstairs, she peeked into her father's study and bedroom, both empty. He might be out on a call, Nora thought, or perhaps at one of his clubs, or having dinner at a restaurant—with his newest protégé, even. She was slightly disappointed, but she hadn't given him a precise date to expect her, after all, only said she would be home in the second week of October. If Calista had already retired, Nora didn't wish to disturb her, so she stayed out of the attic. There was nothing there for her now anyway.

She washed her face in the bathroom sink; how delightfully luxurious to simply turn the taps and have hot water. The bathtub beckoned, but she was tired. Without the energy to undress yet, she lay down to rest until her father came home.

～

But when Nora's eyes opened, it was already morning. She was stiff and disoriented, but the smell of food and coffee lured her downstairs and began to clear her mental fog.

When she reached the dining room doorway, her father was already looking up from his morning paper. He cried out in owl-eyed surprise. "My God, my girl! What are you doing here—and when've you come? I'm not dreaming, am I?"

He sprang from his chair as he spoke, and when he was close enough, pulled Nora to his chest in a nearly suffocating hug. Then he held her at arm's length and grinned. "Aye, solid you are—and looking well, too! Calista!"

She had already come out of the kitchen, drawn by the noise, and came to hug Nora the moment that her father let her go.

"Look at you, Miss Leonora—all that fresh air and fresh cream's agreed with you, hasn't it?"

Nora smiled and let herself be pressed into her old chair at the table, Calista refusing to let her get her own plate—though much more kindly than Kirsten.

"How did you sneak in, then?" her father asked as he replaced his napkin in his lap. "Did your luggage not make it?"

Rather than answer, Nora asked, "Where were *you*? It was late last night, and you were nowhere to be found."

"Urgent case."

"Of whiskey at McCrea's?"

He chuckled. "No, of appendicitis at Murray Hill."

For a second, Nora felt perfectly at home, but then a twinge of nostalgia bruised her contentment. She was glad she was leaving again soon.

She found herself wistful for the farm's large windows and french doors with their pastoral views. It felt strange not to be milking cows, not to start the day in the cavernous calm of the barn.

Her father listened eagerly to her descriptions of it. "You barely scribbled anything on those little postcards," he chided, though fondly. "Wore out your letter-writing arm before you got there, I suppose."

"I made drawings," Nora said. "I'll show you—" And she went upstairs to fetch her sketchbooks, then moved to the chair beside his. They looked through the pages while Calista served them, occasionally stealing a glance herself. Nora worried they might frown at the quirk of Erik's lips in one image, or the slackness of the twins' faces in another. But her father seemed delighted by every detail—said it looked a bonny place. Calista said nothing, until urging them to eat before it all got cold.

They set the books aside and turned to the spread: jellied veal, toast in a filigreed silver rack, soft-boiled eggs in dainty porcelain cups, and the sugar-dusted grapefruit that Nora's father favored.

"I haven't had citrus in a month," she said, digging her serrated spoon into her own portion.

"Haven't had a lot of luxuries, I'd wager."

Nora shrugged. "You'd be surprised at what you don't miss, after a while. What you come to like. And there are things there that . . . I could never have here." She looked down at the glistening grapefruit. "In fact . . . I'm going back."

"Already?"

"To stay."

Her father actually laughed. "You're not serious, are you?"

"Yes, I am." She met his eyes. "Mal and I are getting married."

Her father frowned and put down his fork. "Nora, no."

She put down her spoon and sat up straighter. "What do you mean, no?"

"I mean, it's—madness. For you to be a farmwife? No."

"You don't get to make that decision for me. And I thought you said you wanted me to be happy. That you'd be proud, no matter what."

"I do," he said. "I will, of course, but—you cannae possibly want this."

"I do." Her jaw was as tight as a coiled spring.

By contrast, her father softened. "Nora, love. I know."

"You know what?"

"I *know*. That you still miss him, and it still hurts, but this—this isn't the answer."

"And there isn't a question." Nora scraped her chair out to stand and backed a few inches from the table. "I love him—Mal."

"You barely know him."

The way his words echoed Malcolm's own made her want to scream. "I've written him for nearly a year! I've just lived in his home for a month. You're the one who doesn't know him, but I promise, he is a wonderful man."

"Where he is now, then? Why is he not here telling me this himself?"

"Because I didn't want him to—because I knew you would be apoplectic."

Her father scoffed again, then took a deep breath and nodded to himself. "Well, I admit, it's a great surprise. But even looking at it dispassionately, it seems . . . unlikely, at best. Ill advised, at worst." He held up a finger to stop Nora from interrupting. "You, on a farm—for good. I don't see it. When the novelty wears off . . . And Mr. Colquhoun— however kind he is—he's *my* age, for God's sake—"

"He's ten years younger!"

"And still twice your own age, Nora! *And*—not that I doubt he's become fond of you, but it must be said that he surely finds your station attractive on its own."

Now Nora scoffed. "He does very well for himself, in fact."

"Oh, aye, he's shown you his account books, has he? If he's not in debt now, then he's one bad harvest away from it, I'd wager."

"Well, so what? You were still just scraping by when you married Mama—*her* money paid for this house, and *her* family got you better connections and even richer patients. Not that that's the reason you married her—my point being, money has nothing to do with why Mal wants to marry me either. We won't expect a single cent from you, don't worry."

"I'm not worried about that." The line between her father's brows was severe. He stood from his own chair to better meet Nora's eyes. "You know I'll always help you, any way I can. But there will be a limit to what I can do, once you sign over your freedom. Which I never expected from you. Not like this."

Nora exerted considerable effort to stay stone-faced as she said, "My freedom. There's the crux of the matter. You don't want to cede control of me—not to this particular man, at least."

"Oh, Christ, Nora—don't be daft. Or worse, willfully obtuse. When have I ever tried to—?" He stopped short at her look of furious indignation and emitted a strangled sound. "You'll never let that go, will you? You'll never appreciate that I was only trying to help. And that's what I'm doing now."

"Really? Are you about to threaten me with an institution again?"

Once more, he spluttered. "I never—! Although, now that you mention it, this does seem a very hasty decision, made under some measure of duress."

"You would *never* say such a thing to a son!"

He pinched the bridge of his nose and shut his eyes behind his spectacles as he sank back into his chair. "I just hate the thought of you in the middle of nowhere, miles away from your family, all alone."

"I won't be alone." Nora went to stand behind her father's chair, placed her arms around his shoulders. "And I won't be that far away; I got here in a day. You can still see me. I'll visit. I'll write."

"But what are you going to *do*?" he asked as he listlessly stabbed his spoon into his grapefruit. "You're going to work yourself ragged and wring chickens' necks and forget where the thalamus is."

"I won't," Nora said, and though she felt a sliver of resentment along with shame, she half stooped to hug her father with her chin on his balding head, much as she used to when she wanted to see over his shoulder, as interested in his studies as in being close to him—the center of her universe.

He patted her arm and sighed. "You could always commute to your last year of school, you know. It's not that far, as you say. It's not too late—not nearly. You wouldn't be the first doctor with a family—with a husband, even. And you could take over for Angus whenever he finally retires. Or look into veterinary medicine if you don't want to work with people . . ."

Nora didn't answer as she went back around the table and took her former seat. But she wasn't hungry anymore, and left most of her food untouched.

CHAPTER SIXTEEN

Manhattan & Hoosick Falls, NY
October 1886

Her father's next great disappointment, which Nora delivered as she walked with him to his office after breakfast, was learning that there would be no wedding ceremony.

"Why not?" he demanded. "If it's money, then—"

"I didn't want one. I don't. It's a lot of fuss for nothing. You can always come to the clerk's office if it means that much to you. But twenty minutes ago you didn't even want it to happen."

"Well, but if it *is*, I'd at least like to walk you down the aisle."

"Or have a chance to make a scene when the priest asks if anyone objects . . ."

After a second of genuine surprise, and perhaps real hurt, her father's features slid into amusement and he squeezed Nora in a one-armed hug as he chuckled.

"Your granny's the one to worry about there."

Nora groaned. "She's certainly not invited. Do we have to tell them? Before the fact?"

"I think we do, yes. I'll send a message round today to invite ourselves to dinner at Birdie's. Unless you want to go on in person now . . ."

"No."

"Bette would love to see you, though. And you've hardly met your little cousins."

Nora sighed and considered it. She was already partway there, and if she returned home, she wasn't sure what she would do with herself. "Fine, I'll go. But I'm not telling them yet."

And so she continued toward Central Park and Bette's home, hoping that Ernest would be off at work.

~

Bette was stunned to see Nora in her drawing room, and hugged her so hard it crushed the breath from her.

"Your children are going to be walking bruises," Nora groaned.

Bette laughed and swiped happy tears from her rosy cheeks. "Oh, they're strong, fat little things! Come see them."

The way she towed Nora through the house, up several floors to the nursery, made her think somewhat wistfully of Marie, and of course, the twins made her think of Addie and Bea, though Bette's babies were entirely different.

Even at two months old, they were more engaged; they looked at the adults' faces and smiled and burbled, moved their limbs and heads if somewhat erratically, then at least intentionally. They made endearing noises that seemed to communicate clear emotions.

Nora wondered how her cousin would have behaved had her own daughters been like Addie and Bea. Would she be distressed, or disappointed? Would it be harder to love them? Nora couldn't help but wonder the same about herself—and realized she would be closer to motherhood once she became a bride. Unless she took her womb veil back with her.

Impulsively, she told Bette her news. Her cousin was momentarily speechless. Even once she recovered, her genuine hopefulness still seemed tempered by surprise, and perhaps concern, or maybe disbelief.

"You'll save a fortune on postage, at least."

Nora looked for a rebuke hidden in the remark, but there seemed to be none—and rather than feel relieved, she was a bit deflated. She didn't want Bette to caution her. Still, Nora might have appreciated some expression of disappointment that she would be so far away.

But then, she had been away for some time now, even when she'd lived at Aunt Birdie's for so many months.

Besides, Bette was happy with her babies and her husband, their little group now a nucleus inside the larger cell of their family— everything else was extraneous.

Nora tried to take some comfort from the fact that she might be able to say the same soon enough.

$\sim$

The rest of the family heard the announcement at dinner. Aunt Birdie was delighted, of course, and Grandmama, equally predictably, was aghast. She deployed several of the same talking points that Nora's father had that morning, which he himself now parried.

To Grandmama's peevish question of "What will people think— you marrying a farmer?" Nora and her father scoffed in derisive unison, which made Nora smile.

"Tell them he's a landowner," she said, "and leave it at that."

Grandmama's flat line of a mouth brought Kirsten to mind. "At least the other one was trying to make something of himself."

At that, Nora was struck silent, as was her father.

But after a second, he said assuredly, "The man cares for his family—more than can be said for some."

The table fell silent, but Grandmama was undaunted. "It would be fortunate if he could do it with the trappings of this century instead of last."

"Well," Nora said, "I thought you'd at least be pleased it was marriage. But I suppose we found the one thing worse than having a working physician for a granddaughter. Apparently, I live to disappoint."

～

At the appointed hour, John Garrett picked them up. As the landau pulled away from Aunt Birdie's, Nora's father sighed. "You probably cannae wait to get back to the country after that, eh? Everyone else on the farm is as agreeable as Mr. Colquhoun, I hope?"

Nora made a noncommittal sound and shrugged. "For the most part. They're certainly quieter, on the whole."

Her father smiled and sighed again, a tinge of plaintiveness in the sound. Nora half wished she could have John take her to the station now and get back to the farm by morning.

～

But over the next four days, she busied herself with packing, this time in spare wooden shipping crates, nestling in everything she wanted, from her microscope and some self-prepared wet specimens—a seahorse, a salamander—to her favorite throw blanket and one of the china cats from the downstairs mantel.

She only meant to put in a few medical texts and anatomy books but ended up filling an entire crate with those alone. She was tempted to ask her father where he'd hidden her old leather roll of surgical instruments, but she had Euan's already, so bit her tongue.

After some hesitation, she packed all her letters and drawings.

She dithered for slightly less time before she packed her womb veil. Just in case.

Though Nora considered calling on some of her old friends, she'd been so withdrawn for so long, barely communicating with anyone except Mal, that it seemed too late—and pointless, since she was about to leave again.

Per the legal requirement for all prospective brides and grooms, she did visit a doctor to get her certificate of good health, but chose one she'd never met.

And then she said goodbye to her father and Calista, only slightly tearful—she couldn't help it—and journeyed back to Hoosick Falls, where her new life waited for her.

~

She found Erik more aloof than ever, strangely so, in fact. It bothered Nora more than she might have expected. One afternoon, when he was splitting firewood with no one else around, she approached and asked if something was wrong. Erik looked up and brought his blade down again with a grunt that Nora couldn't interpret.

"Are you put out that I'll be living here?" She watched the split wood fall into pieces. "I can't see how it matters much when you don't even—"

Erik thunked the axe down so it was embedded in the stump, then let go of the handle to fully focus on Nora, his bright-blue eyes narrowed. "Maybe you're used to the whole world revolvin' around you, but it won't out here." When she only gaped in response, he added, "I've got more concerns than whatever stupid mistakes you're intent on makin'."

Nora couldn't even scoff.

"I'm surprised Mal said yes, though." Erik grabbed the axe handle, pulled the blade free, and placed another section of log upright on the stump. "He claims he doesn't believe in it, but I get the sense that's more wishful thinkin' than the honest truth."

Nora frowned, then flinched at the crack of wood beneath metal as Erik swung again. "What are you talking about?"

She thought he wouldn't answer beyond his sarcastic chuckle as he brought the axe blade down again. But then he paused to look back up at her. "Didn't Euan ever tell you? This place is cursed."

Nora's throat went dry, so she couldn't even say *That's ridiculous.* She thought of how evasive Euan had always been when she talked about visiting, and how Mal himself had tried to dissuade her from staying.

But that was because they thought she was a city mouse, not cut out for the country. And then she thought of her own family's curse, which was equally absurd. Euan hadn't died because she'd loved him, and nothing bad would happen to her because she'd come back to the farm.

With a measure more confidence, she said, "I don't believe in curses. Awful things happen all the time, everywhere. Everyone's doomed in some sense from the day they're born."

"Yeah, well." Erik picked up a fresh length of dry wood. "I guess you'll see."

Nora tried to sound calm when she asked, "Why did you come back here, then? If you think this place is . . . ?"

Erik tightened his hands on the haft of the axe. "I ask myself that every goddamn day." He brought the blade down so hard the wood splintered on the first blow. "I think maybe it's just in my blood—the curse—so it doesn't matter where I go. May as well be someplace familiar. But you?"

He pointed the axe at her with no trace of a smirk on his face. "You stay here and I guarantee you'll be askin' the same thing before long. Why you came back when you could've left. Not too late yet, doc."

Nora tried to avoid thinking about what he'd said, and pushed for the wedding to go forward as quickly as possible. She and Mal filled out applications at a clerk's office, had the signing witnessed, and submitted their health certificates. A few days later, the marriage license was granted. They had a month in which to ratify and file it, at which point they would be legally joined. But they arranged the civil ceremony for that same Friday, at Nora's urging.

Mal suggested that they designate a separate afternoon for the special occasion, but she said it made sense to do it when they were in town anyway. He conceded.

When they informed the others at dinner, Erik only quipped that someone was in a hurry. Nora wasn't sure if he meant to implicate Malcolm or herself.

She telegrammed her father half hoping he wouldn't make it, but he arranged to arrive in Hoosick Falls on the Thursday afternoon before the wedding, and to stay with Dr. and Mrs. Burns.

The Burnses insisted on hosting a lavish dinner in honor of the soon-to-be-newlyweds that same evening and invited the whole family. Nora knew that Kirsten would decline, citing the twins as an excuse, and wasn't surprised that Axel elected to stay behind as well. Marie, of course, was ecstatic.

Nora thought Erik would dismiss the invitation, too, but to her dismay, he agreed to come. "I bet they've got good wine," he said.

CHAPTER SEVENTEEN

Hoosick Falls, NY
October 1886

On the afternoon of the wedding dinner, Nora's intestines were a knotted snarl of rope. They grew even heavier in her gut when she saw Erik ride off on Odin several hours before they were due to leave.

She was certain that he was going for a drink and felt faint with anxiety trying to imagine what he might say, how he would act in front of her father. Would he purposefully attempt to disrupt the union? Speak of the curse again?

If she was lucky, Nora thought, he'd lose track of time and drink himself into a stupor, miss the entire event.

～

When she and Mal and Marie arrived at the Burnses' home a few hours later, however, Erik met them looking almost dapper. He'd had his hair washed and cut and combed, his cheeks and chin shaved smooth. Nora could no more compliment him than she could look at him, his blue eyes blazing in an almost boyish face.

Mal smiled and said, "Look at you—a proper gentleman Viking."

From her peripheral vision, Nora saw that Erik grinned wide enough to flash his pointed eyeteeth.

Throughout the dinner, he behaved impeccably, and she felt even more off-kilter, as if she had imagined every off-color comment and rude remark he'd previously made. She could hardly cobble together complete sentences and was glad that she'd already talked her father out of visiting the farm itself.

She'd told him that although Mal would invite him—which, of course, he did—he would only be being polite. In fact, she'd led her father to believe that there was a great deal of farmwork already being interrupted and that his presence would only compound the situation.

Nora wasn't sure if he believed her, but he'd acquiesced, and at the Burnses' table, he only told Mal that he had patients to see, so must be going immediately after the ceremony tomorrow—but that he'd like to come back for a proper visit sometime soon.

Nora's stomach swayed at the notion, but that was a worry for another time.

∼

Outside the Burnses' house, Erik ambled away, and still hadn't returned from town by the time they went to bed.

Nora barely slept. When she did, she had disturbing dreams, in which she found herself standing at Euan's desk, opening the veins along the inside of her arm—or at the mantel, smearing Euan's ashes on her face, where they made a human mud mixed with her tears.

When she actually woke—with a racing heart, to nothing but the blank ceiling and the expectant shadows in the preternaturally quiet room—she turned onto her side and pulled the covers higher, hoped that the next time she opened her eyes, the sun would be rising.

∼

When she did wake for the last time as an unmarried woman, Nora had dark circles under her eyes and a fuzzy feeling in her head—but the morning light would erase that, too, she hoped.

There was still milking to attend to first. A few moments after she settled herself on her stool, Erik dragged himself into the barn, looking far more disheveled than the last time she'd seen him. He'd quaffed quite freely of the Burnses' fine wine, and Nora suspected he'd had harder stuff afterward, in even greater quantities. At least he'd waited until after the dinner.

As they all carried their canisters to the springhouse, he sidled up and squinted at her in the sunlight. "You look about as fresh as I feel." She quickened her pace to get ahead of him.

At breakfast, he sopped his bread in runny yolks and bacon grease, but excused himself from coming into town with them again. "Afraid all this might come back up in the middle of the vows," he said, and ignored everyone's looks of distaste.

Nora was glad that Marie would be their only additional witness, then. Axel had agreed to ride into the village to take Kirsten's place and trade in their butter while Nora and Mal completed their business.

Kirsten herself was staying behind to finish cooking their wedding feast, and to mind the girls, of course.

~

The ride into town felt curiously normal, as if they were only off on another errand—but Nora was glad to feel so calm after the previous day and night. She felt it was proof, if she needed any, that she'd made the right decision, the only one that held any promise of contentment.

Her father had wanted a wedding portrait, and offered to pay, so they met him at the photographer's studio, where Nora and Mal posed together, and then she stood beside her father for another. He was happy to indulge Nora's request for one more, of her and Mal and Marie, an abbreviated family portrait.

She wondered if the others would feel snubbed. *But they could have come,* she told herself, and tried not to care that they hadn't.

～

A few blocks away, at the clerk's office, the wedding took far less time than the pictures.

Nora's first officially sanctioned kiss with Mal was as brief and dry as the ceremony itself—but when she and Mal looked at each other afterward, they smiled at the same time, and Nora was buoyed.

And that was it. She was a wife—a new being, at least in the eyes of the law, and of others.

She didn't feel transformed, but she had been changing for some time now; this was only one more part of the process.

Love made me a stranger to myself, she'd written to Malcolm in one of her earliest letters. *Now death has done it again.*

And though she hadn't told Mal that writing to him, and coming to the farm, had begun to transform her again, Nora trusted that he could tell, and that she had exerted some similarly positive influence upon him. That she made him happier than he had been before.

～

He exchanged a few words with his new father-in-law after the ceremony and shook his hand before taking Marie outside.

Dr. Harris had been dabbing beneath his eyes with a hankie since they stepped inside the photo studio, and now his cheeks shone with tears. Nora led him out of the clerk's office in case anyone else was waiting, but then let him hug her as long as he liked in an alcove in the corridor.

When he finally disengaged, he fished in his pocket and pressed a billfold into Nora's hands.

"Papa, no. I don't—"

"Please. Just take it. For my own peace of mind."

So Nora did, and glanced about to ensure that no one had seen, then looked squarely at the worry still betrayed in her father's face and sighed. She thanked him and kissed his bristly cheek. "Come on, now," she said, "or you'll miss your train. Here."

She gave him her elbow, and they linked arms. Nora smiled at him as they started down the hall. "It's not an aisle, but close enough."

∼

She felt lighter, somehow, once she'd left her father at the little train station, even as the relief itself—and the thought of him sitting alone in the townhouse—caused guilt to lodge itself in Nora's sternum.

It weighed no more than the money clip in her pocket, though, and she thought it would lift soon enough.

∼

They rode back to the farm without Axel, who had disappeared to wherever he went in town.

When they came out of the last stretch of trees, Nora saw Kirsten standing on the porch and thought for a moment that she might ring the dinner bell in welcome, but she only stalked down the front stairs as the wagon approached.

As Mal slowed it to a stop, she said, "The bull broke through the fence again. Erik's after him."

Mal stifled some mild exclamation and jumped down. "When did this happen?"

"Half an hour ago. I patched the fence as best I could."

"Thank you." He looked toward the pasture with another harsh exhale, then said to Nora, "I'm sorry, but—I should go help."

"Of course," she said. "Be careful."

Her stomach churned at the thought of Old Nick on the loose, and at the fact that it had happened on this of all days.

"I'm sure the food's ruined," Kirsten muttered to Marie, "but you go put the wagon away while I try to salvage what I can."

Marie nodded, clearly concerned but always ready to obey. Nora, although nervous at the prospect of encountering the bull outside the pasture, followed her.

She helped Marie unhitch Jasper and heft the tack away, startling at every sound in the barn as she did so, imagining Old Nick stalking through the mazy trees, like a human-flesh-hungry minotaur.

When they finished, Marie wanted to check the pasture to ensure no cows had wandered off.

As they stood, Marie surveying the herd and Nora surveying the tree line, the sound of barking heralded the distant pounding of hoofbeats.

Nora's heart thudded in time. She held her breath as she saw Erik emerge from the woods upon Odin. As he galloped closer—and Mal still didn't follow—Nora saw that Erik was splashed from forehead to shirtfront in fresh blood.

CHAPTER EIGHTEEN

Hoosick Falls, NY
October 1886

Nora clutched the split-rail fence to keep from falling and pressed herself close against it as Erik barely slowed on his approach, only pulling Odin to a reeling stop mere feet from her and Marie.

Erik swung himself from the saddle, tore his stained leather hat from his head, and flung it toward the pasture, simultaneously kicking the closest fence rail so hard the wood cracked.

"Stupid son of a *bitch*," he shouted, and spat.

Nora's heart quavered, along with her limbs. She wanted to ask if Mal needed help, but couldn't speak. For a second, all she could see was Euan, a startled expression and a vast quantity of blood spilling down his chest.

When she blinked the image away, she dragged her gaze over the sodden fabric of Erik's shirt to his crimson-daubed face. His pale-blue eyes froze the breath in Nora's lungs. The way his long, lean body heaved with fury made her feel weak.

"What happened?" Marie asked, and took a halting step closer to her husband.

Erik huffed bitterly and spat again; Nora wondered if he had blood in his mouth. "Nick's dead."

"*What?*" Marie cried. "Oh, *no*. How?"

"Stupid bastard managed to stumble into a ditch. Broke both his front legs."

Nora frowned, confused as to how even the most severe compound fractures could have caused that much blood to end up on Erik—convinced that the bull must have gored him or Malcolm first—but then she realized Erik must have put Old Nick out of his misery. She hadn't heard a gunshot, but perhaps he had a knife. Or maybe he'd simply lifted a large rock.

However he'd done it, the amount of blood that soaked him seemed excessive. And the way he radiated such *rage* . . . Nora took a few steps back.

But finally, she found her voice. "Where's Mal? Is he . . . ?"

Dead, she thought, but couldn't say it. She was convinced that one curse or another had stricken him.

Erik's icy eyes pinned her in place for a moment; they were even more startlingly intense within the smeared mask of red, and with the wild anger that emanated from them. But he stalked off toward the barn without answering, a metallic stench drifting off him as he led Odin past.

Nora's mind swirled. A wife and a widow within the hour. Alone again—always, now. Doomed. Death would follow her until it caught up, and she was weary of the thought of running again. There was nowhere else she wished to go.

Then Solomon barked again from where he'd doubled back into the woods—and this time, Mal emerged from the trees upon his mare at a measured trot, upright in the saddle and unmarked by blood, as far as Nora could tell.

She jogged toward him and, when he dismounted, launched herself into his arms. "My *God,*" she said, "are you all right?"

"Yes; I'm fine. It's all right. Everything's all right."

Nora crushed him to her and tried to believe him.

～

Inside, a rather modest spread waited; nothing appeared to have been ruined. A two-tiered cake squatted on the sideboard, its bright white frosting the color of newly exposed bone. Orange calendula petals speckled the perimeter.

"Kirsten let me decorate it," Marie said, still sniffling over Old Nick. "You don't have to eat the flowers, but you can. I mostly just thought they were pretty."

"They're bitter," Kirsten warned.

"They're beautiful," Nora said, and meant it, and thought how happy she might have felt if such a calamity hadn't just occurred. "Thank you—both of you."

Kirsten gave a single, nearly imperceptible nod, and Marie glumly mimicked the gesture. Erik showed no sign of joining them, so Kirsten said grace, and they began to eat in silence.

Eventually, Kirsten's voice cut through it, sharp and short. "Will you be going back out for the bull, or just leaving it all there to rot?"

Mal stifled a sigh and briefly rubbed the spot between his eyes. "We'll haul in what we can tonight, after milking. So it's not a total loss."

"Speaking of loss," Kirsten answered, "what about next breeding season?"

"We'll get a new bull before then." There was a slight edge to Mal's usually patient tone. He smoothed it out when he added, "We can get a good price, since it's fall."

And they could afford it now, Nora supposed—she could always ask her father for help if it was needed.

❧

She had no wish to eat a slice of cake even before she discovered it was dry. And the achingly sweet icing was almost as hard and thick as bone to match its color, threatening to stick its shards in Nora's throat.

She pictured all of them collapsed dead upon the table—bluish faces planted in their plates, slack fingers curled at their necks, looks of gasping desperation fixed forever in place, at least until the putrid flesh rotted from their skulls.

She choked and grabbed her glass, fought down the gluey mouthful of cake with a long drink of water.

~

Mal went to fix the fence after eating; Nora didn't see him again until evening milking. Erik appeared in the barn, too, cleaned of blood and calmed by whatever was in his flask, she supposed. From his stool, he mused that Old Nick was the only bull he'd ever known to run away from heifers.

He looked down the row to his brother when he added, "Better let me pick the next one."

Mal ignored the jab, only apprised Erik of his intention to harvest Nick's meat and go to Albany for a new bull soon. "Not this Sunday. Maybe next."

"Knowin' you, you'll get a yearlin'. When you ought to pick up a proven stud—hell, maybe two or three now, and another twenty or thirty head of heifers while you're at it."

"We don't have the space for anything like that," Mal said. "Or the hands."

"Then we hire 'em," said Erik, his own hands still steadily milking. "Clear another couple dozen acres of forest and put in more pasture. We'll make a boatload."

"Maybe. In a few years' time—meanwhile, we don't have a fraction of the money for such a thing in the first place."

"Sure we do," Erik said, and looked at Nora.

Though she had just been thinking much the same, hearing Erik say it made her face flame and her jaw clench. She tugged a bit too firmly on the teat in her fingers, so the cow shifted and twitched its tail. Nora flinched, but no hoof kicked out.

"Careful there, doc," Erik said.

When he got no response, he changed the subject, slightly. "So, Albany—that gonna be your honeymoon too? Not the most romantic spot."

"I don't think Nora wants to see the livestock auction," Mal said, then looked at her with creased brow. "If you do, of course, you're more than welcome, but . . ."

"No," she said, though she felt strangely stung. That he had taken it for granted that she wouldn't go. But it was true that Albany didn't sound immensely appealing, even before she imagined hundreds of hooved animals milling about the livestock yards. Besides, Nora knew that she would be needed—for milking at the very least, to help lighten the load while Mal was gone.

On the way to the springhouse—just before true night—Erik said to Mal, "I'll get the wagon hitched when we're done here. Should take me ten minutes, maybe. If you want to run inside for a piece . . ."

Nora, of course, was close enough to overhear, and felt her face burn again in the chill air.

~

Mal didn't come in, though; he only took a moment to apologize to Nora for having to go on such an awful errand. She assured him it was fine. "I'm only sorry it happened."

"Me too." He sighed. "I expect I'll be back late, but I'll try not to disturb you."

Nora tried not to let her eyes well with tears, and tried not to be disappointed by the brief kiss her new husband placed upon her cheek before he went off toward the barn to help Erik gear up the horses and hitch the wagon, to haul back as much meat as they could hack off the bull's carcass.

∾

The rest of them dispersed to their rooms, in no mood to sit in the parlor.

The previous week, when Nora returned from Manhattan, Mal and Erik had carried her packing crates upstairs and deposited them in the hall between the spare room and Mal's. Erik had made a crack about sleeping separately being the key to a happy marriage, which went unacknowledged. When he left, however, Mal had said, "You can put whatever you like wherever you like; the house is yours now, too. But this room—it's yours alone."

Until it would be needed for their children, Nora had supposed. If in fact they would have any. She'd glanced over Mal's shoulder toward the main bedchamber. "And where will I be sleeping?"

"Wherever you'd like," he'd said, unable to hold her gaze.

Nora had blushed, but forced herself to ask, "Where do you want me?" Then rushed to add, "I know you're used to your privacy, and I don't want to intrude, so if—"

"It would be no intrusion," he'd interrupted, and the slight roughness in his voice had raised gooseflesh on Nora's skin. "But you'll be under no obligation here," he'd continued. "I promise . . . I won't expect anything of you."

Nora had swallowed dryly and crossed the few inches of creaking floorboards between them. "I promise," she'd said, "I wouldn't have asked to marry you if I didn't want to be your wife."

He'd looked at her lips then, and she'd looked at his, and they'd drawn toward each other. But at the instant their mouths brushed together, the dinner bell out front began clanging, and they sprang apart, chuckling slightly only after the shock coursed its way through their bodies.

∾

In the days leading up to the wedding, they hadn't come that close again, but Nora had felt heat pooling beneath her skin every time she was in proximity to Mal.

Several times that week, more than at any point in the previous month, she'd wanted to steal across the hall and ease his door open. But he wouldn't have welcomed it, she thought. It would have spooked him.

Now, on what should have been their first night together as husband and wife, it felt strangely invasive to enter Mal's room alone. Yet even stranger to think of staying in Euan's.

Nora hadn't moved any of her things yet, though, so had to go in for her nightgown and brushes and tooth powder, at least. When she did, she took a moment to caress the abalone box, and briefly considered moving it to the mantel across the hall.

But that seemed wrong too. Anyway, Mal already had framed commencement photographs from her and Euan's first and second years of medical school above his hearth.

Nora left the box and the room itself with some degree of sadness, but mostly deepening unease.

She had never been in the house at night without Mal nearby.

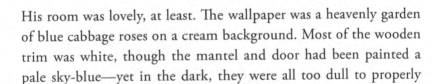

His room was lovely, at least. The wallpaper was a heavenly garden of blue cabbage roses on a cream background. Most of the wooden trim was white, though the mantel and door had been painted a pale sky-blue—yet in the dark, they were all too dull to properly appreciate, and Nora didn't feel like lighting a fire.

A small dressing room had been carved out of the larger chamber, but alone, she simply changed beside the bed. As she brushed her hair, she peered from a window with a view of the barn, a faint light inside. A lantern, she imagined, that Mal and Erik would carry with them as they rode through the seemingly impenetrable thicket of trees to butcher the cold, hulking carcass of the bull.

Nora frowned at the thought, at the freak tragedy that had coincided with their marriage. She didn't think it a bad omen or evidence of any curse, but worse—her own fault. If she hadn't taken Mal away from the farm, he would have been there to assist Erik sooner, and they might have corralled Old Nick before the poor beast met such a grisly end.

She pictured Erik clinging to the bull's massive neck, plunging in a blade, releasing a steaming torrent of blood. Nora clutched her collar tighter and hastily closed the curtain.

She reminded herself, as she often did when the outer darkness threatened to prey on her mind, that she knew precisely what populated it: scattered farms; cleared, well-traveled roads; and a proper village.

Yet it was hard to dispel the sense that there was something in the room with her—even now that she'd moved across the hall. She tried not to give it credence, much less to wonder if it had followed her from Euan's chamber or was an entirely new presence.

Of course it was the same—because it was only in her head. It was old grief and older dread stitched from normal shadows and, now, the knowledge that her husband was out in the woods at night.

Erik's with him, she thought, which didn't exactly reassure her.

She meant to stay awake until Mal returned, but despite her resolve—and her ridiculous anxiety—Nora slept. She woke in the morning still alone in the foreign bed.

Panic propelled her to dress quickly. She peeked into Euan's room—empty—before rushing downstairs, where she could smell breakfast in process. But Kirsten wouldn't have known if the men hadn't come home. Marie wouldn't, either, maybe not for quite a while.

But when Nora made it to the barn, she found everyone in place—even Axel, who had once more walked home sometime very late or very early.

Erik smirked at her. "Sleepin' Beauty finally arose. Presumably without a kiss."

Nora flushed and grabbed her milking stool. She looked at Mal, and they traded small smiles. As soon as his eyes returned to his pail, though, his face changed. He looked exhausted, and rather old.

Nora felt a pulse of sympathy for him. Or something painfully tender. She wanted to care for him, but it occurred to her that she wasn't sure how she would do so. She felt terribly certain that she was the one with nothing to offer.

CHAPTER NINETEEN

Hoosick Falls, NY
October 1886

Mal told her, later, that he'd only slept for a few hours, on the sofa, as he hadn't wanted to wake her. "You could have," she said. *Or slept in the spare room,* she thought, curious as to why he hadn't. Did he also sense some presence there?

~

Though the most intensive farmwork was done for the year—they'd harvested their winter wheat just before Nora came to visit—there was always more to do: caring for the animals, chopping firewood, fixing various equipment and outbuildings. That day Nora didn't expect to see Mal again until dinner.

After breakfast, she and Marie collected the day's eggs. Nora no longer shied from the hens, but gently waded through the muttering mass of feathers and beaks as the chickens swarmed for their feed.

"They won't lay half so many soon," Marie said as she and Nora walked back to the house with their full baskets. "Don't like the cold. And some of 'em are apt to freeze besides."

"The chickens?" Nora asked.

"Well, them too, sometimes, but the eggs, I mean—they'll turn to ice still in their shells some days. The ones what crack, I give to Solly. Make his fur all shiny. Give him awful foul wind, though."

Nora chuckled. "That'll be the sulfur."

"The what?"

"Never mind." She smiled as she shook her head.

~

There were no special chores for the women that day, but there was always cleaning, and the kitchen garden was still producing. Nora gazed out over the land and tried to imagine it frosted white, frozen through. She looked forward to seeing it—as lovely and pristine as a fresh sheet of paper.

But then she thought of frozen eggs and frozen chickens, and Kirsten's son, Johan, dying under ice, and shivered. She'd heard how brutal the winter could be on the farm, but she had committed herself to it, and felt that she would be fine. The house, after all, was cozy enough with the fires lit. And she would share a bed now, have Malcolm's warmth to shield her.

~

That afternoon, she moved her clothes into the main bedroom, where Mal had made space in the armoire and closet.

Nora saw two pieces of blue wool—light fabric folded atop dark— in the back of a shelf and realized they were his old uniform; she often forgot that he had served. According to Euan, it had been to keep Stephen from enlisting. Mal had made him promise to stay on the farm, and ended up in a prison camp himself, very nearly died there. A thing he never talked about, though everyone knew. As Nora touched the fabric, she wondered if she would find any scars upon his body when it was finally bared to her. He would see her own, of course. She felt her mouth go dry and her skin grow hot, and jumped when a loud bang issued from downstairs. It turned into a regular rhythm of pounding that sounded much like the shaping of butter, but it wasn't Thursday.

When she went to investigate, she found Kirsten tenderizing meat, no doubt cut from Old Nick's carcass.

Nora had seen hunks of the bull dangling from some of the spring-house's hooks that morning. And though there was no good reason to be unsettled by the origin of the steaks at dinner, she couldn't finish hers. Kirsten's lips tightened when she cleared the plates.

There would be more tough chunks of the bull in subsequent meals, Nora knew; she would have to get used to swallowing it.

She wondered if they had left Old Nick's butchered skeleton where it lay, to decompose in the elements. She wanted to sketch it and thought about asking Mal to show her, but that might disturb him.

She wouldn't dare ask Erik; he might be too intrigued.

~

Though Nora had been impatient for the remaining hours of daylight to drain away, as they did, her anxiety grew—and it was not just the lengthening shadows that shortened her breath.

She found comfort in the ritual of evening milking, in the radiant calm of the animals and the routine itself, but she also felt her heart thud harder, for it was the true mark of the day winding down.

After dinner and at least an hour in the parlor, it would be time for bed.

~

When they filed in from the barn, without Erik, who said he wasn't hungry, Kirsten pointed out the napkin-swaddled plates she'd placed on the sideboard—sandwiches of beef and sauerkraut, which curdled

Nora's stomach, and a more appealing jumble of potato, egg, onion, and ham.

Kirsten said she was exhausted, and Nora thought she looked it—but also, perhaps, somewhat sad. She took the girls up to turn in early. Axel took two sandwiches back to the barn, and Marie asked Mal if they might eat in the parlor.

As they sat chatting before the fireplace with their plates on their knees, the strains of Erik's fiddle started up outside, one of his slow, sweetly sad folk tunes drifting on the cold autumn air. When Nora opened the french doors to better hear it, she detected the melody of Mendelssohn's "Wedding March" hidden between more baroque phrases, twisted in places into a minor key. She didn't know if he meant it as mockery or tribute, but she shivered, and quickly shut out the chill night air and the darkness before they seeped too far across the threshold.

~

When Marie took their plates into the kitchen, she evidently left through the back door, for a few moments later, the fiddling stopped, and Nora and Mal remained alone.

Suddenly shy, Nora rose to scan the bookshelves. She turned to Mal a moment later and said, half questioningly, "You must be tired."

"Not terribly," he said. "Just—digesting."

She nodded and resumed browsing spines, eventually took *Far from the Madding Crowd* back to the settee.

She read the first four chapters and began the fifth before putting the novel aside and looking significantly at Mal. "Shall we turn in?"

He might have flushed, or it might have been the heat and reflected glow of the flames. "You go on," he said. "I'll close up the house."

In the bedroom, Nora stripped to her chemise and washed the important parts of herself, then waited.

When Mal arrived, he paused in the doorway. She realized that she must have been somewhat indistinct in the dim room, not having lit a fire, her ghostly white chemise the brightest thing about her.

He came in and closed the door, then locked it. As he approached the bed, Nora slowly rounded its foot to meet him. She studied his face, his dark-blue eyes with their fine lines radiating from the corners, his ivory-streaked temples. Older, yes, but handsome in his own right, regardless of any resemblance to Euan. She kissed him, softly, and began unbuttoning his shirt.

She doubted that Mal ever ordinarily let his garments fall to the floor, but they lay in unheeded puddles that night. He stayed Nora's hands when his union suit was only half unbuttoned, revealing a sliver of his pale, freckled chest.

Shyness, she surmised, so to encourage him, she pulled her chemise over her head, her body prickling with gooseflesh from the caress of the chilly air, and from the frisson of being seen.

Watched, by living eyes that she could look back into.

Mal's gaze went to her breasts, then lower, then back to her face, and even in the darkness of the unlit room, Nora could see something like pain in his expression. At least, she thought it betrayed a shade of distress. But she could also see how he strained against the ribbed wool of his long underwear, a slick spot on them, to which she wanted to touch her tongue.

Nora stepped closer and kissed his mouth again, took hold of his arms and turned him, like leading him in a dance. She wondered, not for the first time, if he had ever done this before, and gently pushed him back against the edge of the mattress, then down onto it, meeting nearly no resistance.

A surge of heat licked through her as she straddled him, but before she could make another move, Mal sat up and drew her beneath him. He turned her lengthwise upon the bed and pressed her back upon the mattress with a fluid strength that sent another tingling flush racing through her body. It was a decisive movement, but also surprisingly delicate.

Oh, she thought. *He has done this before, then.* She was surprised, and surprisingly relieved, and both emotions were burned immediately away by another flare of desire.

He didn't bother with the rest of his buttons, simply pulled his thickly muscled arms free from their long sleeves and shoved the one-piece undergarment down his hips. Nora shifted and bent her knees. When he slid himself against her, she drew in a shaking breath. He paused, then did it again, and again, until they were both so wet there was barely any friction. When he fully pushed his way inside her, Nora uttered a louder noise than she meant to.

Mal bent his head to kiss her, or maybe muffle her, then put his lips upon the side of her neck and her ear as he thrust, slowly, surely. His ragged breath was hot against Nora's skin, his strong back warm beneath her hands, but after a few moments, it was as if a window had been opened: an unwelcome chill crept into her limbs and spread implacably inward.

It was the way he moved, she thought, that turned her cold—so determined and methodical. Doing another job. Doing it well, naturally, but because it was expected of him. And how he kept his face firmly buried in her shoulder. Was it so he didn't have to look at her? So she couldn't look at him?

He seemed a different person—than she had expected, at least, than she had wanted. And different, too—of course—from Euan, which Nora tried not to think, which should have been neither a surprise nor a disappointment.

But though she tried to clear her mind of such distracting thoughts and focus on sensations, even what had felt good moments ago now felt like nothing—simply endurable, if not mildly irritating the longer it went on.

She stopped making any sound at all, and stopped moving her hands upon his back, but tightened her legs around Mal's body and kept moving her hips, faster and harder until she drove him to finish.

His climactic spasms and low grunts—sounds that seemed forced from him, as if by blows, or painful exertion, rather than drawn from him in pleasure—sent a lesser flutter through Nora. Not an eruption of her own in any sense, but something like aftershocks at least. Her body was moved, mildly.

And Mal's body, even when he finally stilled and drooped out of his peak rictus of tension, remained carefully suspended slightly above hers, so as not to crush her, Nora supposed.

Yet she felt the air go out of her anyway.

Before Mal moved off her, he kissed her again, an almost comically chaste peck on her lips. Nora draped an arm over her breasts as he peeled himself away, and kept her knees bent, pinned them together for modesty's sake—but Mal didn't look at her anyway once he rose. Nor did she look at her husband, except what she couldn't help seeing from the corner of her eye, as he pulled his union suit back up.

He excused himself, to use the outhouse, she surmised—though he asked, first, if she needed anything. She shook her head. As soon as she heard his footsteps fade down the stairs, she got up and hobbled into the spare room, to use the chamber pot there.

She scrubbed herself dry—harder than she needed to—and looked at the room, the now-familiar bed that Mal surely wouldn't mind if she slept in, but it felt too cowardly, and uncharitable.

So she hurried back across the hall and took her place on the far side of the mattress, her back to the door. When Mal returned, he moved quietly, got carefully into bed beside her. Nora held herself still and waited for him to murmur good night, or put his arm around her, or kiss her shoulder—anything. Instead, he settled into position near his edge of the mattress, without touching her at all. Perhaps she had pretended too well, and he thought she was already asleep.

As she listened to his breathing deepen and slow, tears began to roll over the bridge of her nose.

~

She remembered, without wanting to, the first time she'd been in bed with Euan, just after they'd returned to Washington Square from their first summer apart. It was on a Sunday, while her father and Calista attended church. Nora had coaxed Euan to her bedroom on the pretext of studying, then shut the door and began undressing.

"What exactly are we studying?" he'd asked, watching Nora unfasten her blouse.

"We should brush up on our anatomy."

He'd chuckled, low, and watched her shrug her arms out of her sleeves. She'd paused and raised a prompting brow. "It's my study too."

With a slow-spreading grin, Euan began working at his own buttons.

Not a million dissections could have properly prepared them for the vulnerable immediacy of standing naked before one another. They both blushed and looked away—but both looked again.

"I'll start, then," Nora finally said. "I'll give you the name of a structure—skeletal, muscular, or vascular; all fair game, I think—and you indicate its location. On me. We'll take turns."

Euan let out a breath that was not quite another chuckle and, perhaps unconsciously, licked his lips. "All right."

"Deltoid," Nora said.

"Too easy." He softly caressed her shoulders, looked into her eyes. "Thoracoepigastric vein."

She lightly tapped the side of his abdomen in a line from a spot near his ribs to just above his navel, then smiled. "Inferior vena cava."

166

He held his lower lip between his teeth as he ran his fingertip down the center of Nora's chest. "Terrible name from this view," he murmured.

She laughed. "Your turn."

"Talus."

"Talus?" Nora echoed, with another arched brow. "With a *T*?"

"Yes," Euan said, with a breathless burst of a laugh.

Nora had kowtowed, kissed the top of his foot where it met his ankle—first one, then the other. When she rose, she turned her back to him and went to lie face down on her bed. "Teres minor," she said against her pillow. A moment later, she felt the weight of Euan's body on the mattress, the warmth of him bending over her.

He pressed his lips to the space near her underarm. "Somewhere around there," he added, and dabbled his fingers against Nora's skin until she was squirming with more laughter. She ended up on her back, arms tucked tightly to her sides.

"Gracilis!" she yelped, as if it were a plea for mercy. *"Gracilis."*

"You already went," Euan said.

"Stumped?"

"No." He smiled and sat back, concentration overtaking his face, and then reverence—and a trace of fear—as he eased her legs apart. "Gracilis," he breathed, and traced a faint line down the inside of Nora's thigh, then up the same longitude of the other.

Her lips had parted to permit a ragged inhale, and then she'd sat up to pull him closer and kiss him, again and again.

When the memory finally wore itself thin and faded back into the dark recesses of Nora's mind, she wiped her slick face and sighed.

For the first night since coming to the farm, she realized, she didn't feel watched. She supposed it was Mal's proximity, though he didn't feel as close as he should have.

And now Nora felt the pull of Euan's empty room, if it was truly empty, from the same distance over which she had recently pined for his brother.

CHAPTER TWENTY

Hoosick Falls, NY
October 1886

Mal moved nearer to her in the night, which Nora only knew come morning, when she woke to feel his heavy arm curved over her side, thick fingers slack against her stomach. His legs were angled so his knees fitted into the bend of Nora's own.

She could feel his breath move through his body against her back, and held still for a protracted moment, trying to ascertain if he was indeed asleep. When she was sure that he was, she nestled even closer, softening against his warmth, and dozed again.

~

When they walked into the barn together, Erik eyed them both but said nothing, which was somehow more jarring than any indecent comment he could have made. He seemed relaxed, though, and Marie, Nora noticed, hummed a song that sounded very like the melody Erik had played the night before.

At the breakfast table, Kirsten seemed her usual stern self. The twins, of course, betrayed no awareness of any change. Nora might make a more rigorous study of them now that she was permanently installed in the house, but she assumed Kirsten would balk and stymie any overt attempts. In fact, they might all be opposed. To them, the girls weren't a mystery to investigate or a problem to be solved, but ordinary members of the family. In time, they would become the same to Nora, though she might remain inconsequential to them.

The rest of the day spooled out rather indistinctly, if tinged with melancholy, but that wasn't an unfamiliar feeling anymore. That night was much like the one before. In near silence, her ardor was kindled, then prematurely doused. Afterward, she felt even more alone.

～

The next day, at church, she thought that people smiled more broadly at her. Nearly everyone made a point of greeting her so they could say *Mrs. Colquhoun.* The sole exception was Grace Murphy, who smiled and nodded just like usual and said, "Good afternoon, Nora."

"Good afternoon, Grace." She felt unduly grateful for her friend—though suddenly sad to think she'd see less of her now, since she couldn't go off so frequently, shirking household responsibilities now that she was elevated—or perhaps demoted—from her position as guest.

～

During her first week as a wife, Nora mulled over Mal's behavior some-what obsessively, and analyzed her own as well. She wanted things that he didn't seem able to give, and she didn't feel able to ask for, though she had never before been shy about communicating her desires. His age had something to do with it, she thought, and his deference, his reservation.

Yet they'd bared their souls to each other on paper. Even so, Nora reflected, the genuine rapport they'd forged through letters had remained tempered by convention and the more formal mode of com-munication itself. She'd assumed all such stiffness would dissolve once in each other's presence—and it had, to a degree. But when they should have been closest, they seemed most restrained, by a strange sense of remove they couldn't shed with their clothes.

Naturally, Mal wouldn't pull her into an embrace by the barn or hold her hand at breakfast, but he might have kissed her in the parlor when they were the last ones left downstairs, or undressed her himself when they went upstairs together.

Instead, he would watch her begin to disrobe, which she did neither hurriedly nor seductively, just a matter-of-fact unfastening of her various buttons and ties and then the loosening of her corset laces before unhooking the busk. Before she could finish, though, Mal turned away and kept his back to her as he undressed himself. She'd yet to see much of his skin and still didn't know what scars he bore, if any. He seemed not to have noticed hers.

Though he evinced no entitlement even in private, the way he moved Nora's hands away from certain parts of his body, and always repositioned hers to be beneath his own, was uncharacteristically adamant—if unfailingly gentle. It seemed less an issue of control and more of self-preservation, as if he couldn't bear to look at her or be touched for too long. As much as it frustrated Nora, she didn't want to cause distress or tension, so she acquiesced. And kept quiet.

She found the most pleasure in going up first and changing into her nightgown—it was chilly, after all, without a fire—and lying with her back to the door. Once Mal climbed into bed beside her, she moved closer against his body, until he lifted her hem above her hips and cupped her breast with a calloused hand. Then, she didn't mind the way he pressed his brow against her neck, since he couldn't have seen her anyway.

She did wonder if he thought of someone else as he moved in her, and if it might be someone she had seen in town—and if she knew who it was, whether she would mind.

She couldn't, she supposed. Not when her own mind often replaced Mal with someone else, though it wasn't always who Nora wanted it to be. Some nights, bright-blue eyes flashed behind her own closed lids, forcing them open. She stared hard into the darker shadows then, tried to will another familiar face to materialize from the gloom—though the moment that she thought it might be possible, she lost her nerve and shut her eyes again.

Afterward, she often rolled over and let her forehead touch Mal's warm back, put her arm around him so she could better feel his steady breath.

He might not have been everything that Nora had wanted, but she did love him, and clung to him. He was all she had.

~

The following Sunday, however, Mal was off to Albany for the new bull.

The night before, he asked if Nora was sure she didn't want to go. She said yes, though it was a lie. She was slightly jealous to think of him staying in a hotel and eating at restaurants and being away from all the rest of them.

She wanted to be alone with him in some other place, to see if he was different in private then. But more than that, Nora wanted him to want her to join him. He clearly only asked out of obligation, and perhaps concern. "It'll only be two nights," he said.

She smiled and nodded and turned away, keeping close to her edge of the bed. Mal, of course, didn't move any nearer, and Nora felt strangely satisfied by the self-pity in which it allowed her to wallow.

The next morning, they said goodbye after church, and she was shocked when he kissed her cheek there on the street, in full view of everyone. She wanted to follow him to the station and wave until his train pulled out of sight.

Instead, she walked down to Main Street alone, admiring the jack-o'-lanterns that had appeared on a number of porches in the village over the preceding week. While she stopped to chat with the Burnses and the Murphys, she heard the children running about the church lawns trying to scare each other with promises of ghosts and witches and goblins that were sure to be afoot—or afloat, or a-broom—that night.

~

Back at the farm, as the sun began to sink, Nora felt a faint twist of discomfort to think of sleeping alone again. But the main bedroom had a calm enough air, and she could keep a fire going all night if she wished.

During evening milking, Erik was more loquacious than usual, without Mal there to shoot him censorious looks. He invoked the same Halloween ghosts and ghouls as the children in the churchyards, which clearly made Marie nervous. Perhaps it caused some echo of anxiety in Nora too.

"Stop trying to scare us," she said, striving for a tone of boredom. "It's just the last night of October. Nothing special about it."

"Maybe." Erik shrugged as he continued milking. "My ancestors didn't hold to it either. Not like the Celts. But they still thought the dead were close this time of year. And they huddled up, not just against the cold. Shut their houses to outsiders, made sacrifices to the elves. A lot like what happened with Old Nick, actually. They killed an animal to spill its blood. Humans were even better. Then they shared the meat among the family—"

"Oh, stop it!" Marie cut in.

Erik laughed. "That sound any different from what we do all year round? With the animals, anyway." He looked at Nora again. "You don't believe in curses, doc. Guess you don't believe in ghosts, either, huh?"

"No," she said. "Because they aren't real."

"I bet Marie begs to differ. I know Kirsten does. Maybe Axel, too."

Nora looked at Axel, but he remained as silent as ever, his expression inscrutable.

Erik continued to address him anyway. "The Germans are the ones who came up with that name for the kind of ghosts that like to make noise and knock shit over, right? *Poltergeist.* What's the word for the kind that just lurks all quiet like—"

"Please," Marie interrupted, "can we talk about something else now?"

Before Erik could reply, Nora gave voice to the happiest thing she could think of on such short notice. "Yes—Christmas will be here before you know it, and it's a far better holiday than this. What's your favorite part about it?"

As she'd hoped, her sister-in-law burbled over with cheer too brisk and forceful for even Erik to interrupt.

When they carried their pails out to the springhouse, however, he sidled up close to Nora and said in a low voice, "You sure you're not scared to sleep alone tonight?"

She didn't answer, or even look at him, but quickened her pace to put distance between them.

∼

Naturally, she did have trouble sleeping—she lay awake imagining, once more, Old Nick's great throat being slashed, gallons of blood soaking into the ground, smeared across Erik's face like a mask from some secret sacrificial ritual.

But she knew he had only killed the injured animal to spare it longer suffering. And there were no elves, any more than there were witches massing in the trees beyond the windows, any more than the trees themselves moved closer in the night.

When she finally dozed off, however, Nora had more strange dreams that made her think she was awake when she was, in fact, still caught in subconsciousness. She expected to find herself sleepwalking, but in the morning was still alone in her marital bed.

Only one more night before Mal was back, and she was eager for his return.

CHAPTER
TWENTY-ONE

Hoosick Falls, NY
November 1886

On Tuesday, Nora left for the village on her bicycle shortly after breakfast, to visit Grace before meeting Mal.

Grace answered her door with her youngest child on her hip. "Well, hello, you. Say hello, Alvie."

He did his best, and Nora followed them inside, waving to Ezra, still looking at him too long.

"How was it?" Grace asked as they settled at the kitchen table. "Being all alone with the rest of the in-laws while the mister was gone."

"Oh, fine. They're used to me by now, I think. I'm mostly used to them."

Grace gave a brief huff of amusement. "Well, Marie's sweet, at least."

"She is," Nora agreed.

"Such a shame about her girls," said Grace, letting the words trail off.

Nora faltered; they'd had many frank conversations by then— about subjects ranging from their own childhoods to women's medicine to the surrender of Geronimo, which revealed some pointed political differences—but this seemed a more sensitive topic, and perhaps not Nora's to weigh in on. Of course, she had plenty of private thoughts about the matter. She only made a noncommittal murmur that could be taken for agreement, or perhaps the slightest censure—and was, in fact, somewhat offended by Grace's remark, though she also understood it. The twins were enigmatic, which made people uncomfortable. And when any perceived abnormality was equated with deficiency, kind people pitied; others scorned. Scientists, Nora supposed, might be of either persuasion, but always looked for possible causes and solutions.

She gazed into the other room at the apparently uncomplicated Ezra until Grace said, "It's a wonder you haven't stared a hole in that boy yet."

Startled, Nora looked back at her. "Oh, I—I'm sorry."

Grace only smiled and shook her head. "People can't help it. He's beautiful."

"He is." Nora picked up her coffee and blew on the scalding liquid in a vain attempt to hide the flush she felt prickling her cheeks.

"Takes after his father," Grace said.

Nora paused mid-sip and looked over the rim of her cup.

Grace laughed. "Oh, now *I'm* sorry. But, you see, my sister was dark-haired and darker-eyed, like me. And Ez was hers. Ellen's."

It didn't sound like a secret so much as a sadness, but Grace lowered her voice for the next bit. "She was only sixteen when she had him. It killed her, poor thing. Though I always thought the heartbreak helped her along."

Nora had previously divulged that her own mother died of puerperal fever, within days of giving birth to her—yet it never felt any less gut-wrenching to hear of another woman killed bringing new life into the world. "I'm so sorry," she said now. "But then, Ezra's father . . . ?"

Grace took another sip of coffee. "Oh, everybody has their own theory. Ellen wouldn't say one way or another, but I know she was running around with Erik before he disappeared. She cried for weeks when she realized he was gone, and then again when she realized she was pregnant."

"Does he know?"

Grace shrugged. "I've seen him stare at Ez too. With a strange sort of look in his eyes. That same blue, of course . . . But he's never come to me to ask. Which is just as well. Benji's Ezra's father now. Always has been."

Nora nodded and looked at the white-blond back of Ezra's head.

"And plenty of other names have been floated about," Grace added. "Some people even think he's Axel's." Which made her laugh again, harder than Nora thought it should have.

The talk of youthful indiscretions and town gossip made Nora wonder about her husband. "What about Mal?" she asked. "I mean—well, did he ever . . . have a sweetheart, that you know of?"

Grace raised one eyebrow but readily said, "No, I don't believe so."

"Did you know him well, when you were younger?"

She raised both eyebrows at that. "How old do you think I am, exactly?"

Nora fumbled the beginning of an apology, but Grace cut her off.

"No, no, I'm only ten years younger. But that's an age, when you're children. By the time I was grown, he'd been to war and back. I think that might have made him quieter than before, but people did say he was always like that. Stoic. Steadfast."

Perfect words for Malcolm, Nora thought.

"He was always the shyest of the Colquhoun boys," Grace continued. "I'm not sure I ever even spoke directly to him more than a dozen times in as many years. But he was always well liked. Respected. Admired. Pitied a little, too. For not having enough fun, I suppose. But handsome, obviously. God knows plenty of women in this town would have married him, no matter what state the farm was in when he came of age. But he didn't let himself get drawn into such things—as far as I know. Which is why everyone was so stunned when he married you. And happy, of course. Such a blessing for you both."

"Yes." Nora flashed a smile as she took another sip of bitter coffee.

"So, then," Grace said, "will we be seeing a brand-new head of bright-red hair around here soon?"

Nora choked on a little on her drink, though she'd meant it to come out a laugh. "Get straight to the point, why don't you?"

"Yes," said Grace. "Why not? Life is short and people are curious. I can't stand to pretend I don't care. You're the same, and we both know it."

Nora flushed again, but felt a flare of appreciation for Grace's frank manner and inquisitiveness. In answer to her question, however, she only let herself say, "I don't know."

∽

She took her leave soon after, to reach the train station before Mal arrived. When he stepped onto the platform, Nora felt a startlingly magnetic gratitude that hurtled her toward her husband. He laughed and clasped his arms around her, and Nora nearly sobbed.

When they finally drew apart, Mal looked somewhat bemusedly into her face. "That's the warmest welcome home I've ever gotten."

"I missed you," she said, shaken by how much, or perhaps by the fact that she hadn't truly realized it until that moment.

He smiled and kissed her brow—only briefly, yet Nora almost swooned.

"I missed you, too," he said. "Now, come meet Titus."

∽

Nora had expected a hulking, beady-eyed beast dangerous with muscle and male vigor, but Titus was little more than a large, curly-haired calf, disarmingly precious and easily loaded into the back of the wagon.

Nora stowed her bicycle there too and sat close beside Mal. He asked how things had been while he was gone. She said fine, and little else, and turned the talk to what his trip to Albany had been like, no trace of jealousy left in her.

≈

Back at the farm, Marie was equally taken with the long-lashed new bull. Even Kirsten almost smiled. Erik shook his head and spat, said Mal must have gotten the cheapest runt they had on offer, but Mal himself was confident that six months hence, Titus would be coming into his own quite nicely.

"Give it a little time," he said. "You'll see."

≈

Now that Nora's suspicions about Ezra Murphy's parentage had been bolstered, she couldn't keep from peering at Erik in the barn that evening—and then in the dining room, at least until she worried that he might have mistaken her pointed interest, based on the look he shot back at her.

He knew by now that she was friendly with Grace. Nora thought it plenty likely that he wouldn't care what gossip her friend imparted. Maybe he didn't believe it himself, or simply didn't mind that another man was raising his son, let alone that half the town knew it.

Maybe when Grace thought she'd seen Erik stare at Ezra, it had been a coincidence, or mere passing curiosity. Frankly, it seemed just as likely that Erik might resent the boy's existence, a reminder of yet another thing he'd lost.

It might have been the sort of subject some wives could broach with their husbands, but Nora wouldn't dare ask Mal if he'd heard any such rumors. She could hardly imagine him angry at her, but she thought the subject might at least elicit a flinty expression and a firm declaration that Benjamin Murphy was Ezra's father. Which was clearly true now, whoever had planted their seed in Grace's sister.

Nora didn't know that it wasn't Axel. Anyway, it should be none of her concern, so she tried to put it out of her mind.

～

But the thought of Erik having a sweetheart before he left home did intrigue her—as did the fact that she had died while he was gone, so even if he'd wanted to leave his wife and daughters for Ellen and Ezra, it wasn't an option.

Nora remembered how he'd said his blood was cursed, and wondered if he believed it had tainted others. Ridiculous, but still, she felt a pang of sympathy for Erik. For who he had once been, at least.

～

That night, she asked Mal to light a fire in their room. The moon was only half full and Nora wanted to be able to see and be seen—at least for a moment. While he kindled the flames, she undressed and reclined atop the covers. When he turned, he paused a moment, then came to kiss her as she tilted up her face.

He seemed reluctant, still, to touch her skin, but his lips were soft and branding-hot upon Nora's neck and shoulder and then her breasts. Once he was naked and they were fully upon the mattress, his knee stayed firmly pressed between her thighs, even when she rocked herself against it, which ordinarily would have made him move away. What was more, he looked at her again, his eyes trained on hers until Nora couldn't stand to hold his gaze, almost dizzy with surprise.

She had a flicker of suspicion—that he had been with someone else in Albany, that that was why he hadn't wanted her to come along, and why he was so unlike himself just now, but whatever secrets her husband had, he would surely never commit adultery.

When he was inside her, Nora reached down between their bodies and moved a fingertip in circles upon her exquisitely aching flesh, that wondrous bit that, as she had once half jokingly quipped to Euan, made her believe in God, created as it was for no purpose other than pleasure.

They were both nearly done for, she could tell, perhaps even about to come apart together—when a sudden loud bang made them stop and snap their heads in the direction of the mantel, where both framed commencement portraits had fallen over.

There was no open window to account for it, nor had there been any seismic shaking of the ground; the bed wasn't close enough to have juddered the pictures over. Mal frowned. Nora, startled but desperate not to lose him, tried to recapture his attention, her hand on the side of his face, but when he looked back at her and shifted slightly, his frown deepened and his eyes swept lower, to where their bodies were yet conjoined. "Oh," he murmured. "Nora, you . . . you're bleeding."

She looked down, too, as Mal quickly disengaged and covered himself. He rose to retrieve the washcloth from the pitcher and basin on the dresser.

"It's fine," she said, though she herself was surprised by the volume and brightness of the blood. "It's just—I thought it wouldn't be for another day or two. But—I don't mind."

Mal said nothing, only finished cleaning himself with his back to her before fetching a fresh handkerchief from a drawer. "I'll get another sheet," he said, and pulled on the bare minimum of clothing before stepping quietly into the hall.

Nora lay there dazed and disappointed, slick with her body's various effusions and Mal's sweat, knowing she should get up, too, minimize the mess if only because she would have to clean it later. And they'd only just washed all the linen, she thought bitterly.

Instead of attending to that, however, she put her hand back between her thighs and closed her eyes again, only to see a bright-blue stare made more vivid by a bright-red mask—which she knew wasn't bull's blood this time. In her vision, Erik's entire body was painted crimson.

She couldn't have stopped if she'd wanted to. She was vaguely curious as to what Mal would do if he walked in while she was silently convulsing, if he would take it for some dire seizure.

But he was still gone by the time Nora, finally sated, rose to wash and strip the soiled bedclothes. Whatever had come over him, she realized, had gone. He had been disenchanted. Maybe even disgusted. She felt strangely ashamed.

∼

The next morning, Nora woke alone. She had no idea whether Mal had never returned to bed or had already risen, but she knew that she had slept late.

She scrubbed the dried blood from beneath her fingernails and headed out to milk the cows, using them to block her view of her husband as they went about their work.

∼

And as easily as that, life returned to normal—though it was a normal that had only recently become Nora's own. New enough that it seemed she should have the option to change her mind and hand it back.

But she had made a binding agreement, by law and by vow, and by her own choosing.

She marveled at how adamant she had been, how very certain, as if she hadn't made countless mistakes before. Only time would tell how long she lived with this one.

CHAPTER
TWENTY-TWO

Hoosick Falls, NY
November–December 1886

November's grip tightened and squeezed all the blue from the sky, all the color from the remaining leaves. The whole forest would soon be denuded to a barren tangle of black limbs, a network of branching veins, gone necrotic.

Nora was drawn to sketch them, but she insisted on helping with all the chores now. She dusted and swept and fetched water, and on Thursdays, helped churn cream in the wooden vessel that stood as tall as one of the twins.

Initially, Kirsten still tried to dissuade her, groused that it was harder than she thought, and if Nora ruined the batch, which she surely would, they'd have no butter to eat, much less to sell.

As pleasantly as possible, Nora said that she was sure she would do well with such capable teachers—but if it was a disaster, then she would gladly buy them a month's supply of butter in town the next day.

"I'm sure you would," Kirsten retorted, then added, "It isn't only the cost," but she sounded rather feebly petulant, perhaps even to herself, for she flapped her hands at Marie and said, "Go on, then. If you're such a fine instructor now."

It took a good half hour for the first small clumps of solids to congeal together into a yellow mass amid the white buttermilk, and Nora's shoulders burned, even trading off turns. When they were done churning, she was slightly sweaty and her skirt was speckled with creamy golden flecks that had splashed from the hole in the churn's lid.

She learned that cornstarch would help get the grease out, and that laundry day was the new bane of her existence. Mercifully, it only occurred twice a month, though Kirsten washed the twins' cloth nappies weekly. She didn't try to shoo Nora away from the steaming cauldron and washboard and wringer, though Nora wished she would have.

As she mangled water from sodden chemises and napkins and pegged them on a line to dry, she thought about how Calista had been blessed that they'd sent all their laundry out in messy bundles, received everything back in neatly folded stacks. Nora knew that there was a laundress in the village, but she guessed that Mal would balk at the expense, and Kirsten would never suffer the judgmental gossip that might follow.

She didn't even dare purchase nicer detergent in town, since Kirsten made the hard lye soap they used herself. At least she scented it with rosemary, which still comforted Nora to smell on herself and the others.

As she'd expected, even her most tentative, innocuous questions about the twins drew curt replies from Kirsten—who was quick to admonish Nora when she addressed the girls directly. It was pointless; prodding and poking would only upset them and the carefully regimented order of the household. Furthermore, there was nothing to be done about the way they were, which was surely as God had intended. Chastened, Nora dropped the matter.

In another concerted effort to maintain harmony, she continued to avoid the kitchen except to carry in dirty dishes after meals. It was fully Kirsten's domain, and Nora was glad enough to leave her to it.

She didn't like how the room was tucked away in the back of the house, and still felt discomfited by the padlock on the basement door. Whenever Nora passed it, she felt a creeping unease, a suspicion that the lock kept something out, indeed—but from the other side of the old wooden door.

Then, immediately, she chastised herself. She needed to shake the fantastical idea of mysterious presences lurking about, when it was plainly only the place's isolation and lingering pockets of unfriendliness that made her nape prickle. Erik's invocation of a curse hadn't helped, but of course, that too was nonsense.

Still, Nora was glad that she had Mal to draw close to at night now, whether or not they coupled. She hadn't touched him again until she was finished bleeding, and even then, she was timid, afraid of coaxing him into something that he didn't really want—or didn't want to want.

Though he clearly experienced gratification from their physical union, Nora still worried that he was only performing his husbandly duty. He never seemed to notice her quick decline in pleasure, her ultimate unsatisfaction. She could have said something, *should* have said something, but it felt somehow indelicate, intrusive, impossible, too late.

~

In her free hours, having been discouraged from attempting to engage the twins, and having sketched everything else, Nora searched for the bull's remains in the forest. When she found Old Nick's carcass, though, she was unnerved by the fact that it was missing its head.

Bears roamed the woods, of course, and were scavengers. One of them must have dragged it away. But they killed fresh meat, too, so Nora hurried back the way she'd come.

Besides, Erik was often out hunting now, and he'd cautioned her from wandering. "Wear somethin' flashy if you're out there. Brightest colors you've got. A matchin' hat wouldn't be a bad investment. That brown hair blends in too well."

So Nora, when she wasn't cycling into town to see Grace or doing chores, took to studying the farm's flora and fauna under her microscope, which sat on Euan's desk. She sketched what she saw under magnification: the profusion of translucent bubbles that hid in a creamy drop of cow's milk; the beautifully delicate lace of a sliver of dried straw or corn stem; a slice of a kernel displaying structures more like clusters of frogs' eggs; the scales of a single pig hair like the elongated shingles of a tightly closed pine cone—or the skin of a snake.

She opened the abalone box on the mantel and felt the remaining half of Euan's ashes through their rough-spun bag, but decided against examining any of the fine grains or coarse gravel beneath the microscope, knowing that plumbing their minutest depths would bring him no closer to her now.

And yet she still felt some sense of accompaniment in his room, which seemed too strong to come simply from being surrounded by his things, and which left her unsettled even now, though she willingly exposed herself to it again and again.

At the same desk, under the same sense of observation, Nora continued to write semi-regularly to her father and Cousin Bette, mild missives that mostly described the weather and the place—always changing, so she felt the subjects were not yet exhausted. Her father, regardless of the pace of Nora's letters, sent his own once a week, and enfolded money into the accordioned paper every time.

She asked him to stop, assured him she had no need of it, but he ignored her, and she socked the growing pile away in the back of a drawer in Euan's room.

~

Midmonth, the men killed two pigs to fatten the farm larder. Nora removed herself from the scene before the animals were even fetched from the pen, though their high-pitched squeals still carried a remarkable distance, and the gush of blood stained the ground for days. The drained carcasses, before they were dismantled and processed, were so white they reminded her of pickled specimens too large for any jar.

In another life, of course, she had dissected pigs—human cadavers came later—and so the butchering itself was no real bother. Watching Kirsten remove the brains, no bigger than human children's, Nora was transported briefly back to her father's basement, and felt a pang of nostalgia that made her eyes sting.

As Kirsten and Marie made headcheese and blood sausage with other spare parts, Nora recalled how she'd once practiced sutures on the rind of a pork shoulder destined for dinner—how Calista had fussed. Yet also been impressed with the fineness of her stitches.

Even Kirsten complimented them, on a night when Nora worked on her own mending by the parlor fire. She ruined the moment by telling the anecdote about her needlework practice on flesh instead of fabric.

Even when she stayed silent, she invited disapproval. When she took up her sketchbook on the settee and made enlarged studies of some of the anatomical drawings in her old medical texts, Kirsten's expression evinced clear distaste. Yet now Nora saw how easily her sister-in-law plucked out the pigs' gelatinous eyeballs, the only parts of the animals that they couldn't use.

Kirsten threw them off the porch for the cats or the crows, or whichever scavenger scented the opportunity first.

Nora felt a brief spike of panic—why tempt any hungry things closer? But they were only four tiny scraps of tissue, and she was safe enough inside.

～

She was suddenly eager for mid-December, though, when she and Mal would visit Manhattan—for a mere five days, two of those for traveling, but any respite would be a gift.

Nora became so fixated on the idea that she thought of little else.

She'd arranged for them to stay at Aunt Birdie's, unwilling to share her girlhood room with Malcolm, nor to sleep separately from him— especially when the only other suitable bedchamber was the one where his brother had died.

As impatient as she was to go, she could tell that Mal was nervous. Part of it was leaving the farm, of course, and leaving the others with more work, though even milking should be manageable; several of the pregnant cows had stopped producing, and none were due to calve until January.

He was also anxious about meeting Nora's family. When she reassured him they would all be nice—"Well, except maybe for Grandmama, but she's no worse than Kirsten"—he only vaguely smiled and nodded. When Nora reminded him that it was only three days, she thought she saw a sheen of dread in his eyes.

And to her irritation, his nervousness was catching. The last time she'd gone home to New York City, she'd been alone, unwed. Now that she was a new creature, a married woman, she had no doubt her family would study her and Mal with keen interest. What they would see, Nora wasn't certain.

～

When the day of their departure finally arrived, Malcolm walked in step with her onto the station platform and stared stoically from the carriage window.

Nora tried to read on the train, but her attention was shot. She wavered wildly between excitement and panic, and repeated things she'd already said to Mal about what to expect. She could tell that he wasn't really listening, but the tenor of her voice seemed to help somewhat. Like chanting slowly to a spooked horse—though Nora was aware that she was doing it for her own benefit as well.

CHAPTER
TWENTY-THREE

Manhattan, NY
December 1886

She wasn't sure if her chattering helped, but their proximity to Manhattan soothed her own anxiety. The city lights seemed to make Nora's excitement sparkle brighter, and she started for the door before the train even fully stopped. Upon stepping out into the grand cathedral of the station, Nora felt a sense of unfurling and expanding.

Her father intercepted them near the platform. She hugged him for a long time, then beamed as he shook Mal's hand.

They drove straight to Aunt Birdie's. Mal was quiet in the carriage, but he was quiet everywhere, and seemed glad enough to listen to father and daughter catch up. Nora had expected to roil with nerves upon arriving at her aunt's, if only in anticipation of Grandmama's frank—and, if Nora was lucky, silent—assessment, but her stomach just growled in anticipation of dinner. Her limbs remained loose, her lips curved in a smile.

∽

And Grandmama was nice enough, nicer than Nora had expected. Ernest was far more aloof, but she'd never warmed to him enough for it to matter. Bette and Birdie, of course, were genuinely enthused to meet Mal, and Nora felt not embarrassed or sympathetic at his obvious discomfort but so fond that she reached over and placed her hand upon his arm, which only further ruffled him.

~

She'd had hope for that evening, based on her theory that he seemed more relaxed away from home, as if the farmhouse itself constrained him.

But when they turned in and Nora placed a questioning hand upon Mal's chest, he apologized and said he was tired. She would have been more disappointed if she hadn't also had to stifle a yawn. She had no dreams that she could remember.

~

She woke after seven the next morning, shockingly late—and saw that Mal had already risen and dressed. He looked to have been standing by the window for some time.

"I didn't want to go down without you," he admitted. "I thought I might get lost."

Nora chuckled and stretched amid the abundance of soft pillows and lavender-scented sheets, then got up to stand beside him and look out at Central Park, a mere suggestion of the woods they'd left farther north. "I should have drawn you a map," she said, and chanced to lean against him.

He didn't move away or stiffen, but neither did he put an arm around her or turn his face to kiss her hair. She felt the sadness that she thought she'd left behind well up in her.

It was only compounded by the realization that dawned on her next: the city looked so much like it had when Euan died, cold and gray and desolate, only missing snow and ice.

And it struck her as incredible, that it had not yet been a year—but that it very soon would be.

"We should go down for breakfast," she murmured, and left Mal at the window to go get dressed.

~

Once fed, they walked through the park and visited the art museum amid swirls of snow that amounted to nothing. The best part of the day was spent sitting in the parlor in Washington Square before dinner—Nora's father had extracted a promise that she would eat there at least once. Beforehand, he poured her a little whiskey. Mal declined, and seemed almost to meld with the furniture as Nora and her father talked for hours that seemed to collapse into mere minutes.

When they moved to the dining table, laid with all of Nora's favorites, they switched to wine.

Before they sipped, unable to help herself, Nora raised her drink and recited her old refrain: "To carpenters, smiths, weavers, and women."

Her father smiled, perhaps a little wistfully, and touched his glass to hers.

Mal, who drank water, looked slightly perplexed.

"She read somewhere," Nora's father explained, "that King Henry VIII decreed it forbidden for any of those people to practice surgery. Of course it stuck with her."

Now, Nora felt foolish for reviving it. But it had been a reflex once, a battle cry she had unleashed at countless family dinners, toasting with weak cider in her glass at thirteen, and had proclaimed every time she went drinking with fellow students in later years.

Mal's own smile seemed tinged with pity. Nora looked away and drank too deeply, keenly aware that he said almost nothing throughout the meal, though he sat amiably enough.

~

It was late by the time they returned to Fifth Avenue. In their oversized room with its impossibly high ceilings, Mal looked noticeably more drawn.

"Are you all right?" Nora asked as she began undressing. "We didn't bore you silly, did we?"

"Of course not." He turned away to gather his own nightshirt, which he took into the adjoining bathroom to change into.

Nora decided, after standing naked before the fire for a few moments, not to put anything else on, but scrambled beneath the cold sheets before Mal returned.

When he climbed into bed beside her, he paused at the sight of her bare skin, and Nora saw him swallow.

She moved closer and studied his lined face. He probably found the excess of Birdie's mansion vulgar, her whole family shamefully profligate; not just the lavish clothes they wore and the lavish food they ate—and worse, how much of it they left untouched—but the posing of probing questions, and the volume with which she and her father laughed, not to mention the alcohol they drank, which was still vaporous on Nora's breath.

Suddenly, she felt ashamed, and turned her back to Mal. "You must hate it here."

"No." A moment later, he inched a little closer. "It's very nice. But I suppose I do feel a bit . . . out of my element."

Euan, Nora remembered, had been a little stiff at first as well, but he'd soon relaxed. Erik, she imagined—if mistakenly permitted entrance—would immediately sprawl out to take easy possession of every space available to him.

It made her sad that, even welcomed, Mal felt dislocated. Yet she understood, all too well. She could only hope that time would make things better—in every place where they would be together. But maybe the place mattered more than she'd thought.

She made herself turn back toward him. "You don't believe in curses, do you?"

He forced a faint breath of laughter. "Of course not. Do you?"

"No," she said, and mostly meant it, wanted to fully believe it. Her mind was muddled with a multitude of things she yearned to know but still found hard to say, even off the farm, even with whiskey and wine swirling in her blood.

What finally came out of her mouth was "Do you want children?"

Mal looked rather stunned. "I . . . Do you?"

"Do *you*?" Nora asked again.

He thought for a moment. "Sometimes I feel as if I've already had them."

She was surprised by how much that hurt. "So you don't need any more, then? You don't want any, with me?"

"I would," he said. "If you wanted—"

"*No.*" She pushed herself up on one arm. "What do *you* want? I think you want what you've always had, for things to stay the same, only it's too late for that, because I barged my way into your life and now you're burdened with me—"

"Blessed," Mal countered, and pushed himself up to face her. "You're not a burden, Nora."

"I am. And if we did have children, even if they were perfect, they'd be burdens too. More people to worry about, and probably lose—because curse or not, we couldn't protect them; you can't protect anyone, and I . . . I can't watch someone die again. I can't." She broke off and began to cry.

Mal shifted closer and pulled her to him. "Nora, please. It's all right."

He smoothed her hair and kissed her face. He helped her lie back down and tucked the covers over her bare shoulder, then stroked her arm through the comforter as her hitching breaths slowed and deepened, and she fell asleep.

≈

Embarrassment fastened Nora's gaze to the floor the following morning. She apologized for having so much to drink, and didn't let Mal get in many words at all, afraid of what he might say—or not say.

She'd promised Cousin Bette a private audience that afternoon and was glad to leave her husband to his own devices.

≈

Bette's babies had grown at an incredible rate in the two and a half months since Nora had last seen them. She still couldn't decipher any of their words, but they attempted conversation and smiled and gurgled constantly. They seemed different creatures from Marie's girls, a thought for which Nora felt guilty, but couldn't deny. Naturally, Bette asked her if there were any babies in her immediate future.

"I don't know," she said, far more sharply than she'd answered Grace a month ago. Forcibly softening her tone, she added, "I'm not in any hurry, anyway."

"Well, that might be for the best." Bette lowered her voice and leaned closer. "The doctor did something terrible to me—necessary, I'm sure, and thank you for not telling me about it beforehand because I would have refused to go through with it at all. I'm finally healed for the most part, but *God*, Nora, I think I know what a butchered hog feels like."

Nora blinked away an alarming mental image and watched her cousin's twins stuff their fat little fists in their mouths. They cooed when they noticed her gazing at them. "It was worth it, though?" she asked.

Bette smiled at her babies too. "Honestly, I already want another one. Don't you, looking at these little angels?"

Nora made a noncommittal sound. "They don't all turn out so well," she said, then felt another surge of shame. "Yours are charming, though."

"I know, they are. What does your husband think?"

"Of your children?"

"Of yours."

"He'd be happy if we had them. Fine if we don't."

"Whatever you want, then," Bette said. "Naturally."

Nora was slightly stung.

She gazed at the twins and thought that their helpless appeal was a clever little trick of life itself—luring you with the promise of a happy, healthy child when there were no guarantees of reaping such a bounty from letting oneself be sown, let alone of surviving the process.

If you did, you might be disfigured, or your child might be damaged, or simply disappointing, and you would surely fail them in some way—in many. Life would bring them happiness if they were lucky, but even then, it would also bring them harm. And if they died before you, they must take some piece of your heart with them. How could anyone bear it?

Nora thought she should be glad that Mal had hardly touched her since Albany, but she wasn't. That night, again, neither of them reached for the other.

~

She couldn't fully enjoy their final day in the city, distracted by the knowledge of how soon it would be over. She kept having to surreptitiously swipe at her cheeks while she did Christmas shopping.

Though she wished they could spend the evening in Washington Square again, their premature Christmas would take place at Aunt Birdie's, with her ample space and massive fir tree that scented the entire first floor and threatened to blind anyone who looked directly at its profusion of glittering lights.

The gathering was pleasant enough, though Nora still dwelled on its inevitable conclusion, far too close at hand.

Perhaps her father felt that same prickle of panic, for he lingered well after Bette and Ernest and the babies had said good night and goodbye, and even Grandmama had retired. Aunt Birdie dozed, fluting delicate snores until her head tipped forward and snapped upright again.

She declared that she was too old to host such late confabs and was turning in, and Nora's father sighed.

"Ach, I suppose I should go. You've got to get up early in the morning anyway."

Nora didn't protest, only rose to accompany him out. The temperature had plummeted well below freezing, and her teeth chattered as she stood on the sidewalk and waved him off.

When she came back inside, she couldn't get warm, even standing before the fire roaring in the guest suite's hearth and the radiators gurgling at the perimeters of the room. Mal looked concerned, asked if he could get her tea.

"No, thank you," she said.

After a period of standing and staring at the fire with her, Mal said, so softly that Nora barely heard, "Maybe you should stay."

CHAPTER TWENTY-FOUR

Manhattan & Hoosick Falls, NY
December 1886

"What?" Nora turned her head toward her husband, though he didn't meet her gaze.

"A little while longer, at least. Three days is nothing, really. Not for you. You've barely gotten to see your family—you don't have to come back so soon."

Tears filled her eyes. "You mean you don't want me to."

With a faint frown, Mal finally looked at her. "I didn't say that, no. It's just—you could stay another week and still get back in time for Christmas."

"And how would that look?" Nora asked, rather sharply.

"Like you've missed home," Mal said, with a trace of humor. "Besides, I didn't think you cared much for other people's opinions."

Nora didn't answer, focused again on the leaping flames.

Mal peered at her profile. "I just don't want you to feel like you can't stay. If you want to. You've seemed . . . you seem so happy here."

Now, Nora scoffed and swung about to face him. "Do I not seem happy there? At *home?*"

When he hesitated, she wasn't sure if it was because of her sudden acidity or because the answer to her question was so obvious.

Before she could stop herself, she said, "In case you hadn't noticed, everyone in that house is rather dour by default. Except Marie, because she doesn't have half the sense God gave a chicken."

The look of shock on Mal's face must have mirrored Nora's own, for as soon as she heard the words fly from her mouth, shame coursed through her, along with disbelief.

"I didn't mean that. You know I adore her. I just . . ."

"You're used to more intelligent company," Mal suggested, not quite coldly, though not quite kindly either. "More stimulating conversation. In more comfortable surroundings. I understand. And honestly, I worry . . ."

"About what?"

"That the winter might be hard on you."

Nora shook her head and walked toward the bed, yanking at her clothing as she went. "Don't try to make it seem like it's concern for me when you just don't want me there."

"That isn't true—"

"Yes, it *is*. Oh, the visit was fine, but when you said I could stay, you hoped I wouldn't—"

"That is nonsense, Nora."

"*No*. You might have been fine with *stabling* me—like Kirsten, just another one of your poor brothers' lonely widows. Not that I'm even that. But you . . . you didn't *want* me. You don't."

"How can you say that?"

"You tried to talk me out of marrying you in the first place! Maybe you should have tried harder."

He was silent for a crushing moment, but it felt even worse when he said, "You're right. I should have."

She fought a seismic sob. "Why didn't you?"

"Because I love you."

"No. Because you felt . . . *responsible* for me. Because I pushed you, and you were too afraid to say no. Had my father already written to you, then? Advance warning? Did he tell you that I . . . ?"

"That you what?"

That I wanted to die, Nora thought, but didn't say. Malcolm likely knew that anyway. She suspected that she hadn't been as coy or careful in her letters as she'd thought. "If you love me, then why do you think you should have said no?"

"Because I love you. Because I knew you wouldn't be satisfied with the life I could give you. Or with me, with the way that I am."

"I never said that."

"You don't have to."

Nora scoffed again, but it was a sound of panic more than derision. "Well, *you* don't have to say you're not satisfied with me either. It's painfully obvious."

Mal looked truly befuddled, which made her want to shove him.

"You hardly touch me," she nearly shouted, not caring if her voice carried. "You barely look at me when you do. You don't want me to touch you either. And I know I'm plain, but—"

"You're beautiful, Nora."

"Then what is it? Is there someone else?"

"Of course not."

"But there has been."

When he didn't deny it, she made herself go on. "You still think about her."

He didn't answer, perhaps because Nora hadn't phrased it as a question. "Are you in love with her?"

"No. I wasn't . . . It wasn't like that."

"What was it like, then? Who was it? I deserve to know. Now that I'm your wife."

Mal sighed and nodded. "She was a widow—well, still is. My age. Kitty Spencer. She has a very settled life, and . . . plenty of other acquaintances. She would never have been interested in anything serious, but even if she had been, I never would have . . ."

"Why not?"

He took a slow, deep breath. "When I was a boy, I was too shy to even consider courting a girl. And then, as a man . . . I got used to being alone. That seemed right, somehow. But a few years back, in Albany . . . It was cold. My train got delayed. So I went toward the first bright window I saw. I got a drink, just to warm up a bit. Didn't speak to anyone except to order. Always happy to be on the fringes. But then the proprietress, she made the rounds to greet her patrons, and when she came to me in the far corner . . . she sat down. We talked—she talked, mostly. She took a liking to me for some reason."

"I'm not surprised," Nora murmured as she gazed at his profile. "And then?"

"We went for a walk. It started to snow. When we got back to the saloon . . . she took me upstairs, to her apartment. I knew what was happening, but—not what I was doing."

Nora couldn't speak. To her surprise, Mal continued, "I stayed for two nights. Blamed the weather when I got back."

Nora tried to swallow the lump in her throat. "Did you write to her?"

"No."

"But did you see her again?"

"Yes. Every year after that."

Nora's stomach twisted. "And this October? When you went to get Titus?"

Mal finally turned back toward her and stepped closer. "I did, but we only talked. We stayed downstairs at a table. I told her about you."

That felt worse, somehow—that he had talked to someone else. Nora's tears spilled over. "What did you say?"

"That I love you. And that I'm a poor excuse for a husband, and I feel so guilty."

"*Why?*"

"Because this isn't supposed to be my life. It was supposed to be Euan's. And I feel like I've stolen it."

"He's *gone*," Nora said. "And you didn't *take* anything." *I gave myself,* she thought, then: *No. I forced myself.*

Mal could have been stronger, could have refused her, could have trusted that she wouldn't fall apart without him. But he'd given in, rather easily, really. And so, like Nora, he only had himself to blame. Or they only had each other.

"I'm sorry," she said, and turned away again, resumed unfastening her clothes. She stopped at her chemise and belted a flannel robe atop it, then climbed into bed.

When Mal joined her shortly after, he moved closer than usual, but didn't touch her. "I love you," he murmured.

Nora said nothing, and hoped he thought that she had gone to sleep.

❧

In the morning, Mal was up and dressed by the time she woke. He smiled at her, as usual, but the corners of his eyes were sad, at odds with the corners of his mouth. He murmured good morning and Nora murmured it back. She shivered as she rose to get ready to leave.

They went downstairs together, Aunt Birdie's main staircase wide enough for them to walk abreast, but Mal fell behind, letting Nora lead.

She had a vision of throwing herself down the flight, breaking her head open and emptying everything in it, or at least buying more time in the city with a broken wrist or ankle, then reached out to grip the banister and picked her way carefully down the plush carpeted runner so she wouldn't trip.

❧

She was somewhat distressed to find her father downstairs. If he hadn't come, she could have made it without crying. As it was, she teared up before they even embraced.

While she sniffed and dabbed her face with her cuffs, he produced a fresh batch of cinnamon-raisin biscuits that were, improbably, still warm. "You must have carried these inside your coat," she said as she took the parcel. "And Calista must have been up at five."

"Always is," he said.

"Well, thank her for me." Nora's voice hitched again. "Thank you, too."

Her father kissed her cheek and clapped Mal on the back while Nora put on her coat, then stood out on the still-frigid street to see them into Birdie's carriage. The air was cold enough to hurt, as sharply honed as any scalpel. Nora's jaws clattered and she thought her wet eyelashes would freeze, but still, she opened the little window to return her father's waves until they disappeared from each other's sight, as if he had never done her any harm.

Well, Nora thought, *he hadn't meant to.*

It was hardly warmer inside the carriage, even with its heated bricks and the window shut, so she didn't move away from Mal as he drew closer for the twenty-odd blocks to the train station. They ate the rapidly cooling biscuits in silence, except for Nora's occasional sniffles and stuttering breaths.

She wondered if it would be as cold in Hoosick Falls. She could still change her mind. Mal would be all too happy for her to stay for another few nights of medical jargon and inside jokes and smoky Scottish liquor in her father's snug, coal-warmed parlor. He would likely be happy for her to stay through the remainder of winter.

But Nora would not be separated from her husband now. Part of it was pride—she was barely two months into her tenure as his wife—and part was fear—that it had been true when she told Mal he was her only chance at happiness. But a larger part of it was love, even if it was of a desperate, uncertain sort. If Nora left him now, she would miss him. And no matter what else Malcolm felt, Nora believed that he loved her too.

It should, she thought, be all that mattered.

~

Much later that evening, they trudged inside the farmhouse amid swirling flakes of snow.

Nora fervently returned Marie's welcoming embrace, as if she could transmit an apology for a trespass that her sister-in-law would never even know she'd made, and surely would have forgiven. If the girls didn't shrink from being touched, Nora would have squeezed them close as well.

Still, she discouraged Marie from coming upstairs, as she had presents she didn't want her to see.

Euan's room was as empty as ever, yet it held the familiar sense of a suspended breath, particularly palpable just then. Nora looked to the abalone box atop the mantel and thought, *Hello*, but received no answer.

She placed her satchel on the desk. Nothing seemed to have been disturbed in her absence, yet she couldn't shake the feeling that someone had occupied this space, had stood in the very spot, and touched her things, or at least made minute study of their details: her specimen jars and microscope and medical books, her Newport shells and sand dollars and starfish.

It was entirely possible that Marie had done so, she supposed, or even Kirsten.

She hid her gifts, mostly chocolates and exotic fruit, both fresh and canned, and scraps of grossly expensive fabrics for trimming hats and dresses and making pocket squares, little luxuries that she thought were minor enough to be absorbed into their lives without disruption. She hesitated only briefly before unpacking her personal belongings, restoring them to their former places in Euan's closet and dresser. Then she crossed the hall to remove her things from the main bedroom.

～

Mal came upstairs before she was finished, and though Nora's face burned, she didn't pause.

"What are you doing?" he asked, distress in his voice.

She saw no need to answer.

"Nora, please. I don't want you to—"

"You said I'd be under no obligation here," she interrupted. "That I could sleep wherever I wanted."

Mal was quiet for a moment, then said only, "Yes. Of course."

Nora wanted to say that she still loved him, that she would not make him feel obligated, either, but her throat was pinched and she wouldn't cry in front of him again, so she bowed her head and walked back across the hall.

CHAPTER
TWENTY-FIVE

Hoosick Falls, NY
December 1886

Nora's relocation was as much to protect herself as to show deference to Mal; she couldn't stand the thought of lying next to him, however chastely, now that she knew it caused him such guilt. That she made him feel like a thief.

She hoped he knew it was an act of mercy and not of punishment. But it was lonely, too.

She tried not to think about Kitty, or about Manhattan, much less the rapidly approaching anniversary of Euan's death. She tried not to feel like an utter failure, to focus on the promise of a reasonably festive Christmas, still five days away. But Nora couldn't suppress some measure of melancholy, and sensed it in the rest of them, too, except for Marie and the girls.

In an effort to lighten the somber mood, and to assuage her nagging homesickness, she decided to bake.

She retrieved the biscuit recipe that Calista had given her as a wedding gift and waited until Kirsten took the girls up for their afternoon nap to sidle into the kitchen.

When Kirsten returned and discovered the incursion, she insisted on helping, but Nora dug in her own heels until Kirsten finally flashed her palms.

"Fine—but I'll thank you not to move anything around where I can't find it again!"

"Of course not," Nora said. "And you won't see a speck of flour on the counter when I'm done, either."

Kirsten harrumphed her way out of the room, and Nora shot Marie a look that made her giggle. She continued setting up, but a critical ingredient eluded her. "Do we not have raisins?"

"I'm sure we do," Marie said, and proceeded to open every kitchen and pantry cabinet that Nora had already searched. "Oh. We must be out."

Nora felt almost despondent. "Well, I can't make them without."

"You could ride into town and get some more . . ."

"That would take two hours." A slight exaggeration, but long enough to dispel her determination. Nora turned toward the basement door, feeling the usual slither of unease when she looked directly at the padlock. "Maybe there are some in the cellar?"

"No!" Marie said, but gave Nora an unconvincing smile when she swiveled her head to look back at her. "No," she said again, more calmly, "there's none down there."

Nora narrowed her eyes. "Where's the key?"

"Kirsten has it. But she won't want you going down."

"Why not?" Nora could feel the door at her back as surely as she would sense a person standing behind her.

"Ain't safe," Marie said.

"I'll be careful." Nora reached into her hair and removed a pin, not confident that she would be able to pick the lock, but not willing to ask Kirsten for any favor, especially this one.

Marie wrung her hands as Nora angled the lock toward her and jiggled the pin about in the opening. It would probably break off, she thought—but within a few seconds of random prodding, the mechanism released. Nora was shocked, and somewhat sorry it had worked.

Putting the bent pin in her pocket, she looked back at Marie, as if for a pardon, as if that made any sense.

"It's dark down there," Marie said. "And there are spiders. And centipedes. And mice."

And there were skeletons and human organs and sometimes whole corpses in mine, Nora thought, but only said, "Well, as long as there are no monsters, I'm sure I'll be fine." She turned back to the door and fully opened the shackle of the lock, then removed it from the hasp and set it aside before opening the basement door.

The steep, narrow stairs disappeared into murky shadows.

"You should take a light," Marie said. "Those little windows at the back, they don't do nowt. It's never bright enough."

After a moment's hesitation, Nora said, "Hand me that candlestick?"

Even after she'd struck a flame to guide her, the bottom treads were so indistinct that she wasn't sure it was the bottom she could see.

"Be careful," Marie whispered.

Nora trembled. She knew it was absurd to be scared of a basement—especially an ordinary one, but Marie's keen aversion was catching. And it was so dark . . .

Shielding the candle flame, Nora held her breath and started down the stairs, her sense of dread growing heavier with each step she descended, as the air grew cooler and the smell of damp earth grew stronger. It was like the springhouse, she realized. *Some medieval morgue.* But surely no dead flesh was down here.

At the bottom of the stairs, she stood for a moment to peer into the dark. Smeary oblongs of light in the near distance marked the windows, as useless as Marie had said. But Nora began to be able to discern shelves lining the rough stone walls, stocked with faintly gleaming glass jars and burlap sacks and wooden crates.

As Nora's eyes adjusted, her ears became attuned to the particular silence of the cellar, deep and poised, not unlike the silence in Euan's room two floors above—holding both a sense of expectation and a promise that it might be broken at any second.

All in your head, she told herself, and moved decisively forward, the soft taps of her boot soles and the faint swishing of her skirts far too loud. She was overcome with an urge not to draw attention to herself—but also to finish her business and hurry back upstairs at once. She made for the nearest shelves, then held her candle up and slowly swept the light along the rows of jars, the glass softly winking.

She felt the fine hairs prickle on her neck and glanced over her shoulder several times, but—of course—nothing was there.

Nora stooped to see the labels and contents of the bottles and jars—and at last she spotted a glass canister of wrinkled, dark fruits.

As her fingers brushed the cold, smooth surface of the jar, a puff of air jetted past her shoulder. A breath, which stirred the hair against her earlobe and blew out her candle's flame.

She gasped and spun around, suddenly expecting to see not a ghost but Erik standing there, smirking over his childish prank. But there was no one.

There was only the same shadowy murk that filled the whole cellar, even deeper and darker now without her little light.

She scanned the periphery of the room, and there—in the far corner beneath one of the windows, she discerned the shape of a man, his head bent to one side, as if he'd cocked his ear to listen for the unspoken question that she should have posed in her most strident voice: *What do you think you're doing, you horse's ass?*

But God help her, she couldn't move, let alone speak. She was transfixed, and rapidly pervaded with a jumble of awful impressions. They felt foisted upon her by some dark outside force rather than dredged from her subconscious: an amalgamation of every corpse she'd ever seen; purple slabs of butchered bull; a blood-drained, eyeless pig; poor Euan's startled face and crimson shirtfront; his dear, dead body splayed open like a book for some inadequately reverent first-year students who could have had no notion of how wonderful he was.

That last image lingered, and Nora was terrified that she would see his face when the figure stepped close enough to gain distinction.

Or perhaps it wouldn't have the head of a man at all, but the horned aspect of a beast.

Tears trembled in her eyes and then spilled over.

When a noise from above snagged her attention, she looked instinctively toward the stairs, as footsteps clearly sounded on them. Another dangerous prickle at the back of her neck made Nora swivel her head again, but there was no longer a figure in the far reaches; there never had been, surely.

Still, she rushed toward the staircase as if fleeing something, even as Kirsten clattered down. There was just enough light coming from above to see that she was scowling—but Nora was startled when Kirsten said, "Stop!"

Nora obeyed, though fear rippled through her skin.

"Step carefully," Kirsten ordered, and nodded toward the ground before the stairs.

Nora looked down and saw a white line on the dark dirt floor just beneath the bottom riser. She stepped over it, skirts lifted in her hands, the candleholder still tight in one fist. She hurried behind Kirsten back up to the kitchen, where the older woman practically slammed the door and snapped the padlock back in place.

"What was that?" Nora breathed, meaning not the barrier drawn below the stairs but the human-shaped thing that she had glimpsed in the shadows.

Kirsten fixed her with a look both scornful and self-contained. Nora suppressed another shudder and said, "Who was it?"

When Kirsten still didn't answer, Nora raised her chin. "Stephen?"

"No," Kirsten said, voice as hard as her stare.

More tears prickled in Nora's eyes and nose. "Olaf, then?"

"It's nothing," Kirsten said. "Nothing but a bad memory. Nothing you need to give power by paying attention to. You ignore it. And you don't go down there again."

With that, she turned her back and began tidying away the things that Nora had placed upon the counter.

She looked from Kirsten's narrow shoulders to Marie, who stood with her thumbnail between her teeth and as much guilt as fear on her face—for telling on Nora, she supposed—and then, with her back to the cellar door, felt another wave of fear roll through her like a full-body chill.

CHAPTER
TWENTY-SIX

Hoosick Falls, NY
December 1886

Nora rushed toward the front of the house and out, not knowing where she meant to go. She didn't think she was capable of operating her bicycle, and nothing could have driven her into the snarled woods on foot, so she staggered toward the nearest pasture fence and paced it, trying to calm her thoughts, her breath.

She had only imagined it, of course.

Despite the implications of Kirsten's behavior, and what Nora felt certain she had seen, it couldn't have been real—for any number of logical reasons that had long calcified into bedrock belief.

But she also knew now that even her strongest convictions could be eroded far more easily than she'd once thought.

As a little girl, she had unquestioningly accepted the existence of ghosts and been instinctively afraid of them. It didn't matter how many reasonably trusted adults assured her they did not exist; for years, she was convinced otherwise.

But as she grew older and ever more scientifically inclined, she began to doubt in the other direction. By her teenage years, Nora was comfortably certain that ghosts were no more than wispy lies and wishful thinking. If they were real, after all, surely her home would harbor one or two, at least, with all the corpses that had gone through the basement—and with her own mother dying upstairs.

When the subject of supernatural phenomena had arisen among her fellow medical students—which it had quite early, and quite often—Nora had been stunned to hear so many of them seriously entertain the possibility of incorporeal spirits and life after death. Euan was a staunch nonbeliever—or at least he'd claimed to be—but several of their peers swore to God and Galen that they had *seen* things.

Her father had readily dismissed the existence of such manifestations himself, yet had always allowed that a living mind, influenced by dread or hope or expectation or any highly agitating mix of emotion, could conjure a good-enough ghost to persuade the living body that something of substance was there with it, floating outside of the mind itself.

The eyes connected to the all-powerful brain could be quite convinced that they *saw* something, and the ears that they *heard*, and the body that it *felt* what should not be there. Someone else, standing right beside them, would easily see that of course there was nothing, and yet would be hard-pressed to convince the other that they had imagined anything. Furthermore, the nonbeliever, forever barred entry from the affected person's brain and body, could never unequivocally say that the other's experience was false.

This line of thinking had always frustrated Nora, who wanted a thing to be true or not—provable or refutable. If ghosts were real, then everyone would be able to see them, or someone who could see them could at least demonstrate evidence of their existence—not just flimsy stories and easily debunked parlor tricks.

If one person out of one billion swears that the sky is always green, her father once argued, *even if science seems to prove that such a thing is impossible, no one can ever definitively prove that the outlier's genuine experience is not of a perpetually green sky. Therefore, it is real—to him.*

But that's the logic of madness, Nora had countered.

And that's what I think is in play when people swear they've seen a ghost, her father had answered. *But I don't know. For all our science has uncovered, it's yet to reveal anything where the soul is concerned—whether it exists, let alone what happens to it when our bodies die, if it can take some form or exert some influence afterward. All of us are only operating on belief. And maybe that blinds us to things we'll never know we've missed. Until it's our turn, of course.*

Nora's beliefs had been bowed and broken already, first reshaped and strengthened when her pragmatism had eclipsed her childish faith in ghosts. She had, in a sense, inoculated herself against susceptibility to such fanciful superstitions.

Which had been immeasurably dispiriting after Euan died, to be unable to conjure a convincing shade of him even when she'd tried—or to allow herself to believe that the unease twisting in her gut in the darkness of his boyhood room was from any part of his presence.

Up until that afternoon she had never *seen* anything in the shadows. Even if she had, if her eye had wanted to interpret a shifting beam of moonlight as a ghostly flash of bloodless skin, or her ears to mistake a sigh of wind down the chimney for the whisper of a vanished voice, her mind would never have let her.

Now, though, now that she had glimpsed something—clearly enough to know that it looked human, or like it once had been—no matter how fervently she wanted to dismiss it as a ridiculous hallucination, she could not.

~

She intended to stay outside until it was time for milking, but she hadn't grabbed a coat and soon was shivering. Mal, who had been off mending the roof of the sugaring shack, found her like that and asked what was wrong.

Nora only shook her head, but he pressed, and she was so overfull of wild anxiety that the words burst from her. "I saw something. In the basement."

Mal frowned, but there seemed to be a touch of fear in his expression. "What?"

She looked back at the house and shuddered. Mal took off his coat, and Nora let him drape it over her shoulders but sidestepped when he tried to touch her arm.

"Nora? What exactly happened?"

She turned away from the house again, though she hated the feeling of its windows staring at her back. She paced a little way down the fence, Mal following.

"I was leaning down to look at a shelf when something . . ."

Breathed on me were the words Nora wanted to use to describe the puff of air that had ruffled past her, but she stopped herself, flesh creeping. "There was a draft—but it couldn't have come from the windows, and it didn't come from the stairwell. And then I turned around and . . . there was something standing in the back of the cellar.

"I thought it was Erik at first, but . . . it was someone else. A tall man. I couldn't quite see his face, just that it was pale, and the features—they were too dark. But just smudges, like the beginnings of a sketch. Just roughed out."

When she trembled, Mal stepped closer but didn't attempt to touch her again. Tenderly, he said, "Everyone's eyes play tricks on them from time to time."

"It wasn't just my *eyes*. I *felt* it. And I did see it. Because it was *there*. *He* was. Outside of my head."

The expression on Mal's face had too much pity in it for Nora's liking, but there was still fear, too. "What did Kirsten say to you?"

"Nothing, really. That there was nothing there, but that isn't what she meant." *She said to ignore it,* Nora remembered, *to not give it power,* and felt another shiver run through her, because she was already disobeying that order.

Mal sighed. "Well, there is nothing there, of course—nothing strange, at any rate. But it is the least hospitable part of the house, I know. It's dark, and damp, and—even I've gotten the shivers down there before. But I've never seen a thing besides spiderwebs. And you *know*, Nora—there's no such thing as ghosts."

"Then why are Marie and Kirsten so afraid? Why is there a lock on the door?"

"Because it's dangerous. It's steep, and dark, and . . ." Mal broke off and shook his head.

"And what?" Nora prompted. "Tell me."

"If you want to know the truth, it's where Olaf died."

"What?" Alarm buzzed through her body. "You said it was a fever—"

"It was. He shouldn't have been out of bed, but he was determined to keep working, and . . . he fell. He broke his neck."

More chills quaked through Nora then, at the revelation of such a gruesome truth, and at the knowledge that it had been kept from her, that it would have been buried forever if she hadn't ventured underground.

Mal asked, gently, and entirely reasonably, "If there was a ghost, do you really think a lock would do anything against it?"

Nora looked at him and answered honestly. "No."

But she could still feel the ghastly uncanniness of beholding the bent-necked figure in the basement, cloaked in shadow.

∼

She gave Mal's coat back and went inside to grab her own, then slipped out to the graveyard, where she looked for a long time at Olaf's stone.

O Magnusson

2/2/26–8/26/70

Hannah's marker, of course, was inscribed with the same date of death. But now, Nora wondered if she had truly died from fever too. And of all the people who had died in this place, why would he be the sole one to remain?

Maybe he isn't, Nora thought, and crossed her arms tightly over her chest.

~

During milking, she was quiet. Afterward, she had to force her feet toward the farmhouse.

She couldn't stop thinking of the cavernous cellar below the dining room, separated from the soles of her shoes only by wooden boards and a thin skin of carpet. She imagined Olaf—whatever was left of him—listening, lusting after their liveliness, even on a night like this when they were so subdued.

But again, her rational mind resisted. If he existed in some incorporeal form, could he really be cut off from commingling with them by a line of chalk or ash? Or whatever the substance was. She should ask Kirsten outright, in front of everyone—then the whole absurd notion would collapse in Nora's mind. But she was too afraid.

Erik finally broke the silence. "What the hell's gotten into you all? I didn't know better, I'd think you caught whatever they've got." He nodded toward his silent, detached daughters.

Nora glanced at them and wondered if there wasn't something to the idea—if perhaps they were attuned to presences that the others couldn't perceive. Their furtive head movements and persistent lack of eye contact, she had always thought, didn't necessarily indicate that they couldn't engage but that they didn't want to.

But what so possessed their thoughts? What if they were afraid of something? When they were occupied with sorting objects—beans, buttons, ribbons, though only Bea would touch the latter—they appeared content, or at least fully absorbed. Yet at the table, though they didn't exactly cower or shrink, they maintained something of a self-protective posture.

Nora wondered if perhaps they felt something watching them. Nothing suggested that they suffered hallucinations, auditory or visual, though if they did, of course they couldn't tell anyone. How might Nora test that theory? And test other, less credible ones as well?

And then, whatever she found, how might she relieve it? Or was it possible that merely investigating such matters might exacerbate them?

She was startled from her reverie when Marie blurted out, "She went in the cellar."

Nora looked at her, then at Kirsten, then Mal. As she dropped her gaze to her plate, Erik said, "Oh, so you met my father, then."

Nora had been reaching for her glass and nearly knocked it over.

"Erik," Mal cautioned.

He paid no attention. "That makes three of you now, convinced he's down there. Yet no matter how many times I've gone pokin' around, I've never seen him. Why is that?"

"Because there is nothing in the basement besides last summer's preserves and extra coffee beans," Mal said.

"That's not what Kirsten thinks," Erik countered.

"Everyone has their superstitions," Mal said, in a conversation-quashing tone.

Kirsten looked more wounded than offended, but said nothing.

Undeterred, Erik asked, "How about you, doc? You seem pretty spooked."

Nora flicked a glance at him. "I just got a little nervous in the dark."

He smirked and stabbed another clump of pickled beets, shoved them in his mouth, then waved his fork at Axel. "I've always wondered, is that why you like to sleep out in the barn?"

Before Axel could answer, if he was going to bother, Malcolm said, "That's enough."

Erik regarded him with a sly sort of look, but said, "All right," and abandoned the subject, though naturally it hung like a pall over the table for the remainder of the meal, then followed them into the parlor.

～

Axel didn't join them there, of course. Nora gritted her teeth when Erik planted himself on the other end of the settee after she'd tucked herself into her corner.

He brought a book with him and flashed the cover at her: *A Christmas Carol.*

"'Tis the season. As good a one for ghosts as any."

Nora leveled an unamused look at him and opened her own book.

Erik waited for the length of three paragraphs before he spoke again, in a voice barely loud enough to carry across to the armchairs where Mal and Kirsten held their usual positions. "So, was that really your first time, doc? All those dead bodies you've been wrist-deep in—you never saw any of their ghosts?"

"No," she said, as emphatically as she was able, "because there is no such thing." She sensed Kirsten and Marie and Mal all look at her but kept her gaze on Erik. "Except in stories like Mr. Dickens's, of course—and the ones you like to tell."

"Sure," he said, but let it drop, before Malcolm could intervene. Nora was glad that Erik seemed to dislike being chastised by his elder brother—and, despite his brazenness, disinclined to challenge Mal's authority past a certain point.

～

Soon, she and Mal were the only ones left downstairs. She was torn between wanting to escape to her room, farther from the basement, and not wanting to be alone. She knew Mal would welcome her—wordlessly—if she went back to his bed, but she couldn't, even just for company.

She made herself leave the parlor while he was still reading, though she paused before plunging into the shadow-soaked hallway, the brightly lit room at her back.

Mal must have seen her hesitate on the threshold, for he asked, softly, "Are you all right?"

Nora looked over her shoulder and smiled. "Fine now," she said. "Good night."

In truth, though she was still nervous to be alone, some part of Nora was relieved to not have to lie beside Mal knowing that he'd lied about Olaf's death, suspecting that he might not have told her the full story even now.

Learning that Olaf had died in the cellar only made Nora more convinced that what she'd seen was real, and yet—how could his ghost be contained by a padlock and a line of white grit? Why not simply rise up through the floorboards, or float like smoke through a window slit?

Maybe it did; maybe that accounted for all the strange shifts in the air in this room, and the creaking boards, the feeling of being seen. The falling picture frames the night that Mal returned from Albany.

No, Nora's brain insisted. As unnerving as those things were, they hadn't terrified her like the presence in the dark pit of the basement.

But if Olaf's ghost did dwell there, why not some other spirit on this higher floor? It could be any member of the family whose skeletons moldered in the damp earth past the apple orchard. Nora shrank, half afraid that simply thinking of such things might summon a whole host of apparitions.

She tried to recall what Euan had told her about Olaf. It had been very little, except that he was awful. Everyone else seemed to have felt the same. But as Kirsten had said, he was nothing but a bad memory now.

And Nora had enough of those of her own.

She would do as Kirsten commanded, then, and put Olaf from her head, stay away from the cellar, trust that whatever charms had been deployed would continue working. Convince herself, if she could, that it had been nothing but her imagination after all.

CHAPTER
TWENTY-SEVEN

Hoosick Falls, NY
December 1886

The next morning, despite her resolutions, Nora lingered in the barn and the chicken coop, not wanting to be inside. After breakfast, she cycled to Grace's house, if only to leave the farmstead for a few hours. On the ride, she considered what she might say or ask, but speaking of ghosts at all seemed ill advised—not because it might embolden them, but because word might get around.

Grace welcomed her with a grin and a loaf of molasses bread. She cleared the parlor table of the half-made paper chains that her children had been fashioning. "Mam picked them up for the afternoon so I can finish my baking. But I'd much rather eat it with you instead."

Nora smiled and stood in the hall while Grace made tea. They chatted about the upcoming holiday and how Manhattan had been. Only when they were seated in the parlor, on their second cups and slices, and the conversation lulled did Nora say, "Can I ask you something?"

"Of course you can."

"What do you know about Erik's father?"

Grace's eyebrows rose as she sat back against her sofa. "The Swede," she said, and licked a bit of butter from her thumb. "That's what people called him when he first showed up. I was just a girl then, eight or so. I don't think he was particularly disliked at the time. That only came later, after he married Hannah."

"After her first husband died," Nora said.

"Not even a full year later," Grace confirmed. "But she needed help, God knows. She had a new baby and the whole farm to run—and Stephen was only maybe fifteen then; your Malcolm was already off fighting, so he had no idea it had even happened. She was desperate. And Olaf Magnusson was the only one interested in stepping in, as far as I understand. In fact, the way I heard it, he'd been interested in Hannah well before then. Had her big with Erik almost straight away; Irish twins, him and Euan Jr."

When Nora looked down at her plate at the mention of Euan, Grace paused. "I'm sorry. I always seem to forget you knew him first."

Nora shook her head. "So, after Olaf married Hannah, that's when he started . . . gaining a reputation?"

"Well, that's when people started to see less of the family. Poor Hannah in particular. And they started to see bruises on her, here and there, when she did come into the village. It got a little better once Malcolm came home, I think—even though he was just skin and bones when he did—but Hannah never really went back to how she was before. She was just too broken-down by then, run ragged."

"But they never had any other children," Nora asked, "besides Erik?" It surprised her, but perhaps something had happened to Hannah to physically prevent it; Erik might have been a difficult birth, caused irreparable damage.

"Well," Grace said, "she was pregnant at least two other times that I know of after, but nothing came of it. Not that that's unusual. There was talk. About why not. But that's all there was, really, for the next few years. Whispers. Conjecture. They had their blessings, too, of course. Stephen got married and moved Kirsten and her brother onto the place. Their people were in Troy, but they fell on hard times, so that was a boon to them both. And Malcolm got his strength back. Things seemed to settle. It was quiet until, all of a sudden, Hannah and Olaf both died."

"On the same day," Nora said.

Grace nodded. "I was sixteen by then, so I remember that much better. It was a fever, so the boys buried them right away."

Nora couldn't detect any hint of suspicion in Grace's tone.

"They all kept away from town until there was no chance of spreading the sickness. I suppose they're lucky that no one else died. It was awful for them to lose their mother, of course. The Swede, maybe not so much. Well, Erik might have missed him. And then their luck held out for a while after that."

"Until Johan," Nora said.

Grace nodded again and sighed. "Poor boy was only ten. And he was the sweetest little thing. Spirited, but not with that devilish streak like Erik always had. But oh, Johan *loved* him. He loved everybody, I think, but I expect Erik was the most fun in that family. Not that your Euan wasn't. But he always had some of that Colquhoun seriousness about him. Goes right along with the red hair, I think."

Nora felt her throat constrict but kept a faint smile on her face.

"Anyhow," Grace said, "I remember how the whole town mourned Johan."

"And he drowned?"

Grace hummed affirmation. "Out in the pond in their woods." Her face darkened as she added, "Most folks didn't hear much in the way of details."

Nora's mouth went dry. "But did you?"

Grace hesitated. "I'll have you know, I've never repeated this to anyone else, and I'm only saying it now because you're a part of the family, so I suppose you should hear. Ellen told me Erik was there. Not doing anything nefarious. Just playing at being brave and daring—walking out on thin ice. And of course little Johan would have followed along. Erik was old enough to have better sense at seventeen—but boys that age, they don't think they can die. Even if they've seen it happen to their friends. Or children younger than themselves. Well, Erik saw his sweet little nephew slip under the ice, and he couldn't get him out in time. Who knows what he thought then."

"My God," Nora said. "He must have felt so guilty."

"And even more so," Grace answered, "when Stephen couldn't bear the loss. He and Malcolm, you know, they were like fathers to Erik and Euan both. I believe Erik always favored Stephen. So to have that weight added to his shoulders . . . I don't wonder that he ran away. But there's no escaping the things you've done, is there? Or the things that've happened to you. He only dragged his sorrows all the way across an ocean and then back again. Had new ones waiting for him when he came home."

Grace's sister, Nora thought; how Ellen had likely borne Erik's own son while he was gone and died in the process, leaving him with both more than he'd left behind, and so much less. *Doesn't matter where I go,* she recalled Erik saying, the day he'd told her about the surely nonexistent curse. *It's in my blood.*

"How did Stephen die?"

Grace sighed louder than before and stared at the crumbs on her plate. "Broken heart."

Precisely what Nora had heard before. "Meaning what, exactly?"

With a slight shake of her head, Grace rose to tidy their dishes. "I'm sure I've already said more than it was my place to. You have a way of loosening my tongue, Mrs. Colquhoun. But you can ask your husband about all that."

"I can't. I won't. I'm asking you."

From the kitchen, Grace said, "Well, I don't even know for certain. Only what Ellen told me, and she wasn't meant to. But it was that Stephen slung a rope over one of the beams in that old cabin and hung himself from it. And Erik found him dangling there already purple in the face."

Nora drew in a deep breath and held it.

"Every life has its hardships," Grace mused, and turned around at the sink to face Nora across the hall. "Every person suffers tragedies. But they have had more than their share, it seems." She gave a humorless huff of a laugh. "It's no wonder some folks say they're cursed."

"What?"

"Oh, what else is there to say to explain it?" Grace shrugged as she came to sit back down. "Some even say the Swede started it. That he was so jealous of Mr. Colquhoun he cursed him and his land—I've even heard some crazy things about blood sacrifices and other such nonsense—and then he got it for himself—the farm and Hannah both, but he couldn't keep them either. Because curses come back to you."

Nora felt her body break out in gooseflesh. "Do you believe that?"

"Do *you*?" Grace answered, apparently thoroughly surprised, though also amused. "A woman of science and logic like yourself?"

When Nora only continued to stare at her, brows slightly knit, Grace shrugged again. "Does it matter? What happened happened. But if you put stock in what people say, then you should know some think you broke it. The curse, I mean."

That only further unsettled Nora. "Who said that?"

"Oh, just people." Grace chuckled. "It's just village gossip. People trying to make sense of things. Looking for hope. For comfort. When they're not looking for a reason to feel superior." She tilted her head. "What's got you asking about all this now, anyway?"

Nora looked down at her lap. "Just—curiosity. No one else talks about it—about any of them. And I wondered what Erik's father was like. Since he's so . . . different, from his brothers. The ones I met, anyway."

"Mm," Grace murmured. "He is that. Always was." She squinted at Nora again. "Has he made himself a nuisance?"

"No," she answered, far too quickly. "He's just . . . different."

"Well," Grace said, "whatever his faults, he did right by his children, I suppose—"

The girls, at least, Nora thought.

"—and Marie," Grace continued. "Erik Magnusson is no Colquhoun, but he isn't Olaf either."

"No," Nora agreed.

~

Before heading home, she wandered into a few stores, her pocket fat even with a mere fraction of the money her father had continued to send her.

She ordered a phonograph to pick up on Friday, to give as a gift to everyone, to fill the house with music even when none of them felt like making it.

And then she went into one of the druggists—not the one where Mal had an account—and bought a few small things, including a bottle of laudanum, just in case she needed help drifting off, quieting her mind.

~

Back at the farm, Nora stole into the graveyard again. She imagined the hasty burial of Hannah and Olaf, perhaps to prevent spreading a fever, or perhaps to cover up a harsher truth.

In four days, it would be Christmas. In ten, it would be the sixth anniversary of Johan's death—which, if Grace's gossip was correct, Erik had witnessed, and possibly precipitated. And the day after, the arrival of the new year would mark the sixth anniversary of Stephen's suicide.

Precisely one week later, it would be a full year since Euan's death. An age, and an instant.

She returned to the quiet house, aware of everyone else's silence, even Marie more subdued than usual now that the cellar's secret had been revealed. But Nora could almost believe that only grief haunted the farmhouse.

~

Christmas itself shone brightly enough, with spice cake and recorded carols after the exchange of gifts. Though Kirsten seemed displeased with Nora's extravagantly wasteful purchase of the phonograph, even she rocked slightly in her chair to the music.

Marie was enchanted, of course. Nora believed even Bea and Addie cocked their heads toward the disembodied voices and invisible instruments that emanated from the strange new object on the side table, though Kirsten insisted she was imagining it.

She was glad to attend church the following day, and back at the house, grateful for the music streaming from the phonograph, the only thing that helped dispel the lowering atmosphere of a tomb. Marie seemed to spend every spare moment cranking the handle and reverently changing out discs. Nora vowed to send away for every record she could find so they would never run out.

~

It seemed to agitate Erik, though, who spent increasingly less time in the house after Christmas. Even at meals, during which Kirsten prohibited music, he bolted his food faster than usual and left still chewing his final mouthful. He barely spoke at all, even in the barn during milking, which at least meant he'd given up needling Nora about ghosts.

She was less relieved than she would have expected, and surprised to feel such acute sympathy, unable to stop thinking about what Grace had told her, how Erik's demons must be clinging to his heels like his long winter shadow.

He might have borne some responsibility for Johan's death, but ultimately, it had been an accident. To feel responsible for Stephen's suicide, too, and maybe even Ellen's demise in childbirth . . . It was no wonder he possessed such a turbulent personality. No wonder he felt cursed.

He should be as somber as Mal—and perhaps he was. Perhaps it only seemed like callousness from outside. Nora had thought, at times, that Erik's flippancy and crudeness were belabored. That he made too great an effort to put people off.

But some inner voice tempered her. She remembered how Euan said Erik had always had a wild streak—and Grace, too, had called him devilish, but that didn't mean he'd been wicked. He'd undoubtedly been influenced by his monstrous father, via example or genetic inheritance, or both.

Should that not also be cause for sympathy, though? Erik couldn't help his parentage, or what might have been done to him as a boy. Nora tried to recall if he'd sounded disappointed when he said that he'd never seen his father's ghost.

Admitting to looking for it was enough to make her feel like they were, in some respects, kindred spirits. She wouldn't be surprised if he'd looked for Ellen's ghost, too, in vain.

CHAPTER
TWENTY-EIGHT

Hoosick Falls, NY
December 1886–January 1887

When it came to the existence of ghosts in general, Nora wavered between belief and dismissal by the hour, even the minute. She continued to argue with herself, to postulate theories and hypothesize experiments that she might conduct.

She even considered a quick trip back to Manhattan, to gather equipment and resources. She could consult a Spiritualist society, if only to amass a list of books she might order, and the names of paranormal experts to whom she might write.

But truthfully, Nora still felt skeptical of such things—so-called authorities, any claims to have uncovered the secrets of the supernatural. She only trusted her own experience.

And she knew that the first step to any further investigation was to simply go into the cellar again, to observe what was there, if anything.

Yet she was far too frightened. The visceral, unearthly feeling that had paralyzed her in the presence of the shadowy figure still fizzed in Nora's body when she thought of confronting it again.

If Olaf's ghost was there, it seemed contained, corralled in the cellar like a bull in the pasture, though she remembered how easily Old Nick had broken the fence.

She came, then, to the same conclusion as before: that it was safest to simply ignore the issue, to trust that it was either her imagination, or under Kirsten's control.

~

Two days after Christmas, laundry took them outside. Nora was glad, despite the cold; at least they could warm themselves in the rosemary-scented steam while they were exposed to the winter wind. The girls had been left indoors with enough buttons to fascinate them for a while.

Nora's thoughts drifted as she watched swirls and billows of white fabric, and when Marie ran to the outhouse, she heard herself say, "Have you ever seen any other ghosts?"

Kirsten's thin hands went still in the soapy gray water. She peered at Nora for a moment. "I thought you didn't believe in that."

"I'm not sure," Nora admitted.

"Well, it's best to leave them alone," Kirsten said, firmly, yet not unkindly.

"Do you really think they could hurt you?" Nora asked.

"Maybe."

"But how? They can't touch you, can they?"

"I wouldn't know—I don't get that close. But maybe, if they got strong enough. And if you let one too deep inside your head . . . well, people speak of possession. And people have been frightened to death, haven't they?"

Nora's heart lurched at the idea; it was true, if rare. Yet she couldn't suppress another question. "So you put down chalk, to keep him out? Or keep him in?"

Kirsten pressed her lips together. "Salt. On the cellar windowsills too. And rosemary—in the soap, in the cupboards, in the food. Iron locks. Iron crosses here and there. Prayer, of course. You'll think it's all nonsense, but—"

"It doesn't hurt," Nora interrupted. "'An ounce of prevention . . .'"

And though it seemed ludicrous that such common substances could constrain or repel a ghost, rosemary had been used in medicine for ages. Salt was a powerful preservative; if it could stop the decay of dead flesh, why not the advance of a spirit as rotten as Olaf's?

She glanced back at the outhouse. Though Marie hadn't reappeared, Nora still lowered her voice. "But isn't there a way to . . . banish him?"

"You think I didn't try?" Kirsten scrubbed so hard she splashed water out of the tub. "Some wills are stronger than others. As I'm sure you know."

Nora frowned. "But you mentioned possession—so what about an exorcism? Of the house? With a priest who—"

"They don't know what they're doing. And what good are God's laws against a devil who never thought he was beholden to them?"

Nora thought again of physical sickness; a disease didn't have to believe in medicine to be eradicated by it, but then a disease was not sentient. Olaf was, it seemed, nothing but. And he had apparently been superstitious. Perhaps Kirsten's charms and prayers did keep him from infecting the rest of the house.

"But why would he be the only one?" Nora asked. "Was it . . . the way he died?"

"What do you know about that?" Kirsten snapped, and before Nora could stammer an answer, said, "It was the way he *lived*. But I told you not to speak of it. That's *enough*, now."

She yanked another dripping piece of fabric from the water and fed it into the wringer.

Nora briefly bit her tongue, then said, "But did you really never see any others? Never sense them? Never Stephen, or your son?"

"No." Kirsten's gray eyes grew wetter as she viciously cranked the wringer's wheel. "And that should be a comfort," she added. "To know they aren't caught here."

Nora felt the truth as a strong tug on her heart, yet disappointment wrenched it too.

~

Privately, Nora returned to more practical questions. If Olaf's ghost *was* in fact real and *there*, in the cellar, why could only some people see him?

Her father, of course, thought belief could blind a person—but Nora's belief, her certainty that apparitions could not exist, had not done that. Maybe because it had been worn away and undermined without her realizing, by talk of curses and sacrifices, and the uncanny atmosphere of Euan's room, opening up new channels in her mind.

Or it could be something simpler, innate. Some people were color-blind or ambidextrous; others had perfect pitch—but the vast majority were not and didn't. Couldn't it be something as vexingly ordinary as that?

And just as nature made every living person distinct, perhaps it only made some of them into ghosts. Did it require that a person possess an uncommon strength of will, as Kirsten thought? Or a combination of that and a violent death? Or had Olaf broken even God's own laws and bound himself by blood to this place, in body and in spirit?

~

Four days later, the anniversary of Johan's death dawned and drew to a close with no mention made, no memorials, save the ones each of them held in their own heads. No one, Nora presumed, would speak of Stephen either—or of Euan when his time came.

In his room, where Nora tried harder than ever to ignore the awareness in the air, she looked at his scalpels and her unopened bottle of laudanum and remembered Mal's first letter to her, in which he wrote that only time could truly heal, but even it was powerless to completely cure a person. Nora had agreed, had believed—not without comfort— that only death would ultimately mend them, by undoing everything they were, and freeing them from consciousness.

Now, she didn't know if that was true.

~

It had been eleven days since she'd seen Olaf's ghost, or thought she'd seen it, in the basement.

If it was there, she believed it trapped. But in case it could send malevolent psychic tendrils into other parts of the house, as a seed sent questing rootlets through the soil, seeking purchase, Nora tried to make her mind inhospitable territory.

Living in a haunted house, she'd decided, was like living in a body with a chronic disease. She imagined it had been similar when Olaf was alive.

An angry shout might echo through a window, or a cold draft blow through a closed room—just as the occasional shock of pain might sear through one's side—but after the initial prickle of alarm, the body could calm. The brain could insist it was nothing, really.

And such habituation could allow the afflicted to continue dismissing more intense and frequent symptoms, sometimes up until the point of death.

But it was also true that not all incurable ailments were fatal. A person might be plagued by allergies that made them miserable all their life without true danger, as often as they might harbor a malignant cancer that gave them a similar wheezing cough.

Without investigating, Nora couldn't determine what sort of threat Olaf's ghost might be, mere nuisance or silently metastasizing doom. She took some solace from the fact that Kirsten and Mal had lived in the same house for sixteen years since Olaf's demise without suffering grave harm.

Perhaps the unlikely remedies of rosemary and salt did have a mitigating effect. Nora couldn't prove otherwise without removing them, and was unwilling to take that risk, either, no matter how ridiculous it seemed. She knew enough to admit, privately at least, that however intelligent she might be in some matters, there were countless things beyond her ken.

These particular mysteries of life after death, she didn't want to plumb any longer—for fear, in part, that they would never yield to her what she most wanted: some tangible reconnection with more of Euan than his memory.

The longer that she lived on the farm, in fact, the farther away he felt, even in his boyhood room, for Nora remained unconvinced that the uncanny presence she sensed there was truly any part of Euan.

Even if it was, it remained formless and uncommunicative, and so was not enough.

She no longer glimpsed his ghost in Malcolm either—but now she knew that Mal was haunted.

Nora should have stayed away from him, so they could have kept some semblance of Euan alive with their regular exchange of stories. Failing that, she should have left well enough alone in Manhattan—not given greater power to her fears and discontentment by speaking of them.

She should have met Mal's gentle suggestion of extending her stay with gratitude instead of hostile suspicion. Then, while she might still yearn for things to be different between them, she could at least still take comfort from his warmth at night.

Instead, she'd forced him to admit his guilt, which had proved communicable. It would have been better for Nora not to know—but would that have been fair to Mal?

It wasn't fair to blame him, surely, yet she wished he'd kept certain things quiet too. If he'd confessed solely to self-doubt and shyness and a sense of unworthiness, then Nora could have been magnanimous and consoling—and hopeful for their future. She would have been emboldened to take charge of the situation, to reassure him that he was loved, and wanted. She could have tolerated knowledge of Kitty.

But Mal's admission of guilt, though no less sympathetic than his diffidence, was unforgivable, because it was Nora's doing.

So she'd been angry with him for not being forceful enough, for not refusing to marry her when it had clearly been the wrong choice—for him.

Yet Nora knew that wasn't fair, either, that Mal's emotions were as complicated as her own. And that she would have brushed off any talk of his guilt on the night of the husking bee, besides. She'd dismissed every other worry and caution.

And she knew that Mal's refusal to turn her away was not weakness, but love.

Perhaps they could be one and the same.

Nora should have learned that by now.

She wondered what might have happened if she'd let herself be kindly dissuaded and left the farm in October. Perhaps, as she'd threatened then, she would have stopped writing Mal. And perhaps by now, with a new year on the horizon, it would have become a bearable pain. Her determination to marry him and stay on the farm might strike her as faintly horrific and dreadfully embarrassing, but even that would fade with time.

Mal would have weathered any anguish with his usual forbearance. He would have wished Nora well, and kept her in his thoughts.

She would be back at school now, she was certain, busy with final-year studies, exhausted from long days but excited to start each morning—freed from the tedious grind of domestic drudgery, and revitalized by new associations with other ambitious, intelligent young women.

She might be back in contact with old friends too.

Nora envisioned meeting Townsend and Pruitt for drinks in some glowing, smoky pub, toasting to Euan with tears in their eyes but smiles on their lips and laughter in their throats as they reminisced.

Instead, she curled up alone in a cold bed and felt tunneled through by disappointments and regrets, with vast distances sprawling between herself and all those she loved.

CHAPTER
TWENTY-NINE

Hoosick Falls, NY
January 1887

On the first morning of the new year, Erik didn't appear in the barn. Nora expected him to sway in, glaring his way through a crushing hangover, perhaps. But he didn't, and no one else mentioned it, so she assumed the others had anticipated as much.

As they took their milk canisters to the springhouse, she looked toward the cabin and wondered if they should be concerned.

At breakfast, she warmed her hands on her coffee cup and bit her tongue to keep from asking if they should take something to him. Surely Marie would, if she or anyone else thought it wise.

Marie herself, however, was under the weather; she and Kirsten had caught a post-Christmas cold circulating with the holiday spirit through the Episcopalian congregation. Kirsten remained indomitable, despite her coughing fits and stuffy nose; she refused to let the common illness be more than a minor bother, but Marie looked as if she might tip over when she rose to help clear the table. Nora took the plates from her and said to go lie down.

Kirsten might have raised an eyebrow, but didn't say a thing. After another nod from Nora, Marie went with murmured thanks.

Jen Wheeler

Since it was Saturday, no special chores or scheduled trips to town awaited—and Kirsten wanted no help washing up. Nora was glad not to linger any longer than necessary by the cellar door, though across the room, Bea and Addie sat as indifferently as ever.

Mal and Axel had already gone off to their own tasks, so Nora bundled up again and stepped back into the numbing cold.

In all her time on the farm, she had scrupulously avoided the cabin. That day, she cut straight for it and leaned her ear against the rough, unpainted wood of the door but heard nothing.

It should have been easy to knock, or even give an experimental push to see if it swung open. She didn't expect to find anything worse than Erik sleeping off the last of the old year, but she thought of Stephen hanging from the rafters—and then of Erik lurching up and staggering over to tear open the door—and couldn't raise her arm.

Moving to the nearest filmy window, Nora cupped her hands around her face to better see inside. It was a single room with a sleeping loft, and it was neater than she'd envisioned. A spindly thicket of antlers bristled from one wall and a low fire burned in the stone hearth. Nothing dangled from the beams but a few household items stored on pegs and hooks.

Erik might have been abed, but Nora sensed that the cabin was unoccupied, and was rather relieved to be discharged from her sense of duty.

⁓

Since she was already out and didn't relish returning to the house, despite the miserable cold, she decided to walk a while in the stripped, stark forest. It would warm her up, consume some time. And the sun wouldn't sink for several more hours, so she trusted that she wouldn't lose her way.

A white scrim of snow covered the ground and obscured familiar details, though. If she were to sketch the scene, it would be a chaotic slashing of hatchmarks upon a blank page.

The sun shone low through the trunks, spears of shadow stretching across the shimmering snow. Nora was lost in close study of the hieroglyphic tracks of birds and voles and other creatures when the sound of something much larger made her pause, look up.

All the bears should be hibernating now.

A mountain lion, if there were even any left, wouldn't make its presence known, as Erik had happily told her once.

A deer, probably. Nora held her breath as she scanned the thicket of bare trees, trying to see what might be standing just as still as she did among them.

A person, perhaps—Erik himself, most likely. But she saw nothing, and reassured herself that a ghost wouldn't make so much noise, if any.

Still, she had an image of the thing she thought she'd seen in the basement, and then of a headless, lumbering bull.

Her heart fluttering faintly, Nora pressed on. When the pond came within sight, she saw immediately that the snow had been disturbed by something, and a soft, irregular lump marked the bank. At first, she thought it was an animal, or an alarmingly large pile of scat, but then she saw it was a heap of clothes, a woolen blanket sliding off the top.

Nora's heart hammered as she hurried toward the ice-rimmed pond. A jagged path had been broken through it, where Erik had clearly walked out until he was submerged. She recognized his patched trousers and knitted sweater and wool coat, his battered boots, though she'd never seen his heel-chewed socks or waffled union suit before.

She meant to plunge into the water herself, to haul his body out and rub warmth back into stiff limbs, breathe air back into sodden lungs—at least try—but she froze. Even his name stuck in Nora's throat, not that he would have heard her shouting underwater anyway.

It would be stupid to go in after him; the cold would be a great shock, and the water would saturate Nora's heavy winter layers until it dragged her down too. If she managed to scramble out, she could easily succumb to hypothermia before she made it back to the farmhouse, especially if she went the wrong way in her confusion. She could hurry to get help—but however fast she ran, it would be too late.

And then in a great sparkling splash of water a body surged upward. Nora stumbled back a few steps. Her heel caught on the abandoned boots and she fell, landing on her backside so hard it jarred the breath from her lungs.

With a violent gasp, Erik shook his head, casting prismatic droplets of water from his hair. His shoulders heaved. Most of his body was deathly pale, but the stinging cold had turned it red in places. Nora's own skin shrank tight against her flesh. She averted her eyes and pushed herself up off the ground as Erik began splashing toward her, more and more of him revealed with every step.

She saw a hint of blond hair as unruly as his beard below his navel and turned her back, but could plainly hear the smirk in his voice when he said, "You come to spy on me, doc?"

Anger flashed through her and she turned back to him; he had picked up his blanket and was scouring his bare skin with it, but made no effort to conceal himself. His breath rolled toward Nora in a cloud of steam, his blue eyes brighter than ever.

"What are you doing out here?" she asked, and turned her head again as he moved the makeshift towel lower, wielded it more gently between his long, leanly muscled legs.

"Swimmin'."

Though Nora's face flamed, she said, "It's freezing."

"Vivifyin'," Erik answered.

She heard the soft sound of the blanket falling to the ground and closed her eyes, made herself stay angled away from Erik as she heard him start to dress. When she judged him at least fully in his long underwear, she turned again and faintly shook her head.

"It's incredibly dangerous, to do that."

His wet hair dripped like snowmelt, but he didn't shiver. Nora felt overheated, herself, more so when he slid his icy gaze down her wool-bulked body and back up to her face again. "You ought to try it."

It ached just to imagine baring her skin to the air, let alone immersing herself in the water. And yet there was a different ache that came along with it, that she tried to ignore.

She wondered how long Erik had stayed under, holding his breath as the cold tried to claw through his chest and steal the air from his lungs, to freeze everything inside him solid. Nora imagined that he'd kept his eyes open, trained on the sunlight past the surface, corneas burning as they crystallized on a cellular level.

Penance, she presumed. But as he fastened his trousers and pulled his suspenders over his shoulders, then bent for his sweater, there was no sign of anguish or contrition or anything but amusement in his expression. Perhaps she had imagined his sorrow, then, and he truly felt no remorse, much less regret.

"Do you do this all winter?" she asked.

"Why?" He balanced on one huge, bone-white foot and yanked his sock over the other. "You hopin' to stumble across me in the raw again?"

Nora huffed and turned to walk away.

"Aw," Erik drawled, "I do believe I've got the good doc blushin'."

She whirled back around and let herself shout in the middle of the empty woods. "I am not blushing—it's *cold*. And you are impossible. You can't ever have a serious conversation, can you? Everything's a joke—or else something to be angry about. And I'm not a goddamned doctor, so would you stop calling me that!"

"Whoa there," Erik said, and laughed. "Who's angry now, doc?"

She was absolutely furious, inordinately so, but at least she wasn't scared, or sad.

Still, she couldn't stand to look at him a moment longer, and strode back into the woods toward the farmhouse, glancing over her shoulder every few feet, convinced that he would come chasing after.

Some part of her wanted him to pursue—and to catch up, and then . . . well, to do whatever he wanted. Or whatever she did, whether that was to leave her in bloody pieces on the forest floor, or simply splayed open in the snow and panting, the echo of another sort of scream fading in the bare trees.

~

Nothing untoward had happened.

Nora kept reminding herself of that. Yet she felt guilty and couldn't look at Erik during dinner, or in the barn at evening milking. She claimed to be chilled, worried she was coming down with something, and skipped supper.

Upstairs, she wanted to stoke a fire, but feared its sinuous heat writhing through her, making everything worse.

Instead, she changed into her nightgown and robe and lay in bed, thinking of the laudanum bottle hidden in the dresser.

~

The next morning, in church, she participated in the silent confession, which she usually spent daydreaming, having rejected the idea that most sins needed to be pardoned, or that any truly grievous ones ever could be. But Nora was compelled to ask the universe at large for forgiveness.

Not that—as she reminded herself yet again—anything had happened. She had not transgressed. In her thoughts, perhaps—but that couldn't count, especially when so many of her mental images came unbidden.

When she saw Grace an hour later on Main Street, they wished each other a happy new year and Nora worried that she tried too hard to seem normal, to not act suspicious.

Dr. Burns peered at her too intently, she thought, and remarked that she looked a bit piqued. Nora murmured something about the time of year, and he seemed to suddenly remember what day was just around the corner. He wouldn't be wrong in ascribing her pallor, at least in part, to grief.

~

For the next five days, Nora leaned into the lie that she felt unwell—which wasn't entirely untrue. She held Euan's name in her mouth like a stone that kept her from speaking, except to thank Mal and Marie for bringing her toast and tea. She let herself skip milking sessions and meals.

But she was still hungry, and she snuck downstairs to steal morsels from the kitchen, trying not to let Kirsten catch her, nor wanting to spend any extra time near the padlocked basement door.

On Saturday, one week since her encounter with Erik at the pond, and one year since Euan's death, Nora set out for a walk after breakfast, while Mal went to chop firewood.

She took her sketchbook with no intent to use it—in this weather, Marie wouldn't want to come if she thought Nora might sit drawing too long. She felt slightly guilty for the subterfuge, but she wanted to be alone.

Though she wasn't quite sure of the way, having only been there twice, Nora struck out in what she thought was the direction of the rise where they had scattered Mal's half of Euan's ashes.

She knew she had the right place when she reached the top, slightly breathless, and saw Erik sitting on a broad, flat rock. Irritation rippled through Nora, as did bittersweet surprise—that they had both thought to come to the spot when no one else had. Less welcome was her body's pulse of arousal.

Whatever Erik felt sitting there was unfathomable; all he betrayed was amusement. "Hell, doc, you follow me again?"

Nora gripped her sketchbook harder and approached the rock, because it was the only natural seat besides the bare ground, but she didn't bother to reply.

Erik looked up and offered an open flask.

She raised an eyebrow. "It's not even nine thirty in the morning."

He shrugged and took another drink. "It's cold."

Nora reached for the flask, glad she was wearing gloves, though when Erik's bare fingers brushed the leather, she could still feel his touch, and fought not to let her breath hitch. She swallowed a burning mouthful of moonshine and blew out as hard as one of the horses, but took another slug before handing it back.

"Not my father's Scotch."

Erik chuckled. "Good medicine, all the same. Gets the job done."

Nora sat beside her brother-in-law, keeping as much distance between them as possible, but the rock was much smaller than the settee. She accepted the flask again, handed it back.

She wanted to ask if Erik missed Euan, but his presence on the frozen hill where half the particles of her love had scattered seemed proof enough. She wanted to ask about Stephen, and Johan, and Ellen, but that seemed too cruel. So she let the silence gather, until Erik spoke.

"So, did my prediction come true?"

"What prediction?"

"That you'd end up askin' yourself why you stayed here when you had the chance to go."

She waited a beat before posing her own question. "Do you really believe in curses?"

Erik drank. "Aw, hell, I don't know. Hard not to sometimes."

"And do you really believe your father's ghost is in the basement?"

"Fuck, no. Do you?"

Nora didn't answer that. "Do you miss him?" she asked.

Erik looked surprised, and Nora couldn't interpret his soft huff. He gazed out over the valley for a long while before finally saying, "He taught me to play the fiddle. Started to, anyway. I had to figure out the rest on my own once he croaked. Seemed like somethin' worth carryin' on."

She peered at his profile and felt her eyes well.

He looked back at her. "You miss the city? School? Medicine?"

She took the proffered flask and sipped. "I miss everything. The way it was."

Erik let his fingers rest on Nora's as he took back the flask. "It's stupefyin', ain't it? How your whole life can change in a goddamn instant?"

She blinked away tears and looked at him too closely, his bright-blue eyes and plush pink lips. The feeling of being seen—from inside her head, as on those nights when his image had come to her—made her stomach flip. He seemed to know what she was thinking, or feeling, but before he could lean toward her, she stood and began to walk away.

Erik rose, too, and gently caught her sleeve. He said, more softly than she had ever heard him speak, "Nora."

She bowed her head as he moved in front of her and took her in a loose embrace. She meant to pull away or push against his shoulders, but instead she closed her eyes and leaned against his chest. After what seemed a long while, she tilted up her face.

And then he kissed her.

CHAPTER THIRTY

Hoosick Falls, NY
January–February 1887

It was nothing like Nora had ever imagined—not forceful, nor posses-
sive, nor rushed. It was soft, and warm, and gently probing, though it
became more intense when she returned it with a muffled whimper.

Erik brought one of his hands to the side of her neck, and Nora
dropped her sketchbook so she could clutch his arms. His palm seemed
hotter than it should have against her skin. His mouth too; the moonshine on their commingled breath made the kiss feel flammable, and
Nora had to stop it before it flashed over.

She might yet save them from destruction.

But she didn't want to.

She pressed her mouth against Erik's and let her tongue seek his,
tugged off her gloves and let them fall to the ground with her book so
her bare hands could mold themselves to his body, slip inside his clothes
wherever they could find an opening, or make one. He propelled her
back against a tree and a huge pair of ravens burst from the branches
above them with loud, grating caws.

Nora gasped, her heart stuttering, and slipped sideways out of Erik's
grasp. When he reached for her again, she said, "Not here."

And so he followed her back into the trees and down the hill,
closely and quickly to match her steps. She realized that she'd forgotten

her gloves and sketchbook, but didn't care. She pushed on toward the sugaring shack, counting on its being empty; it wasn't maple season yet. They'd have to wait for daytime temperatures to rise above freezing while the nights still plunged below. For now, the world was frigid at every hour.

Yet Nora was surprised that she didn't melt a clear, steaming path in the snow as they approached the small wooden shack with its steeply pitched, shingled roof. Its tiny windows barely let in any light, but there wasn't much to see besides the long, hip-high brick oven, which supported a huge metal pan, under which the fire would be stoked when it was time to boil sap.

It was plenty big enough for Nora to lie down in, but first, Erik maneuvered her so she was half sitting, half leaning upon the lip of the stove and knelt between her legs. As he pushed her skirts up out of the way, she leaned back with one hand splayed upon the cold metal to support herself and placed the other on Erik's warm head where it fit so well between her thighs. He seemed to know exactly what she wanted, and made her come so quickly she was almost disappointed.

But then he did it again, with his mouth and his hands and a stream of encouraging, inflammatory words, and finally, as he kissed her again, he unbuttoned his trousers and pushed himself inside her. She lay back with one burning cheek pressed to the cold metal and her knees pinned to his sides. The blunt pain from the hard surfaces only seemed to underscore Nora's pleasure, which she felt building in her again.

She thought, dimly, that she should caution him to be careful, but she couldn't speak, dumb with gratification, and as with her abandoned gloves and sketchbook, didn't care to exercise any shred of prudence now. She wanted all of him, and watched his face as he let go.

～

They parted ways in silence. Outside, Nora stooped to palm a stinging handful of snow and scrubbed the bottom half of her face, where Erik's mouth had left her own scent on her skin. She would wash herself, and her underthings, in Euan's room.

The reality of what she had done—the magnitude of her trespass—seemed inordinately unmoving; Nora supposed she was in a sort of shock, or stupor. But she already knew that if she had the chance, she would transgress again, and that was what made the first pang of guilt twist her insides.

All she could do, she realized, was ensure that they were never alone together again. It seemed easy enough; she would cling to Mal or Marie on the way to and from the barn, and stop using the outhouse, contrive to empty her chamber pot only when she knew Erik was busy elsewhere. She would stop all her solitary walks and sketching expeditions and bicycle rides into town, all opportunities to be ambushed. She would feel the loss of those excursions, but some part of Nora was grimly satisfied by the idea. She didn't deserve her freedom if she was going to do such unforgivable things with it.

Late that afternoon, before milking, she was at the desk in Euan's room, gazing vacantly out the window, when a board creaked out in the hall. Her breath caught, not at the notion of ghosts but at the prospect of Erik having crept upstairs—but it was Malcolm, and his appearance gave Nora an even greater fright, for he held her snow-dampened sketchbook and gloves in his rough hands.

She stared at them and couldn't speak.

"I was worried," he said, and gave them back, concern and sadness in his eyes, but no disappointment that she could discern in the brief moment that she was able to hold his gaze.

Sorrow hollowed Nora's chest—that they had both been up on the hill, but not together. That had he gone a little earlier, he might have caught her and Erik sharing the flask, if not embracing—and that he hadn't, hadn't saved her from her own terrible choices.

Though she wanted to lean into her husband's arms and not let go, it felt too awful to imagine, to even be in his presence when another of his brothers had only two hours before been inside her.

And he seemed to have no inkling, which made it even worse.

∿

She hid again that evening, skipped milking and dinner, though her stomach growled. When Mal came up to check on her, she claimed not to be feeling well, and he sent Marie up with a tray of soft, warm foods fit for an invalid.

Nora could barely look at her, either, and ducked away from the gentle hand that Marie laid upon her brow to check for fever.

∿

The next day was Sunday, and Nora would not be left alone with Erik. She went down for breakfast and tried not to look at him. The avidity with which he regarded her was alarming—for how much it immediately aroused her, and for how obvious she feared it was to everyone. But no one else seemed to notice.

In church, Nora didn't ask for forgiveness, but numbly prayed for the strength to be better, knowing that it was not in anyone's power but her own.

And even there, and then, she wanted Erik. The hard edge of the wooden pew beneath her thighs brought back the lip of the oven, and she became short of breath. The bit of nerve-rich flesh for which she'd half seriously given glory to God made its existence known, and Nora spared a wild, unholy thought for that barbaric amputation that certain male doctors found so useful for curing feminine ailments, including hysteria and wantonness. She could do it herself, she thought, in secret; Mal would certainly never notice.

But she would no more do that than cut off her finger or her nose. She would rather die. And that, she thought, was still an option.

She tried to act sane and sanctified when they walked down to Main Street, where Grace and Dr. Burns both scrutinized her—or so it felt. She forced a smile and said she was fine. "But I'll be better when spring comes."

It sounded convincing, but didn't feel true. It would be harder to keep herself shut inside when the weather changed, Nora thought. For now, she was glad they were still mired in winter.

∾

At home, she spoke as few words as possible when Erik tried to draw her into conversation at the dinner table, or during milking, or in the parlor, where—despite Marie's continued fascination with the phonograph—he resumed sprawling on the settee beside Nora some nights, which paralyzed her too greatly to concentrate on anything.

She managed to read or write letters only at Euan's desk, but still froze at any sound of shifting boards, expecting Erik to materialize and slip inside, shut the door and lay her back upon his brother's childhood bed. But he never came upstairs, never had since Nora had arrived, so she felt reasonably safe there, alone.

She still missed Mal, but in some sense, she always had. She didn't deserve the comfort of his presence now, and was glad she'd left his bed before she'd ever touched Erik.

Worse was the fact that Mal plainly missed her too. But Nora hoped he was more relieved by her absence than not.

∾

When the cows began giving birth, he often spent long nighttime hours keeping vigil in the barn with Axel. Nora sometimes wanted to go too—to offer help if she could, to observe, if nothing else, to simply be accompanied. But she stayed in bed and listened for footsteps in the hall.

She heard Mal's going away, and if she stayed awake long enough, his coming back, though sometimes the tread sounded different, and she held her breath. She tried not to picture Erik—or Olaf—in the darkness, of the hallway, or the cellar, or her own head.

～

Outside, she stuck close to Marie, who seemed thrilled by Nora's new willingness to spend more time together; Nora had often sensed her sister-in-law's disappointment when she'd cycled off to see Grace. She felt monstrously callous to use Marie as a shield, especially when her innate good cheer grated. But Nora didn't trust herself to go about alone.

～

All through the rest of January and most of February, the relentless cold and gloom and stretches of fresh snow bound them to the house, except when they had to hurry through the numbing drifts and stinging flurries to tend the animals or go to town. They skipped several Friday marketing excursions and were forced to miss a few Sunday services, though Kirsten let nothing stop her. She trekked through weather that made Nora fear for her safety, though the others seemed to trust that she'd be fine. She put the girls down for their naps early on those days and went to afternoon services.

～

In late February, one lunchtime's talk turned to tapping the maple trees, which would likely happen soon. Nora kept her eyes on her plate and tried not to feel Erik's bright-blue gaze upon her, but it was harder to staunchly ignore him when he addressed her directly.

"You know why there's a separate shack for it?" He must have known she wouldn't answer, but he paused, then supplied a hypothetical reply for Nora. ""Cause it's closer to the trees, and you don't have to haul buckets full of sap back to the house?' Nope—not just that, anyway. It's because when you boil all those gallons down to syrup, that steam sends vaporized sugar all over the place. Coats the walls, the windows, whatever's in there with it. You get this sticky film all over you. Lick the back of your neck and it'll taste sweet. Gets all in your clothes too. Kirsten's probably thankful I usually take mine off."

Nora's whole body prickled with heat.

Marie giggled. Mal only lightly cleared his throat. Kirsten's disapproval was obvious, but her own discomfort made her look down at the table too. Nora chewed her bread until it turned into a paste and eventually dissolved before she could attempt to swallow.

~

She'd noticed that, with the number of farm chores so reduced—ditto the number of cows needing to be milked—Erik had taken to riding off on Odin more often, and staying gone for several hours at a time. Working out his frustration, Nora supposed.

At first, she didn't trust that it was safe to brave a brief walk in the graveyard by herself. But she wanted so badly to simply stand alone among the softly clattering tree limbs for a moment, to feel briefly unburdened, that one afternoon, she took a chance.

Erik had trotted away on Odin half an hour before, and the women had finished dusting for the day. Kirsten actually sat down in order to peruse a seed catalog. Mal was in the orchard, pruning branches, and Axel was somewhere in the barn, as far as Nora knew. She didn't quite mean to wait until Marie was in the outhouse, but the moment she was, Nora hurried to grab her coat on her way out the front door.

She made for the trees, only slowing to a proper walk when she was deep enough to be hidden. She considered veering toward the pond, or perhaps the hill, but instead, she was drawn to the sugaring shack.

Inside, it smelled like weathered wood and dust and cold stone and snow, a hint of the damp ground just outside—no trace of sugar, nor of sex. She looked at the oven and the metal pan, thinking that it looked like a dissecting table, or a crematory, with its chimney that funneled smoke through the roof.

She ran a fingertip along the cold edge of the metal and brought it to her lips, but tasted nothing on the tip of her tongue. It wouldn't surprise her if Erik had been lying, just to get her blood boiling. And Nora couldn't forget what he'd said, couldn't help imagining the warm, humid atmosphere that must pervade the space when the fire was roaring and the sap bubbling, the sweet steam clouds rolling over everything.

When she closed her eyes and raised her hand to touch her jaw and neck, she caught a hint of rosemary and smoke from her own sleeve, a bit of sweet hay and animal musk. That was her own scent now, and it wasn't enough to make her think she wasn't alone.

But then a soft creak behind her made her freeze, and slowly turn. Erik stood just inside the door. The shack was small, mostly filled by the oven in its center; there was just enough room to walk in front of its narrow end, with comparatively larger spaces to either side. But there was no easy exit with him filling the entryway, and then he stepped closer.

Nora could attempt to scrabble through a window, but she'd get stuck, or caught—and she didn't want to escape anyway.

"You followed me?" she breathed, not quite angry—or not only that. "You just pretended you were leaving? Is that what you've been doing every time? Just . . . lurking in the woods? Lying in wait?"

Erik licked his full lips in a seemingly unconscious gesture, his voice low and rough when he replied, "You've been keepin' tabs on me. You wanted to be found."

Nora stood her ground as he neared; otherwise, he would only back her up against the far wall, and though the thought sent a pulse of pleasure through her, she felt a touch of fear as well.

"You've got the patience of a goddamn saint, doc. While you torment me like the devil."

A scoff started and died in Nora's throat.

"I'm afflicted," Erik said as he closed the last few inches between them and placed one hand on the small of Nora's back, the other at the base of her skull, his fingers sliding into her hair. "You're in my head all the time now. And I know I'm in yours. But that's not enough. I *need* you. And you want me, don't you? You miss me?"

She tilted her face up in reply, but though he brought his lips close to her own, he didn't let them brush her mouth. "Say it."

"No." But she moved her lips closer to his, and it was all the provocation he needed, or could stand.

They sank onto the dusty floor and Nora thought she'd have to say she'd fallen if anyone commented on the state of her skirt. But then she thought of nothing except what was happening, inevitably, ecstatically.

CHAPTER THIRTY-ONE

Hoosick Falls, NY
March–May 1887

There was no sense, after that, in denying themselves. No chance.

The following Friday, Nora opted out of going into town—claiming to be too cold and tired—and as soon as the wagon was out of sight, she went to Erik's cabin.

He wanted to undress her before the fire, but she worried Axel might walk by and see through the window. So they climbed the ladder to the sleeping loft, where Nora discovered that no bear or other four-legged beast had taken Old Nick's head. Erik had carted it home and boiled it down to polished bone, then placed it on a shelf above his bed. The skull was angled such that Nora got the full effect of one empty eye socket and the toothy grimace, made all the more disturbing for the fact that Erik's leather hat perched between the bull's horns. But his attention distracted her soon enough.

They pulled at their clothes, their own and each other's, and he looked long and close at nearly every inch of Nora.

He ran a fingertip along the pale line on the inside of her arm and said, "What's this?"

"A mistake I almost made."

He kissed the scar and moved on from it, touched her elsewhere, and tasted, and told her everything he liked and wanted to do to her and how she made him feel, and Nora felt ravenous, felt foolish to have ever thought she could starve herself to death, any more than she could have bled herself dry.

She was alive with Erik's eminent pleasure, so freely felt and expressed, as well as with her own. And she was grateful that he evinced no shred of guilt even afterward. Only satisfaction, and hunger to have her again, and again.

∼

Now, she looked for any opportunity to slip away from the others' notice. She and Erik came together in the woods, shielded only by the trees, insensible to the cold; in the sugaring shack again; in the barn loft when Axel was away for a night in town. Never the cabin unless Marie and Mal and Kirsten and the girls were gone—though Erik assured her Marie wouldn't come there unless he'd told her to. When the weather kept the rest of them from going into town, Nora was put out.

It was like it had been with Euan, in that all their best time together was stolen and secret—and when they were in the presence of others, it was excruciating to act like nothing had changed.

The incessant desire they had for each other was as it had been with Euan, too, and as it never had been with Mal. Even when such thoughts made Nora unutterably sad, it only lasted for a second before desire burned it away. Likewise, her guilt: it struck her as bottomless in moments of clarity, then vanished the instant Erik had his hands on her again, his mouth.

The cure was not to stop but to keep giving in. To stop would kill her, and now all Nora wanted was to live—for the next clandestine meeting, the next brush of her brother-in-law's eager tongue, the next insistent thrust of his hips.

She went about as wet and tender and exquisitely raw as some freshly hatched thing, newborn to all sensation.

~

Still, she had to keep up appearances, and maintain her routines. She marveled that none of the others appeared to notice anything strange.

Mal and Marie seemed rather pleased that her attitude had improved—that she stopped claiming to feel unwell, and smiled and laughed and went for walks again, even if she also seemed jumpier, more brightly agitated, and didn't visit town on Fridays. When Mal initially expressed gentle concern about that, she'd said, "I've seen every inch of Hoosick Falls there is to see by now; I don't feel the need to reacquaint myself twice a week."

His auburn brows had knit, and Nora looked away in shame as she mumbled an apology.

"It's all right," he'd said. "I'll pick up your mail, then."

Kirsten, she noted, took her old place on the bench seat beside Mal on the days that Nora stayed behind, but she didn't look long enough to confirm if there was smugness, much less pleasure, on the woman's face. She was harder to read anyway; she looked at Nora as coldly as she always had, but Nora no longer cared, and forgot all her sympathy for the woman, since Kirsten hadn't wanted it.

She hoped that the others—Grace and Dr. Burns included, for she still went to church on Sundays, fearing that it would be too obvious otherwise—would ascribe the change in her to spring, which began to assert itself, to release the world from its season spent locked in snow and ice.

Water dripped from the trees as buds swelled on their branches; the white carpet of winter became ever more moth-eaten, though in the coldest pockets where the shadows clung fast, there were still frozen drifts, and an icy breeze often blew across them. But the land shifted and softened and the damp roofs and fences steamed under the warming sun. Everything was unfurling, stretching itself out toward the light, toward life.

When Mal smiled at her, she felt terrible, but out of his presence she could almost forget. When she caressed herself at night in Euan's bed, no longer denying thoughts of Erik, she felt guiltier to imagine what Euan would think of her now. If he did think of her, from someplace where Nora could not sense him.

But she barely noticed the familiar disembodied presence in the room, much less thought about whatever might lurk in the basement. Neither of those things could touch her, after all.

In March, mud reclaimed all the land the snow had so jealously covered. Its abundance was astounding, and incredibly aggravating. Fed up with having it glom onto her skirts and drag down her hems, Nora took to wearing a pair of Mal's old trousers around the farm, held up with a pair of his suspenders. Kirsten despised the getup, and even Mal seemed somewhat disconcerted, but Marie laughed and Axel barely gave her a second glance.

Erik loved Nora in trousers. In part, she thought, because she dispensed with her corset, too, no longer needing it to support multiple layers of skirts, never having needed it, really, to support her modest breasts. So now all he had to do was pluck her blouse's buttons free and slip the suspenders off her shoulders to bare the rest of her.

She resurrected her womb veil, but usually insisted Erik finish elsewhere to be safer. He was happy enough to oblige.

Nora was careful, too, to wash away all the substances and scents he left on her as soon as possible, worried that Kirsten would lift her nose in the air when she passed and fix her with a pointed gaze, a keen-nostriled greyhound.

Even if she'd still slept with Mal, Nora didn't think she'd worry much about his noticing the marks that Erik left on her. Marie, however, she could easily imagine tracing a fingertip over scratches on her husband's back or touching suction marks upon his neck and asking what had happened, then readily believing whatever lie he told her. But as far as Nora knew, he'd hardly taken his wife into the cabin in the past few months. Sometimes, she looked for signs of sadness in Marie, but if they were there, they passed quickly.

∼

By April, the last of the cows had given birth. Titus, once angelic little bull himself, was now almost fully grown. He'd at least doubled in size. Nora no longer liked to walk too near him, though his temperament was as mild as ever.

Erik often sucked his teeth and speculated that he'd be a poor stud.

One or two female calves would be added to the herd for milking, while the others would be sold. Locally, if there were buyers, or else Mal would take another trip to Albany. Nora hoped he would, and that he would see Kitty, and do more than simply talk.

She felt only slightly disgraceful for it. In a patch of woods where bright sunlight leaked through the gently fluttering new leaves above them, as Erik's fingers, slicked with Nora's own saliva, worked between her thighs and his mouth worked upon her breast, she felt the tremulous light and the fluttering of the leaves inside her too.

What guilt, however dark and filthy, and what worries, however persistent, could survive such bliss?

But Nora knew that it could not last either. Nothing did.

She couldn't imagine what might come after.

∼

She continued to dress appropriately for church, and to trade pleasantries with Grace, whom Nora perceived as the greatest threat to her

263

secret. Grace asked one Sunday, "Have the wheels finally fallen off that contraption of yours? We hardly ever see you anymore."

Nora blushed, tried not to stammer. "Well, it is getting to be the busy season." She made herself narrow her eyes in a teasing manner at her friend. "But maybe you don't know that. A well-to-do village lady like yourself. Us country folk have work to do. Sunup to sundown."

Grace smiled, a little thinly. "Well, try to get some sleep, at least. And come see us when you can."

Nora just managed to smile back, to say, "I will."

And she did, every other Tuesday after that, the most that she was prepared to give up of her precious private hours.

Over tea and sweets on the Murphys' back porch, Grace fished for information, but never directly challenged her.

Nora was glad that Ezra was at school now, for she thought she would have stared even more intently at him, acutely aware that despite her precautions, she could easily end up in a similar position as Ellen.

～

Alone with Erik, Nora sometimes asked innocuous questions about his childhood, but never dared mention his adolescent affair. With so little time to steal, they didn't waste much of it talking at all.

～

The daily farmwork increased with the fecundity of the growing seasons—the excuse she'd given Grace had at least been founded in fact. As the men prepared the fields, the women prepared the kitchen garden for their own small summer vegetable crops. Nora was glad to think that the seeds she poked into the soil would sprout and grow and nourish them soon enough. That not every one of her actions was destructive, or deceptive.

~

Later that month, the subject of Newport arose. Bette and Birdie had both written to ask when she was joining them in June, and for how long—she was welcome to spend the entire summer, of course. But the very idea was unimaginable to Nora.

When Malcolm mentioned it at supper and she casually said she wasn't going, the look on his face reminded her too much of her father's expression when she'd told him she might not return to school.

"But it's your family tradition. I don't expect you to give it up—"

"Well, I'm not going to go laze on the beach for three months while you all break your backs."

"Even if you only wanted to go for a week or two," Mal said. "I think everyone would understand."

Marie's crestfallen look proved that false, though to her credit, she tried to hide it behind a smile. Kirsten's expression seemed to be at war—one part of her resenting the mere thought of Nora relaxing while the rest of them worked, the other wishing she would leave, even for a brief spell. Erik seemed simultaneously intrigued and smug.

Nora set her teeth while she tried to choose her next words, but before she could, Erik said, "What, you don't want to go with her? You've still never even seen the ocean."

"I have too much work," Mal said.

"Well, hell, I'll go for you." Erik looked across the table again at Nora. "If you need a chaperone to get you there and back."

She looked down at her plate. "I'm not going anywhere. I'm not cut out for Newport anymore, anyway."

Which felt oddly, alienatingly true.

CHAPTER
THIRTY-TWO

Hoosick Falls, NY
May–August 1887

Aunt Birdie expressed heartfelt regret that they wouldn't see Nora that summer. Cousin Bette was more affronted.

> *Never in your entire life have you not summered here.*
> *Even before you were born—you came to Newport in*
> *your mother's belly. You belong here—with us.*

~

I'm afraid I belong now in the green inland sea of the forest, Nora wrote, *and the waving fields of corn and wheat, which, in fact, sound rather like the ocean if you close your eyes and stand among them.*

~

In truth, she was a bit wistful about missing out, about forfeiting what had once been a great pleasure, but was also afraid she wouldn't enjoy herself, wouldn't even fit, having been warped out of the shape of herself that had left a hole in her family.

Her father still wrote regularly, and still sent money in every letter. In early June, after he'd heard that she wasn't going to Newport, he expressed his own surprise, and asked if he might visit her. *I would, of course, impose upon Angus and Hattie and not you all.*

Nora replied promptly, for once, to say that she was very sorry but it wouldn't be fair to everyone else to accept.

> *It will be far too hectic to entertain or to take an evening away for a dinner. But perhaps in the fall, when things start to quiet down, we could plan a visit. It is the most beautiful time of year here, too.*

That seemed to mollify him, though she was terrified that he might show up anyway; he could easily drop in on Angus and suggest he run him out to the farm.

∼

Even Erik harped on Nora, as they lay under the stars glimmering in the twilight one evening. "I mean, this is nice, but I can't believe you're gonna pass up the chance to stay in that fancy mansion and be waited on hand and foot. But maybe that'd make it too hard to come back here."

When she didn't answer, he said, "Don't get me wrong, I'm flattered. That you'd miss me that much. And I hate the ocean, but even I wouldn't say no to pokin' around tide pools and havin' picnics all summer . . ."

Nora frowned at him. "It's not because of you. And how do you know where I'd stay? Or what I'd do?"

"Euan told us." His name rolled far too easily off Erik's tongue for Nora's liking. "He sure liked the taste he got."

Her brow furrowed deeper as she sat up, knees folded to her chest.

"He talked about you all the time," Erik went on. "I only half listened, truth be told. But my ears do perk up at certain words. *Huge house. Full staff. The Astors.* And he wrote all about you too. From his first letter home—'Dr. Harris's daughter, Leonora, is a rather fascinating figure.'"

Nora scowled at Erik. "How do you know that? You weren't even here when Euan first came to Manhattan. Mal wouldn't have told you."

"You sure about that? He is my brother. We do talk."

"Well, he didn't quote Euan's letter. Much less show it to you."

Erik shrugged, as best he could with his arms crossed behind his head. "Maybe I'm paraphrasin'."

Nora snatched her clothing and stood up. "Or maybe you *snooped.* Did you? Go into his private things—?"

"Sure did," Erik snorted, which only made Nora angrier.

And then she stopped, midbutton, suffused with a bodily recollection of the atmosphere in her room—Euan's room—when she and Mal first returned from Manhattan before Christmas. As if someone more substantial than the familiar formless presence had just been there, and might at any moment peek over her shoulder. "You went into my room, too, didn't you?"

"What, you mean the one I slept in every night when I was a little boy?"

"Well, you don't now. You don't even go upstairs." She shivered, faintly, at the recollection of all the nights she'd been so assured of that, mostly unafraid of Erik sneaking into her room—Euan's.

She trembled with fury, too, at the thought of Erik reading her own letters, and Euan's, touching all those papers upon which they'd poured their souls, studying all the private drawings she'd done. It didn't matter that Erik had seen Nora's body in the flesh, had plumbed the depths of it with various parts of his own—the very notion was violating.

And then she realized—the reason that he seemed to instinctually know so much of what she liked was not proof of some fateful connection or particular prowess but more evidence of his prying.

"How *dare* you," she choked out. "You sneaking, lying *bastard*."

He only laughed. "Look, I was curious. You can appreciate that, can't you? And I finally got it." He sat up and peered at her. "All that smut hidden in your room? That was intriguin' as hell, sure, but readin' all Euan's letters home? I finally understood how Mal fell in love with you before you ever even met. Maybe it took me a little longer, but—"

"Don't say that," Nora snapped, voice breaking.

"What?" Erik smirked. "That I love you? Or that your husband does?"

"*You* don't." She yanked a blouse button too hard through its hole and pulled it off. "And I hope he doesn't," she added. "Not now. Not after . . ."

Erik stood and cocked his head; in the gloaming, his outline was blurred and shadowed, and Nora had another horribly visceral memory, of how Olaf had tilted his head at her when she first perceived him in the cellar shadows.

"You know, a bull won't ever choose one cow if there are more around. And if there's more than one male in a herd of heifers, every one of them'll lift her tail for whichever stud comes callin'. They know how to share."

Nora huffed as she struggled with her shoes. "Well, some of us are humans, not animals."

"Aw, come on now." Erik leaned against the nearest tree like some faun. "You must know better than anybody, we're all animals too. All just meat and urges. Every livin' thing wants to keep on livin'. And make more of itself so it never really dies. Maybe people like to have a little more pleasure in the process. But we overcomplicate it too. Make ourselves miserable when there's no need."

Nora studied him, though his features had receded further into shadow. "It's that easy for you, though? You wouldn't be sorry if Mal found out and had his heart broken? Or Marie?"

He shrugged one shoulder. "They'd get over it."

"They wouldn't. They wouldn't forget it, even if they forgave."

"And?" Erik said. "They'd live with it anyway."

The urge to shove him made Nora's fingers curl into fists. She forced herself not to turn and go but to press back. "You must love Marie, or you wouldn't have brought her back here."

"She's pleasant enough. Doesn't give me any trouble. And I felt sorry for her, I guess."

Nora felt sorry for her now, and for Mal, both oblivious to the betrayal of their faithless spouses—but she felt unfairly sorry for herself as well. "Neither one of them deserves this," she said. "Deserves *us*. We're terrible people, you know that?"

Erik chuckled. "Guess that's why we're drawn together. But I've already made peace with it. Once you do, you'll feel a whole lot better."

Nora had felt so much freer in the beginning, when passion was enough to burn away snarls of guilt and regret and even worry about what would come next.

Now, though, the tangled undergrowth grew quicker, and thicker, and might be scorched, but could not be so easily obliterated. Feeling unburdened was the last thing Nora should want anyway, she knew. She turned to walk away.

He said, "Marie, I get; she's an innocent. But you think Mal's some pure soul, too, never sinned a day in his life?"

Nora stopped but didn't turn around.

"I mean, I don't know for sure," Erik continued, "but I always thought he had somebody in Albany. And he sure as hell didn't want you to go there with him."

Nora fought a rising tide of indignation. "I already know about that."

"Oh, really. And what do you think he knows? He's not stupid. Not naive."

Nora thought of Mal standing in the hall with her snow-stained gloves and sketchbook, and of every time he'd looked at her since then, but if he knew anything, then Erik was right: he forgave her.

∽

She combed through her room when she returned to it, seeking evidence of Erik's prying. But her letters and drawings were all tucked back in their proper places; her money was accounted for; the remaining half of Euan's ashes appeared undisturbed.

She wanted to hunt for Mal's secrets too—his letters from Euan at the very least; they were about her, in part, so it seemed Nora had some right to them. But she felt too contaminated by Erik's trespass to perpetrate the same intrusion. And keenly aware that she already had, in some sense, when she'd read Mal's letters to Euan so many months ago.

∽

Grief dully gnawed at Nora, but anger chomped and tore. Her temper grew shorter as the heat increased; she almost longed for the icy fingers of winter reaching under her collar again. She traded her trousers for comparatively airier skirts that she could hike up over her knees when she sat somewhere semi-private. At home, she still left off the bulky layers of petticoats beneath, and the corset, too, rolled her long sleeves up above her elbows and undid the buttons of her blouses halfway down her chest.

One afternoon, Marie said, "Oh, you've hurt yourself!"

Nora was confused, and startled. When Marie reached out to trail her finger along the shining, pinkish line inside Nora's arm, she flushed and jerked away, mumbled that she'd had an accident a long time ago but it was fine now.

Kirsten never mentioned it, nor did Mal—indeed, he never had, though he'd surely noticed the scar before. He frowned to see it bared in the daylight, but Nora couldn't tell if it was concern or disapproval, and tried not to care.

≈

She stopped seeking Erik out, and when he managed to catch her alone now, she was less receptive, more severe. It sometimes lent a contentiousness to their coupling. Even when she let herself give in, hoping that everything would be swept away in the violence of a cataclysmic climax, Nora's agitation returned moments later—shimmering through her like the fireflies that flashed in the pasture on muggy nights.

"We can't keep doing this" became her favorite refrain, "Speak for yourself" Erik's usual answer.

"I *am*," Nora said. "This is awful. And stupid. And it can't go on forever."

"Uh-huh."

"It won't."

"So, what?" he said. "We'll just . . . stop? Keep sittin' across the table from each other, and on opposite ends of the sofa, and never do it again?"

"Exactly. Unless you'd rather leave."

Something brightened in Erik's eyes at that. "Leave?"

Like he thought she meant together. To disabuse him of the notion, Nora said, "Light out for whatever territories you haven't seen yet. Like you did before."

He huffed, but only half amused; Nora thought he might have been genuinely, if mildly, offended. "I came back, though, remember? I'd sure as hell come back again now."

I might not still be here, though, she thought, but didn't say. It was a half-formed idea that had more than one conclusion, and she didn't truly want to examine any of them, at least not yet.

~

Nora wanted the impossible: for everything to change—to return to what had passed for normal—without requiring that she take any decisive action.

In the absence of divine intervention, she simply continued to delay the inevitable.

One Friday afternoon, as she and Erik lay in his loft under the eyeless gaze of Old Nick's skull and a summer storm pounded on the roof just above their heads, Nora turned the conversation toward his going away again.

"You hate it here, anyway. You said so yourself."

"That was before you let me in."

She shoved him rather violently and drew away, crossed her arms over her breasts. "I can always shut you out again."

Undeterred, Erik casually stroked himself. "Keep tellin' yourself that."

"You think I need you?" Nora asked.

"I know you want me. You're here, aren't you?"

"Well, we can't both be."

He gave that half-insulted, half-amused huff again. "I thought you wanted me to be loyal to poor Marie. But now I should abandon her?"

"Would it make that much of a difference? In the end?"

"Ask her, why don't you."

Nora turned away from his irritating smirk and the irritatingly stirring sight of his erection in his large, lovely hand—and from the bull skull's frozen grimace—and gazed out the tiny window at the rain-lashed landscape. The lightning flashed bright enough to blind her for a second. "You never did say you loved her. Marie. You don't seem all that fond of your daughters either." It was a subject she'd never broached before, but now thought worth it, if only to break the spell Erik still seemed under.

His answering burst of fury, however, made Nora physically shrink back.

"'*Daughters*.' They're overgrown *dolls* come to life—and barely. At least they don't scream all the time anymore, I guess."

He raked both hands through his damp hair, grown too long again.

"I should have left them all there," he said. "Let Marie's crazy old father and his crazier old mother drown 'em if they wanted. Changelings, they said. Ignorant fucks. Well, so was I, I guess. I didn't know shit about babies. They all screamed and cried, far as I knew. I thought it was a good sign, even, that they hardly ever stopped. They went all red in the face and hoarse and an hour later, they were at it again. They were strong. Smart enough to be pissed off at bein' brought into the world without any say-so. And maybe that's still true. But there's somethin' wrong with them. And no cure for it, either, is there, doc?"

"I don't know," Nora said.

She thought she detected a hint of pain beneath Erik's bitterness, but it could have just been what she hoped for. If only because it made her let him come closer and brush her hair behind her ear.

"They're better off here," he said, then kissed Nora's mouth the same way he had the first time—disarmingly tenderly. "And Marie'd be fine if we went," he said, and gently pushed Nora back on the mattress. "So would Mal. They want so much less than we do. But I can't live like this—with you only half the time. Not even that."

Nora couldn't speak, and anyway, Erik kissed her again as he moved on top of her. "Leavin's easier than you think," he said. "And you know you don't belong here. So, we can go—anywhere. We're still young. We can start over."

"And do what?" Nora asked, strangely ashamed of how stridently her inner voice derided the notion, because she knew that, however alike they were, Erik wasn't good enough for her.

He kissed her throat, and then her clavicle. "Whatever we want. You can go back to school, get your license. Every damn place needs doctors. You can practice medicine somewhere while I . . . I don't know."

He kissed Nora's sternum, and then her breast. "I'd like to be someplace where no one knows me—or *thinks* they do. I could have another farm, a small one, that belongs to me alone. I don't mind the work. *That's* why I came back—I couldn't stay over there on some other man's land one more minute, bustin' my ass to fill up his pockets faster than my own."

He looked up from Nora's navel. "You know Marie's father owns a mill? Whenever he dies, it's supposed to go to her—so, me. No other family left. Part of why I agreed to marry her—I wouldn't mind ownin' my own business, sittin' back while other people fill my pockets up. But who the hell knows how many goddamn years that'll be. That bastard probably wrote us out when we left, anyway. Even though he didn't want to be saddled with them either."

He dipped his head again even as Nora squeezed her thighs together to shut him out. But she let him ease them apart a second later.

"I couldn't take *that* one more day," he murmured against her before he kissed her again. "Livin' under his yoke. So I didn't. But I couldn't leave Marie there either—sense of duty, I guess." He ran his tongue through Nora's equally slick flesh. "Blame Mal for that."

Erik's lips closed around her then, and he left off talking for a while. But when he drew back to move himself face-to-face with Nora, he picked up where he'd left off. "Blame you for the rest—all this. I could have lived like that for as long as I needed to. Worked the way I always had worked. Provided for my sad little family, 'cause that's what I'd got. But now I've got you."

"No, you don't," Nora said, then drew in a deep breath as Erik slid himself inside her. She closed her eyes and wrapped her legs around him, sank her fingertips into his smoothly muscled back and hoped it hurt.

The situation was untenable. So was Erik's far-fetched solution.

∼

He grew surlier in July and August, rougher with Nora when they were together. She hadn't disliked that before, but now felt genuine alarm when he pushed her—though the instant she conveyed displeasure, he pulled back, and placated her again.

She still wanted him, or at least her body did, even as her head and heart grew heavier with dread, and the certainty that she had seen more goodness in Erik than was ever warranted.

If he left, Nora was certain that she wouldn't want to follow. And she would never run away with him.

She couldn't conceive that he might truly think otherwise. Yet she feared that Erik was intent on having her—on holding her for his own.

One sleepless night, she paged through her well-worn copy of *Frankenstein* to a passage that now made her queasy: *If I cannot inspire love, I will cause fear.*

And if that failed to move Nora, Erik might well wreak destruction.

~

She thought of Olaf more frequently than she had in months—but not his ghost. Now, Nora hazily envisioned him alive, working some sinister spell to gain possession of the farm and Hannah Colquhoun. Then, losing everything. His curse coming back to him. But outlasting him, too.

In mid-August, it would be the seventeenth anniversary of his and Hannah's deaths. And earlier that month, the twenty-fifth anniversary of Euan Sr.'s demise would come to pass. She'd never paid much attention to the fact that those events had all occurred so closely on the calendar, because they'd been separated by nearly a decade. But now that Erik's possessiveness had begun to prick at her, Nora wondered if there was more to it. She believed Mal had told the truth about Olaf's broken neck, but suspected there had been no fever—not when it killed husband and wife on the same day yet left everyone else unscathed.

Perhaps Hannah had still mourned Euan Sr. and it had infuriated Olaf enough that he'd attacked her. As a medical student, Nora had seen cases of domestic violence, the results sometimes fatal. Maybe they'd both fallen down the stairs. Or maybe someone had pushed Olaf after discovering whatever he'd done to Hannah.

It struck Nora that Mal was both an unlikely and a perfect suspect—he was loyal to a fault, after all, and though he seemed incapable of violence, he had been a soldier before coming home to his new stepfather. He'd certainly killed men in the line of duty. What if a similar impulse had moved him to avenge his mother?

It would make sense for him to lie about it, then.

But he would also lie to protect anyone he loved—so it could have been Stephen, or Euan himself.

Nora could more easily imagine Erik pushing Olaf, though, even if he had only been six at the time. Not too young to shove a grown man at the top of the stairs—gravity would have done most of the work. Helped by the hard packed-dirt floor.

She'd never asked Erik if he recalled anything about the circumstances of his parents' deaths and wouldn't dare now. But if he had murdered his father—which was ridiculous, Nora told herself—then it had surely been an impulsive act triggered by anger, and maybe fear. The lashing out of a stricken boy.

Johan's death, years later, had been a common-enough tragedy; it felt spiteful to even question whether it had been an accident, yet now Nora wondered that a seventeen-year-old Erik hadn't been able to rescue his younger nephew.

And there *was* anger in Erik, deep and dark. She worried that it could erupt far more dangerously. If he was denied what he wanted. If he was hurt again.

Nora told herself that she was being dramatic, simply looking for more drastic reasons to end the affair, not that she should need them.

And even when she looked at Erik with trepidation, it wasn't enough to keep her from cleaving to him.

∾

That, in fact, began to trouble Nora too. The pull that Erik exerted—that she'd felt from the very beginning, and chafed against even then—seemed too strong to be natural.

Nora had felt intimately seen by him long before he ever snooped, much less disrobed her. And all the disturbing visions she'd had of Erik, so often drenched in blood . . . was it possible that he'd cast some dark enchantment on her?

If Olaf had taught his son to fiddle, then perhaps he'd taught him other things as well.

Nora realized that such fantasies were even more far-fetched than her unfounded fears of Erik harming her.

And she suspected the root of it was still her desperation to shift the blame again.

~

Idly, she daydreamed of divorce, as a means of getting away from the farm and of freeing Mal in the bargain.

But she still thought it would hurt him, and hurt her too.

Besides, if Nora left now, she felt certain that Erik would follow.

There was no point in causing more pain for no benefit. And she would feel far less safe away from Mal.

CHAPTER
THIRTY-THREE

Hoosick Falls, NY
September 1887

On the final Saturday in September, Nora took a new sketchbook out to the woods, still humid despite the storm that had just rumbled through.

Less than a week ago, she'd last shoved Erik away, then turned her back and hiked up her skirts for him. She sat in the damp, dappled shade for some time, ambivalent as to whether she hoped he would find her again. He didn't, and she was slow in walking back. Admiring shafts of golden sunlight angling through the heavy gray clouds, gilding pools of standing water in the pasture, she only belatedly noticed the figures in the near distance: two women and two tiny children leaning over the perimeter fence, reaching out to a couple of the cows. Nora recognized Marie immediately, but it took a long moment to realize that the other woman was Cousin Bette—and the little girls were Nora's toddling nieces.

Alarm immediately gave way to outsized anger as Nora strode closer. The grin that split her cousin's face wavered as Bette took in Nora's overall appearance: partially unbuttoned blouse, unsupported skirt, disheveled hair, and thunderous expression.

When Nora came close enough not to have to shout, she said, "What are you doing here?"

"Well, hello to you too! We missed you so much we thought we'd stop by on our way back to the city. Mother's on the side porch having lemonade with—Kristin, is it? Grandmama, too."

"What?" Nora looked toward the house. *"Why?"*

"Because they were thirsty," Bette deadpanned. "But the girls wanted to see the animals."

The girls smiled and babbled what sounded like hello when Nora looked at them. She flashed a smile and nodded. Marie looked ecstatic for the unexpected company, and Bette's expression had gone expectant, but Nora turned her back on all of them and beelined toward the house.

Bette and Marie came after at a more leisurely clip. Nora made the porch well ahead of them, and was glad for fewer witnesses to Grandmama's keen look of displeasure, and Birdie's surprise. Nora instinctively raised her sketchbook to cover her chest. *Thank God I'm not wearing trousers,* she thought.

"Nora!" Aunt Birdie cried, and rose to enfold her, despite her sweaty disorder. "Oh, what a lovely home you have, dear—and how welcoming."

Nora glanced at Kirsten, wearing an identical expression to Grandmama's, then looked out toward the fields. "Mal's out working," she said, as if they had come for him.

"Yes, Kirsten said. Marie wanted to ring the bell, but we didn't want anyone to think there was an emergency."

"No notion if you were even close enough to hear it," Kirsten muttered.

"I was out drawing," Nora said, wishing she didn't sound so defensive. "We're between chores."

Kirsten pressed her lips together and went inside.

Nora heard Bette and Marie come up onto the porch behind her, and turned to see that each woman carried one of the girls on their hip.

"You're not staying, are you?"

Bette laughed. "So much for social graces!"

"Not that she had many to lose in the first place," said Grandmama.

"Just for a spell," Aunt Birdie answered. "We just wanted to say hello and see you—it's been so long since Christmas."

As if they had any idea, Nora thought.

～

She was relieved to hear the village carriage driver who'd brought them to the farm would retrieve them in a few hours. Still, that left plenty of time for the men to come in from the fields and meet them.

Mal, of course, they had met before, though not in his natural state of sweat-sheened brow and labor-bent back, clad in rough, patched clothes. He was gracious, though, far more than Nora, and Erik was fine, though not as mannered or well groomed as he had been when he'd met Nora's father.

Bette seemed rather intrigued, but also wary of getting close. Nora wanted to pull her cousin aside and beg her to take her back with them. But she bit her tongue and tried to avoid looking at anyone. Secretly, and shamefully, she was glad Marie's girls were already napping; Kirsten wouldn't wake them until Nora's people left.

When they finally did, Nora went straight upstairs and shut herself inside the spare room. She wondered what they would tell her father, what she looked like now to those who used to know her best.

～

She remained on edge for the next few days, and Kirsten seemed rather nervy, too, as if equally afraid they might come back. She seemed to blame Nora for their intrusion, despite how abundantly clear it was that she hadn't welcomed their presence either.

She thought that was why Kirsten carped at her and Marie when she saw them pop a few stray Concord grapes in their mouths one afternoon. The girls were upstairs again, asleep, while the women stripped fruit stems in preparation for making Kirsten's peerless jelly.

All summer long, when the kitchen garden crops were at their most profuse, the women had canned various produce. Whole tomatoes, pickled cucumbers, corn relish. It involved as much boiling water and steam as laundry day, but had to be done in the close, hot confines of the kitchen.

This step was pleasant, though, washing and picking through the grapes out on the porch, where a faint breeze stirred. It seemed harmless to snack on a few as they went, and impossible to resist. When Marie spat out another few minuscule seeds, Kirsten said, "If you're going to eat half the fruit before we cook it, then what's the point? I won't get three good jars. Why don't you go do something else?"

Marie shrank as if physically struck, and Nora furrowed her brow at Kirsten, whose hands seemed to be shaking slightly.

In a soft voice, Nora said, "I noticed some weeds in the cabbage when I walked by earlier."

Her poor, sweet sister-in-law nodded and slunk off the porch to go into the garden. Nora continued picking through her own vast bowl of grapes without eating any more.

After a moment, Kirsten said, "I wonder that you can even speak to her without your tongue bursting into flame."

Nora looked up, alarmed, and saw Kirsten trembling all over. She felt a similar tremor start in her own limbs.

When Kirsten rose and carried her mixing bowl of grapes into the kitchen, Nora understood that she should run as far as she could in the opposite direction, but instead, she picked up her own grapes and followed.

"You're shameless," Kirsten said as she thunked her bowl down on the counter and took up a wooden spoon to begin crushing fruit. "You've barely been here a year—though God knows it feels far longer than that—and look what you've done. You think other people don't see it? Don't know what you are?"

Nora held tightly to her bowl and tried to breathe normally.

"Your own family knows now, too," Kirsten said, with something bordering on satisfaction, spoon driving down and splashing bright-purple juice up onto her wrists. "A full half hour they sat on that porch and I had to pretend I couldn't fathom where you might be, or what you might be up to."

"I was sketching."

Kirsten scoffed and turned to lunge; Nora recoiled, but Kirsten only grabbed her bowl and yanked it from her hands.

"You're a whore, and I knew that from the first time Euan wrote about you—a *doctor*. Going to the men's school, prodding a bunch of men's bodies. Thinking you could do whatever you wanted."

As frightened as Nora was, she still nearly choked on scornful outrage.

"Mal felt sorry for you," Kirsten sneered. "He couldn't see the truth. He worried, about what might happen to you—as if you were some poor, helpless thing. He wrote to you like your life depended on it."

"It did," Nora said.

"I suppose you liked the attention. Having him in your thrall. Just like Euan before him. And now Marie and Erik too. You almost fooled me, even. Because Mal was happy—I have to admit that. For a time, at least. But you weren't ever cut out for this life, and you don't even have the decency to lie in the bed you made. Which shouldn't be a surprise, considering how you gave up everything else you were so invested in. You lose interest and you abandon a whole life, don't you?"

Nora couldn't defend herself, and didn't try.

Kirsten sighed. "If it were any other man, I might say he deserved it. For being foolish enough to marry you. But Malcolm Colquhoun is the kindest person God has ever put on this earth, and he's only ever been punished for it."

When she turned abruptly away, Nora stared in wonder at the rigidity of her narrow shoulders. "You love him."

"Of course I love him," Kirsten answered. "He's been a brother to me. And a keeper. And a helpmate. And a best friend. He's been everything."

"But not a husband," Nora said, not quite meaning to be cruel.

Kirsten's thin shoulders and neck tensed, and twitched, and the hitching, strangled breaths that escaped her as she tried to stifle her tears were horrifying.

"I'm sorry."

Kirsten whirled back around, her gray eyes almost silver with their sheen of tears. "Don't apologize to *me*. I wouldn't forgive you anyway."

Nora nodded, swallowed against her rising fear and guilt. "Mal would, though. Even if you told him. So—"

"I wouldn't dare. I expect he knows already—though I hope he doesn't. The real question is, what will *you* do?"

"I'll stop. I will."

"So what?" With a bitter exhale, Kirsten turned back around and began mashing grapes again, though without her former vigor. "It's too late to undo anything. You ought to leave—you and the devil's own, slink off in the dead of night together. You'd manage, I'm sure. And so would we. Malcolm would be devastated, of course; Marie too. But— they'd manage."

Now Nora scoffed. "And you'd be there for both of them? With your cold, scrawny old shoulders to cry on?" She knew she was being wretched, but Kirsten had been too—and now that Nora knew why, knew that the woman had hated her before they'd ever met, when she had not yet deserved it, she felt her insides glow with anger. Her voice was calm, though, when she said, "Maybe you're the one who should go. Has it ever occurred to you that you've overstayed your welcome? You're what now? Fifty?"

"Forty-two."

Just one year younger than Mal, then. Nora went on, "Old enough that you'll start to be a burden soon. You're lucky Marie brought children with her, or you'd hardly have an excuse to stay. With the boys grown and gone."

"With Euan *dead*, because of you!" Kirsten spun to face Nora again. "You and all your kind, making him think this life wasn't good enough for him."

"It wasn't!"

At that, the basement door thumped, and both women gasped and turned toward it. When nothing more happened, Nora looked back at Kirsten, who raised her sharp chin. "Well, thank God I did stay. Marie's a sweet soul, but she can't take care of those girls alone, much less manage a household. Especially not this one. And *you*—besides being faithless, you don't have a truly kind bone in your body."

"Says the woman with a skeleton carved of ice."

"Oh, that's very clever. Clever is one thing you are, I'll grant you. And crafty. But I hope you're washing yourself out with vinegar, because you're certainly not cut out to care for a family. You leave and everything will go back to normal, soon enough. But do you have any idea how quickly things would fall apart without me here?"

Nora felt the back of her neck prickle at the thought of the cellar beneath their feet. But there was a lock, and salt, and she made herself sound braver than she felt when she said, "Please, *go*. I'll hire a nanny—and a cook, and a cleaner if I have to. Send the laundry out."

"With what money? Generous as Malcolm is, I don't think he'd allow all that. And he does have *some* say. And some sense."

Nora turned on her heel, strode upstairs to Euan's room, rummaged in the back of the closet where she'd socked away all her father's money; in fact, the wad of bills and weight of coins had grown so cumbersome that she'd stuffed it into an old stocking to contain it. She took it back downstairs and thrust it at Kirsten.

She looked at the lumpy stocking like it was a freshly filled chamber pot. "What is that?"

"Money," Nora said. "*Mine*. I thought I had no use for it, but now I do. Take it." She tried to shove it into Kirsten's gnarled, juice-spattered hand. "There's enough for a train ticket to wherever you want to go. And plenty left over—to buy a house of your own, or whatever you want. You can rent an apartment in Paris. Start a vegetable stand. Found an orphanage. Live your *own* life, however you want. Wherever you want. Just—far away from here."

She knew, of course, that Kirsten's life was there—that she wanted to be nowhere else, only wanted Nora gone from it.

Kirsten turned her back. "You don't need to buy my silence—I told you, I wouldn't be so cruel as to tell Mal the truth."

"I don't care about that," Nora lied. "But *this* . . . I can't stand to live here with you anymore, and I'm not going anywhere. Mal wants me here. He loves me. You didn't even know me, and—you've been a horrid old witch to me since the beginning. I'm *sick* of it." She stepped close enough to place the money-stuffed stocking on the counter by Kirsten's elbow.

She weighed and measured her next words, knowing they were barbaric, but feeling they were also necessary. Lowering her voice, Nora said, "I think Mal's a little sick of you too. Or haven't you noticed, the way he grits his teeth sometimes when he answers you? Usually after another complaint, or another criticism. Haven't you seen the way his shoulders tense when you talk? Of course you haven't seen the way he relaxes when you leave a room."

Having delivered that dose of poison, she stepped back and watched Kirsten's own shoulders tense in response, and then begin to shake. And though Nora took no satisfaction in having made her cry—again—she did feel slightly better, in a thoroughly awful way. Like a wild animal that had lashed out to defend itself as violently as necessary.

But an animal wouldn't feel guilt for it. A monster might, Nora supposed. That seemed as good a word for her as any.

CHAPTER
THIRTY-FOUR

Hoosick Falls, NY
September–October 1887

Nora half expected to find the stocking on her dining chair, or on the dresser or the desk in Euan's room. But it didn't reappear, so she could only assume that Kirsten had pocketed it. Or maybe she'd thrown it down the cesspit, or in the pond. Because she was still there, every morning when Nora woke and held her breath as she came downstairs.

They stopped speaking to each other, and Nora resumed her old practice of sequestering herself from Erik, which was surprisingly easy, though she sensed his agitation was even greater than before. Now that she knew he'd gone upstairs while she and Mal were in Manhattan, she began to fear—again—that he might accost her in the house, if only to demand to know what was going on.

But it should be clear enough; she'd told him it would end. He didn't need to know that Kirsten had guessed their secret, or that Nora had tried to drive her away, and failed. Or that her money was gone—for Erik surely knew it existed. It undoubtedly fueled his fantasies of absconding with Nora.

And Kirsten didn't need to know that her refusal to cede ground rankled Nora, twisted her intestines into snarls and made her seriously think of draining her bottle of laudanum, to soothe her nerves past the point of ever feeling anything again.

It might be best, she thought. Mal might be devastated—so might Marie, and even Erik—but they could continue on. And Erik couldn't follow her, wherever she went.

The thing that stopped her wasn't guilt, or concern for any of them, but the paralyzing fear that she might not in fact be freed. That she might open her eyes and stand up from bed, or the forest floor, and look back to see her own body still lying there.

~

Kirsten's own attrition was mostly silent, but on a Saturday not quite two weeks after their hideous confrontation in the kitchen, she paused at breakfast and said, "It would have been Euan's birthday today. His twenty-fifth."

It seemed to surprise everyone, save the twins. Nora felt her throat close and her eyes fill. She had, of course, been conscious of the date already, and was certain that Mal had been too.

"I suppose he would have been a doctor by now," Kirsten continued, gazing at her eggs. "Married, maybe. With a child, even."

"Kirsten," Mal said, his tone a mix of disbelief and warning.

She ignored him, looked up at Nora. "Did you ever talk about names you liked? If it had been a boy—"

"Enough," Mal said.

Even Nora flinched. Her fork clattered against her plate as her tears spilled over and she pushed back her chair. She rushed from the room and ran upstairs, slammed the door of the spare bedroom behind her, then grabbed the abalone box from the mantel, so she could place it on the bed beside her, where she curled up to cry. She heard raised voices below—Mal's, and Kirsten's—but only briefly, and too muffled to discern any words.

∽

Whatever had been said, Kirsten didn't apologize that evening, nor did anyone else mention what had happened at breakfast. Nora went to bed early, and alone, thinking of Mal across the hall, wishing she could join him, wishing that he wanted her to.

If he had, she reminded herself, he could have knocked.

∽

And then, he did. Nora didn't trust the soft tapping at first, until it came again, and then Mal's low, soft voice speaking her name.

She rose and opened the door to her husband, so kind and somber and ill treated. She felt overwhelmed with love and shame. Her face crumpled, though she didn't mean to let it. Nor did she mean to let Mal hold her, but when he reached out, Nora stepped closer and leaned into his broad, warm body.

He pressed his lips against her hair. "I miss you."

Nora shook and held him tighter. When she finally managed to curb her tears, she tilted up her face to kiss him, and they moved back across the hall to their room.

They undressed efficiently, and Nora gently pushed him back upon the mattress, held him there with her palms against his chest as she climbed astride his hips. "Please," she said, and whether or not he knew what she meant, he didn't try to move her beneath him, or close his eyes.

She took Mal's hands and pressed his palms against her breasts, and rolled her pelvis against his, seeking only friction for the time being, seeking to build herself up against him. She bent over to kiss him, her hair falling in a curtain around his face.

She had a disconcerting image of herself as a succubus—and her husband's almost stricken expression might have been fear, or pain, but she knew that features twisted in strangely similar ways when one suffered nearly unbearable pleasure. When Mal sat up to kiss her again, it exorcised all Nora's fear, and all her guilt, if only for a short while.

∼

When she woke cuddled close beside him and he smiled and said good morning, Nora's heart fractured in both pleasure and pain.

"I love you," she said.

He said it back, and she felt undeservedly reprieved.

Far more so than she did at church later that morning, though she did take part in the silent confession, and prayed fervently for forgiveness. It couldn't hurt.

At home, she strove to treat Kirsten no differently than she had before—to behave neither more obsequiously nor more imperiously. She would show her that, despite Kirsten's victory the other morning, Nora could not be defeated. But that she was willing to live in harmony for the foreseeable future, or at least without further discord.

What did change was her relationship with Mal, who seemed unduly grateful to have Nora back. He told her one night that he was sorry.

"For what?" she asked; she took his face in her hands and kissed him. "You've done nothing but be wonderful."

It wasn't that she forgot all the private disappointments and criticisms that she had stored up against him, but that they seemed petty and childishly unfair now.

Yet, for once, he insisted on being heard. "I shouldn't have told you—"

"About what? Kitty? I asked, and it doesn't matter—I realize you had a whole life before me."

"No," he said, "I didn't. And I didn't mean that . . . her. I shouldn't have told you that I felt guilty—that was never your fault."

Nora's throat was too tight to say anything: that she knew he couldn't help it, that she'd always wanted to know the truth.

"And that isn't all I feel," Mal went on. "I feel inordinately lucky, and absolutely terrified, and I want you to be happy—not just be taken care of. I want you to know that I love you."

"I do," Nora said, and kissed him again as tears filled her eyes. "I do."

~

And, crucially, Mal seemed determined to let Nora love him, too. Things weren't wildly different, but he didn't hold so much of himself back when they lay together, which still wasn't often, but was more than enough, Nora told herself. More than she deserved.

He made more time for her, or gave more time to her, during the days as well, easier now that summer's relentless grind had slowed with the advent of fall. He asked if she cared to join him for walks or wanted company on her own excursions, and Nora was surprised by the intensity of tender gratitude she felt for the question alone. She always said yes.

She should have felt entirely tarnished, worthless with the sins she'd committed, but the way that Mal looked at her and how he treated her made Nora feel like some newly discovered treasure. She only wished her happiness wasn't underscored by regret and shame along with grief—but at least the happiness itself was there, and bright.

Some nights, when Marie cranked the phonograph in the parlor, Mal offered Nora his hand and danced her about the room, turning back time to the husking bee.

Kirsten couldn't stand it, and went upstairs to bed with the twins in tow.

Erik didn't like it, either, and stopped coming inside except for meals, which made Nora even happier and more hopeful, that he might finally give up and leave. Marie would be sad, but he'd been right; she wouldn't stay that way for long, not for good.

~

Nora was genuinely pleased that her father was due to visit for her and Malcolm's first wedding anniversary, when the beautiful blaze of the forest canopy would be most impressive too.

He had arranged to stay at the Burnses' for a few days, and they'd insisted on hosting an anniversary dinner. Nora looked forward to that as well—confident that neither Erik nor Kirsten would come.

And indeed, on the second-to-last Saturday of October, after they finished milking, washed up, and changed into finer clothes, only Mal and Nora and Marie set out for town. Axel rode along but planned to skip the celebratory dinner.

~

At the Burnses' house, Nora discovered that it was more of a small party; several Hoosick Falls acquaintances had been invited, including Grace and Benjamin Murphy, who had left their children with Grace's mother.

A month ago, Nora would have been frightfully surprised and irrationally annoyed, but now she was all smiles and profuse apologies for not having seen her friend in so long. And Grace, who seemed somewhat reserved at first, soon warmed and smiled back and said she hadn't seen Nora look so well in some time. She leaned closer to murmur in a lower register, "Nor Malcolm, for that matter."

As was so often the case now, Nora's happiness brought with it the threat of tears—but she managed not to let them fall, and hoped they only enhanced the sparkle in her eyes.

~

They returned home to a dark, quiet house, but brought their own light inside and upstairs.

In the morning, they discovered Axel already in the barn. Nora wondered what lonely time of night or day he'd walked home. After milking, he stayed behind to finish watering the animals while the rest of them filed inside to find the dining room empty, the table bare of plates.

Only then did Nora notice the profound silence of the house.

Marie darted back to the kitchen and returned to report it empty, the stove still cold. "She must be sick."

Mal stopped her from rushing for the stairs and traded a worried glance with Nora. "Er, Marie—would you mind putting on some coffee, please?"

Erik dropped himself into a dining chair and grimaced; he seemed not hungover but still somewhat drunk. "Yeah, and see what's left from last night. I could eat a goddamn horse."

"Language," Marie murmured, but after a moment's hesitation, said, "All right."

While she headed back toward the kitchen, Mal and Nora went wordlessly toward the stairs. A flutter of panic unsettled Nora's insides. Kirsten never slept in, even when she was under the weather, and it would take true disaster to keep her down on a Sunday morning.

She stood behind Mal as he tapped softly on Kirsten's ever-closed bedroom door.

When there was no answer, he knocked a little harder, said Kirsten's name, asked if she was feeling all right.

Nora felt certain that there was no one in the room—then thought it might be entirely possible that Kirsten's body was still abed, her spirit sundered and released to heaven. She didn't believe Kirsten would ever harm herself; she was too pious, too desirous of being reunited with her husband and son. But she could have had a stroke, or a heart attack, some acute ailment brought on by stress and heartache. Which would still be Nora's fault.

When Mal opened the door, however, the room was empty, the bed neatly made, a key ring and two envelopes placed upon it. One, with Axel's name on it, was much thicker. The other, thinner one was blank. Nora clenched her fists to keep herself from snatching both. Mal frowned and picked up the envelopes, tucked Axel's into his pocket and opened the other.

Nora held her breath as he scanned it. When he said, "I don't believe it," her stomach flipped.

"What is it?"

"She's left. I didn't think—it hasn't been that bad, has it? I know I was a little short with her—"

"It isn't your fault," Nora said, and calmly took the letter when he offered it.

She skimmed the words, and though her own name wasn't among them, she felt it hidden behind every phrase: *perhaps it is no longer my place.* The last sentence Kirsten wrote was: *So I will move on.*

She'd left no indication where.

Nora began to follow Mal back downstairs to tell Axel, but then remembered the girls. Kirsten usually got them up and dressed just before serving breakfast, once the bulk of cooking was done.

For a moment, Nora wondered if they might be gone too. But they were abed, and she only had to look for a moment to be certain that Bea and Addie were still breathing.

~

Since they were asleep, Nora went to help Marie in the kitchen. They made eggs and griddle cakes; that would have to be enough for Erik.

Mal returned to apprise them of certain key details contained in Axel's letter. Kirsten told her brother that she was striking out for some new place without knowing precisely where and would write as soon as she had settled.

Nora had been the one to suggest it—though *suggest* was far too gentle a word for what she'd done—yet it boggled her mind as much as it plainly boggled everyone else's, that Kirsten had actually gone.

She felt no relief. Instead, her stomach was leaden, her throat parched, her entire body hot, even before Mal privately told her that he'd glimpsed money in Axel's envelope. Kirsten's wool and butter money, he'd surmised. Axel had saddled Aggie and ridden off to the village to try and intercept his sister, to speak to her in person at least.

Belatedly, Nora realized that her father expected to see her in the village, after church—but there was no chance of going. Mal asked if he should ride in and let him know, but she said he'd surely hear soon enough, and would have Dr. Burns bring him out as soon as he did. She didn't want Mal to leave, the fear of being left alone with Erik overriding any worry about what her father might think when they failed to appear.

She and Marie left the dishes for later. Under the circumstances, Nora told herself, it was a reasonable slipping of routine, not proof of Kirsten's prophecy that everything would fall apart if she left.

They roused the twins after clearing the table, and Nora entertained fantasies of Axel trotting Aggie up the lane with Kirsten clinging to his waist, returned to her senses, and her proper place.

It might be no more than a cry for help of sorts—Kirsten might want to be pursued and entreated to return. To know that she would be missed, and was needed. Perhaps Nora should have told Mal to go after her.

If Kirsten did come back, she thought, then she would apologize, profusely. Even though she'd said no end of unforgivable things—but so had Kirsten.

They could count themselves even, Nora thought, rather desperately. She'd naively assumed that they already had.

CHAPTER THIRTY-FIVE

Hoosick Falls, NY
October 1887

Nora's father and Dr. Burns arrived in late morning, by which time the girls were becoming agitated. They knew something was different, she supposed, that Kirsten was missing, though she and Marie had kept their routine as intact as possible.

It felt to Nora like she and Mal both tried to downplay their surprise at Kirsten's departure. They recounted what the note had said—that she was moving on to someplace else, that it finally felt like time to do so.

Dr. Burns seemed astonished but rather tickled by the idea. Nora's father wasn't worried, not knowing Kirsten. "People do upend their lives," he said, with a grin at Nora. "Just look at you, eh, hen?"

She hoped she looked less ashen than she felt.

Axel returned from town to report that no one had seen his sister. The consensus was that she had likely gone another way, not wanting to be noticed. She must have set off through the woods, toward another nearby hamlet where she would be less likely to be recognized. Axel headed north next, in his quest to track her down.

With apologies, Nora suggested that her father return to the village; he was disappointed, but understanding. "I'll come back tomorrow. Things should have settled down a bit by then."

Nora hoped so.

~

At the afternoon meal, Erik was the only one who still seemed unconcerned.

"Honestly, I'm surprised she stayed as long as she did," he said, with a flick of his eyes at Mal, who ignored him, and barely ate.

When Axel finally returned from inquiring in nearby towns, with no sign of Kirsten, his anxiety had taken on a greater shade of fear. "Something could have happened," he said. "I searched the woods as best I could, but we should call in more men."

"It seems a bit early for that," said Mal, though he sounded uncertain. "I highly doubt anything would have happened—"

"A twisted ankle, even," Axel interrupted. "She could be out there trying to crawl back home in need of help."

"Let's not assume the worst. But even if that happened, it's not getting all that cold at night yet. She won't have been without food and water for more than a few hours—there's no need to panic. I'll saddle up Jasper—we'll all go out, cover more ground that way."

So they did, and Nora was relieved that Erik went with them, though her nerves were still frayed, by the anxious waiting, by the twins' increasing restlessness, by Marie's fretting.

"It's not like her," she kept saying, and it was all Nora could do to stop from snapping that Marie had no idea what Kirsten was really like.

~

They tried to feed the girls, but they knocked food and forks to the floor, and uttered combative sounds through tightly closed lips. When

Adelaide began abruptly vomiting after Marie nudged a boiled egg toward her, Beatrice began shrieking, hands clapped over her ears, eyes shut tight. Nora had to stifle a scream herself.

Attempting to comfort the girls only seemed to make matters worse; when Marie or Nora touched their tiny shoulders, they drew violently away.

A superstitious observer might have thought them possessed, but Nora knew that was ridiculous. They were only distressed, though greatly so. "Where are the medicines?"

"Kirsten's room," Marie said, her voice wobbling on the edge of tears.

"I'll see what I can find," Nora said, and dashed upstairs.

It felt transgressive stepping into Kirsten's room again, going through her things, but there was no other choice. All Nora had was her unopened bottle of laudanum, which she preferred not to resort to. A ginger tonic might soothe Addie's stomach, if Nora could get her to swallow it.

In Kirsten's closet, she found a basket of bottles and vials and jars. Ointments, liniments, pain relievers; nostrums, cordials, and patent elixirs with no powers beyond the placebo; cough syrup that was almost pure morphine. That would certainly work, though the magnitude of the girls' outburst made Nora doubt she could force a sedative past their jaws even if she wanted to.

And as she had that thought, she picked up a bottle of laudanum. Nora couldn't imagine Kirsten taking the drug herself, but the bottle was half empty.

They used to squirm and scream, she remembered Mal saying of the girls. And Erik had spoken of how, as infants, they'd shrieked themselves hoarse, cried constantly. They'd come a long way with Kirsten's care.

Could they have been transformed so dramatically by nothing more than Kirsten's firm yet caring oversight? Nora thought of her leash system, how Kirsten had claimed the twins might otherwise dart into the street—yet she had never seen them move any faster than a shuffle.

Because she's been drugging them, she thought, the fact so immediately clear and obvious that Nora felt humiliated for never having seen it before.

Their unfocused eyes and often slack jaws, the way they moved as if through deep water or a dream. Some of it might have been their nature, but when Kirsten came to dress them in the mornings and when she put them down for afternoon naps, and then again for bed, she must have been administering at least a few drops of laudanum to keep them quiet and pliable, make them no trouble.

Nora felt another scream rising in her chest, but choked it down.

She gripped the laudanum bottle in one hand, a bottle of stomach bitters in the other, and went downstairs, leaving Kirsten's door wide open.

~

Despite the twins' wriggling bodies and lashing limbs, they were small and slight, easy enough to remove from the sullied table and deposit in the parlor, where Nora and Marie managed to strip Bea's soiled dress as well.

Then they stepped back and let the twins wail and rock.

"They'll calm down eventually," Nora said. Even if it was only sheer exhaustion that did it.

She knew they would be thirsty too; they drank great quantities of water in general, so she briefly left the parlor to prepare two glasses, with modest measures of laudanum.

It was for their own good, of course—which must have been what Kirsten told herself, just like Nora's father had, and which was absolutely true; it was certainly better than strapping them down to their beds. But Nora couldn't deny that it was also for her own peace, for the entire household's. She knew that it would work, and was duty-bound to make them as comfortable as possible, expeditiously.

Still, she hesitated once the girls' screams and tears subsided, aware that she was medicating them against not acute symptoms still presenting but the threat of their reoccurrence.

A valid practice, too, Nora reassured herself, and set the glasses on the floor in front of them, then watched them gulp down every drop of laudanum-infused water.

~

By the time the men returned, with no news to share, the girls were calm, in their beds for their afternoon nap, if a little early, and Nora and Marie had cobbled together a quick meal. Deceitful though it felt, Nora decided they shouldn't mention the girls' episode; there was already enough for the others to fret about. So the table discussion centered on Kirsten's likely whereabouts, and whether they should report her missing—which was Axel's idea, though Erik and Mal both thought it unnecessary.

She'd left a note, after all, explicitly outlining her intention to move on, and promised to write as soon as she could. It was shocking, perhaps, that she had taken such a drastic and uncharacteristic step, but she was a levelheaded and capable woman whose decision seemed to have been a long time in the making, regardless of the fact that none of them had had any notion. Nora shifted in her seat and felt her face flush.

"But why do it in the dead of night?" Axel asked.

"She didn't want to be dissuaded," Mal said.

It might not have been the dead of night, Nora thought. It could have been at any point after the rest of them had left for the anniversary dinner in the village. Except, of course, Erik hadn't gone with them. She glanced at him but kept quiet.

Axel continued to fret. He'd said more in that one day than on all the others during which Nora had known him—though she supposed she didn't know him, really.

She was somewhat surprised at the depth of his concern; his habitual distance seemed to separate him even from his sister. But Kirsten had brought Axel to the farm, away from a bad situation in Troy, if Grace's gossip was correct. Of course he cared for her.

And of course Nora hadn't spared a single thought for Axel when she'd pushed Kirsten toward the idea of leaving, in hopes of making more room for herself.

~

After supper, while she and Marie washed dishes, Nora felt a skin-creeping consciousness of the padlocked cellar door to her side—and of what other things might indeed fall apart without Kirsten.

Nora could keep Kirsten's physical protections in place, but had no chance of matching her prayers. What if they were necessary to keep Olaf's spirit corralled?

She'd barely thought of him since reuniting with Mal, which had given her a greater sense of protection from Erik too. She had blithely forgotten to be afraid of spirits or of curses, but she sensed that—suddenly, and irrevocably, and thanks to all her own evildoings—everything had shifted again.

~

That night, she and Mal held each other for comfort. Nora listened to the house breathe around them. She slept poorly and woke often—both within her dreams and eventually without.

In the morning, she was alarmed to find that Mal had already risen without waking her. Judging by the light, he would already be in the barn.

As Nora dressed, she realized it was wash day. She had no intention of attempting to tackle that chore yet. On her way past the girls' room, she paused. She would bring them more doctored water as soon as she finished the milking, but perhaps she should do it now.

She doubted they would wake, much less get up, while everyone else was in the barn, but it seemed better not to chance it. She fetched Kirsten's laudanum, then turned back and opened the twins' door.

Nora started at the sight of Marie standing at the foot of their narrow beds, having assumed that she too would be in the barn—and then, just as Nora was about to speak, she realized that the figure was far too tall and thin to be Marie.

"Kirsten?"

No sooner had another wave of knee-weakening relief washed over Nora than she felt strangely unnerved again. Kirsten's clothes and hair were soaking wet, her sodden skirts hanging heavily around her ankles. Thin hanks of silvery hair slipped from her usual neatly braided and pinned-up style and shed more water down her shoulders.

Frowning, Nora glanced toward the gap in the curtains to confirm that it wasn't raining. When she looked back to ask what had happened, and where she'd been, she saw that the floor around Kirsten's feet—like the hallway itself, in fact—was completely dry.

Nora held her breath and backed up a stealthy step, but the floorboard creaked beneath her boot.

Kirsten's ghost turned far faster than any living human could have. One second, her drenched back was to Nora, and in the very next, her ashen, water-beaded face with its cold gray eyes was pointed at her.

Nora only managed a choked syllable of a scream, and nearly stumbled as she hurried backward through the door, fearing that the spirit would be upon her in the space of another blink. Kirsten's mouth opened a fraction of an inch, as if she might try to speak, but there was no sound, not even the lowest moan. The expression on her face—*its* face—was more sorrowful than stern. It—*she*—seemed confused.

Nora should have stood firm, or dropped to her knees to beg forgiveness as she'd planned, ask her—*Dear God, what happened?* She should have at least stayed to make sure that the girls were safe, but she turned her back on Kirsten's specter and ran.

~

Downstairs, Nora left the front door gaping and pelted across the yard, burst into the barn, startling everyone. Cows sidestepped, two of the horses spooked in their stalls, several cats scattered and hissed.

Mal rose immediately. "What's wrong?"

Nora didn't know what to say. She couldn't tell the truth. None of them, save Marie, would even believe her. But she couldn't keep quiet either.

She looked from Mal to Axel to Erik to Marie and back again, said, "I think . . . we need to check the pond."

"The pond?" Axel said, at the same time that Mal asked, "Why?"

Marie looked concerned. Erik, in the brief second that Nora spared a glance, seemed strangely wary.

Axel started for the barn door and ordered the dog back, but Nora followed, as did Mal.

"You stay here," she heard Erik tell Marie. "I'm not doin' all the damn milkin' alone."

"Nora," Mal said, as they hurried along after Axel, "what's this about?"

She shook her head, didn't look at him. "I just—I had a dream." When he began to protest, she cut in: "It felt so real. We should have checked there, anyway."

It should have been the first place they looked, in fact; but none of them had thought that Kirsten might harm herself, especially since she'd left letters that spoke of an earthly future. Maybe that was why, Nora thought, because she didn't want them to worry, or find her.

She and Mal both lagged behind Axel. When they reached the clearing, he was wading into the pond, not having paused even to take off his boots.

They shouted his name, called for him to come back, to wait—but he didn't listen.

At its deepest, the pond was perhaps eight feet, and its bottom was covered in vegetation. Nora watched Axel draw in a breath and duck under the water. She already knew, in the hollow pit of her stomach, what he would find.

~

It was horrifying to behold, but even worse to witness the others' shock and despair. Axel broke the surface of the pond and sucked in a breath that was also a sob. When Mal realized what he was seeing—his sister-in-law's limp body, heavy head dangling on a seemingly boneless neck, bedraggled tendrils of hair trailing in the water—he uttered a weak, low noise.

"Oh, Jesus," he said, and went forward to meet Axel, his boots gaining purchase on the slippery bottom, his face wet with water and tears.

Nora focused on the tips of Kirsten's fingers as they rose above the water. For a brief moment, they kissed the shining surface, like she was gingerly touching a mirror, seeking an intimation of what was on the other side.

And then they separated, her body and its reflection pulling away from one another one final time. A moment later, Axel gently placed her in the reedy grass. He and Mal both crouched alongside, and Nora looked behind her, half expecting Kirsten's dripping ghost to come gliding out of the whispering trees.

CHAPTER
THIRTY-SIX

Hoosick Falls, NY
October 1887

"It might have been an accident," Mal said, softly.

Axel rejected it outright. "She was in the goddamn *middle*." He thrust his hand into one of his sister's pockets to pull out a rock—then another, and another, and more from the opposite side.

He piled them in a cairn beside her body, let them speak for themselves. By then, he was weeping too hard to talk anyway.

When he could manage to draw a few hitching breaths to form words, they were: "Why *now*?" And he looked fiercely at Nora, who braced herself for an accusation, though none came.

She looked into the trees again—for the ghost that wasn't there. She should go check on the girls, but she felt compelled to stay, to look again at Kirsten, having run from her once already, from some other version of her.

Nora gingerly approached and crouched near Mal.

Kirsten had been dead for at least a day, Nora thought. Why, then, had her ghost only just appeared that morning? Had her newly shelled spirit taken time to gather its strength, pull itself together from the ether? Or had it lingered here by the pond, trying to make sense of what had happened?

There was no sign of the spirit now; it must have stayed behind at the house. However unnerving it had been to see, Nora felt certain that Kirsten's ghost would not hurt Bea or Addie, if it was even capable of such a thing.

But if the girls woke up, and their last dose of laudanum had worn off, would they see Kirsten? Would they be terrified, or comforted?

Nora took note of Kirsten's swollen fingers, leeched of color and heavily wrinkled from long submersion. Kirsten's face was pale gray, including her cloudy eyes and parted lips, which made her look almost like a figure formed from damp clay. There was some marbling where the blood had pooled in her veins. Nora frowned and reached for the collar of Kirsten's dress—the purple shadows there looked strange.

Axel pushed her hand away, but her troubled expression must have given him pause, for he looked back down at his sister and tentatively folded aside her collar himself. "What is that?" he asked. "Are those finger marks?"

"I'm not sure," Nora said, and glanced at Mal. "They could be."

Mal frowned and shook his head. "From whom?"

Erik, she thought, and wondered if Axel did too.

But he said, "Anybody could be passing through these woods," and shot up to his full height as he looked wildly around. "They might have robbed her—she had money—and then tried to hide her body."

Nora felt her own panic rising, along with a fresh surge of guilt. She tried to say that the marks might not be anything unusual, simply evidence of livor mortis, but Axel cut her off with renewed ferocity:

"Wait—why did you say we should come here and check the pond in the first place? How did *you* know?"

Nora could only repeat her earlier lie, even knowing how insubstantial it would sound. "I had a dream."

"*No*—you *knew.* And you must have known yesterday, but you didn't say anything then. *Why?* Because you—"

"Stop," Mal interjected. Though he barely raised his voice, it carried the full weight of his authority. "I know this is upsetting, but we can all see what happened here. Please don't make it worse by saying something you can't take back."

Axel, his massive shoulders beginning to shake again with sobs, dropped back into a crouch beside his sister and clutched his head in his hands.

"We'll have to get Dr. Burns," Nora murmured to Malcolm. "Or my father. He can examine her and see if . . ."

To her surprise, Mal turned a look of impatience upon her. "This was no crime." He pushed himself up to stand.

Nora rose, too, lowered her voice. "Probably not. But we should make absolutely sure. They can see if there's any water in her lungs. If there is, then—"

"We're not cutting her open," Mal said, loud enough in his vehemence for Axel to hear.

"She had money," Axel said again. "She left me half—she said in the letter she'd been saving up, but she took the rest, for train tickets and food and whatever else. She wouldn't have done that if she meant to kill herself, would she? And where is it?"

He'd emptied her pockets already.

Nora wondered, with a sick sense of dread, if the money might now be in Erik's possession. But if so, then why would he remain on the farm?

Because he doesn't have you yet, she thought, and shuddered.

Meanwhile, Axel stood and splashed in the pond again, deaf to Mal's entreaties to stop and come back.

He dove down once, then again, and came back up with a valise, which he brought onto dry land and set beside his sister's body. When he opened the case and dug through the upper layer of sodden clothes, he found a small satchel, full of money.

Nora was surprised, and strangely crestfallen not to have more fuel for her wild suspicions.

Axel looked defeated.

"There," Mal said, his voice gentle and frayed. "She did this to herself. And she deserves our respect, and our forgiveness. Let's take her home."

~

Axel walked at a plodding pace, his sister's bony, broken form cradled in his arms. Mal carried Kirsten's valise. Nora went empty-handed, eyes full of tears. She hurried ahead as they neared the house, intending to fetch a quilt in which they could wrap Kirsten—but as she passed by the cabin, she saw Kirsten's ghost on the farmhouse porch.

Afraid to approach any closer, Nora went back to the barn to break the news.

Marie was as distraught as she had expected.

Erik seemed strangely flat—not unaffected, but numbed. Grief could do that, Nora knew, and he'd just lost the only mother he'd ever known.

She stole sideways glances at him as she sank onto the dusty, hay-strewn floor and held Marie while she sobbed.

~

Mal fetched the blanket in which Axel wrapped Kirsten's body. After a brief, hushed discussion as to where they should take her—her bed, the parlor, the barn, the springhouse—they simply placed her on the porch. Her pale, sodden spirit stood beside the shrouded form, transfixed. It didn't glance up at Solomon as he stood at the bottom of the steps and barked. It didn't glance up at Nora, either, as she edged past to guide Marie inside.

She led her upstairs, where the girls were awake but still in bed, and Nora didn't hesitate to dose them this time—there was simply no question of risking another outburst with so much else to deal with. Her father, she realized, would turn up soon. Besides, it would be dangerous to simply stop their medicine; she would need to taper the dosage over time.

She did hesitate before offering Marie a laudanum-laced glass, but that seemed suddenly necessary too. And then she sat with her until her sobs faded into something softer, and her breathing slowed, though every second Nora spent on the edge of the mattress made her neck prickle more fiercely, certain that when she looked toward the door, Kirsten would be standing there.

~

The newborn ghost was still on the porch when Nora glanced out the front window downstairs. She lingered in the parlor, knowing she should finish helping with the animals, or go collect eggs, but not wanting to go outside. Not that she was safe indoors.

It was clear that Kirsten had committed suicide, wasn't it? Nora could easily fathom why. Kirsten had lived under a great burden of pain for years. Even now, her brother dug a grave beside the stone that she'd inscribed to mark the boundary between her husband's and son's resting places: *My heart lies here.* It was a wonder that her body hadn't gone to join them sooner.

And yet the letters that she left were not suicide notes, and she had taken half the money—which made it even more absurd to entertain the thought of murder. Why would someone kill her if not to take her things?

Hatred, Nora thought.

But she didn't think anyone had hated Kirsten. Except, perhaps, herself.

Nora thought then of the strange dreams she'd had—in which she'd thought she was awake, but wasn't. She hadn't dreamed at all after the anniversary dinner, though, and she couldn't have followed Kirsten through the night woods to throttle her and sink her corpse.

Not without waking Mal first, or finding some evidence later—her own wet clothes, scratches on her face or hands where Kirsten surely would have fought back.

And the marks on Kirsten's neck were nothing more than normal skin mottling. It would be rash for Nora to suggest otherwise to Dr. Burns or her father—and they were experienced enough to recognize them as suspicious, if indeed they were.

But even if Kirsten had drowned herself, Nora was still responsible. She knew she had hurt her, with her carefully chosen words, and then with her inconsiderate happiness.

She should have remembered that, however stern Kirsten's manner, she had cared for so many of the people that Nora cherished. Nora should have been kind, at least, but instead, she'd done what she'd always done in the face of opposition: bucked and bristled and exerted the force of her own will until she broke whatever barrier she faced.

Yet Kirsten's will was strong, too, and even if her body had been destroyed, her spirit persisted.

∼

Nora's father arrived alone in Dr. Burns's carriage; Angus was seeing patients in town.

He seemed stricken when Nora relayed what had happened, and she watched him perfunctorily examine Kirsten's corpse. When she was able to draw him aside out of anyone else's earshot, she asked if he'd noticed anything strange, or concerning.

His brows knit above his spectacles. "Like what, love?"

Nora swallowed and shook her head. "I just—I never thought she would do such a thing."

Her father sighed and squeezed her arm. "We never know another's true experience. It's often the ones you'd least expect. There was nothing you could have done."

He offered to stay, but Nora suddenly wanted him gone, before this haunted place—cursed or not—had a chance to harm him too.

She promised to write, and wished him a good journey home, and hugged him tight before he left, hoping she would see him again.

∾

She'd lost track of Erik. While she checked on Marie and the girls, Mal went to join Axel in the graveyard. Not wanting to pass by Kirsten again, Nora let herself out of the parlor's french doors and walked up to the edge of the orchard, slowing to listen to the conversation that filtered through.

"Don't you think she would want a church service?" Mal asked.

Axel grunted as he stabbed his shovel into the soft earth beyond the apple trees. "She wouldn't want everybody knowing her business—not that it won't get around anyway. And once it does, they won't even bury her in their consecrated ground. They can go to hell, then."

His voice broke.

Mal stayed silent.

"Unless you want to lie again," Axel finally added. "Make up another sad story for people to tell in town . . ."

Nora frowned, then turned toward a flicker of movement in the corner of her eye, half expecting Erik to have sneaked up behind her.

But it was Kirsten's dripping spirit, now beside a nearby tree, the ground beneath her dry. Thankfully, Nora's gasp was covered by the shovel's scrape and the soft shush of loose dirt cast onto a pile. She backed away and stole inside the farmhouse again.

∾

Her father's examination must have relieved Axel of any worries about foul play, and in town, Dr. Harris would sign a certificate officially confirming the cause of death. Nora was surprised, though, that Axel didn't want to wait even a few more hours for Mal to hammer together a rough casket before the burial.

She let the girls sleep but roused Marie, whose despair had been blunted by the laudanum. Silent tears rolled down her face as freely as the phantom water streamed from Kirsten's ghost, which stood among them, watching its body be interred.

Nora tried not to look at it—at her—and kept a firm grasp on Marie partly for her own benefit. She still felt greatly unnerved by its presence. Even glimpsing Kirsten's ghostly form in her peripheral vision caused an electric ripple of *wrongness* to course through Nora's body; it felt as if someone had wrapped wires around her bones and touched them to a battery. She decided that she would finally administer her own modest dose of laudanum when she went back inside. Not so much that she would lose her wits, but enough that she might relax.

In the spare room, however, she couldn't do it. Her fear of letting down her guard was greater than her fear of total consciousness. At least Kirsten's sodden spirit had remained in the graveyard, standing nearly shoulder to shoulder with her brother, though Axel clearly had no idea.

Solomon, for all his valiant attempts to alert the humans to the presence of an unearthly being, had been tied up inside the barn, where he had finally stopped barking, though occasionally he let out a mournful howl.

∼

Nora dosed the twins—in a smaller measure—again that afternoon, then fed them crushed potatoes and changed them before leaving them once more in bed. Dinner was a sparse affair, which seemed to disgruntle Erik, who saddled Odin and rode off afterward, perhaps in search of a proper meal, or something more to drink. Or simply seeking distance.

Nora wished, vainly, that all the things she'd said to him and her avoidance of him had finally driven him off. Maybe Kirsten's death had been the final piece.

A sacrifice, Nora thought, then rejected the idea, along with the dull hope that Erik wouldn't return.

She and Mal went to bed early and lay awake for a long time. Nora kept thinking of what Axel had said about lying again, making up a story for people to tell, but couldn't bring herself to ask Mal what he meant.

It didn't matter, whatever secrets Malcolm still kept. They couldn't be worse than Nora's own, and wouldn't change how grateful she felt to have him beside her.

CHAPTER
THIRTY-SEVEN

Hoosick Falls, NY
October 1887

She tiptoed through the house the following morning, bracing herself to see Kirsten's ghost around every corner. But it must have remained in the graveyard.

Nora didn't see it at any point between waking and returning to the house after milking, which took longer than usual, since Erik still hadn't returned and Axel moved at half speed.

She'd collected the last two days' worth of eggs and made more griddle cakes to go with them for breakfast.

Nora hadn't expected anyone to call so soon, but the news had already spread through the village and outlying areas. People came bearing pies and chicken casseroles and pots of stew. She was glad to take the food, if only to be spared the burden of cooking, though she had no wish to speak with anyone.

She was surprised that Grace didn't come, and relieved that Kirsten's ghost still stood vigil near the cemetery.

Unless it had gone, though Nora felt it was too reckless to hope so.

~

Nightfall earned them a break in the steady stream of visitors. A spell of rain released the intoxicating scent of wet earth, which Nora normally loved. Now it reminded her too much of the muddy banks of the pond, and the rich dirt of the graveyard.

She listened to the patter on the roof and thought of Kirsten among the apple-laden trees, raindrops falling through her as the pond water rolled forever down her face. Nora cast a thought toward her: *I'm so sorry.*

Knowing, of course, that it was inadequate, having as little impact as those phantom runnels of water that never dampened the ground.

～

But it seemed that Kirsten might have heard her, that the direct thought might have summoned her. For when Nora woke on Wednesday, her sister-in-law's ghost stood in the bedroom, by the mantel.

She gasped and scrambled up to a sitting position, startling Mal. "What is it?"

Nora forced herself to look away from Kirsten and shake her head. "Bad dream," she murmured, and got up to dress.

When she went to give the girls their morning draught, she jumped to see Kirsten's ghost in the corner, watching. The spirit didn't follow Nora to the barn, in that she didn't see Kirsten when she looked over her shoulder—yet when she stepped through those vast doors, Kirsten was already there.

So was Erik, oblivious to the ghost. But Nora thought the nearest cows were more restive than usual. The barn cats, for once, were nowhere to be seen. She missed a more blatantly obvious thing.

"Where's Axel?" Mal asked. "And Solomon?"

"Haven't seen 'em," Erik answered.

"Maybe they went for a walk," Marie sleepily mused.

"Not into the pond, I hope," said Erik.

While Nora started milking, as far from him as possible, Mal climbed into the loft.

"There's no note," he said when he came back down the ladder. "No money, either."

"Hell, Axel's probably been waitin' for the chance to get out of here for years now," Erik said. "You think he stayed for any reason other than Kirsten?"

No one answered, but the absence of the dog, and of all the money that Nora had once pressed upon Kirsten, reassured her that Axel had likely gone elsewhere. Not into death.

Though it occurred to her that Erik could have disposed of them both, could have her savings in his cabin or his coat pocket even now.

For God's sake, stop, she told herself. But gooseflesh roughened her skin.

~

Later that morning, more people arrived with food and condolences. Kirsten's ghost stood in a corner of the parlor while neighbors visited.

Nora wasn't sure if Kirsten listened to them speak of her, or if she could even hear them. She sensed that Kirsten's eyes could see, though, and that they were trained unblinkingly on Nora herself.

Periodically, Nora went upstairs to look in on the girls, whom she had decided should stay in their room, fearing that they might be disturbed by all the unaccustomed company. Marie had readily agreed, though Nora didn't think she would object to any suggestion, subdued as she was.

Kirsten, even when Nora thought she'd left her downstairs, was always in the room when Nora entered; it still made her jump at first, then only made her shudder slightly. While the ghost stood protectively between the headboards of the twins' beds, Nora averted her eyes and told herself that she would ease up on their dosage soon.

As soon as things settled, which, as impossible as it seemed now, they eventually would. People could get used to anything, after enough time. For better or for worse.

~

In the meanwhile, Nora tried to keep her eyes mostly on her own feet, for Kirsten was everywhere she went.

When she drew fresh water from the springhouse pump, the woman's ghost gathered itself out of the shadows. When Nora sloshed back inside to start boiling the kettle, Kirsten was already standing before the cellar door.

Each faint electric shock wore Nora's nerves down a little more. She wondered if she might find a way to banish Kirsten—or release her. But she remembered that Kirsten herself had tried to expel Olaf and been unsuccessful.

Still, she had kept him contained.

Nora might be able to lure Kirsten into her old room before pouring salt across the threshold and stepping over it. But that seemed too cruel after everything else she'd done to Kirsten. Besides, Nora thought her too savvy to fall for such a ruse.

And she wasn't entirely convinced she wouldn't incur the woman's wrath. She recalled what Kirsten had said about ghosts: that she thought they could gain enough strength to harm the living, that they could frighten you to death, at least. That they might even be capable of possession, if you let them too deep inside your head.

Nora had essentially invited Kirsten into hers by beaming her a message of apology, not believing it would work. It hadn't with Euan, after all.

But here Kirsten was, giving Nora her full attention, even when she tried to divert her own.

~

Dusk fell and clouds gathered with the threat of more rain; the kitchen was dark enough that Nora could see her reflection in the window above the stove.

Marie still looked alarmingly sleepy; Nora worried that she had misjudged her last dose. But she knew that grief itself was wearying, and bade Marie sit at the table while she finished heating supper.

When thunder rumbled and Nora looked up at the window, instead of her own reflection, she saw Kirsten's face in the glass.

She jumped and burned her wrist, sucked air over her teeth.

She could have sworn Kirsten's gray lips twitched in something like a smile. "Is this fun for you?" Nora muttered. The ghost certainly looked less distraught than before. Perhaps because it was getting the hang of haunting.

Nora bowed her head and carried the soup out to the table. Erik was mercifully absent.

While she spooned up broth and Kirsten stood before the china hutch, Nora observed Marie, to see if she noticed the ghostly presence, but she didn't. She wanted to ask if Marie had ever seen anything in the cellar, or if she had only been afraid of Olaf because Kirsten had taught her to be.

Nora didn't want to think about Olaf at all—in part, lest she draw his attention too.

Eventually, however, she would need to venture into the basement, once the neighbors' funereal foods ran out.

She would have to remember to take down some salt, and crumble more rosemary in the corners. She shuddered at the thought, and put her spoon down, pushed her bowl away.

~

Though Nora was tired, she couldn't sleep. She buried her face in her pillow and felt Kirsten's gray eyes on her, burning like cold coins pressed into Nora's flesh.

~

When Grace finally came by the following afternoon, Nora realized why she'd waited—she'd wanted a private audience, to not have to censor herself in the presence of neighbors.

"It's no great wonder," she said of Kirsten, once she'd gotten Nora to tersely confirm that the rumors of suicide were true. "Poor woman. May she rest in peace."

Nora flicked her gaze to the opposite wall, where Kirsten's ghost stood beside the grandfather clock.

"I may be Catholic," Grace continued, "but I don't hold with that cruel doctrine about being barred from heaven if you do yourself in. God is far more merciful than people, I think."

Nora sipped her tea and nodded automatically.

"And then Axel," Grace said, with an arched brow.

"What about Axel? Do you know where he is?"

"No, but he's not the only one who's suddenly gone. Harvey McGinness is too . . ."

"Who is Harvey McGinness?"

"A nice young fellow who works at the factory. Who seemed fairly friendly with Axel. Only person he ever said hello to when he came into town. He always stayed at Harvey's apartment too. If he didn't feel like coming back to the farm for the night."

Nora recalled with a jolt how peculiar she'd found it that Grace laughed so hard when she relayed the rumor that Axel might have fathered Ezra.

Most women—proper ladies, at least—mightn't have understood the implications, but it gelled for Nora in a flash.

If Kirsten had known, then she certainly wouldn't have approved. Yet she was the only blood family Axel had left, and so he'd stayed near her. But now, grievously freed, he'd gone. Taken the money and the dog—who had always liked him better than anyone else—and apparently set out for some new place with his lover.

"Good," Nora said. "I hope they get far away from here and end up someplace happy."

Now Grace sipped her tea, both brows arched.

Nora glanced again at Kirsten. *Why don't you go follow your brother?* she thought, not meaning to think it *at* Kirsten, but to herself. Then she wondered if having driven the woman's only blood relative away had made her angrier. For Nora sensed that the spirit was angry now, was growing more so every hour, the initial confusion and despair having fallen away like scales from its unblinking eyes.

∽

It was a Thursday, but Nora didn't even consider making butter. "I'm sure you're livid about that, too," she muttered once Grace had gone, unable to help herself.

Though it felt dangerous to directly address Kirsten, it was satisfying, too, like scratching a painful itch. The temporary relief, however, could easily lead to an even worse condition—suppuration, rot, slow death.

While butter could wait, Nora would need to boil the laundry kettle soon; the girls' underthings were nearly all soiled. She'd resorted to making a few hasty new pairs from a couple of old blouses.

I should have used your clothes, she thought with another glance at Kirsten, whose dresses hung in the closet like empty skins.

∽

On Friday, they all skipped going into town and ate more of their neighbors' food, including the molasses loaves that Grace had brought.

That night, Nora retired to the spare room, telling Mal that she didn't want to keep him awake again, which was partly true. She'd been restless for the previous few nights. She intended to remedy that now.

She was surprised, and at least momentarily relieved, that Kirsten's ghost wasn't there when Nora entered Euan's room. Not that she couldn't appear at any second. But maybe Kirsten wanted to be alone with Mal, forever oblivious to her worshipful adoration.

In private—shut away from the living and the dead—Nora finally uncapped her secret bottle of laudanum. She'd have needed to open it soon anyway, because Kirsten's bottle contained only dregs.

Nora took a few drops directly on her tongue, then lay down with a scarf draped over her eyes, so even if she was tempted to open them, she wouldn't be able to see anything in the room's shadows. When she heard faint murmuring, her arm hairs prickled upright, but then she realized it was only Marie, talking to her girls again. A bit later, as Nora dozed, she heard muffled crying, but not from the next room; it came from across the hall, where she should have been, but her limbs and her head were too heavy now to move.

She woke with her nightgown fluttering against her legs in a chilly breeze, damp, uneven ground beneath her bare feet, and a scalpel, of all things, in her hand.

Another one of her strange dreams—she closed her eyes and took a deep, slow breath, waiting to be transported back to her room.

But then a low voice said, "What the hell are you doin', doc?"

CHAPTER
THIRTY-EIGHT

Hoosick Falls, NY
October 1887

Nora jumped, half turned to see Erik in the middle of the orchard with her. She closed her eyes for another futile moment, but it slowly dawned on her that she was truly awake, and outside. She looked down at her hand and dropped the scalpel. What *had* she been doing?

"I was sleepwalking," she murmured.

Erik frowned at her, kept his distance. "You do that a lot?"

"Never . . ."

It seemed that Nora had been headed for the graveyard. Perhaps to exhume Kirsten's body and slice into her shriveled chest, to see if there was water in her lungs after all—or if they told a more sinister tale, of death occurring before she was dragged down beneath the surface.

By now, though, her body would be full of leaking fluids, and the marks on her neck would no longer be legible. Kirsten's ghost might not know that, though, and so it might have propelled Nora toward a truth it wanted known.

She shivered as the breeze blew the smell of damp earth and sweet apples into her face, pushed her nightgown against her body. A shadow shifted in the moonlight, and she saw Kirsten, of course, standing not far behind Erik's shoulder, staring at her.

For a second, Nora wanted to cling to Erik, if only for warmth, for protection. For the illusion of it, at least.

She considered that she might have brought the scalpel out with another idea—whether her own or Kirsten's—of sacrificing herself upon the altar of the raw grave. Spilling her own blood on the thirsty ground.

Or maybe, Nora thought, she'd brought the instrument outside with her in case she might need a weapon.

As if he knew what she was thinking, Erik nodded at the silver blade shining in the dirt. "You just gonna leave that there?"

Nora felt a silvery, cold flash of panic as she bent to pick it up. She looked again at Kirsten's ghost, as if it might give some indication—of whether Erik was culpable. But even if he hadn't physically harmed Kirsten, just as Nora hadn't, she must have resented him for so many things.

Nora considered asking Erik if he really thought that Kirsten had killed herself, but she knew how evasive he could be, and so instead said, "She knew. About us."

Erik's expression didn't change. "Not surprised." Entirely unaware that the woman's spirit stood mere paces from his back.

Nora wondered that the breeze on the nape of his neck didn't feel colder than it should.

"We argued." She glanced over Erik's shoulder again, but saw no change in Kirsten's expression. "I told her she should go. But I only meant to leave, not—"

Erik shook his head. "Whatever you said, you didn't make her do what she did. That was a long time comin'."

Nora remembered what Axel had said after he'd dragged his sister's body from the pond. *Why now?* As if he too had thought Kirsten might do such a thing, and only marveled that she had waited so long.

"So, it was the last straw, then. What I said to her." She looked at Kirsten again. "I'm sorry."

"Even if it was," Erik said, "what good is guilt gonna do you now? It's guilt that got to her, too. She thought every bad thing that ever happened to her was some divine punishment. But like you said yourself, bad things happen all the time."

Nora frowned. "Punishment for what?"

Erik hesitated a moment. "My mother didn't die of any fever. My father didn't either. He shoved her down the basement stairs and she broke her neck. And Kirsten . . ." He stopped and wiped his mouth, as if trying to rid it of a bitter taste. "She saw it happen. And she pushed him after. That's how they both ended up dead at the bottom of those stairs."

Nora swallowed and glanced at Kirsten's ghost again. It looked angrier.

"If that's what happened," she said, "then she should have been *proud*. Justice rarely gets served so quickly, if at all."

Erik huffed a sort of laugh and shrugged. "Well, it was murder all the same. And everybody agreed to lie about it—no use makin' things even worse for the family, right? She was about to pop her own baby out any minute. No sense puttin' her on trial. But she lived with that every day—a capital sin—just waitin' for the other shoe to drop. Took a while, but then it did. Surprised she lasted so many years after all that."

Nora's fingers tightened on the scalpel stem. The fact that Erik knew that Kirsten had killed his father gave her pause. Perhaps he had exacted retribution by letting Kirsten's son slip beneath the pond ice. Or pushed him under.

"You must have hated her, then."

Erik looked both genuinely surprised and reproving. "No—he deserved it, like you said. Not like she planned it out, anyway. But what exactly do you mean to imply by that?"

"Nothing." Nora glanced at Kirsten, still behind Erik's shoulder, as if for encouragement. "It doesn't seem like you're all that upset that she's dead, though."

He scoffed. "Well, that's your opinion. But, sure, there wasn't a whole lot of love lost between us. Doesn't mean I fuckin' drowned her."

"I didn't say you did."

"But you've been actin' like you don't want to get within five feet of me even with everybody else around, like you're scared—"

"Should I be? You were home the night it happened. And you were there when Johan died too. At that same pond."

Erik's face momentarily went blank before pain and anger twisted his features into a frightening mask. "And that was a goddamn accident."

"Still," Nora said. "It wasn't an accident, what happened to Stephen after."

"Well, that wasn't my fault, either," Erik snapped, and stepped abruptly closer.

Nora stepped back and gripped the scalpel tighter. "It doesn't feel that way, though, does it?" She thought of her own guilt over Kirsten's death, and Kirsten's guilt over Olaf's, and asked Erik with something like hope, "Do you ever see them? Their ghosts?"

"Thought you didn't believe in those," he said, and he looked over his shoulder again, where Nora's eyes kept straying. "You said you argued with her. And that she knew about us. And *you're* the one who came out of nowhere sayin' we should check the pond. And that money she had—I know that was yours. Hidden in your stockin', wasn't it? Did she steal it? 'Cause all that and now you're talkin' like you want to accuse *me* of somethin'—well, it makes me wonder if you did do more than just tell her she ought to go."

"Like what?" Scorn sharpened Nora's tone. "You think I managed to drag her all the way out there without anybody noticing?"

"Hell, you're strong enough. You could have slipped somethin' in her food to make it easier, or killed her some other way—shit, maybe you were sleepwalkin', didn't even know you were doin' it."

Nora scoffed, but looked again at Kirsten's silent ghost, as if it might confirm or refute the implication.

"The *fuck* do you keep lookin' at?" Erik stepped closer again, though this time he seemed driven by the desire to put space between himself and the trees at his back. "You're actin' crazy," he said, "and you came out here with that thing in your hand and no idea you were doin' it. What do you think? You losin' it? Or is the curse comin' over you too?"

Nora's arm tensed with a vicious impulse to slash out at him, open his veins to release whatever poison coursed through them. Then she would do her own.

"You'd better get back inside, doc. Before you catch your death."

She watched Erik turn and walk straight through Kirsten, who broke apart into a puddle of shadows that re-formed itself the instant he'd passed, and continued to stare at Nora with pale, unblinking eyes.

∼

The only benefit to that strange nighttime encounter was that, afterward, Erik seemed inclined to keep his distance, even if he had no intention of leaving the farm itself.

But there was still time, Nora thought. She could wait him out.

Kirsten's spirit, however, continued to follow her, and how could one outlast a ghost?

∼

Nora didn't truly think that Kirsten's specter had propelled her into the orchard; that had been the laudanum and her own subconscious. But she feared that the spirit would acquire greater powers, exhibit some startling new behavior at any second.

She was tempted to try and run, test how far Kirsten could follow her, hoping she might be tied to the farmhouse and the woods between it and the pond.

But Nora feared that Kirsten was tied to her instead, and was afraid to stray far enough to find out.

∼

She stopped slipping laudanum into Marie's drinks, but continued to give small measures to the girls, just enough to keep them calm. *Compliant,* Nora's inner critic corrected.

On Sunday, she stayed home to watch them, unwilling to attempt Kirsten's leash gambit on her own, much less entrust it to Marie, though perhaps that wasn't fair. Nora didn't want to see Kirsten's ghost among the congregation, either—unless her spirit would eschew the Presbyterian church even in the afterlife and glide down to St. Mark's.

It occurred to Nora, after the others had left, that if Kirsten was tethered to her now, then she was keeping her from her favorite place in all creation.

"But I couldn't possibly keep you from church," she mused when they were alone again, "much less from heaven. You're here because you want to be. To teach me a lesson, or make me pay." That was fair enough, she supposed.

The last few days of October slipped by in a blur of chores. Nora was glad all the canning was done—intentionally or not, Kirsten had provisioned them for one last winter before she left.

When Nora finally went into the basement, she averted her eyes from the far walls where the thick shadows seemed to writhe and reached into her pocket, which she'd filled with salt before descending. She scattered grains before her like she scattered seed for the chickens. Before briskly returning upstairs, she refreshed the line of salt at the bottom of the flight, trying not to imagine broken bodies piled up in the same spot, much less little Euan peering down from the kitchen.

I've seen too much death, he'd told her when they'd first discussed their reasons for pursuing medicine. Nora had had no real idea what he'd meant.

But if Erik, one year younger, knew what had happened to his parents, then Euan must have too. Would he ever have told her? Nora wondered. If they'd married and made a long life together, would he have confided in her eventually? Or would he have shielded her from the full truth like Mal?

Though Nora hadn't said anything to him about what she'd learned concerning his mother's and Olaf's deaths, and how the family had covered it up, it was difficult to reconcile with the man she knew.

The knowledge that they had all conspired to keep such a secret made her feel set apart. It was a familial cohesion, born of care for each other, a desire to keep their own safe. They had closed ranks to cover an ugly wound and were knitted together in their pact.

It made more sense to her now, why Euan had been so reluctant to bring her to this place. And why Mal had resisted Nora's wish to marry him.

She didn't blame him, or any of them, for hiding what Kirsten had done. Nor was she disturbed to imagine Kirsten—a young woman then, still getting used to a new home, heavy with her first child—lashing out and shoving Olaf, himself a murderer, to his deserved death.

But had Kirsten yoked herself to Olaf by killing him, in a sense that transcended mere guilt?

It made Nora ferociously sad to think that one impulsive, understandable act on Kirsten's part had chained her to a dark spirit, even if she had managed to barricade it.

Then Nora felt briefly hopeful—that maybe Olaf's ghost wasn't even there now; it might have died forever with Kirsten. As Kirsten might with Nora.

∾

She must have looked exhausted, for Mal, whose own sad eyes were likewise shadowed, asked if they should get help.

Nora hesitated, afraid of what he meant. But then he clarified—"It's too much work; just the cooking takes all day. We could hire someone from town. To come in a few days a week, or even to stay. We could clear out Kirsten's room . . ."

"No." Nora glanced at the eternally dripping ghost by the mantel. "We can manage."

Mal sighed as he situated himself beneath the blankets. "We'll have to hire another hand next summer, though. I doubt they'll want to sleep in the loft. So we'll have to clear the room out anyway."

"I'll do it," Nora said, and resisted looking at Kirsten again. "Over the winter."

What she wanted to do was suggest they leave—beg to leave, now, together.

But Nora knew she wouldn't be able to make him understand, much less convince him, without telling far more of the truth than she wanted to. If she admitted to seeing a ghost, he might send her away. To her father if she was lucky; to an asylum if not. If Kirsten followed her there, Nora truly would go mad. And if she confessed her fear of Erik, and had to explain why, Mal might well cast her out for her betrayal. Which would only make it easier for Erik to come after her. Better to bear both burdens in silence, then. To hope for the best, however wretched it might be.

CHAPTER
THIRTY-NINE

Hoosick Falls, NY
November–December 1887

A few nights later, thinking of the girls' impending fourth birthday, Nora finally asked Mal if he knew that Kirsten had medicated the children.

"No," he said, clearly surprised, though he allowed that it made sense—the change in their behavior had been remarkable after Kirsten took over their care. He didn't seem unduly troubled, and asked with nothing more than interest if Nora had continued doing it.

She said yes, but admitted—all the while aware of Kirsten skulking in the corner—that she worried it might have stunted them. That they hadn't been afforded a proper chance to learn all the things they might have, even at their still young age.

"I know she wanted to help them, but she wanted them to be easy, too. It's no wonder she stopped me asking questions. And she barely let Marie be with them; she talks to them, you know, at night, but Kirsten never did—except to give them orders. And them in a fog all the time. What if that's why they don't speak now?"

Mal frowned. "Euan seemed to think it was just . . . how they were made."

"Well, even so," Nora said, "even if they never talk, they could still learn to read, or write. They could *communicate*—not just obey instructions. Did she ever even think to try and teach them?"

"I suppose there wasn't much time for that."

Nora felt the shadows seethe but avoided looking toward Kirsten's ghost. She vowed to herself that she would make time, even if it meant sacrificing other responsibilities. They could leave the laundry a little longer, she thought, and eat simpler meals, and let the windows go unwashed, the stairs undusted.

~

But there were only so many hours in a day, and Nora was no teacher. She and Marie did start talking constantly, naming every object, narrating every thought and action. And the girls slowly became accustomed to their new minders. They usually listened when asked to sit at the table, or to go up for bed—not alone, of course; Nora and Marie had to help them change. They tolerated the assistance, but still wriggled and ducked away from every touch, including the hugs and kisses their mother attempted to bestow upon them. Nora bit her tongue to keep from telling Marie to leave them be, as Kirsten often had.

Bea protested somewhat less, she noticed. Bea also seemed more attentive to both the women's voices and the phonograph music; she lifted her head and closed her eyes for sonorous strings, whereas Addie perked up for piano—but flinched at the higher, plinking notes. The women gladly played the girls' favorites on repeat, even during mealtimes.

Through similar trials and observations, they learned that Bea and Addie liked different foods, though Kirsten had always fed them the same purees. Nora started a diary so they would remember how both girls happily ate mounds of sweetened whipped cream in lieu of birthday cake, and stridently refused all cooked green leaves and oatmeal. Addie evinced a methodical enjoyment in rolling individual peas around her mouth before smashing them against her teeth, while Bea only ate them if passed through a food mill and a sieve, completely free of skins.

Both girls liked watching the rotation of records and the wool-spinning wheel. They still ignored their rag dolls, but Bea accepted Nora's pastel crayons, deliberately striping sheets of paper with blue and green and orange, eschewing red and yellow. Addie, disinterested in art, became enamored of stroking the soft nap of the settee's velvet fabric while humming tunelessly.

For the women, such small discoveries all seemed monumentally significant surprises, yet Nora's every pang of excitement was slivered with sadness—for how long it had taken anyone to realize, much less appreciate, that the girls were far more complex than assumed, and not at all interchangeable.

There were still challenges, bouts of difficult behavior, but wasn't that so with all children? Dulled by drugs, Bea and Addie were infinitely easier to deal with, yet also impossible to truly know.

She sometimes wondered if Kirsten had ever loved them, or had even tried.

But Nora knew that she had, in her own perplexing way. And who was she to judge someone else's failures? She wouldn't think of her own actions as corrections, simply as different approaches. She wasn't above employing the waist tethers in the house when her attention was divided and she needed the girls to stay put, either, and only somewhat guiltily locked their bedroom door before milking, in case they woke and tried to wander.

Teaching them in any formal manner remained unsuccessful. When Nora placed cards with simple words and objects and individual letters and numbers before the girls, they didn't focus. If she gave them something they enjoyed, however, they would at least listen to her read while they completed their task.

She began doing so in the parlor in the evenings and on Sunday afternoons, while Marie and Mal were at church.

The first time Erik slipped in, she'd just begun narrating *Alice's Adventures in Wonderland*.

Nora faltered when the front door opened, but continued reading aloud as Erik walked into the room and studied them.

For once, she was in an armchair—Mal's, not Kirsten's, which no one else had sat in since her death. And yet when Erik lowered himself to the settee, Nora could feel the shifting of the cushion, the sense memory of all the times he'd sprawled beside her on the sofa.

"Cozy little scene," he said.

She continued reading.

After a while, Erik added, "Anybody looked in on us right now, we could almost pass for a happy little family."

Nora lowered the book and looked at him. "I can see her, you know. You asked what I was looking at that night, in the orchard. Well, Kirsten was standing behind you the whole time. Until you walked through her at the end. Didn't that feel strange, at all? I've never tried. Right now, she's over there, under the painting of Euan."

Erik narrowed his eyes, looked from the wall back to Nora. "If that's true, you're takin' it pretty well."

She shrugged. "I've had a while to get used to it. It's curious, though. I've never seen her sit or lie down; she only stands. It's not quite floating, but . . . her feet don't quite touch the ground either. And she's not transparent like you might expect, but somehow . . . murky. Like pond water."

"Yeah, I don't believe you, doc."

Nora couldn't tell whether it was true or, perhaps, what he wanted to think.

"Anyway," he said, "you know I've got a taste for loony women. So don't think that's gonna put me off."

∾

In fact, speaking to Erik seemed to encourage him. He started coming to the parlor again, even when the others were there, and Nora went back to pretending, as best she could, that he didn't exist.

But he must have known his presence unnerved her, which seemed to be enough to satisfy him for the time being.

Suffused with his own patience, and with power, he sat and watched and waited.

$\sim$

As late November set in and the trees shed their last leaves, Nora could scarcely believe that winter was so close again; she had only just survived the first one. The thought of trudging through another frozen five months with Kirsten's ghost hounding her and Erik still thinking he could have her back made her increasingly frantic.

She should have been overjoyed when Mal brought up a Christmas visit to Manhattan, but it was impossibly impractical. Besides, Nora was still afraid of finding out that Kirsten could follow her that far, that she would truly never be free. Conversely, if she discovered that Kirsten couldn't leave the farm, Nora feared she might not return, herself. But she felt duty-bound to stay—and wanted to be with Mal, besides.

All she said was "We can't. And leave Marie alone with Erik and the girls?"

"We could ask someone from town to stay with them," Mal suggested. "Or I could stay here while you go . . ."

Nora bit her tongue to keep from saying that the girls needed her, if only for the sake of routine—and to keep from betraying the hurt she felt at the apparent ease with which Mal would still separate from her, even if only temporarily. Finally, though, she let herself say, "Or what if we all left?"

"What, you want to bring them with us, to your family's?"

"No. I mean, what if we—you and I, at least . . . what if we left the farm? For good? For someplace else. It wouldn't have to be the city."

339

"Nora . . ."

She shifted onto one elbow and looked at him, his dark-blue eyes and their radiating lines, his auburn hair and the places where it faded into that aged-cream-silk color. He wasn't young, but he still had time. They did. Only, time itself would never be enough. They had to make good use of it.

"I know it would be hard to leave," she said, "but . . . with all the awful things that have happened here, sometimes I don't understand how you can want to stay."

"It's all I've ever known," he said.

Except war, Nora realized. And Albany, for a few nights at a time.

"It's all I have," Mal went on, "of my mother and my father. My whole family."

Nora shook her head and caressed his cheek. "You have them in you. You'll take them with you, wherever you go. And you—*we*—can't go on like this forever. This place can't. Even if we had a dozen children—"

When she broke off, Mal turned his head away, a sheen in his eyes.

"I can't leave," he said.

As if he couldn't bear it, or the farm itself wouldn't let him.

But a moment later, his voice thick with the threat of tears, he asked, "What about Marie and the girls, then? If we left. And Erik?"

Again, his tone was difficult to interpret—it might be a challenge to Nora's impossible idea, or it might be a prelude to actually considering her suggestion.

Her voice was strained. "He owns half the farm now, doesn't he? You could just . . . give him the whole thing. We'd be fine, financially. Or if you both agreed to sell, then they could live in town. Or buy a smaller plot. Either way, we could help them if need be. Hire a nurse to help Marie with the girls, too. And they'll own her father's mill someday. They could go back to England if they wanted—or sell that place too and move to Fifth Avenue."

It sounded false and flimsy. It sounded like Nora didn't actually care. And she was secretly afraid that she would still forsake Marie and the girls for her own safety and security. Her better human nature should have made her selfless, but Nora had come to accept that she was more animal, at heart.

Crafty, though—if Mal gave Erik the entirety of the land to do with as he wished, it might be enough to make him forsake Nora. It might be the only thing that could.

~

Erik seemed ever more animalistic, too, growing restless with the change of season, and with Nora's continued refusal to engage with him, his patience finally fraying.

He'd discarded his relatively innocuous comments laced with sarcasm in favor of distressingly sincere confessions: that he missed her, that he loved her and she was heartless, that he felt like she was a million miles away again and couldn't stand it, that he wanted her but more than that, he *needed* her—and when those words had no effect, he tipped into vulgarity, aided by increasingly generous amounts of whiskey, judging by the ever-sharper fumes he emitted.

"Sit there and pretend you don't care all you want, but I know better. I know you want me. And I know Mal doesn't know what the hell to do with you. I bet you're slippery as the inside of an egg right now. Ought to throw you down on the floor and find out."

Though it took considerable effort, Nora continued reading, at least until his descriptions became even more detailed and she finally broke. "How can you be so disgusting in front of your own daughters?"

"They don't understand a goddamn thing! Includin' any of that shit you're readin' to 'em."

"That's not true," Nora said, and opened the book again, but before she could continue reading, Erik sprang across from the settee and snatched *Alice* from her hand.

Nora flinched, and the girls made soft noises of distress.

"See?" she said as she stood from her chair and backed away from Erik. "You're scaring them. They understand that."

He looked like he might lunge toward her again, whether to smack her across the face with the book or grab her by the throat and drag her to the floor like he'd threatened—it wouldn't matter that the girls were there, she knew.

But after a terrible moment of raw tension, he threw *Alice* on the settee and stormed out through the french doors, leaving Nora as rattled as the panes of glass.

She looked to Kirsten's ghost with a mixture of shame and fear and something like rebuke—as if the spirit should have helped her somehow. And though it was likely only Nora's imagination that made Kirsten's face appear mildly smug, she didn't glance at it again to check.

∼

The following Sunday afternoon, Nora's hands trembled as she turned the pages, but Erik didn't appear. She assumed he was hunting, judging by the long periods of silence punctuated by the sharp cracks of gunshots some distance away in the woods.

Nora thought of the other rifle hanging over the study fireplace, and of the poker by the parlor hearth, and the knives in the kitchen. It seemed sensible to be aware of the nearest weapons, wherever she might be in the house. Though if Erik burst in with his gun or his axe, there would be nothing she could do.

But he only shot animals, and brought home a few rabbits, peeled off their pelts, which he would turn into gloves and sell in town while Nora and Marie cooked the meat.

In early December, he dragged a field-dressed deer from the trees, his striking hands stained red from pulling out its innards.

∼

Nora's own insides felt like they'd been forcibly jumbled, like she might bring them up in a steaming gout of blood at any moment. But when she did vomit, it was only bile and the small amounts of food she managed to eat.

Other places bereft of blood: Nora's bloomers and her chamber pot, unspotted with any shade of red for more than three months now. She'd been late before, but never so long. Another secret to keep. Another thing to intensify her disheartening anxiety.

~

Her father returned to Hoosick Falls to see her for the holidays. He stayed with the Burnses, who invited the whole family to Christmas dinner, but Nora—politely, apologetically—said no, they would have to do it at the farm.

She couldn't leave the girls alone, and feared that bringing them to the Burnses' would result in disaster; Addie and Bea didn't like leaving their familiar surroundings or breaking routines. And Nora was no longer willing to give them an extra measure of laudanum so she could tote them along like oversized dolls.

In the months since Kirsten's death, she'd gradually decreased their daily doses to an acceptable minimum but found it impossible to take them into town without incident—unless she drugged them more heavily. She had tried twice but couldn't stomach doing it again.

At home, Nora gave up on the teaching cards for the time being and provided more absorbing busywork, better than the same old jars of beans and buttons and less messy than pastels. Both girls liked puzzles, so Nora had purchased as many as she could find. Though the twins hadn't mastered the knack of fitting the pieces together, they seemed to enjoy grouping similar colors and patterns. When they were done, she and Marie would press the pieces into place, and the girls would watch in flickering looks from the corners of their dark eyes, Bea's gaze steadier than Addie's.

Nora made simpler puzzles, too, by drawing branches and veins, overlapping tendon structures and plantar nerves, resembling roots in the garden, on long rolls of paper that she then cut into strips or squares. When she scattered a pile on the parlor rug, the girls would patiently shuffle about, placing the disparate parts in proper order, softly hooting to each other.

Nora and Marie became surprisingly fluent in their largely silent tongue, and came to recognize certain subtle gestures that indicated specific things: thirst; a need to eliminate; a wish to go to bed. Gradually, some of the girls' sounds began to resemble words. One day, Bea spoke a few quite clearly, if entirely out of context, as far as Nora could tell. Still, they encouraged her to babble.

Mal was pleased, she thought—and so was she, by every tiny triumph. Yet worry still thrummed through her, every day that she did not bleed, every day that Kirsten's ghost and Erik still waited to greet her. Her anxiety reached its highest pitch as the sun sank below the trees, earlier and earlier as the year drew toward its end.

Ignoring unpleasant things might not make them go away, but it was Nora's only option while she remained unwilling to tell Mal that she saw Kirsten's ghost and feared that Erik meant to kill or claim her.

When she was eventually forced to acknowledge those awful truths, they would be even worse for having waited, but there was still a chance Nora might be reprieved in some way.

Failing that, she would delay facing the consequences of her actions for as long as possible.

~

Erik made himself scarce when Nora's father came, and didn't join the rest of them for Christmas dinner. "A bit under the weather," Mal said when the Burnses asked.

Part of what troubled Erik was surely the way winter had sunk its icy claws into the world again, and pulled time inexorably onward toward some of his coldest, darkest memories.

Nora tried not to think about the previous year, much less everything it had led to. She half hoped—again—that Erik might simply disappear, whether on a train or ship or by letting himself succumb to the cold beneath the surface of the pond. And she still half feared that he might decide to slaughter every one of them.

She tried to take comfort from her father's genuine gladness, to not feel like a fraud and a failure when he hugged her on the porch after their dinner and fireside festivities and said, "You look well, love."

She wished she hadn't gotten so good at lying.

CHAPTER FORTY

Hoosick Falls, NY
December 1887–February 1888

On the last day of December, Nora studied Kirsten's ghost in an attempt to work out whether it knew the significance of the date, wanting to ask it: *Don't you want to see your son? Can't you find your way to him?*

It did seem as if the woman's water-speckled face was more downcast than usual, her gray eyes more morose, but Nora never knew how much her own expectations changed her perception of that spectral visage.

～

The next day, the first of the new year, was a Sunday, so Nora was left alone with the girls after breakfast. Once again, Erik hadn't come to the barn for milking, and she assumed he was back at the pond, though she wondered if he would hesitate to go in now that it had claimed Kirsten too.

Too distracted to read to the girls, Nora entertained more fantasies of Erik giving himself over to the cold. He could be floating in the tainted water even now, a thin skin of ice forming above his head.

She kept looking up toward the french doors, expecting to see him standing there, wondering if she would be able to tell at first glance whether he was still alive or had become another unholy ghost.

~

One week later, on the second anniversary of Euan's death, Nora felt wistful, but not racked with grief, nor even particularly guilty for that, as she might have expected.

She cast no thoughts out toward him, and took some comfort in the fact that he had not been trapped at the farm—as Kirsten had once taken comfort from having never seen Stephen's or Johan's spirits.

Malcolm's guilt, as far as Nora could tell, had never entirely diminished, despite the considerable effort he'd made until Kirsten's death undid so much. They hadn't made love since then, but they lay lovingly beside each other every night, and Nora could accept—could cherish—a lifetime of that.

Mal hadn't noticed any changes in her body, which weren't yet drastic. She could no longer convince herself she was imagining them, but nor could she be sure how far along she was. The dreadful math she did only confirmed that it could be either Mal's or Erik's. She wore her flannel robe to bed, another layer of concealment that would fail to be enough in the near future.

When she changed her clothes or bathed, she felt Kirsten's unblinking eyes on her belly and placed a protective arm across it, as if she could shield the child from anything fate had in store for it.

Sometimes, Nora hoped the baby would perish—or, better, kill her, either before it was born, or when it made its entrance into the world. It would be a fitting punishment, she thought, but it would also be an undeserved pardon, from everything: grief, responsibility, love, fear.

Unless, of course, death only released Nora's spirit from its bodily confines so it was left to wander the same rooms, and bear the burden of the same memories and emotions, without even the potential comfort of being seen, and touched, and spoken to, and understood.

Even when she wasn't certain that she wanted to live, she was now overwhelmingly afraid to die.

~

On the second Sunday in February, she dozed off by the parlor fire as she read *Gulliver's Travels* to the girls.

She came to with her head slumped and a crick in her neck, the book splayed open in her lap. A minute might have passed, or an hour. She blinked to clear her vision, and sudden, total alertness jolted through her—for the rug before the fireplace, where the girls had sat working on their puzzle, was now empty.

Nora stood and looked around the room. "Addie? Bea?"

Not only were the twins gone, but Kirsten was conspicuously absent.

"Girls! Where are you?"

A quick circuit of the first-floor rooms, all empty—the lock still engaged on the cellar door—and then Nora hurried upstairs, calling their names with increasing desperation.

Mal and Marie weren't yet back from church, which meant either that Erik had come and taken the twins or that they had wandered away on their own.

All the upstairs closets were empty, as were the spaces beneath the beds and behind the curtains. She'd never known them to hide, but they were exhibiting new behaviors all the time. Nora couldn't draw in enough air as she ran back downstairs and burst from the front door, but managed to shout the girls' names, trying to decide where to look next. She clanged the dinner bell for good measure, for the purpose of raising an alarm if the wagon was close enough to hear it yet. Or in case Erik might.

Nora dashed over the snowy ground to the barn and tore inside to peek into every stall and corner, disturbing cats and disquieting calves. She climbed into the hayloft as well, but found no twins, no Kirsten.

On the verge of hysteria, she half slid back down the ladder and swept out of the barn to hurry toward the cabin—wondering if she should check the springhouse first.

She didn't think they would go there—she didn't think they would go anywhere, though. But if Erik had taken them, it might be to his cabin.

Maybe just to teach her a lesson. Nora prayed she would be that lucky, that the twins would be sitting mesmerized by the antlers on their father's wall or petting the pelts from the animals he'd hunted and skinned.

Hope and anger built in her chest, fighting against doubt and fear. She didn't believe that Erik could have coaxed them out without waking her, much less taken them by force. But maybe . . .

Nora shoved against the door with all her strength.

It crashed open. The cabin too was empty.

A frustrated cry erupted from her chest, but turned into a mere whine in her constricted throat.

Dutifully, shakily, Nora checked the sleeping loft, knowing they wouldn't be there—reeling under Old Nick's empty-eyed stare and charmless grin—then climbed down and lurched back outside, scanning the tree line.

"Bea! Addie!"

She checked the dark and deeply chilly springhouse to no avail, then thought of the pond. It seemed too patently terrible, too dismally obvious, but that was precisely why Nora feared they would be there.

~

What if it wasn't Erik, she wondered, but Kirsten who had coaxed the girls outside? Or some inexorable pull exerted by the land itself, to which they were more susceptible now that Nora had sharpened their senses?

And so, calling for the twins in an increasingly hoarse voice, she hurried through the woods toward the cursed, killing water.

She would strip off her clothes and kick away her boots before she plunged into the icy pond, lest she be weighed down, tangled up in dead and dormant reeds and roots on the muddy bottom. It would cost precious time, every second she took another millimeter of ground ceded to disaster, to death—but in the back of her mind, and the depths of her heart, Nora already knew she was too late.

Yet when she reached the clearing, the pond was frozen over, its surface mirror-smooth, if cloudy, like the eye of a corpse. She could see no dark path or black hole with ragged margins where someone might have slipped through and under. There were no small, silent faces pressed up against the opaque ice.

Which was even worse, in a way. Nora had no idea now where to look, or what to do. The sugaring shack was the only other nearby structure. Before she could get even a few feet into the trees, she heard a sharp crack of sound, then ringing silence.

Nora veered in the direction from which she thought the gunshot had come, and quickened her pace when, some moments later, a distant but distinct shrieking began.

"Bea!" she screamed back. "Addie!"

She couldn't tell which one of them it was, only that it was a singular voice.

The screaming came closer faster than Nora expected. What she finally saw was not a little girl running toward her but Erik hastening through the creaking trees, his crimson hands and blood-streaked forearms clamped around Addie's wriggling body, his face in a grimace as she shrieked.

Addie's face was speckled red. Nora's stomach dropped.

"Put her down!" she called.

Erik looked toward her but didn't slow his pace.

Nora ran after, but when she tried to grab him, he shrugged her off and a tree root tripped her up, as if the forest conspired to help him get away.

"What did you do?" she shouted as she pushed herself up off the snowy ground and tried to catch up. "Where's Bea?"

Erik didn't answer, no matter how many times Nora repeated the questions, but then they emerged onto the clearing around the house, where they could see that the wagon had returned from town.

Nora, legs cramping and knee aching, let herself slow down as Mal and Marie ran toward Erik. He didn't try to evade them but shoved his writhing daughter at Marie. "Get her to shut up!"

"Erik!" Mal said. "What happened? *Nora?*"

She stopped a few paces from them, tried to catch her breath.

"Nora!" Marie cried, and fought to keep hold of Adelaide, but lost her grip and watched Addie drop onto the ground to curl into a ball and rock herself.

"What *happened?*" Mal repeated.

Erik's shoulders were heaving with labored breath. "Mountain lion. I was out trackin' it, saw it stalkin' . . . I thought a deer, or—" He paused to draw in a deeper breath and wiped his mouth. "Didn't believe my eyes at first. When I saw the girls. And then—it pounced. Had the other one in its teeth . . ."

"*What?*" The horrified incredulity in Malcolm's voice matched the feeling that surged through Nora's body.

"I shot at it. Stopped it for a second. Managed to grab that one"— at which Erik gestured to his still-moaning daughter—"but it took the other. I'm goin' back out there, to find it. I'll fuckin' kill it. I'll bring 'em back."

Before Mal could respond, Erik turned and glared at Nora, his voice both raw and, itself, abrasive. "You were supposed to be watchin' them, goddamn it. This is all your fault."

She knew it was true, and might have collapsed if Mal hadn't stepped closer to support her.

"He's lying," Nora murmured. "About what happened."

She didn't believe that any mountain lion had attacked poor Beatrice.

And then she knew, because she looked toward the cabin as Erik went inside and saw two figures there: Kirsten, and beside her, Bea, staring at the ground.

The wound she'd suffered made Nora's stomach turn. She clutched her abdomen as fresh tears spilled down her cheeks.

~

Mal seemed tempted to go after Erik but scooped Addie off the ground instead, her small, furled form vibrating with terror as he carried her inside, up to her bed. He asked Marie to fetch some water. Though she was sobbing, too, she got the pitcher and basin from the dresser, and began to dab at the blood on Addie's head.

Gently, Mal peeled Addie's hands away from her face so they could inspect the damage. But the blood must all have come from her sister's wound, which Nora couldn't bear to look at, though Bea's and Kirsten's ghosts stood just inside the room.

When Mal asked—gently—what happened, Nora shook her head. "I fell asleep. I'm sorry, I'm so sorry. I woke up and they were gone. I couldn't find them anywhere, so I went into the woods, and . . . I ran into Erik bringing Addie back. I don't know what happened." Which was a lie, but how could she expect him to believe the truth?

His brows knit in sympathy for the moaning girl. "Can we give her something?"

Nora prepared a glass with a judicious dose of laudanum. "She won't take it in this state. Trying to force her will only make it worse. But she'll be thirsty when she calms down."

Mal nodded, deferred to her.

Marie asked, "Is Bea all right?"

Nora couldn't speak.

Mal said, "We'll pray that she is."

Nora noticed, and appreciated, that he hadn't lied, at least.

CHAPTER
FORTY-ONE

Hoosick Falls, NY
February 1888

While Marie knelt beside Addie's bed, hands hovering just shy of touching her daughter before clasping in prayer instead, Nora tugged Mal down the hall. She pulled him into their bedroom, shut the door, and finally said, "He shot her. Erik. Bea. I heard it when I was in the woods."

Mal shook his head, face paler than usual.

"He said he shot—at the mountain lion."

"There was no mountain lion!" Nora said before forcing her voice lower. "You don't believe that, do you?"

Mal's eyes were glazed with tears. "What else do you expect me to believe, if not that? There are mountain lions out there. Not many now, but . . . there are."

"That's not what happened."

"And how do you know that?"

Nora hesitated, fully aware that she had nothing even halfway convincing to say. But she had to try. "Because I can see her. Bea."

With the invocation of her name, the girl flickered into being inside of the bedroom, just in front of the closed door. Nora shut her eyes.

Mal glanced behind him and saw only empty space. "Nora—"

"I can see Kirsten too. I've seen her since the morning after she disappeared. That's how I knew we had to look in the water."

Naked desperation contorted Mal's features. "She spoke to you?"

"No; she doesn't speak. But it's clear from looking at her. And it's clear from looking at Bea . . . she was *shot*."

"Nora . . ."

"I *know*. But I'm telling the truth. Erik isn't."

Mal moved to sit on the edge of the mattress and dropped his face into his hands. "Why would he lie?"

"Because, if he shot Bea—"

"Then it was an accident," Mal interrupted. "Why wouldn't he say so?"

"Maybe he can't bear to take responsibility for another death." Nora sat beside Mal and took his hand. "I know he was there, with Johan. I know Stephen hanged himself because he couldn't bear it. Everybody else seems to know it too. So, maybe he's afraid they'd find it too suspicious, if he killed his own daughter on top of everything else. If he can convince everyone a wild animal took her, then he only gets sympathy . . . and maybe enough people believe in the curse on this place that it would make perfect sense."

Mal, one hand pressed to his mouth, brushed his other calloused thumb across Nora's knuckles and said in a soft, choked voice, "I should have insisted."

"About what?"

He stood, letting go of her hand to rub his face again, dash away his tears. "That we hire someone to help you and Marie. Or that you stayed in Manhattan for the winter. Or that I couldn't marry you. But I didn't, and so it's all my fault."

"No, it isn't." Nora rose but hesitated to step closer to him. It was her fault, of course. Erik's, too. And Kirsten's, even. But not Mal's.

"I should go help look," he said.

"No!" Nora grabbed his arm, held tight. "So he can 'accidentally' shoot you too? Then God knows what will happen to the rest of us."

"Nora . . . why would you think such a thing?"

She couldn't answer, of course.

But Mal persisted. "Why would Erik want either of his daughters dead?"

"They didn't turn out to be what he'd hoped for," Nora said.

Her husband looked almost disappointed in her. "Then he could have just left them here. Gone away again. But he didn't."

"Because he wants this *place*," Nora said. "All for himself. And he wants to rid it of every bothersome little distraction that doesn't square with how he thinks it should be."

Mal frowned. "Including me? And, what, he came in and took the girls while you were asleep? Or they just happened to wander out to where he was, so he took the opportunity?"

"I don't know . . ."

Mal's voice softened into a more tender register. "Either way, why bring Adelaide back from the woods, then? Why not shoot both girls at once?"

Nora's stomach dropped. "I don't know. Because it would be harder to explain?"

"But he wouldn't have had to—he could have just . . ." Mal sighed. "I don't even know why I'm entertaining such a terrible idea. It's absurd. You can see that, can't you? When you think about it logically? And you know, Nora, there are no such things as ghosts. We've had that conversation before."

"And I wasn't certain then, but now I am. I can see them."

"Why can't I?"

"I don't know that either! Some people can't hear a high-pitched note that will drive another person mad with its shrillness—but it's a matter of perception, not existence."

The look on Mal's face made her wish she hadn't spoken of madness, but he only said, "Then there should be some way to verify it, with scientific instruments or—"

"There may be yet," Nora cut in, fighting to stay reasonably calm. "We didn't have microscopes four hundred years ago. Now we can see the organisms in a drop of pond water, completely invisible to the naked eye. A hundred years from now, we'll see even more that isn't apparent yet."

"But those organisms *are* there," Mal said. "And no one can see them with the naked eye."

Nora was as frustrated by her imperfect analogy as he was, and yet she watched him pace toward the door and nearly bump into Bea, who seemed to shimmer like an image in rippling water but did not offer resistance, or break apart.

"I obviously can't leave you here like this," Mal muttered, anguished.

Desperate to turn his doubt away from her, Nora said, "What are you going to do when Erik comes back here without a mountain lion, much less Bea's body? When he's had time to bury her someplace no one will ever find her? So no one will ever know the truth?"

Mal's brows knit. "You want me to go after him now?"

"No, I don't. I just—I need you to believe me."

Concern was deeply etched on Mal's face, but it was impossible for Nora to tell who it was for.

~

When he left the room, he walked straight through Bea's and Kirsten's ghosts, without a hitch in his step. Nora edged around them as they re-formed themselves, and went back to the twins' room.

Marie had given Addie her medicine, the water glass empty.

Now that the girl was sedated Marie stroked her daughter's long, dark hair and soft, unblemished cheek. "Do you think Bea's all right?" she murmured.

I hope so, Nora wanted to say. It would be true, even though she knew the poor girl was dead. But she only sank down next to Marie and held her as they cried.

~

No matter what else went on in the world, the cows must be milked. Mal and Nora took on the task that evening without assistance. It wasn't so burdensome, with several calves still suckling. But the somber atmosphere was awful. And their silence felt tainted, tense.

~

An hour after supper, fully dark outside, Erik still wasn't back.

Nora didn't want Bea's death to be the price for his departure, but if he never returned, she would be relieved. Mal would have to hire at least two men—or they would all have to leave. Maybe he would be less resistant to the notion now.

~

That night, she slunk away to the spare room and tried to sleep but couldn't keep from staring at Kirsten and Bea, turned softly luminous in the moonlight, still blurry through Nora's tears. She'd thought that Kirsten's spirit wanted to torture her, punish her, but perhaps all she—and now Bea—wanted was for someone to see them, acknowledge them, affirm their existence in the world.

"I'm sorry," Nora whispered, over and over, and they only stared in inscrutable silence, Kirsten at her, Bea at the floor.

~

In the early morning hours, Addie woke up moaning, which quickly ratcheted into proper wails. They waited through it until she was willing to take her glass of water, which soon sent her back into a laudanum-softened sleep.

"Stay with her," Nora said to Marie, who was still sniffling and looked exhausted.

She nodded and knelt by Addie, stroking her brow with the backs of her fingers. Nora had a horrid image of herself bent over Euan's deathbed, and then a horrid thought: that perhaps, in some ghastly way, Bea had been luckier than her sister. Her ghost didn't seem distressed, at least.

Nora and Mal trudged out to the barn and began milking the cows in more silence. They were nearly done when a strange sound became audible over the soft animal chorus of the morning, and they traded questioning looks. They stood and stretched their backs as they went to peer from the mouth of the barn.

Erik was approaching, dragging behind him a tawny, long-tailed corpse with massive paws and delicate whiskers, a bloody hole just beneath its shoulder.

"Jesus," Mal muttered, and went out to look more closely at the cat.

Nora felt faint. She saw Bea's ghost shift closer to Kirsten's where they had materialized in the snowy yard.

Mere feet away, Erik let the carcass come to rest and spat before looking pointedly at Nora, dark circles under his pale-blue eyes.

"Where's Bea?" she asked.

"In my pack," he said, his voice breaking, a glassy sheen brightening his haunted gaze.

Nora's own voice wavered. "Let me see her."

"You don't want that, doc. Trust me."

She drifted closer to the animal, its thick fur rippling in the cold breeze. Its jaws were bloodstained, but that could have been an after-effect of death.

When Erik turned and started toward the cabin, Nora saw the bloodstains seeping through his pack and nearly buckled.

She wanted to chase after him, wrestle open the bag to see if Bea's body was still a twin to its ghost, but she knew Erik would easily stop her. Mal might help him. Nora would have to be stealthy if she wanted to examine Beatrice.

But no one was guarding the mountain lion. She strode back to the house, retrieved a scalpel from Euan's room, and marched back out to the frozen yard.

Mal stood transfixed by the creature: a monster, slain. Precious, gruesome proof of his brother's innocence. Nora crouched beside it and sliced it open before Mal realized what she was doing. The blade barely seemed to touch fur and flesh, fat and fascia before they neatly parted for her, and then the stomach itself opened. Nora emptied it of unidentifiable lumps of flesh and fragments of bone, pulling them out like some arcane scryer.

"There's no hair." She looked up at Mal, who seemed too stricken, or afraid, to stop her rummaging.

Numbly, he said, "Lions pick all the fur off their prey before they eat it."

"And the hair off a little girl?" Nora countered. "But not *one* strand in its stomach? Not one scrap of fabric?"

"Maybe it's another cat, then . . ."

Nora scoffed, but she wasn't certain—about anything now; she felt quite unhinged, and knew she looked it. She'd felt in her bones that there was no chance a mountain lion even existed in their woods, let alone attacked Bea, but now she had one big cat's blood all over her hands and wrists and sleeves. She stood and staggered back from the reeking mess, left the scalpel on the ground, her hands too slippery to hold it now.

She went back toward the house, where Marie, who had come out to gaze in dull horror at the scene, shrank away behind a porch post.

Nora was still scrubbing her hands in the kitchen when Mal came in.

Before he could speak, she said, "Do you really think there are two mountain lions out there? Close enough that one ate Bea and Erik killed another?"

"It might be a mated pair," Mal answered.

Nora scoured her fingernails with a stiff-bristled brush. "When you look at her, if the top right part of her skull is missing, then you'll know."

Mal paused, then said, "I know mountain lions can crush bones more thoroughly than you might think. I know they'll eat a deer's entire spine. All you'll ever see of it is pieces that look like chips from a broken plate."

"Well, Erik must know that too." Nora's voice rose and splintered. "So if he's smart—if he's committed—then I suppose he just brought back those pieces. But he'll have ravaged them himself. It'll be too horrible for you to look at too closely, and when you do, you'll see what you want to."

Mal had no rebuttal.

Nora threw the brush down to clatter in the sink. "I know you only want to protect your family, but surely not at the expense of endangering any of the rest of them. And how many crimes are you willing to cover up?"

"Excuse me?"

She turned fully toward him. "Maybe Johan's death really was an accident. But I *know* . . ."

"You know what?"

"That Olaf pushed your mother down the stairs, and Kirsten pushed him after. There was no fever. Despite what you told me. And everyone in town. I still think it's possible that what happened to Kirsten might not have been what it looked like. If Erik blamed her for his father . . ."

With a grimace, Mal said, "*No*. She didn't—" He took a deep breath and pinched the bridge of his freckled nose. "I was out in the field with Axel and Stephen when it happened. The boys were on the side porch. Shelling beans, I think. Kirsten was here, fixing dinner. And Olaf . . . well, he was drunk again, upset about something. He followed Mother into the kitchen, presumably while she was on her way to fetching something from the cellar, and when she was at the top of the stairs . . . yes, he shoved her. Kirsten said she landed at the bottom without touching a single step."

He and Nora both looked toward the basement door; only Nora saw the ghosts who stood sentry.

Mal took a moment to gather himself before going on. "There was a skillet on the stove, and Kirsten—the way she told it—she was just so shocked, so incensed, she picked it up. Olaf was still standing there, calling down to Mother as if she could hear him. Telling her to get up. And Kirsten swung. He ended up at the bottom of the stairs, too, but the fall didn't kill him. Neither did the blow to the back of his head."

"What did, then?"

Mal took a deep breath. "Kirsten came out and rang the dinner bell. We could tell as soon as we came up that something was wrong—the boys, they were used to shouting, so they hadn't gone in to see. She sent them off to the springhouse. When she told us, we went down to check. And I could see that Mother's neck was broken—she didn't suffer. Not at the end, at least. I don't know if Olaf was on his way or not—he was in bad shape, but he was breathing. He was trying to talk. I think his jaw was broken. His eyes were wide open. I went to get the wagon hitched so we could take him to the doctor. Axel came to help. By the time we came back in, maybe ten minutes later, Olaf was gone too. I was never sure, but—well, I always thought he'd been strangled. Stephen hated him."

Nora's voice wavered. "Well, that makes a certain kind of sense, then, doesn't it? That Erik would kill Johan to punish Stephen, and then strangle Kirsten when—"

"*No.* He wouldn't do that. He didn't."

"But he *was* there with Johan. Alone. And he was here the night Kirsten died, and there *were* marks on her neck. And I swear to you, he *did* shoot Bea—"

"You don't know that. You can't. And Kirsten—you said yourself it might be normal bruising. Your father looked at her; he didn't see anything concerning."

"He saw what he expected to. And he didn't check her lungs—that would have been the only way to be sure—"

"What difference would it make?" Mal's hoarse voice broke.

Nora's own words were almost inaudibly soft. "If your own brother was a murderer?"

"Yes," Mal choked. "Another one of them. So am I."

"No, you aren't. If you mean the war, then—"

"That wasn't different. Killing is killing, Nora. Even if it wasn't, *I* decided we should lie about Mother and Olaf. I came up with the story. I helped Stephen carry their bodies up and bury them before sunrise the next morning. We didn't even take the time to make them coffins."

His dark-blue eyes shone with tears. "I shouldn't have been capable of that."

"Anyone might be," Nora said. "But Erik . . . I'm afraid he's capable of so much worse."

Mal looked at her with a measure of sorrow. "Why do you want to think so badly of him? Or why do you want me to?"

Nora's stomach dropped, for she was certain that her husband knew. The words *I just want you to know the truth* were too thorny to get out.

"If he did shoot Bea," Mal went on, "then it was an accident, and by God, I pity him. And by God, I will protect him." He studied Nora's face with obvious tenderness and a sort of resigned determination as he added, "I'll protect you too."

"From what?"

"From everything I can."

She felt a strange chill race through her limbs.

CHAPTER
FORTY-TWO

Hoosick Falls, NY
February 1888

While Mal went to fetch Dr. Burns, Erik guarded his cabin like a predator might its cache. At least Nora knew he wouldn't come near her or Marie as they watched over Addie, who became agitated every time she woke. What horror must have filled her head. If only she could tell them.

Nora's nerves were utterly frazzled, yet she was also deeply tired; she felt she might tip into sleep at every other second, but then jerked back upright in alert alarm.

~

She ruminated on the probable state of Bea's remains. For them to fit inside Erik's pack, he must have committed an act of desecration. Brought only some fragments back, so no one would be able to solve the full puzzle of his crime.

Even if the killing itself was accidental, the aftermath was not. Abuse of a corpse, willful deception. Punishable offenses.

Yet Nora couldn't forget what Mal had said about mountain lions' feeding methods—and about all the holes in her own fearful logic. It was entirely possible that Erik was telling the awful truth and Nora had driven herself to new flights of macabre fancy.

If anything was amiss, she hoped that Dr. Burns would notice when he came to look—but knew he could be blinded by his own expectations and assumptions.

When she heard him arrive, she ran downstairs but went out only when he and Mal entered the cabin. Trusting the doctor's carriage driver not to interfere, Nora hurried over to the cabin and crept up to a window.

The men's backs blocked her view through the glass. If she sidled around for a better angle, they might see her. So she retreated a few yards and waited for them to emerge, hoping it would look like she was only just approaching. When Dr. Burns was close enough, she seized his sleeve.

In a low voice, she rushed her words. "Were there cut marks? On the bones? Or did he smash them? That would have been smarter, so the edges were jagged. But were there tooth marks?"

"Nora." Dr. Burns's tone was one of mystified unease.

And already, Mal was pulling her away. "She's been extremely upset," he said, "as you can imagine."

Nora wasn't shocked by his inexorable strength, only by the fact that he exerted it so fully upon her when he'd always been so gentle.

She spoke louder, even though it meant Erik could hear her too. "What was left of the skull? That's where she was shot; the right parietal and temporal bones were shattered, but—"

"*Erik,*" Mal said, and swung Nora around toward his brother, who had come closer too. "Take her inside."

"No!" Nora struggled but was easily passed from one man to the other. She supposed Mal didn't trust Erik to speak as diplomatically as he would to the doctor, but how could he trust him to take charge of his wife?

Did he not see, or not care, how viciously Erik gripped her, how he nearly yanked her off her feet as he towed her back toward the house and up the porch steps? He dragged her inside and then into the parlor, where he shoved her down onto the settee and pushed a hard hand into the center of her chest when she tried to rise, driving the breath from her lungs.

"What the *fuck* are you tryin' to do? You want me arrested? Executed?" He stood so close his knees touched Nora's; she was trapped. "You want to get me out of here that bad, huh? You want to punish me, like I'm the only one who did wrong? Or is this the only way you can stop yourself from wantin' me every goddamn second of every day?"

He'd leaned even closer, and pressed his knee between her own as he held her arms.

Unable to move away for all her writhing, Nora spat in his face.

Erik bared his teeth and grabbed her jaw hard enough to bruise it, wrenched her face upward as he brought his own closer. "Stop fightin' yourself."

Footsteps in the hall—Nora prayed that it would be Mal. Even if she had to explain everything that had already happened.

But it was Marie, to whom Nora had given a small measure of laudanum again, to help her rest. Now, she murmured, "What are you doing?"—sounding as if she might believe herself in a dream.

Erik let go of Nora and backed away, then turned and stalked out the french doors.

Nora remained seated, tense and trembling, massaging her jaw and trying to steady her breathing. She didn't look up at Bea and Kirsten as Marie scuffed partly through them on her way to sit down.

"Are you all right?"

Nora nodded, vision wobbling.

"Did he bring Bea back?"

At that, Nora's tears finally spilled over. "I'm sorry," she said. "She's gone."

~

Nora didn't attempt to leave the house again that day; Mal and Erik handled the milking, and constructed a coffin, judging by the sounds of sawing and hammering. She served her drawn husband a silent dinner. Erik must have eaten in his cabin, if at all. Later, Nora tried to sleep in the spare room but couldn't, so moved her chair into Marie and the girls' room, unwilling to indent Bea's empty bed.

In the morning, she shambled to the barn—momentarily arrested by the sight of the mountain lion's eviscerated carcass now hanging outside Erik's cabin.

She only glanced at him and Mal long enough to see that their eyes were as red-rimmed as her own. It was easy to read sadness and sleeplessness into Mal's, though for Erik, Nora wasn't certain. Guilt, she imagined. Anger. Drink exacerbating rather than assuaging either.

It was almost a relief when Dr. Burns's stately black carriage returned before milking was finished—except, this time, Nora's father stepped out after him.

"What are you doing here?" She shot an accusatory look at Mal, but saw that he was equally surprised.

Her father approached to gently embrace her, teary at the mere sight of her. "I'm so sorry to hear about what happened, love." Indeed, he looked almost frighteningly distressed.

Nora had a wild moment of hope—that Dr. Burns had noticed something suspicious about Bea's remains after all, and planned on questioning Erik further, that her father had come to help protect her, but then her fear flared; they should have brought the police. Nora looked toward the margin of the woods, as if she might see more men hidden there.

But no human figures shifted among the skeletal trees.

Mal asked if Erik could finish up alone. He grunted assent, though Nora thought he tensed in anticipation of being discussed in private. She walked back to the house with anxious hope building in her, but quickly understood she was to be excluded, too, meant to make breakfast while the men talked. "Marie can manage," she insisted. "And whatever you have to say you can say in front of me."

So they all settled in the parlor. Nora had the distinct sense that they were poised to grab her if she made any sudden movements. As if she was the one who had done wrong—which, dear God, she had. Still, her stomach dropped when her father finally spoke.

"We're concerned about you. Angus telegrammed about the poor wee lass—such an awful thing. But . . . he mentioned you said some troubling things as well."

Nora stayed quiet now.

Her father forced himself to hold her gaze as he continued. "I've kept certain things from you, love. As any parent does. As we try our best to protect our children. And I didn't worry about you, not for a long time. After Euan . . . even after you first came here, I did. But then I saw how glad you were, how content, and how much Mr. Colquhoun clearly cares for you. But you've suffered several great shocks now, a series of terrible losses, and . . . being isolated here, I don't think it's good for you. It's compounded all your other troubles, and I believe it's clouding your mind."

"You're clouding it," Nora finally said. "Still not saying whatever you mean to. What have you kept from me? What does it have to do with any of this?"

With a glance at Dr. Burns, her father muffled another sigh and leaned slightly forward. "Your mother, Nora . . . she didn't die of fever. There were complications from the birth—but not of the body. It was her mind . . ."

"She tried to harm you," Dr. Burns said when his friend faltered. "When you were just an infant. She suffered delusions, Nora. And when treatment—"

Nora's father cut him off. "She thought she could see things that weren't there; that she could hear our other bairns crying, when they'd been dead before they were born. I tried to help her. And she seemed to get better for a while, but then . . ."

"Then what?" Nora breathed.

"She took her own life," Dr. Burns said.

Nora wanted to strike him.

"I didn't want you to think poorly of her," Nora's father added. "I didn't want to burden you with that. But I should have warned you . . ."

"What? That I might be crazy too?" Nora felt numb. Bea and Kirsten stood not far behind her father's chair, but she looked at Mal, and wondered if he had heard this painful secret before she had; he didn't look surprised, only sympathetic.

Her father said, "I simply think you should be in a more familiar environment for now. Less taxing. Less . . . lonesome."

"I can't leave," Nora said. Not without the rest of them, she meant. Mal, and Marie, and Addie; her family. Erik could rot.

When she rose from the settee, all three men stood too; she was certain they meant to converge on her, propel her out to the waiting carriage and cart her back to town, then Manhattan, and who knew where. They would bind her, drug her, do whatever was necessary to keep her calm. She would never be able to reason with them again.

She dashed away and brushed past Marie, who had come to stand and listen from the hall, then ran upstairs and shut herself inside Euan's room, where Bea and Kirsten appeared a second later. Nora was aware of the scalpels behind them, in their leather roll near the desk.

She braced the chair beneath the doorknob, and though she readied herself for the pounding of a half dozen feet in close pursuit, and then the battering of hands upon the door, there was only silence—that deep, expectant silence from which the house observed.

And then, softly, Mal's knock, and his voice speaking her name.

Nora let him in, and shut the door again behind him, then clamped his arms in her fingers. "Please. Don't let them take me. You promised—to protect me."

"From yourself, too," he said.

Nora looked deeply into his troubled eyes. "We can hire someone to come help keep up the house and cook, like you said. We can send out the laundry, and get a nurse for Addie. I made a terrible mistake falling asleep, I know, and I am so tired, and so sad, but I am not crazy. And I can't go—not where they want to take me. Please."

When she saw him waver, she took his rough, broad hand and placed it upon her stomach, still not dramatically distended, still easy enough to conceal under clothing, but prominent enough to communicate the truth by touch.

"Please. Let me stay with you. Please."

A welter of emotions passed over Malcolm's face, but when he enfolded Nora in his arms, she knew she had been pardoned—yet again.

It would be in her best interest to go back down and tell her father that she understood his concern but would be fine with rest and the return of spring, that Mal would take care of her in the meanwhile, and always. But she was shaken, and incensed, not only at what he wished to do with her but at the revelation of what he had withheld, at the fact that he had actively lied for years to cover up the truth that should have been her birthright. She couldn't even begin to wonder what it might mean, if anything; she needed time, perhaps an eternity, to digest its very existence.

And she couldn't face him just then, so Mal agreed to speak with him alone. Surely, they had conferred that way before, sometime prior to the marriage. Nora's father must have said enough, at least, to make Mal concerned, watchful.

Yet Mal hadn't been the one who summoned him. He mustn't have divulged Nora's claim to see ghosts yet, either.

"Don't tell him," she said, pressing Malcolm's palm to her stomach once more. "Or he'll come back with a court order. He has lots of wealthy friends. And rich patients who like to do him favors. You won't be able to help me then."

~

Only a few minutes after Mal left Nora with a brief kiss on her lips and another on her forehead, Adelaide woke, and her moans swelled until they filled the house.

Nora's father and Dr. Burns both rushed up. Though Nora's face flamed for her father to see her administering the laudanum, she had no other choice.

To forestall any questions, she told them what she was doing, like an instructor on rounds describing their actions for attentive students. "Just a few drops, diluted in water—she'll drink it right down once she stops crying. But she's been like this since poor Bea . . ."

When the doctors pressed closer, Nora interposed. Mal and Marie flanked her, maybe only by happenstance, but she was glad that they presented a united front. "She'll only get more upset if you try to touch her. She'll wear herself out in a minute." More quickly now that she was more regularly and heavily dosed again; Nora sometimes wondered that Addie ever managed to wake.

"She needs medical attention," Dr. Burns observed.

"That's what she's getting," Nora answered, rather sharply. "What more could you do? Except agitate her with useless experiments. She's not some fascinating case for you to work up in a journal, or an animal to study. She's a little girl. Who's just seen her poor sister—"

Shot, she almost said, but bit back the word and let the silence ring out.

The doctors exchanged more looks that made Nora bristle. She turned back to Addie, the room far too crowded—the ghosts, too, pressed into the corner, forced to fit where they could.

When Addie calmed and flickered her thin little fingers, made a soft half-coo, Nora offered the water glass. Addie took it and gulped its contents without stopping for breath.

"There," Nora said. They all watched Addie slowly slump as her eyelids flittered. A moment more and she was fully relaxed upon her pillow, Marie once more petting her flushed cheek.

～

Nora, reasonably certain now that Mal wouldn't let her be hauled away, went back downstairs to attend to chores; she needed something to occupy her hands, and the house was a mess. She was embarrassed that her father and Dr. Burns had seen it in such a state.

No mourners came by. She wondered if Mal had put out the word that they wanted no company, or if people were so horrified by what had happened that they instinctively stayed away. The snow and the cold helped, Nora supposed. No one wanted to venture out. And perhaps they didn't know how to sympathize with the loss of such a strange child, oblivious to how precious she had been.

Nora was streaming tears again, washing the french doors in the dining room—scrubbing away all but Bea's and Kirsten's wavering reflections—when Malcolm came to find her. Her name was dreadfully soft in his mouth.

"I need to tell you something," he said.

She was certain that he'd changed his mind, that the other men had swayed him, that disclosing her condition had backfired, been exceedingly misguided after what her father had only just revealed about Nora's poor, delusional mother.

But what Mal said was "We've agreed that Adelaide should go back to the city with your father and Dr. Burns."

"What?" A confusing mixture of relief and horror churned through Nora's body.

"They can secure a . . . more consistent level of care, in a proper setting—"

"In an *institution*," Nora hissed. "In a cage. Maybe literally."

"They'll choose the best facility—"

"No *facility* is the best place. The best place is with her mother."

Mal faltered; his voice frayed. "I know that Marie loves Adelaide with all her heart—we all do, but—things are . . . precarious, right now. We're all grieving, and exhausted."

Those truths were so heavy, Nora felt she might crumble. But it seemed dangerous to send Addie away, as final as death itself.

"Once things are settled," Mal went on, "then we can bring her back, of course. You and Marie could go visit in the meanwhile. And who knows how much they might be able to help her?"

"Help her with *what*?" Nora retorted. "You know she's never going to be a normal little girl, don't you? Who sings and smiles and picks you flowers? They can't make her into that. And she'll be so confused and scared, to be in a new place without anyone she knows—and after what's just happened. That won't make her any better."

"She'll be taken care of," Mal said, his voice strained, but sincere.

Nora studied his face and wondered if this was the bargain—they would take the broken little girl instead of the damaged woman. They had come to solve a problem, and were clearly determined to leave with some blighted soul that they might cure.

She wondered if Mal believed that Addie might really come back, or if he felt relieved at the thought of her being permanently removed from their lives. Even she could see how that would make things easier. And she wondered if he worried that, if Addie stayed, Nora might hurt her. She could still feel how closely he—and everyone—had watched her administer the laudanum.

Maybe it was smart to send Addie away—from Nora, and from the house, from the cursed land that seemed intent on taking as many of them as it could. She knew that was a damningly mad notion, but it struck her as quite sane. So she dipped her rag again and drew a deep breath as she wrung it out. "All right, then. If you think that's best."

≈

Though Marie was inconsolable, Nora restrained herself from offering the forced relief of opiates. Instead, she sat on the edge of the bed and stroked Marie's shoulder until she cried herself into a state of torpor.

Erik seemed mildly surprised but not angry—nor, for that matter, regretful or particularly relieved—when he was informed that his remaining daughter was to be taken away. He shot an inscrutable look at Nora and then walked off.

≈

Bea's coffin was sealed before Erik carried it from the cabin. Nora stared at the unvarnished lid and then the dirt that covered it, as if she might yet see through to what lay beneath.

That night, she stared at Bea's ghost as it stood by Kirsten's in Euan's room. "Tell me what happened," she whispered. "Please. Did he hurt you?" Pointlessly, Nora pushed paper and pastels toward the little spirit's bare feet. "Can you draw me a picture?"

Of course it couldn't. And even if Bea's ghost were capable of such a thing, Nora doubted a legible scene would be sketched. Instead, she envisioned stripes of bright blue and deep crimson covering the page, bleeding off its edges to mark the floorboards and be swallowed by shadows.

CHAPTER
FORTY-THREE

Hoosick Falls, NY
February–March 1888

The next morning, the bruises Erik left on Nora's jaw finally bloomed. Convenient that they'd hidden from her father and Dr. Burns—though she didn't know if she would have told the truth about how she'd acquired them had they noticed.

Mal didn't see them, or at least didn't mention them, but then Nora kept her head down. Perhaps it was so gloomy in the house and barn that the marks blended in.

She only glanced sidelong at Erik, who said nothing else to her.

But Nora felt more frightened by his silence—and plagued by even more wildly frightening ideas that seemed terrifyingly plausible.

For instance, perhaps Olaf's pernicious spirit had not been destroyed by Kirsten's earthly passing but released. Nora had only half-heartedly attempted to keep it contained, after all. She'd spent more effort ignoring it—and then become distracted by more pressing matters, more urgent hauntings.

If she felt that the cellar was truly empty now, perhaps it was only because Olaf's specter had made a new den.

Erik's pervasive aura of malefic possessiveness might indicate more than inherited tendencies and spent patience.

He might be critically infected.

~

After morning milking and breakfast, Nora mounted her bicycle and pedaled through the patchy snow to town, to Grace. There was no one else she could possibly talk to about the things on her mind. And though she knew she shouldn't, she had to purge them, if only to relieve some of the nauseating pressure in her gut.

Grace answered the door wearing her coat. The smile slid from her face even before her eyes went to Nora's jaw.

After an excruciating beat of silence, Nora said, "I'm sorry—were you going out?"

"Just to the grocer. It can wait."

So they went inside, where Alvie sat beside his own coat on the floor, twisting at a loose button. Nora automatically looked for Ezra, then remembered that he was in school with Annie.

"I'm so sorry," Grace sighed. "To hear about Marie's poor little girls."

News of both developments must have circulated through the village already, then: Beatrice's passing and Adelaide's removal.

"Still," Grace said, "it might be for the best."

Nora frowned, confused. Surely Grace couldn't mean to include Bea's death in that statement—though Nora vaguely recalled a similar thought flitting darkly through her own mind not long ago. She hadn't really meant it. She never would have said it out loud.

Since Grace clearly wasn't going to take off her coat, Nora didn't remove hers either. She had so many questions it was difficult to choose one to speak aloud. She was too afraid to ask if Grace had ever experienced any difficult emotions after giving birth—afraid to offend her, and afraid to intrigue her. Nora had no intention of divulging what she'd only just learned about her own mother, much less admitting that she herself was pregnant so Grace could speculate on the father; suddenly, Nora was glad of her bulky coat and Grace's strange inhospitality.

"Do you believe in ghosts?" she finally asked.

Grace looked surprised, then wistful. "No," she said. "Do you?"

"Yes. But I don't understand what they want. Or how they come into being. Or don't."

Grace blinked at her. "Well, you're a smarter woman than me, I'm sure. So I couldn't possibly tell you."

"Maybe it has something to do with guilt," Nora mused. "If you feel it strongly enough, maybe it binds you to them. But I can't tell if they're really *there*, if they *know* they're there, or if they're just . . . like a photographic image. An impression I made. Some people have stronger wills than others, though; so why couldn't they persist, after death? And what could they do, if . . . ?" She fidgeted with her gloves. "Your church . . . you believe in possession, don't you?"

"Some do," Grace said.

"Olaf's ghost . . . I saw it once, in the cellar. And then, after Kirsten died, he seemed to disappear. But what if she just wasn't there to keep him shut away? What if he got out?"

Grace took a subtle step back.

"You said, once," Nora went on, "that Erik wasn't like his father, but . . . I'm not sure that's true. I'm worried that Olaf . . . got inside him."

Grace pressed her lips together. "Does this have something to do with those bruises on your face? Malcolm didn't put them there, I know." She pulled her shoulders back, spine perfectly straight. "Maybe you shouldn't have let yourself get close enough to be harmed. You dance with the devil and he plays the tune. On his fiddle, of course."

Nora's face flushed with heat. Her throat pinched. "I suppose nobody says I broke the curse anymore, do they?"

Grace looked somewhat sympathetic, as she must have looked when Ellen came to her with her troubles—but there was also haughtiness in her expression, which Nora hoped she'd spared her sister. "I'm sorry, Mrs. Colquhoun, I can't have this conversation with you. I can't help you. I have to go."

But Nora couldn't leave without some succor, or at least confirmation, encouragement. "Do you think there's a way to exorcise a spirit from a body that doesn't belong to it? Without getting too close? Or—"

"Go talk to your pastor," Grace suggested, softly, as she motioned Nora toward the door.

Obediently, Nora went, but turned again with her hand upon the knob. "The whole town will be talking about all this by Sunday."

Something like shame flickered in Grace's expression, but she raised her chin and said, "Not that you would know. You don't even come in for church anymore. Maybe you should."

Another spear of shame lanced Nora, and she nodded faintly. Before she let herself out, she glanced over Grace's shoulder, where Bea and Kirsten stood, dripping blood and water on the unmarked floor. Proof they could follow her off the farm. She supposed that was good to know.

~

At home, she studied Erik to see if she might divine any damning signs, but he seemed the same: tetchy, angry, suffused with sarcasm and resentment and frustrated entitlement. His father had been in his blood since he was born; Olaf's ghost didn't need to slip through any crack in Erik's armor.

But Hannah Colquhoun had surely contributed some tempering characteristics, and Erik's elder brothers had exerted more positive influences upon his developing person.

Nora had always thought herself so much like her father that she might have sprung fully formed from his forehead. In the back of her mind, she'd known that her mother made her, too, and had seen evidence in her sprinkled freckles, and her narrow feet, the bow of her upper lip so much like Grandmama's and Aunt Birdie's and Bette's.

Yet she'd given little thought to what ineffable psychological or spiritual qualities her mother might have passed on.

Now that Nora's father had told her the truth about her mother's sad end, however, she was consumed with thoughts of what else she had given her, and what else might have happened.

Had her mother succeeded in killing her, as brutally and instinctually as some animals ate their young, then so much suffering would have been averted.

Other sorrows would have been created in their stead, of course—Nora's father and her maternal relatives would have mourned her, or some idea of her, for the remainder of their lives.

But Euan, even if he had come to stay in Dr. Harris's brownstone as a young medical student, wouldn't have come under her destructive influence, and might not have stood in the path of Babcock's blade. Certainly, Mal would have gone on with his life as it had been—steady, reasonably serene.

Kirsten and Beatrice would still be alive, and Addie at home, and Marie as happy as the day on which she and Nora had met. Erik would never have become fixated on her, and might have remained content.

Nora saw herself in a new light now: she was the infectious agent that had forced its way into the farm and the family, and slowly poisoned them all.

There was one obvious cure. But she'd waited too long, and touched her growing belly with a tender despair.

She tried not to think about what might happen if the baby came and was blond and blue-eyed in that icily piercing manner.

Mal would love the child anyway, but Erik would covet it, and surely claim it, by whatever means necessary.

After he had stamped his fingerprints upon her face, Nora wouldn't have stayed alone on the farm with him for anything, and since Addie was gone, she resumed attending church easily enough. Kirsten and Bea appeared along the wall. Nora prayed for them. It couldn't hurt.

Despite the balm of worship, Marie still cried daily over her daughters, asked constantly when Addie would come home, or when they could at least go see her. "Soon," Nora said, because it was the kindest thing.

She felt grossly guilty for all her lies, and for everything she'd done. She didn't want Marie to trust or love her, or seek comfort from her, but Nora couldn't deny her, so on the nights when Marie's weeping carried down the hall, Nora went to lie beside her.

One such night in mid-March, after Nora had held her until she stopped shaking, Marie sniffled and turned and gingerly touched her fingertips to Nora's belly. "I wish I had more," she murmured. "But Erik says no 'cause they don't turn out right."

Then Nora cried, and Marie nestled closer and held her until they both fell asleep.

∾

The next night, Nora sat vigil in Euan's room, where she'd taken to passing her most restless hours, not wanting to disturb Mal.

She listened for Marie but heard no sobs. When it began to rain, the loud, steady drumming on the roof lulled Nora to sleep.

She dreamed of jumbled images: soft mountain-lion fur, blood-soaked, and Addie's smooth, pale cheek, spattered crimson; Kirsten's wrinkled, water-dripping hands; Old Nick's gleaming skull. And then human eyes, unblinking, bright blue and silver-gray and almost black. They revolved in Nora's mind like unchanging patterns in a broken kaleidoscope, faster and faster, until she began to twitch and toss.

What finally woke her was a thunderous crash.

The roof caving in, she thought, or a rifle blast that she would momentarily discover had punched a hole in her body—unless it had blown apart Mal's chest in their bed across the hall, and where was Marie?

But when Nora sat up with a gasp and a flurry of rapid, flinching blinks, she saw that the source of the noise was even more improbable.

The shimmering abalone box that always sat pushed back on the mantel had not *fallen* off but apparently been pushed, or else picked up and dropped, and landed in the middle of the bedroom floor. It had cracked, and though the burlap bag remained intact, Nora's eyes opened in time to see a faint cloud of dust—of ashes—still hanging in the dim air. Through it, she saw Kirsten and Bea by the closed door, and thought there was some special urgency in their eyes.

For once, Bea's gaze was trained on Nora too.

The instant that her toes touched the floor, however, both spirits flickered out. She found them in the hall, at the head of the stairs, and hurried toward them, only pausing for a second when Mal, woken by the bang of the abalone box, stepped into the corridor and groggily asked what had happened.

"Something's wrong," Nora said as she continued toward the staircase and started down.

He came after.

The ghosts blinked in and out of being, but they were easy enough to follow. When Nora reached the bottom of the stairs, they vanished and rematerialized in the entryway of the dining room—then before the door to the kitchen.

They stood by the cellar door when Nora stepped inside and saw Marie, slumped against the base of the dry sink, a glint of silver on the ground near her limp fingertips. It was dark—the night was without a moon—but Nora's eyes had adjusted enough to make out the knife, and to see the dark blood that sleeved Marie's arm from wrist to elbow.

Mal, close behind her, uttered a strangled sound.

Nora spoke surprisingly calmly. "Go get Matilda saddled. Don't bother with the wagon; there isn't time—you can prop her up in front of you."

He went, and Nora almost asked aloud for a needle and thread, hot water and rags—but even if the ghosts had managed to move the abalone box to wake her, she didn't think they could boil water.

"I'll be right back," she told Marie, and hurried to the parlor to fetch the sewing basket, knowing she should make some attempt at sanitation but fearing it would take too long. She struck a match and lit a candle, held the needle point in its flame for a few seconds, for all the good it might do.

With shaking fingers, in the guttering candlelight, Nora threaded the eye, and murmured reassurances to Marie as she knelt beside her and dabbed at the laceration with a clean kitchen towel. She stopped the bleeding and sewed up the most vulnerable edges. Pressure wouldn't be enough once Marie was jouncing down the forest paths atop a horse at full gallop. Sutures would keep the wound closed until she could get to Dr. Burns, at least. They couldn't wait for him to be fetched and brought back.

"You'll be all right," Nora said, and pierced Marie's pale flesh, pulled the thread taut.

Though Marie's nightdress was dry, her hair was wet and her bare feet dirty; Nora had a clear image of her donning a coat and visiting the cabin. And leaning so close, Nora could smell Erik's scent. Another phantom in the room with them. If she turned, she felt certain she would see him there. Or maybe Olaf, in some form—whether his broken-necked shadow or his indestructible spirit glaring out through Erik's eyes.

CHAPTER
FORTY-FOUR

Hoosick Falls & Hudson Valley, NY
March 12, 1888

Nora finished tying off the stitches and helped Mal half walk, half carry Marie to the door, where they bundled her in warm layers—for the temperature had dropped dramatically, and the rain had turned to snow, fine flakes drifting thickly from the sky.

They maneuvered her out to the porch and down the steps to the waiting horse, Matilda's breath steaming in the cold, her ears twitching in the flurries. Mal mounted and pulled Marie up into the saddle, where she lolled against him. He looked at Nora for a tenuous moment and promised to be back soon.

She watched them go, then looked toward the cabin, from which Erik had not emerged. She was tempted to retreat inside the farmhouse, lock the doors and barricade herself inside Euan's room, where his ashes lay like dust upon the floor.

But ignoring a problem never made it go away. So Nora went through the cold swirls of snow to the cabin and pounded on the door until Erik opened it, looking like he might have been asleep.

"What did you say to her?" Nora demanded.

"What?"

"Marie just carved a furrow in her arm. I hope I closed it well enough. Mal's taking her to Dr. Burns. But—"

"What are you talkin' about?"

"She took the sharpest knife we have and sliced her veins open—and she came here first. You must have said something—"

"I didn't say shit." Erik's expression hardened as his posture straightened, swelled. "At least nothin' I hadn't already said before. And she carved her arm—how would she even know how to do that, huh? She saw all your morbid goddamn textbooks and your nasty little pictures. Or maybe she just saw your scar and got the gist."

Nora's stomach dropped. No matter how desperately she still wanted to blame Erik for everything that had happened, she knew she was culpable—perhaps in more ways than she'd realized.

"We have to go," she said.

Erik glanced up, blinked against the snowflakes that blew in his open door. "There's no point sittin' in the doctor's parlor when we can wait just as well back here. Gotta tend the cows in another few hours anyway. If it keeps on like this, Mal's liable to get delayed. We all get stuck there, then everything's fucked to hell and back. But you go ahead and pedal in if you want."

Nora did want to—to flee the farm and take Mal and Marie with her, and never look back. But Erik would follow. She had to ensure that he couldn't, that he would cause no further harm. She kept her voice calm and even. "I mean we have to leave, together. Now. We'll never get another chance like this."

Erik's surprise made him look oddly young.

"You were right," Nora said, her teeth beginning to chatter in the cold. "We don't belong here. We shouldn't have stayed this long. But it isn't too late to go."

"What are you playin' at?" Erik asked.

"I'm admitting the truth," Nora said. "If I'd done it before, I might have saved us all a world of trouble. I don't even know if—" Her voice broke. "I don't know if Marie's coming back. She lost a lot of blood before I found her. And who knows what got into the wound."

Erik looked down at Nora's bloodied hands. "*You* found her, doc. Imagine that."

Nora tucked her hands closer to her sides. "Why would I hurt her? I was sound asleep. They were clean when I woke up in bed and went downstairs. *You're* the last one who saw her before she started bleeding; I *know* that."

"And if you think I had any damn thing to do with it—any of it— then why the hell would you want to go anywhere with me?"

"Because we're the same," Nora said. "We're awful people."

Erik's face relaxed somewhat, but he was still guarded. "You wouldn't do such a thing to Mal."

"I already ruined his life." Nora didn't have to try to make it sound like a harsh truth. "It's just going to get even worse."

She loosened the belt of her flannel robe and opened it, pulled the slightly thinner fabric of her nightgown taut against her swollen stomach. "He can live with a lot, but he shouldn't have to. And there'll be no pretending once it's born."

Erik stared at her belly as hungrily as Kirsten's ghost did when it caught Nora exposed. He reached out one huge hand, and Nora forced herself not to flinch as he touched her—gently, with a sort of wonder.

"We might only have a couple of hours' head start," she said. "If you're right about the snow, then maybe more. We can leave the calves and cows together; it won't be so bad if they don't get milked in time. And we'll go away from town—we could make Eagle Bridge before Mal got there. My father's sent more money, at least enough for a couple tickets. I can wire for more when it's gone."

"We don't have to run," Erik said, surprising Nora. "We can just . . . explain it to him."

She scoffed, a ghostly puff of breath in the cold. "You want to watch his heart break? I don't. And it's less humiliating if we don't say it to his face. We can send him a letter, later. Sort out all our thoughts on paper, make sure he understands. Besides, he prefers writing to talking." Though she felt a bolt of shame, it was tipped with genuinely bitter resentment, still there in some deep, dark well within her.

"I can't live like this," she said, voice shaking with the cold and with the threat of tears—and the weight of the truth. "I can't. I know you can't either. So let's go. Before something even worse happens."

Erik huffed and dragged the back of his hand across his lips. "Jesus Christ. If you're serious, all right. Go pack, then." He glanced at the sky again, still spilling snowflakes. "Warm. Expect to spend a few nights sleepin' rough. Just in case."

Nora packed in a careless hurry, under Kirsten's watchful eyes, though Bea's gaze remained upon the ground. She bit her tongue to keep from muttering to them, not knowing quite what she would have said. *It isn't what you think?* She had no idea what they thought, or if they did at all. If they were indeed projections of her own brain, or whether that mattered.

She hesitated only briefly before scrawling a note to leave on Mal's pillow: *I'm sorry, for everything.* It wasn't enough, but she needed him to know that much. She made sure the laudanum bottle was still in her pocket and went back downstairs, ducked into the parlor to glance at the time: after one o'clock. They still had several hours of night through which to travel, in which to stay concealed.

She considered cleaning up the blood from the kitchen floor, but there wasn't time, and it was hardly the worst thing Mal would find when he returned.

Nora made herself leave the house without looking back, and found Erik in the barn, saddling Odin. His hunting satchel was slung on his back, as was his rifle. She'd layered a long, fur-trimmed wool cloak over her coat, over which he swept his gaze.

"You need better boots."

"We'll be riding," she said. "Not walking."

They opened stalls to let the heifers and their babies mingle. Erik forked out hay enough to tide them over, and enough for Aggie and

Jasper too. They didn't bother with the pigs or sheep or chickens, conscious of every second that passed.

They briefly debated closing the barn door behind them or leaving it open in case the animals needed water before Mal got back. They settled on leaving it propped halfway, and opened the horses' stalls too.

In the yard, Erik mounted first, then helped Nora into the saddle behind him and clicked his tongue, tapped Odin with his heels to start them on their way.

The snow was unrelenting. It quickly covered the ground and continually blew into their faces, making Erik curse and Odin toss his mane and snort. Nora bent her head into Erik's back and clung to him, fought to stop from shouting that they should turn around nearly every second.

Soon enough, she sensed that it was too late. She didn't know exactly where they were, nor did she know how Erik kept his bearings, if he did.

He kept them mostly under cover of the trees, where they were afforded some protection from the snow, though the wind tore through and downed branches of considerable size—Nora thought they would be struck at any second.

Perhaps an hour or two into their trek, Erik brought them into a clearing where the wind howled and drove the blinding snow into their eyes—but through the streaks of white, Nora could see a homestead, long abandoned, dilapidated.

"We'll have to hunker down here awhile," Erik said, and steered them toward it, then helped Nora dismount. Rather than hobble Odin outside, Erik led the horse right inside the small, half-collapsed house, and looped his reins over a chair with a seat that had rotted out.

Within the interior walls, the shrieking wind was substantially muffled, reduced to strange moans and shrill whistles.

Nora looked around. "What is this place?"

"Some poor sap's busted dreams," Erik said, and shrugged. "Been empty since I was a kid—we used to camp out here. Wish it still had the whole roof. At least there's this."

He uncovered a stash of firewood by the hearth, surrounded by broken tiles. He set to work lighting a blaze, and Nora turned in a slow circle, peering into the deeply shadowed corners, some portions bright with drifting snow.

She hadn't seen Bea or Kirsten in hours, but then, she'd kept her eyes closed for most of the journey. Now, when they didn't emerge as she expected, she felt a strange sort of panic, as if she'd lost track of her friends in the storm.

There was nothing to do but wait out the weather and try to stay warm.

It was obvious that Mal would be stuck in town. *Unless he was on his way back and got caught out in it,* Nora thought. *He could have gotten turned around, or bogged down, and . . .*

She pushed the thought away and leaned closer to the fire, tried not to tense too noticeably when Erik sat close. He'd unfurled a bedroll, and Nora knew they would both have to sleep on it, but at least it was too cold for him to try to undress her. Not that he cared if they kept their clothes on.

She managed not to flinch when he placed his palm upon her stomach again, and asked how long it had been. She wasn't sure, but told him otherwise, that it could only be his.

And it could have been—just. Just as it could have been Mal's, conceived on the night before Kirsten's ghost appeared.

"Do you think it's a boy or a girl?"

Nora answered honestly. "I don't know."

Erik's hand covered too much of her belly, made it seem a thing that naturally belonged to him. He rubbed his thumb over it, like he might absently fondle a dog. Nora felt herself on the verge of tears again, or vomiting.

"I can make a good one," he said.

She looked at him and felt a rush of sympathy, and rage. *The girls are good,* she thought. She said, "I know. Ezra. Ellen. I'm sorry."

Erik's Adam's apple bobbed as he swallowed, brightness pooling in his eyes. He finally removed his hand and looked away, toward the snow whipping past a broken window; Nora looked the other way, and could see a bedroom—and past it, the snow whipping past the half-fallen exterior wall.

They slept, a little. Not well, or for very long. The musky smell of animal hide suffused her nostrils from the bedroll, but at least it was soft.

The snow did not abate, though eventually, the world outside grew lighter, as did the interior of the house.

Nora surveyed the remaining firewood. It wouldn't last long, but there was other material they might repurpose for fuel. Food was another matter. Unless Erik decided to butcher his beloved horse, which Nora could quite easily imagine, though he'd always been gentle with Odin.

He'd brought some rations—*cowboy food*, he called it. Beans and dried meat and a few jars of Kirsten's tomatoes and pickles, the last hard heel of a loaf of bread, a bit of cheese and butter. He scooped snow into a small iron pot he'd packed and added a few bits of leathery meat, some beans.

"May as well let it simmer. Stew for dinner. Doesn't look like we'll be goin' anywhere for a while yet."

Midmorning, they ate the bread and butter. Nora took a bite of corn relish, but all she tasted was the dank breath of the farmhouse cellar. She wondered if Marie was alive. If Addie was all right. If Mal was. If the animals had frozen yet.

She swiped at her cheeks and gazed at the stewpot, wondering when she would have a chance to tip the laudanum into it. But she wasn't sure if cooking would render it ineffective. Best to wait and stir it in at the last moment, then.

Meanwhile, they watched the snow pile deeper and white out the world.

"Will you tell me the truth?" she asked Erik in late afternoon.

"About what?"

"Everything." She touched her stomach in hopes that it might move him.

"Shoot," he said.

Nora paused a moment at his choice of word. "Did you kill Bea? I know it was my fault that she was out there in the woods. I shouldn't have fallen asleep. But it was an accident. And if you shot her . . . then I know that was an accident too."

Erik sighed and sat back down to poke at the fire. "I was out trackin' that lion, like I said. Half blind by then from starin' at the ground so long. The brush was all blurrin' together. And then I saw this dark shape in the trees, low down—thought it was either the cat or a deer. Not a fuckin' person. So I fired."

He dug a flask out of his pocket. Nora was surprised that he'd waited so long.

"Why didn't you just admit it?" she asked. "That it was an accident."

"Like anyone would have believed that? I wasn't about to risk it— jail, maybe even the rope?"

Nora imagined him finding Stephen hanging from a beam, only the day after seeing Johan slip under the ice. "Why didn't you just bury her, then? After?"

"I don't know. I thought maybe you'd find her anyway, like you did Kirsten."

Nora's breath caught. "And Kirsten? Did you . . . ?"

With an exasperated huff, Erik took another drink and looked Nora squarely in the eyes. "I saw when she left the house that night—while you all were on your way to dinner—and I followed, 'cause I wondered what the hell she was doin', leavin' the girls. With a goddamn suitcase. Trailed her all the way out to the pond, watched her stand there for a while. Finally stepped out and called her name—and she was scared as all hell. But she recovered. And she had a whole lot of choice words for me then. I'll admit, it riled me up pretty good. So I stepped up close to her, and I . . . I grabbed her. I squeezed her neck for a good five seconds.

Then I let go. Walked away and left her there and she was damn sure still breathin'. But hell, I might've killed her if I'd known she had all your sock money on her."

Nora believed he was telling the truth, which meant that they were both accountable for what had happened, and that he was capable of worse.

She decided that she would empty all of what was left of the laudanum into the stew before she served them. She would eat her fill too.

That way, Erik wouldn't be suspicious. And both their harmful legacies would be stamped out.

They were if not themselves natural agents of destruction, then irreparably diseased, and should be extirpated before they caused any more contagion.

It was a kinder end than they deserved, perhaps, but they had suffered too—and who was to say what was enough pain, or adequate punishment?

For all Nora knew, they might continue to suffer afterward anyway.

CHAPTER
FORTY-FIVE

Hudson Valley, NY
March 1888

Erik only had one bowl—or at least he brought only one out from his pack. Nora wondered if it was a tactic, was convinced of it when he handed it to her and nodded at the pot. "Time to dish it up, I think."

He watched too closely for her to try the laudanum, and she felt a pang of desperation twined with fury. She filled the bowl and brought it back to him, folded herself onto the floor by his side. The stew looked too red in the firelight, like a bowl of blood, and Nora's stomach churned.

She looked at Odin; Erik had removed his saddle, which rested on the floor with the pack and rifle propped against it. She didn't think she could get to the gun fast enough. Even if she could, she didn't know how to use it. She might pick up the heavy, blazing stewpot and swing it at Erik's head, stun him at the very least, maybe kill him—a broken skull, a bright-red mask of blood flowing down his face.

But she couldn't walk out of that place, with no idea where she was, and with snowdrifts swallowing the trees. Nor was she certain she could manage to saddle and ride Odin—yet images of all these things flickered through her head. Darkly enchanting, despite her determination to kill herself along with Erik.

And yet, as he had once remarked, they were animals, driven by the urge to live. When he proffered the bowl of stew, Nora made herself take a bite as she studied him. It didn't seem to matter now if Erik was or ever had been possessed by his father's spirit, or if he had only inherited savage traits from him. The Swede. Rumored practitioner of animal sacrifice and blood curses. Doomed by his own avarice and malice.

Well, Nora thought, weren't they all?

She tried to imagine what life might be like, if she and Erik did manage to make it out of that otherworldly, half-snowed-in hovel, but her mind was as blank as the clearing outside, covered in frozen white.

"We shall be monsters," she thought, *"cut off from all the world; but on that account we shall be more attached to each other."* She shivered.

The only thing that she could clearly picture was a small, smooth head, covered in bright-red hair; fat cheeks that would surely freckle the moment they spent any time in the sun; smiling eyes the color of the deepest ocean.

She was seized by terror to imagine what might happen if she gave birth to such a precious baby, wherever she ended up with Erik. She was dreadfully certain that he would have no love for such a child.

And whatever he felt for Nora, she knew that she had no love for him. But she wasn't heartless, as he'd said. She felt, just then, that she was nothing but her heart. A great fist, still fighting.

"I have to use the bathroom," she said, and walked to the far corner of the house that they had chosen to use as a latrine.

Hidden from Erik by an interior wall, Nora reached into her pocket and withdrew the flannel-wrapped scalpel that she'd slipped inside the previous night.

She left the flannel on the floor and held the scalpel close to her side, attempting to make it look like a natural posture. She tried to calm her ragged breathing and gather her courage before she walked back into the main room.

Erik's eyes were on her the instant she appeared in the doorway. Just inside it, Nora stopped, abruptly placed her free hand on her stomach.

"What is it?" he asked, and immediately rose to come to her side.

It was too late to change her mind, and so, when he was within inches of her, looking worriedly between her belly and her face, Nora lashed out and caught him just underneath the jaw with the razor-sharp blade.

He didn't seem to even feel it, was only startled and confused by the sudden movement. But he became aware of the wet warmth of blood, and glanced down at his chest as he touched his neck, then held his palm out to see it gloved in red. When he looked back up at Nora, his face smooth with little-boy surprise, enough of his long, lean throat was exposed that she easily made a broad stripe of crimson across it, a clean, deep cut, with one decisive movement of her arm.

Erik clapped a useless hand to his opened neck. Blood spilled between his fingers, down his shirt.

"I'm sorry," Nora said—it came out of her mouth as automatically as the tears came from her eyes. But even as she said it, she shoved him, and he stumbled back and fell.

Odin danced sideways at the noise, at the smell of blood, his reins still over the chair, which jerked across the floor and frightened him again.

"Easy," Nora said as she approached, slowly, scared herself. She meant to try and saddle the horse—she'd seen it done enough times to think she could manage.

But then a sharp crack made her flinch and Odin reared, the chair slamming into the wall and splintering. Nora cringed, expecting to be trampled, then felt another surge of fear as she turned and saw Erik had a pistol in his bloody hand, the left one now clamped around his throat.

He must have had a weapon in his pocket, too, Nora thought, and closed her eyes as he fired again.

Odin screamed. His hooves clattered on the rotten floor, and the broken chair flailed and fell from his reins. Nora looked back to see him bolt through the ruined house, a trail of blood marking his route of escape.

But Erik didn't shoot again.

When she looked toward him, Nora saw that he'd lowered the gun. He hadn't been aiming at her, she understood. He'd meant to hit Odin, to prevent her from fleeing.

"Help me," he said now, blood still seeping through his long, lovely fingers. "Fix this, doc. Please."

Nora didn't think she needed to tell him that she couldn't. But she began to approach, pausing when he raised the gun again and gestured toward her hand. "Put that down."

She dropped the scalpel and he lowered the gun to the floor, though he kept his fingers wrapped around it, one on the trigger.

Nora walked to him and lowered herself to the floor by his side.

"Sneaky bitch," he murmured, his voice growing weaker, his color paler.

Nora placed her hand upon his cheek, then stroked his filthy blond hair. He let go of the pistol and groped for her hand. She took it and watched his bright-blue eyes, full of fear, start to lose focus.

Soon, they drifted toward the empty corner, and his grip grew slack, both upon her hand and upon his own throat, the blood only slowly oozing now, a final pair of tears trickling down his temples. The sound of his death rattle was lower than the wind, but would echo in Nora's head forever.

She was shaken by a primal sob, and then a concussive series of aftershocks; she rocked herself through them as Bea and Addie had so often done. When she finally let go of Erik's cold fingers to dry her face and push herself up, she wasn't surprised to see his ghost standing in the corner, the last place his own living eyes had looked. And for a moment, his spirit gazed not at Nora but at its own empty body. When it did finally look her way, she saw anger in its eyes—his eyes—but, unless it was Nora's imagination, there was a shade of smug amusement too.

∾

She had enough food to sustain her for another day, but the snow wouldn't melt for at least a week. She had the rifle but assumed trying to hunt would be a waste of energy, and wanted to leave the broken, newly haunted house at once.

And she still had the laudanum, so after another night of dubious refuge and a final full meal, she set out with some measure of bittersweet comfort, if not hope.

The crimson trail of Odin's blood had long been covered by snow, which, while no longer falling, still blew in heavy curtains of obliterating white.

Nora considered turning back before she lost her way, but if she did, she knew she would die there, which seemed far worse than dying in the woods. She would at least try to find her way through them.

Bundled up in heavy layers—including Erik's stiff, blood-drenched coat and his fur trapper's hat—she wasn't all that cold. In fact, she was almost too hot; she was sweating with the effort of fording the deep drifts when she couldn't go around them. Only the exposed parts of her face tingled, scoured by the blowing snow. The icy, particulate wind seemed to want to infiltrate her body, wrap its freezing tendrils around her veins.

Her feet soon grew numb. She'd decided against Erik's too-large boots, which had been better insulated, because she'd feared they would constantly trip her up. Now, she suspected it wouldn't have mattered.

When she stopped long enough to catch her breath and her sweat began to cool, Nora shivered. She remembered how hypothermia worked and supposed, among many options, it wasn't the worst way to die. But she wasn't done yet. She pushed on with bleak determination, even though her legs grew heavier with every hard-won step. She thought of walking through the soft sand in Newport, backsliding a little for every inch gained. She thought of taking off a layer or two, as she did on the summer-baked beach, and knew that was a bad sign.

The blowing snow shrouded her and further weighed her down. Her strength faded with the daylight.

She stopped in a somewhat sheltered area among the trees, the shadows thickening, though the snow itself emitted a strange luminescence in the eerie gloaming. The instant that she sat down, she realized she would not get up again. She fished the laudanum bottle from her pocket, half expecting it to be frozen, but it was well insulated, and high-proof besides.

She would sip just a little, just to get to sleep before the hypothermia made her start undressing; she wanted to keep whatever shred of dignity she could—and if she did become a ghost, she preferred not to go around naked for eternity.

Clumsy with her gloves on, yet too tired to take them off, Nora unstoppered the bottle and brought it to her lips—then paused, and lifted the laudanum in the direction of Erik's blood-bibbed ghost, which had followed her every step of the way, leaving no footprints or red droplets in the snow to testify to its presence.

It was curious, she thought, how it still wore the same unbuttoned coat that now clad her body. *Ghost clothes,* she thought, and almost smiled a little.

"One last toast," she said, still somewhat breathless. "To carpenters, smiths, weavers, and women."

The ghost did nothing but stand and stare.

"And to the dead, of course," Nora added, then took a small sip of alcohol-and-opium, and sighed as she settled back into the snow, covering her face and head against the cold one last time, against the sight of the outside world.

She was full of wistful sorrow for Mal and her father, and everyone else she loved and would leave behind.

As for those who had already gone, Nora didn't quite dare to hope for reunion, still uncertain where she was headed.

But she wished—with all that was left within her—that she would see Euan again, if only as her dying brain played its kindest tricks and finally freed him to stand before her, if only for an instant.

CHAPTER
FORTY-SIX

Bennington, VT
March 1888

Nora woke in a strange bed—she couldn't see it, but could feel its for-eignness, and smell the unfamiliarity of the air. Fire burned through her hands and feet and face. She felt muzzy-headed, and feared she'd gone blind, but when she patted at her eyes, she felt gauze coverings, which she began to pull at.

Blunt, calloused hands gently stopped her. A familiar voice that she didn't trust to be real said, "Nora. Nora. It's all right. I'm here."

"Mal?"

"I'm here," he said again, and held her hands, raised them to his lips and kissed them. "I'm here."

"Where?"

"Vermont. Just outside Bennington. It's a miracle that someone found you. No one should have been out in that weather, but thank God they were—"

"Where's Marie?"

"Back in Hoosick Falls. She's all right too. Thanks to you and Dr. Burns."

"What happened? Why am I like this?"

She had a horrid image of a pair of croaking ravens plucking out her eyes—but she'd shrouded her face.

Mal stayed her hands again when they flew to her bandages. He kissed her fingers. "You have some frostbite, love, and snow blindness, some swelling—but the doctor says you should be all right in a few more days. You've been here for a week already."

"A week . . . ?"

"You've been sedated, I suppose. I've been searching for you—it took a while to even try to look. All the telegraph wires have been down; the snow drifted nearly sixty inches deep in some parts. How did you even manage . . . ?"

Nora whispered the only word that would come to her just then. "Erik . . ."

Mal hesitated. "You were wearing his coat. The doctor showed me. All that blood. But they haven't found him yet—when was he last with you?"

She could barely speak, but assumed Erik was there now, some-where in the room. If she was really in a room and not hallucinating, or dreaming, or in some strange version of heaven or hell. How would she know?

"There was a house," she murmured. "Nearly tumbled down. He said he used to play there . . ."

"I know it," Mal said. "But you weren't anywhere near there."

"I left. On foot. He's . . ." Nora trailed off and tilted her head as if to hear if anyone was in the room.

"We're alone," Mal said, in a lower voice. "What happened? Your note . . ."

I'm sorry, Nora remembered writing, *for everything.* She swallowed and took a moment to find her voice again. "He's dead. I . . . They'll know, when they find him. That it was me."

She felt Mal's stillness in his hands, but he didn't let go of hers.

"They won't find him, then," he said. "I promise."

∾

He asked no further questions, not wanting to know the truth, perhaps. And he left shortly after, to do whatever was necessary to uphold his vow. Nora imagined another quickly dug grave, but the ground was far too cold for that, so another hiding place, maybe an abandoned well.

Whatever it was, Mal shouldn't have had to do it. That he was willing to made her feel faint with gratitude.

∾

Meanwhile, she better acquainted herself with her surroundings through smell and sound and sensation. She wasn't in a proper hospital, but a nurse came between visits from the kind-voiced Dr. Putnam to bring Nora food and help her to the bathroom.

"The angels are surely looking down on you," she said. "And this little one."

Nora tensed in ambivalence at the woman's soft words and soft touch upon her stomach, then slumped in relief. She'd probed her own belly repeatedly since waking, when she knew she was alone, but hadn't felt any responsive movement yet, and had feared that whatever was still inside her was dead.

Acutely conscious of the fact that Mal hadn't said anything, Nora had assumed the worst—and part of her had been relieved.

But when her sedatives were stopped and began wearing off, the baby finally twitched its limbs again, and Nora cradled her stomach and wept, mostly with more gratitude.

∾

When the bandages were finally removed from Nora's eyes, she rolled them too quickly around the room and felt dizzy, nauseous—but she saw no Kirsten, no Bea.

She saw no Erik, either, until the smiling nurse moved from directly in front of her to reveal him standing by the far wall, staring at Nora. The nurse noticed her jump, and looked toward where Nora's gaze was fixed, then turned back with a questioning frown.

Nora forced herself to look away and smile.

A faint smirk lifted one side of Erik's lips, while bright-red blood sheeted from the livid line cut across his throat, and the shorter nick beneath his jaw.

～

The greatest shock was trying to stand on her own and falling to the floor. Nora's feet had been badly damaged, but she could hobble on the bandaged lumps with the nurse's help, or Mal's, and thought she should be strong enough to manage on her own for a moment.

More startled than badly hurt by the fall, Nora unraveled the windings around one foot and found her toes black, a more horrific sight than Erik eternally bleeding in the corner.

She felt repulsion so intense, she nearly reached down and broke the dead tissue off herself. They had to know the digits were unsalvageable. But she remembered—it came back to her in fragments—that they would wait a while longer, to see if another miracle might occur. It was still possible that life would come back into some or all of the shriveled flesh.

Meanwhile, even rewrapped, the knowledge that it was there, inky black, like a shadow slowly devouring her, made Nora's skin crawl.

"I guess I should have taken your boots," she muttered.

"What's that, dear?" asked the nurse, who had waltzed in at that moment and tutted to see Nora on the floor.

"Nothing." Nora let the nurse gently scold her and help her up and back to bed.

～

Her father came soon after, and covered her with tears and kisses, but once he'd purged that from his system, he talked profusely about the blizzard, strangely elated, not by the storm but by his daughter's surviving it.

"We had over two feet of snow drifted to the door, but that was nothing! It took out all the rails and telegraph lines. I'm only grateful I didn't know you were gone for most of that time. I would have been beside myself!"

He relayed tales of stranded elevated trains in the city, people carrying out ladders to rescue the passengers—"some scoundrels for a fee, if you can believe that. And it's been nigh impossible to get any food for a price that's not highway robbery."

He didn't speak of the less amusing aspects—the four hundred people who had died, half of them in Manhattan alone, an incredibly awful fact that Nora had gleaned from a newspaper she'd convinced the doctor to bring her.

She was glad, though, that her father's preoccupation with the storm and his gratitude that she was alive seemed to eclipse whatever concerns he must have had about how and why she'd ended up out in the blizzard in the first place. Eventually, the police would come, Dr. Putnam unable to hold them off any longer. Nora would tell them that she and Erik had ridden out in search of lost livestock, then gotten disoriented in the rapidly deteriorating weather. She'd say that his horse had bolted, and Erik had been impaled by a broken branch, that in pulling himself free, he'd opened a grisly throat wound that bled profusely. She'd say that she'd stayed with him until he was gone, then taken his coat and started walking, with no idea where she was. It would be plausible enough. Erik would be recorded as one more snowbound body yet to be recovered. And, in time, all but forgotten.

Nora's survival would be thought a miracle. She certainly couldn't understand it, even with her heavy layers and a tiny flame of alcohol in her bloodstream—but even more perplexing than *how* was *why*.

Something even worse in store, she thought. But that didn't feel inevitable either. Not anymore.

"I think I'll lose my feet," she told her father, and felt that it should be more satisfying, or at least more horrifying, but it seemed almost too small a price to pay.

"You don't know that," he said, and squeezed her fingers. "At least your hands are safe."

〜

Nora assumed his immediate thought was that she might pick up a scalpel again—if only he knew—but then supposed he might have been imagining any number of other things.

His daughter turning the pages of a book, or playing the piano, or picking up shells, sketching an illustration; or holding her own child, offering a pointer finger for its tiny, dimpled hand to wrap around.

Maybe that was why she had survived, Nora thought. To bring forth and nurture life at last, to make a better person than herself.

Or maybe it was only random chance.

Whatever the reason, she felt duty-bound to make the most of the unearned time that she had been given. To do good work, as her father had always suggested.

〜

When Mal returned, not long before she was discharged from Dr. Putnam's treatment rooms, he told Nora that he was selling off the farm. "However much of it people are willing to buy, at any rate. But we'll move, wherever you want."

She swallowed a bitter surge of guilt and shameful satisfaction and said immediately, "Washington Heights—it's less than an hour's ride from my father's, but there are woods there, and some lovely homes—or we could build one, have some land. You could plant a garden, at least.

Keep a horse or two. Even a cow, if you want. And we'll bring Marie with us, won't we? And Addie too?"

"Yes," he said, and brought Nora's hand to his lips again.

She was sure that he'd kissed her more times in the last few days than in all the previous ones they had spent together, and she cried as she clung to him.

CHAPTER
FORTY-SEVEN

Manhattan, NY
March 1888–March 1926

Sometimes, for years afterward, Nora had the terribly clear thought: *You won.*

And it was true, whatever the awful costs to her and others, whatever the collateral damage done to her soul, that she had gotten nearly all the things she wanted, at least after losing Euan.

She did lose her feet, but it wasn't long before she was fitted for prosthetics, which every year became more advanced. She could have run after her son if she'd been that sort of mother, but she tended to let Mal and Marie play with James while she studied or read or worked.

Nora did love her son, of course, with his wayward mop of dark-red hair and deep-blue eyes, but she trusted other people to take better care of him, including the nurse who lived with them and was wonderfully patient with Adelaide as well.

Mal wanted more children, Nora knew, and she said maybe, but she had been fitted for a new womb veil and usually wore it when they lay together. She was afraid to press her luck, but also afraid to be derailed again.

Back in Manhattan, she returned to school at one of the women's colleges and received her medical degree, then joined her father's practice. He was giddy when the new sign went up and the new stationery arrived—and glad to have Nora spend several nights a week in her old room in Washington Square.

Nora was pleased, too, though for the longest while still caught off guard when addressed by one of her new titles: *Mother*, or *Dr. Colquhoun*. She would become aware of the speaker awaiting a response and realize, *Oh, yes; that's me.*

Only Calista seemed to look at her with any misgiving, Nora thought, as if she knew something of what had happened. Or maybe she simply didn't understand how Nora could willingly spend so much time away from her son. But if she knew what had happened to Nora's own mother, then perhaps she thought it was best.

As a boy, James naturally loved his father and Aunt Marie more than he loved Nora. She didn't blame him, or begrudge his shyness around her, but when he grew older, they forged a bond that surprised her, and broke her heart a little all over again; it seemed such an indiscriminate gift, and such a curse, of sorts.

She couldn't help but be proud when James went into medicine planning to specialize in neurological diseases—and then couldn't help but be terrified when the Great War swept across the globe and caught her son in its roiling tide.

Nora felt constantly sick to her stomach. She awaited James's letters with terrific impatience and looked for him in every young face she saw on her own wards.

The shortage of male doctors meant that—finally—medically trained women were welcomed into every facility in the city. It had only taken most of Nora's life and a staggering amount of death.

She was fifty-three then, somehow, which never failed to astonish her. That was her father's age, she always thought. It had been, once.

James was already thirty, older than Nora was when she had him. He'd begun telling her, as Cousin Bette and most of her six children constantly did, that she ought to retire already—but Nora was happy to still be of service, especially when she got to show her own prosthetics to veterans who had suddenly found themselves amputees.

"I've been getting around on these for the past thirty years, almost," she told them. "You'll be fine."

They all asked what happened, of course. All she had to say was "I got lost in the snow in eighty-eight."

The Great White Hurricane. Everyone knew of it. Everyone understood how lucky Nora was, or thought they did.

～

She was luckier still to be reunited with James in 1918. Unscarred, at least in ways that she could see.

Mal was a truly old man by then, seventy-four, but still puttering around his flourishing miniature farm, feeding the chickens that their neighbors thought so quaint, grooming his horse and the donkey that Marie had chosen for herself.

When James returned home they hugged their son breathless—he always seemed as much Marie's as theirs—and that night, Mal and Nora held each other, keenly aware of how fast time slipped away, no matter how tightly one held on. And yet aware that it never really vanished, as long as one's memories remained with them. It only became disordered.

～

Marie became increasingly disordered, too, and apt to wander, though could usually be found scratching the donkey, which she'd named Nelly. She forgot and now called it Old Bob.

I wonder where Erik's gone off to, she said sometimes, or *Where are Bea and Addie hiding?* And then: *Who are you? You look like my sister, Nora, except you're much older! Sorry. I love your sprinkles.*

It was especially distressing to see her grow anxious or angry, as the outbursts common in so many dementia and Alzheimer's patients affected Marie too. They made her seem like a different person, possessed. But they cleared, like storms, and she had many good days, many good hours.

She was calm when she died in her bed from pneumonia. Nora could only thank God for that.

Adelaide was a grown woman then; she still spoke few intelligible words and disliked venturing from her velvet-draped room—except to play the parlor piano, which she'd taught herself, entirely by ear, not long after they'd moved to Washington Heights. Nora had been astonished to hear her rapid progression from simple notes to full songs. Most were from the phonograph records, but a few were older tunes that Erik once fiddled.

She was never sure if Addie knew Marie was her mother, or even understood what a mother was, and then couldn't tell if Addie knew Marie was gone, but hoped her heart and mind were mostly peaceful— and would remain so when Nora herself passed on. Addie seemed likely to survive long after.

James would see that she was well cared for. But would Addie miss her most familiar faces? Nora wondered. Would she be lonely? Sorrowful? Would she be able to surmount those terrible emotions when she couldn't even articulate them?

But then, could anyone?

They all simply endured what they must.

∾

Death was never far away, of course.

Nora's father had succumbed to a heart attack in 1896, at sixty-one, in his favorite chair, with a glass of whiskey and a medical journal beside him, on a night when Nora wasn't there.

She kept the brownstone, and saw that John Garrett and Calista would never have to work another day of their lives. She offered them the use of the place if they wished to continue living there, but they declined and retired to a house together in another borough.

Nora hired no other staff, as there was no need, though it felt strange to be all alone in the townhouse.

It made her feel impossibly young and sad. And no matter how hard she hoped that something might yet shift, she never saw any sign of the other people who once lived there.

She should be glad of it, she reminded herself.

She still had to remind herself.

～

She had to do so again in 1926, when she lost Mal to cancer. He was eighty-two, and Nora was dejected to see no shade of him after his body had been buried. Except, of course, when she looked at their beautiful, kind son, though James's thickly pomaded hair plastered to his skull and his wire-rimmed glasses blunted the effect a bit.

She'd never shed all her guilt where Mal was concerned, but Nora supposed it had lessened considerably over the years, which had largely been happy. She'd stopped feeling so much like she'd forced his hand, or tricked him, or even bested him, because she had come to believe that he was truly content, and had finally let herself be, too, whether or not she deserved it.

When he died, Nora was sixty-one. She'd been keenly conscious of her mortality for decades, but now, at the same age that her father had gone from the world, she detected a new fatigue, a shortness of breath, a fluttering of her heart.

Anxiety, maybe, concomitant with grief.

Or something worse.

She thought of dear Dr. Mary Jacobi, her father's former friend and colleague, the first woman to be admitted into the Academy of

Medicine, a great inspiration to Nora. A handful of years after the turn of the century, Dr. Jacobi, then sixty-three, had developed a brain tumor. She'd written a detailed account of her progressive symptoms, posthumously published.

Nora dimly imagined doing the same. But she wouldn't write about whatever common illness she might have. She would write a monograph on ghosts.

She could never quite finish it, though, even in her head.

∼

She had seen Kirsten and Beatrice again when she returned to the farmhouse to pack her things. They'd watched her cry over the broken pieces of the shimmering abalone box, then gather one shard and the burlap bag and place them in Euan's Runkel Brothers treasure chest, which she'd slid into her leather satchel.

James, she supposed, would find that sometime after her own death. He'd be in for a surprise. Nora could affix a note warning him not to open it, but he would anyway. She couldn't bring herself to destroy the contents while she lived.

Kirsten and Bea hadn't seemed to know that they were being abandoned, but Nora had still apologized to them. And she'd comforted herself with the fact that they could have followed, if they'd wanted.

She supposed the farmhouse was their home. Or, perhaps, they were simply done with her—or she with them, at least in such sad forms, though, of course, she carried their memories.

∼

On a quiet night in Washington Heights several years later, Mal told her, out of nowhere, that he was sorry he hadn't believed her. Nora tried to shush him, but he seemed to need to speak.

"I never told you this, but . . . sometimes . . . well, sometimes I thought I caught a glimpse of him. Euan. His ghost."

Nora had frozen. "What? When? Where?"

"So many times," Mal murmured. "Usually upstairs, in the house. Only after we were married. But . . . never since we left."

It felt heinously unfair. Nora wept privately and raged inwardly for days. But the longer she turned it over, the more certain she became that one of her hypotheses was correct, at least in part: guilt created ghosts, or at least contributed to who could see them, why they did, how long they lasted.

And however broken she had been by Euan's death, she had never felt that it was her fault.

~

Erik, however, had followed her everywhere, from the snowy wilderness of upstate New York to the small town in Vermont where she convalesced, back to Hoosick Falls and then to Manhattan and beyond.

His ghost never faded, never spoke, never aged, of course. It never blinked those ice-blue eyes or took them off Nora for a second.

He shadowed her through the halls of every hospital and house she walked, tailed her down every busy city street and bucolic park path. He came along to Scotland when the family took a rare overseas trip, and visited Newport with her.

Erik was in attendance on the day that James was born, and on the day that James was married. He was there at Nora's father's funeral, and at Grandmama's, and Aunt Birdie's too. He was there at Malcolm's, and at Marie's. He was there when Nora sipped a Scotch by the fireplace and paged through a medical journal, and there when she bathed, and had been there every time that she and Mal made love.

He was often in her dreams. He was there, always, when she woke.

~

He would be there when she died, Nora knew. She could only hope that that would be the last of him—of anything—that she would ever see.

She hoped that she would never be seen again, either, except in memories and photographs and drawings, and in the slope of James's nose and the bow in the upper lip of his youngest daughter, Lily.

∾

She would be seen, of course—in full, at length, on a microscopic level, better than she had ever seen herself—by whichever young women received the gift of Nora's corpse to study. But she was grateful that, even in the deepest channels of her brain, they would never discover her most precious or most damning secrets.

Mal wanted Nora to reconsider donating her body altogether, but she insisted. She hoped her addendum that her ashes be scattered next to his grave was some consolation.

"At least a little of me will stick," she told him. "Work its way down into the ground and feed a clover seed, or a dandelion. A blade of grass."

He never found it as romantic as Euan would have, but Nora held Mal's rough hand and brought his swollen knuckles to her lips. "You already have me in your heart, anyway. You'll take me with you, wherever you go."

∾

In the meanwhile, she did as much good as she could manage, and tried her best to ignore Erik's still beautiful and forever unnerving ghost, and to not think of what else might come after, for she could never know until she got there.

She could only hope that what she said—what she tried to believe—was true. That her own consciousness would flicker out with her body's last electric impulse, and her physical end would be truly that.

The end, and not the beginning of some imponderable eternity, on earth or elsewhere.

AUTHOR'S NOTE

This book began germinating over two decades ago. It was heavily inspired by Michael Lesy's *Wisconsin Death Trip*, which I came to via *A Prayer for the Dying*, an excellent novel by Stewart O'Nan. Around the same time, teenage me became enthralled by the vibes of *Edge of Madness*, an indie film that was itself inspired by Alice Munro's *A Wilderness Station*.

These all gave rise to my mental image of an isolated farm where terrible things would happen, especially while it was locked in snow and ice—and I could vividly picture its core inhabitants almost immediately, though Euan Colquhoun once went by Andrew and was a law clerk in Boston, and Kirsten and her brother were Swedish (since the farm was originally in Wisconsin).

It may sound like a cop-out (or an outright lie) to say that I rarely feel like I *invent* my characters, but so it is; I meet them in my mind and begin a process of discovery. Sometimes it takes longer to discern all their details, but just like Mal and Erik, Marie and her daughters appeared fully formed. Honestly, they caused me some trepidation, because it was clear they were what we would today call neurodivergent. Specifically, we would probably say the girls are on the autism spectrum and Marie has a mild intellectual disability, or IDD. Such people have always existed, of course, but depicting them both respectfully and authentically within a historical context was a challenge I might have shied away from had it felt like a choice at all. I hope my love for them is clear, even when their fates were unkind.

Nora only came to me last year, when it became apparent that my original main character (Siobhan, who had a ghostly childhood in Ireland, and whom I hope you get to meet in a future book . . .) was just in the wrong story. I needed a science-steeped skeptic to take her place, and imagined a medical student might do. Nora took shape rather quickly, and fit perfectly into the narrative, as if she was always meant to be there. She experiences far less overt misogyny and on-page sexism than you might expect, but *Women in White Coats: How the First Women Doctors Changed the World of Medicine* by Olivia Campbell provides a fascinating (and often infuriating) look at the history of Western female MDs.

While I briefly mention the real Dr. Mary Jacobi as a tertiary character in my book, no one else is based on actual historical figures. Any errors are entirely my own, and probably unintentional.

ACKNOWLEDGMENTS

Making a book takes a LOT of people, many of them behind the scenes, so I know I'll miss some names, but I extend my deepest gratitude to everyone involved in this endeavor. In particular:

My lovely agent, Abby Saul, continues to be wonderfully supportive and essential in navigating this art/business (and making my dreams come true); I'm so glad I get to do this with you.

Erin Adair-Hodges has also been instrumental in changing my life—most especially by championing (and strengthening) both this book and my first. I am eternally grateful to you.

Chantelle Aimée Osman has been so enthusiastic, encouraging, and insightful that I'm once again stunned by my luck, personally and professionally. What could've been turmoil turned into excitement instead.

Jodi Warshaw is another absolute treasure, and a delight to work with. This book is infinitely stronger, better, truer, and more itself thanks to your brilliant and sensitive input.

I'd also like to thank Ashly Moore for an invaluable sensitivity read and fresh perspective; Elizabeth Cameron and Abi Pollokoff for more generous, insightful copyedits (and for saving me from some truly humiliating mistakes); Patty Ann Economos for patient, on-point proofreading (I deeply regret my math-related messes); Karah Nichols for kindly keeping the production on track; the Lake Union and APub marketing team; and Shasti O'Leary Soudant for another heart-stopper of a cover. I won't get to hear the audiobook until after this goes to print, but I know I'll want to thank the narrator, as well as Laura Stahl and the entire Brilliance Publishing team (I'm sorry I forgot you all last time)!

My family and friends have all been so genuinely jazzed about my writing; it's incredibly gratifying to have such support, and I thank every one of you for making my heart so full. Special shout-outs, though, to Sarah Tierney (for being the first "outside" reader to say she loved book number one, which almost made me cry), Lannie Tierney (for the Driftwood Library hookup), Lee Ngo and Nicolette Christianson (for ridiculously kind words and bonus live-reading reactions), Lauren Eichelberger and Jess Vess (for enthusiastically talking me up online and off), Courtney Gailey and Kelly Schupp (for Zooming me into your fabulous book club), and my mom (my OG reader and first/forever booster).

Thank you, too, to Neil Tierney, for more than I can say—but in no small part for letting me rant and ramble (not just about writing), bouncing around ideas (even helping me find the right words—sorry I didn't manage to work in "thunderplump"), cooking lots of fabulous dinners, getting me out into fresh air, always believing in me, and making me laugh every damn day, no matter how gloomy they might get. I'm still not sure I deserve you, but I'm certainly glad I've got you.

And finally, thank you to every reader who has taken a chance on my words and dreamed this dream with me.

ABOUT THE AUTHOR

Photo © 2022 Neil Tierney

Jen Wheeler is a former managing editor of food website Chowhound and currently lives in Oregon. *A Cure for Sorrow* is her second novel.